A LOVE OUT OF TIME

Myles found her mouth, the full lips soft and sensual beneath his own, and abandoning all restraint, he kissed her, exploring, experimenting, nipping, licking, parting her lips with his tongue and showing her with lips and tongue and teeth the near violence of the desire that raged in him.

And with each new caress, Paige answered in kind.

He was more lonely than he could bear to admit. He wanted this woman, he'd wanted her since that very first night, when she'd worn his nightshirt and cursed at him for locking her up. But the habits of years, the hard-won peace that had come from locking his emotions away and tossing out the key, were too deeply ingrained to overcome with just a kiss.

In some silent, simultaneous agreement, they moved apart, their breathing loud and uneven in the stillness of the afternoon.

"I apologize, Paige," he said when he could speak at all. His voice was thick, barely in control. "This is not a good idea."

"You're right, of course." She sounded almost flippant. "Besides, the last thing I want is to become emotionally involved with anyone from around here. From this era, I mean. I have to find a way back, sooner or later. To my own life, my own time."

Now And Then

BOBBY HUTCHINSON

LOVE SPELL ◆ NEW YORK CITY

LOVE SPELL®

December 1994

Published by

Dorchester Publishing Co., Inc.
276 Fifth Avenue
New York, NY 10001

The name "Love Spell" and its logo are trademarks of Dorchester Publishing Co., Inc.

Printed in the United States of America.

Thanks to Peggy Cooper and Lori Balch, my good and true friends, for their help with research. In memory of NWMP Constable James Hutchinson, participant in the Riel Rebellion and recipient of the Northwest 1885 Canada Medal.

Now And Then

Chapter One

Dr. Paige Randolph was grateful that at three in the morning, the rain-washed Vancouver streets were almost deserted and driving was easy.

She shivered a little in the predawn chill and switched the heater on; she'd leapt out of bed and pulled on corduroy slacks and a heavy sweatshirt, but she hadn't stopped to grab a jacket. August was supposed to be summer, even in the damp reaches of the Pacific Northwest, but it felt more like January this morning.

Paige stepped harder on the gas. Her powerful little car responded with a surge of energy, and she sailed through yet another yellow light, thinking more of the patient waiting at Grace Maternity Hospital than her driving.

Liz Jackson's husband had called half an hour earlier.

"The pains started five minutes apart, and her water broke right away, Doctor. I thought we'd get more warning. Should her water have broken so fast?" Terror was evident in Dave's husky voice.

Paige had asked detailed questions and then done her

best to reassure Dave and calm him down, but the whole time her own heart was pounding as it always did when the phone ripped apart her sleep. It had been happening regularly for years, all during her internship, her residency in obstetrics and gynecology, and certainly since she'd opened her own clinic three years ago, but she'd never become even remotely used to it. She doubted she ever would.

She'd suggested an ambulance for Liz, but Dave Jackson insisted he could drive to the hospital in the time it would take to summon one. As she pulled into staff parking on the hospital lot, tires screeching on the wet tarmac, Paige hoped fervently that the expectant father had managed to calm down before he got behind the wheel.

"Mornin, Doc." The sleepy-looking parking attendant waved and grinned at her. She gave him a distracted smile and an absent nod. Her thoughts were now all on Liz, reviewing the woman's history, trying to anticipate what could possibly happen during the next few hours.

Trying to second-guess a delivery's just plain stupid, she reminded herself as she bailed out of her car and jogged into the hospital. *When are you ever going to learn to just take it as it comes?*

The elevator seemed to be waiting for her, and she emerged a few seconds later at five, the delivery floor.

"Mrs. Jackson's in labor room three, Paige. The resident examined her; her cervix is five centimeters dilated." Annette Evans, a nurse Paige knew and liked, greeted her and added, "The monitor indicates that the fetal heart rate's a little low, around one thirty-five. Mother's blood pressure and pulse are good, though."

A normal fetal heart rate was 140, so nothing was too serious yet.

"I thought you were on leave, Dr. Randolph. Someone

said you were going to Saskatchewan for a conference this week," Annette commented as they hurried down the hall.

"I'm leaving tomorrow," Paige confirmed. "Today," she corrected, squinting up at the clock. "I'm supposed to be flying out at noon. I'll be gone a week; I'm looking forward to it. My brother and his family live half an hour's drive from Saskatoon, on a farm. I haven't been there in a year, and I'm looking forward to seeing how much my two nephews have grown."

It was the first break she'd taken in months; her partner, Sam Harris, had bullied her into filling out the application forms and making the plane reservations.

"You're getting bitchier every day, Randolph," he'd accused with a grin that belied his words. "My prescription is either a holiday or a hot love affair. God knows I've offered my services often enough for the latter, but you keep turning me down. I can't believe you'd choose Saskatoon and a midwifery conference over my body, but I guess it's better than having you stick around here and alienate my patients as well as your own."

Sam was a great partner and a good friend. He and Paige had known each other since their early days in med school, and she often wished she found him sexually attractive. She knew he was more than half in love with her, and that his suggestive bantering was just his way of admitting that he reluctantly accepted the parameters she'd drawn for their relationship; the occasional, casual dinner, a rare game of squash, or a jog together around the park on Sunday.

"Too bad baby Jackson decided tonight was the big debut; you could've had a good night's sleep before you left, Paige," Annette remarked. "You're gonna be wiped right out tomorrow, probably snore your way through most of the lectures."

Paige grinned at the nurse. "Me, get a good night's sleep?

You want my system to get totally out of whack?" They both laughed, and Paige added, "Anyhow, I'm glad I was still around for this delivery. Liz Jackson's sort of special."

Annette gave Paige a teasing look. "I've heard you say that about nearly every one of your patients, Doctor."

"Yeah, but this time I really mean it," Paige joked. She was fond of Liz, and she wanted nothing more than to deliver her of a robust, healthy child. This was Liz's second pregnancy, and she wasn't supposed to be due for another two weeks. She was 37, and her first baby, a boy born two years ago, had been stillborn. According to all reports, the pregnancy had seemed relatively trouble-free, gone full term, normal delivery, and then inexplicably ended in tragedy.

Paige hadn't been Liz's doctor at the time, but she'd studied all the lab reports with meticulous care, searching for a reason. As sometimes happened with still-births, no definitive answer was evident. There were no congenital defects, no real basis for the baby's death. It seemed a perfect baby, but it had simply never breathed.

A shiver ran down her spine as she washed up. Perfect babies who didn't breathe were her special nightmare. She'd had one herself, a long time ago.

She made certain she had a wide, confident smile on her face a few moments later as she breezed into labor room three.

"Hi, you guys. So I hear this kid's in a rush to meet all of us."

"Gosh, you got here fast, Dr. Randolph." Liz tried for a casual note, but both husband and wife looked profoundly relieved that Paige had arrived quickly.

"Lucky thing young Jackson decided to do this tonight instead of tomorrow," Paige commented. "I think I told you I'll be away for a couple of days, and I'd have hated to miss this."

"I'm glad too. I really want you to deliver me." Liz's smooth blonde hair was fashionably cut and even now in far better order than Paige's own wildly curly, disheveled dark mop.

Propped on pillows in the high bed, wearing a hospital gown, belly huge and encircled by the external fetal monitor strapped around her abdomen, Liz still managed to look attractive. Her color was good, and she returned Paige's warm smile with one that was only a trifle strained.

"Well, let's see how we're doing here." The monitor used ultrasound waves to record the baby's heartbeat on a console beside the bed, and Paige checked the black needle that marked on graph paper each beat of the baby's heart. It was holding pretty steady at 135 beats per minute.

Paige examined Liz next, and felt a bit disturbed when she found that the baby's head wasn't descending into the dilating cervix the way it ought to be. It was still high in the pelvis, which meant that birth was a long way off. Paige remembered that Liz's first labor had progressed rapidly.

Obviously, this one wasn't following that pattern.

As Paige finished her examination, Liz had a contraction. It was powerful and lasted a full two minutes. Liz panted through her mouth, face contorted. Toward the end she lost control of the breathing and cried out with the pain.

"How often are they coming?" Paige directed the question to Dave, who was monitoring his wife's labor. His rugged face was drained of color, and Paige felt a pang of sympathy for him. He looked in far worse shape than her patient did.

"They're still five minutes apart; they haven't changed one bit since the beginning. She's in a lot of pain, Doctor. Can you give her something?"

Paige'd been over this before with both Liz and Dave during one of their early office visits, but she patiently explained again why she preferred not to use drugs on her laboring mothers unless it was absolutely necessary.

"No matter what I give her, Dave, it's going to have a depressive effect on the baby. I'd really like to avoid that if we can. And the drugs don't take the pain away; they often just make it harder for the mother to cope. They make her groggy, less in control. But as I told you before, the decision is Liz's to make. If she truly feels she can't manage a bit further down the line, then certainly I'll give her something."

The contraction ended, and Liz shook her head from side to side vigorously. "I don't want anything, I'm okay, I'm not taking anything that might harm our baby." She curled her arms protectively around her belly, careful not to disturb the monitor.

Paige put an arm around the other woman's shoulders and hugged her close, feeling the tension in her body. "Good for you, love. Dave, why don't you try getting on up the bed behind Liz and holding her against you, cradling her between your legs, rubbing her tummy for her so she really feels your support when the next contraction comes."

In practical terms, it wouldn't help the pain a damned bit, Paige mused, but being held in her husband's arms would be emotionally comforting for Liz, and would also make Dave feel as if he were doing something constructive beyond timing contractions. This was a husband and wife whose love for one another was palpable, and it touched Paige to see that visible bond between them. It made her sad and envious as well; it pointed up the emptiness of her own solitary life-style as nothing else could.

Dave did just as Paige suggested, kicking off his worn

Adidas and carefully clambering up behind his wife. He had a hole in one blue sock.

Another contraction came and went. Liz seemed more relaxed now, propped against her husband's body. But the monitor indicated that the baby's heart rate was fluctuating more than ever, dropping to 120 and then 110. Paige went out of the room and found Annette.

"I'm not sure what's happening with this kid; the heart rate's pretty uneven. I think you'd better get me an infusion setup and make sure we have her blood cross-matched and a supply on hand, just as a precaution."

It made sense to have everything in place in case things went bad fast and she needed to rush Liz into surgery for a c-section, God forbid.

Paige fervently hoped it wouldn't be necessary. She wasn't fond of cesarean section. Surgical delivery, although essential and lifesaving in many instances, still should be treated only as an absolute last-ditch emergency measure, in her opinion. She was all for letting nature take its course, if at all possible.

Annette quickly found the infusion setup, and she followed Paige back into the labor room, not batting an eye at the sight of husband and wife curled up together on the high bed.

Grace Maternity Hospital believed that people came first, which was why Paige had her patients admitted here. She'd had a blind lady in labor a few months ago, and the hospital had routinely admitted the seeing-eye dog along with the patient.

"What's that for?" Liz looked at the infusion setup with alarm, and Paige explained calmly what it was and why she felt it was necessary.

"The baby's heart rate is fluctuating more than I'd like, so we want to be prepared." She'd carefully explained her stance on cesarean birth to the Jacksons at one of their office visits, and now she told them what exact circumstances would make a section necessary.

"I want to be ready just in case your baby gets into serious trouble. You know I prefer vaginal delivery, but we also don't want to take chances."

Paige did her best not to alarm them unduly, but she explained about the combination of the baby's head not descending, and the fetal heart rate being low. After all, it was Liz's body, and her baby. In Paige's opinion, that entitled her to the whole truth, and the right to be clued in to whatever was going on. As she talked, she set about finding a vein in the back of Liz's hand and inserting the needle and drip.

Liz had another contraction, and Annette, who was watching the baby's heartbeat on the monitor, said in a soft voice to Paige, "Down to one hundred."

A rate much below 100 signaled fetal distress, but sometimes the fetal heart rate slowed considerably and then picked up again. There was no telling ahead of time what might occur.

C'mon, baby, don't do this to me, Paige pleaded silently. Give me a little help here. But even as she watched, the heart rate dropped to 90, then within minutes, down to 80.

She felt tension in every fiber of her being, but outwardly she stayed calm and spoke in a quiet voice to the Jacksons. "I'm going to scrub. Annette will keep an eye on things here and keep me posted. Liz, honey, the baby's heart rate is dropping pretty fast; it looks as if we might have to do a cesarean after all, but we'll let you know exactly what's going on every minute, all right?" She squeezed her patient's hand.

Liz swallowed hard and nodded, face drained of color, tears evident. There wasn't time to linger, however. Paige hurried out to the sinks in the alcove adjoining the delivery room, instructing one of the nurses to tell the resident what was happening so he could make the calls necessary for an operating room and a team to assist should they be needed in a hurry.

She started scrubbing. Before she'd donned her sterile gear, a young nurse hurried in. "Doctor, the heart rate's down to sixty and still dropping rapidly."

"Damn. The kid's not far enough into the cervix for us to get it out vaginally. Hit the emergency switch. We'll have to do a section."

She hurried into the operating room a few moments later. Two other doctors were already there, waiting to assist, as well as the anesthesiologist, Dr. Larry Morgan, and the operating-room nurses. A call was out for a neonatal specialist. Paige hoped he'd be arriving any moment.

Liz's abdomen had been washed with disinfectant and shaved. She was still awake, looking terrified. The anesthetic would affect the baby, so it wouldn't be administered until the very last possible moment.

"We're going to put you to sleep now, Liz, and then we'll have your baby out in a couple of minutes," Paige assured her. "You'll wake up in about an hour."

"Is my baby going to be okay?" Liz's voice trembled.

"I'm sure he is," Liz lied. Honesty surrendered to compassion at times like this. "You know we'll do everything we can for her, and for you too. And we'll tell Dave exactly what's happening."

Paige nodded to Larry, and the procedure began.

As soon as he indicated that Liz was under, the nurse handed Paige a scalpel. Aware of the dual needs for speed and caution, she went down quickly and carefully through the abdominal layers, and when she reached the uterus she cut across the front and pushed the bladder out of the way while the other doctor suctioned out the fluids that accumulated. Making a small incision in the uterus itself, she used her fingers to carefully spread the incision wider so she wouldn't cut into any large blood vessels.

At last her hand encountered the baby's head, facedown. She cupped the tiny skull in her hand, carefully turning the child so it was faceup, and lifted. The head emerged slowly, covered with wet, dark hair, and the other doctor immediately inserted a bulb syringe in the tiny mouth and began suctioning mucus in an effort to get the baby breathing as quickly as possible, before it was even out of Liz's body.

Paige slid her hand down the wet little body, supporting the shoulders, easing them out sideways. The rest of the baby, slippery and blood-streaked, slid out easily as Paige cupped the minute buttocks in her hand and lifted.

The child was a good-sized boy, but Paige didn't like the way he looked or felt. Beneath the sticky white coating of vernix, his skin was white and his body limp, without muscle tone. Paige clamped and cut the thick, blue umbilical cord as quickly as possible, but in spite of suctioning, the baby made no effort to breathe.

There was palpable tension and an ominous silence in the room as one of the delivery-room doctors rushed him over to an adjoining table. The specialist had arrived, and he immediately inserted a tube down the baby's trachea.

Liz was doing well, and Paige surrendered the next step in the procedure, the delivery of the placenta, to her assistant and moved over to the table where the minuscule boy lay inert and lifeless except for the oxygen being forced into his narrow chest.

Nausea swirled in her stomach as she watched the specialist squeezing oxygen into the baby's lungs. Losing a baby was horrendous; it didn't happen often, but each time it did, she went through days of silent agony, wondering what she could have done to prevent it.

"C'mon, kid, c'mon, you can do it, breathe a little here," she entreated half under her breath as the seconds ticked away and cold sweat beaded her forehead, trickled down between her breasts and under her armpits.

She glanced up at the clock. They all knew there wasn't much time left before brain damage would occur. Her mind went frantically over the possibilities; was this child congenitally damaged, heart, lungs . . . brain? He looked all right, but there was no way of telling for sure.

The stethoscope now confirmed that the baby's heart rate was slowing. Paige prayed, hard and frantic, willing the small form to breathe, and another long moment passed, and then another.

The specialist shook his head. The silence in the room seemed to deepen as his shoulders slumped and he slowly removed the equipment. The baby was gone.

Nausea swelled inside of Paige as she watched a nurse bundle the lifeless form in a towel and carry it off.

Behind their surgical masks, several of the nurses had wet eyes. Paige had to squeeze her own eyes tightly shut to clear them of tears as she turned to the operating table.

She went back to overseeing the long procedure necessary to clean and repair Liz's uterus and abdominal cavity, ruthlessly blocking out the emotions that would envelop her later. Right now, there was Liz to see to. Then she'd have to go out and talk with Dave. In about an hour, Liz would be allowed to wake up at last—and Paige would have to tell her that her baby was dead.

Paige swallowed hard, and as her hands deftly completed the surgical procedure; her mind drifted back to Liz's first office visit eight months ago.

Liz had stared at Paige and then blurted out, "But nobody

told me you were so young." Her fair skin had then flushed with embarrassment at her own gauche words, but Paige was accustomed to patients commenting on her youthful appearance.

"Actually, I'm on the sunset side of thirty-something, not really all that young," she'd joked. The truth was, she was only 34, but she found patients preferred to believe she was older than they were . . . and with so many women having babies in their late 30s, she'd learned to perpetuate a white lie about her age.

"I just got stuck with looking eighteen and can't seem to age decently," she said to Liz with mock chagrin. "But I intend to get around to it one of these days when I have more time." She'd given Liz the wide, crooked grin and overdone wink that usually managed to both charm and reassure.

Liz had relaxed somewhat. "My husband and I heard from lots of our friends that you're the best obstetrician in Vancouver," she'd said next.

Liz meant it as a compliment, but Paige wished like hell they hadn't heard anything of the kind. It would be so much easier if her patients didn't expect miracles; she did the very best she could, but she was all too aware she wasn't omnipotent.

She glanced over at the empty table where Liz's boy had lain a few moments before.

God, at times like this she didn't even feel competent.

Liz and Dave Jackson had relied on Dr. Paige Randolph to see them safely through this delivery . . . and present them with a healthy baby at the other end. And she'd failed.

Forgive me, she whispered under her breath to the inert form on the table below her. But Paige knew it wasn't Liz and Dave Jackson's forgiveness she needed.

It was her own.

* * *

It was after nine that morning when she finally left the hospital; she'd taken Dave for coffee and done her best to comfort him until Liz awakened. Then they'd shared the awful task of telling Liz.

Paige had settled them in a private room and asked Annette to bring them their baby and leave them alone for as long as they desired.

They needed a chance to say good-bye.

Paige, sick to her very soul, had then visited her other patients, pasting a smile on her face and deliberately taking more time than usual on rounds to chat because this morning she had no office hours. Sam was filling in for her.

At last, the necessary paperwork finished, she left the hospital and walked slowly over to her car. It was still raining, a gray, ugly drizzle that chilled her to the bone.

She got in and slammed the door. She glanced into the rearview mirror, and her own bleak face stared back at her, haunted green eyes with dark circles beneath them, normally creamy skin pasty white.

With a muffled groan, she rested her forehead on the steering wheel and released the tears that she'd subdued for hours now. Sobs shook her, and the acid taste of the coffee she'd drunk came burning into her throat. After a few moments, she sat up and blew her nose hard, wiping away the tears, and anger took the place of sorrow.

What was wrong with her, that she couldn't develop the protective shell that other doctors had? Why did every dead baby remind her on this visceral level of her own baby, so long ago?

She'd never been able to admit, even to Sam, how losing a patient made her feel, how it affected her for days and weeks afterward.

21

God, maybe she needed a psychiatrist. Well, she didn't have time to consult one this morning, that was certain.

She started the car, drove out of the lot and into heavy morning traffic. There was just about enough time to drive home, shower, pack, and hurry out to the airport to catch her flight to Saskatoon.

She pushed the morning's tragedy to the back of her mind and mentally went over her wardrobe, planning what to take. Business stuff for the conference, her plain black silk chemise for dinners.

Jeans and boots for the ranch; her spirits rose a little as she reminded herself that she'd get to spend a couple of days with Tony and the kids when the conference was over.

And Sharon, she reminded herself. She and her sister-in-law had never been close, but maybe this time it would be easier.

She was even going to pack her running strip. She hadn't had a chance to go for a good long run in over a week. She'd learned way back in medical school that hard physical exercise was a good release for tension.

A taxi pulled out directly in front of her, and she hit the brakes to keep from broadsiding it, swearing as her car swerved and the tires screamed in protest. Heart pounding, she stopped for a light, the taxi directly in front of her.

Idiot. Maniac, she silently screamed at the driver. She was trembling violently. She even considered getting out and hammering on his window before sanity claimed her.

You're turning into a nut case, Randolph.

No doubt about it, a relaxing couple of days at Tony's ranch, far away from women in labor and Vancouver's congested traffic, was exactly what she needed. And if Sharon wasn't exactly overjoyed to see her, well, Tony and the little boys would more than make up for it.

Chapter Two

"So was this conference you were at worthwhile, Paige?" Sharon ladled cold soup carefully into her best china, handing the bowls to Tony to serve, not looking at Paige as she spoke.

"It was interesting. There were a couple of seminars on midwifery that—"

"I don't like this green stuff, Daddy; do I have to eat it?" Matthew's plaintive voice interrupted Paige's comment, and she stifled a grin at the martyred look on her seven-year-old nephew's face as he stared at the bowl of vichyssoise in front of him.

"Yes, you have to eat it. And don't interrupt again or you'll go to your room without supper." Tony's voice was harsh and he glared at his son. Matthew's fair skin turned fiery red, and as he bent his tawny head over his soup, Paige caught the hint of tears.

She glanced over at her brother, surprised at Tony's bad temper. Normally he was easygoing, lenient, and good-natured with the boys, but ever since her arrival several hours ago, she'd been aware of an undercurrent of tension in the household.

Tony and Sharon had sniped at one another from the moment she'd arrived, and as usual, Sharon had gone to a great deal of trouble with dinner, managing to appear martyred and overworked in the process.

Paige was sure her sister-in-law didn't really have time to prepare this kind of special meal, and undoubtedly resented doing it. Even a city person knew that late August was a busy time on a ranch. Harvest was in full swing with extra hired men to feed, garden produce needing to be frozen or canned for winter, the boys undoubtedly needing a million things done before they were readied for another school term.

So why, Paige thought now, had Sharon refused to accept her invitation to take all of them out for a special, fancy treat? Or, if that wasn't convenient, why couldn't her sister-in-law just relax with her for once and serve a simple meal on the wide wooden table in the comfortable kitchen, as if . . . as if Paige were really part of the family?

It hurt to be treated like a formal visitor. They were eating in the narrow dining room. The silverware shone, a soft linen cloth covered the oak table, and her nephews wore white shirts, their small faces and hands gleaming from a recent and severe scrubbing.

They'd been told they couldn't wear the fancy western hats she'd brought them to the table, but both boys sported their matching tooled leather boots and belts.

At least the kids are glad to see me, Paige reflected.

She crossed her eyes at six-year-old Jason and he giggled at her, his kelly green eyes an echo of her own.

Matthew was blond and blue-eyed, inclined to be a trifle plump, like Sharon, but Jason had inherited the spare Randolph build and Irish looks that she and Tony shared:

thick black hair, fair skin dusted with a few freckles, high cheekbones, firm chin, lean body. Tony was a few inches taller than Paige, well over six feet, and his hair was straight while hers was curly, but apart from that Paige and her brother looked dramatically alike.

"Are the crops good this year, Tone?" Paige knew that the summer had been unusually wet all across Canada. Maybe Tony was worrying about money again—farming had been anything but lucrative the last few years.

Tony and Sharon exchanged a long, telling look, and Paige felt more like an outsider than ever.

"Crops aren't bad, considering all the rain," Tony said shortly, and changed the subject to the coming election.

The meal seemed to progress in painful slow motion, with stilted conversation among the grown-ups and impatience between the two boys. They wanted to go out and play with the Chinese kites Paige had brought them. At last, Sharon served apple pie, after which the boys were excused.

"Change those shirts before you set foot outside," Sharon hollered after them as they hurried away with a huge clatter of boots.

Sharon began to clear the table, and Paige and Tony got up to help her.

"Why don't you two take your coffee in the living room? I'd really rather do this by myself." Sharon's tone made it clear that she didn't want help. Paige tried not to feel like an unwelcome guest, although Sharon's manner was anything but warm.

Tony glanced at her and shrugged, and they picked up their cups and moved into the other room. Seated in a worn armchair in front of the empty fireplace, Paige took advantage of the few moments of privacy to cut through the polite, impersonal facade Sharon imposed. She reached across to the sofa where Tony sat and caught his work-roughened hand in an affectionate grip.

"What's up, little brother? Anything I can help with?"

Tony was her only close relative; their mother had died when Paige was five and Tony three, and their father had remarried less than a year later, to a woman Paige and Tony came to despise and fear. Their miserable childhood had forged a bond between them, and until Tony's marriage, her brother had been Paige's best and closest friend. She missed him, most of all when they were together, like now . . . and the old closeness just wasn't there.

Tony shrugged and blew out a long, exasperated breath. "I'm just a little on edge today, sis."

Paige shot him a look. "If my being here is a problem, Tone, I can go back to the hotel. You can level with me, y'know."

"You?" Tony shook his head. "Hell, sis, it has nothing to do with you. It's this crazy stuff that's happening in my fields that has me freaked."

Paige frowned and shook her head. "You lost me somewhere, Tone. In your fields? What crazy stuff in your fields?"

"Crop circles. You ever heard of crop circles?"

Paige shook her head. "I don't think so. What is it, some kind of problem with the grain from spraying or something?"

Tony gave a grim laugh. "Don't I wish. Crop circles are unexplained phenomena, according to the stuff I read today in one of my old news magazines. You know, flying saucers and all that garbage. Aliens from outer space." He snorted. "What happens is, a farmer like me finds unexplained flattened-down circles in the middle of his wheat fields, big round circles, all the grain bent the same way as if a whirlwind or something came along and blew it all down, but all in the same direction, and all in one small area. Seems it's happened in different parts of the world for years. Hell, the one I've got even has a pattern inside, the shape of a big triangle." He shook his head, exasperated. "Y'know, Paige, you go to bed at night and the world's going along normal. You get up in the morning, and there's this mysterious damn pattern in your fields that nobody can explain."

Paige stared at her brother. "So what you're telling me is that this . . . this flattened-out ring or whatever it is just appeared out of nowhere in your wheat field? When did this happen?" It gave her a strange feeling, seeing her usually unflappable brother upset.

"This morning. I was driving the pickup over to where we're bailing. I've been driving past that particular field morning and evening, so I know it wasn't there even last night. I had Bert Myschluk, the hired man, with me. He spotted it first, figured maybe some kids had had a party out there or something. We got out to look, and it gave me the damnedest feeling. Like the area was full of . . . I don't know, some kind of electricity." Tony's voice was strained.

"There was this big, perfectly round circle right in the middle of the field. The wheat was all flattened down, but it was flat in a definite pattern, with a triangle shape in the middle." He ran a distracted hand through his hair, setting it on end. "It had to have been done from the air, because none of the rest of the crop was disturbed at all, there wasn't a sign of footprints, and anyway there's no way kids could make anything like that. We spent a good hour checking every inch of the field, and I'd bet my life nobody had walked or driven anywhere near that circle. It was weird. Next thing I knew, Bert up and quit on me, right then and there, right in the middle of harvest. Made me drive him back to the house and settle up his wages. He figures it's

27

the work of the devil." Tony snorted in disgust and took a long sip of his coffee.

"It's damned near impossible to get another good hired man this time of year, and worse yet, he'll be spreading the whole story all over the countryside, if I know Bert. He's a talker. By tomorrow, I lay you odds we'll have television trucks and reporters all over the bloody place, tramping over my crops, delaying the harvest, upsetting the guys I've still got working, and generally causing me a whole pile of shit I don't need."

Paige didn't know what to say. The whole thing sounded like something out of a science-fiction movie. But she was curious as well. "D'you think I could have a look at this thing, Tone?"

"Why not? By tomorrow, it wouldn't surprise me to have the whole of Saskatoon out here. Soon as the boys are in bed I'll drive you out." He was quiet for a few moments, and then he said, "I don't want the kids to know anything about this quite yet, so don't mention it to them, okay?"

Paige nodded.

"Sharon's already seen it; I drove her out today while the kids were away swimming. She can't understand why I'm upset over the whole thing; she just figures it's exciting."

Two hours later, Tony bounced them over a rutted road in his battered pickup. The prairie sky was still tinged with the colors of sunset, scarlet and orange and gold, and a wind had sprung up, moving the stifling air without cooling it.

"I hope Sharon doesn't mind us taking off like this," Paige said, pitching her voice over the roar of the truck motor. It was wonderful to be alone with Tony for even an hour, but she felt guilty as well about leaving Sharon behind. Guilty, and more than a little angry at her sister-in-law for making her feel that way.

"I don't want to go out there again," Sharon had said. "You two go ahead; I'll stay here and watch TV."

Well, it might be the only time during her visit that she'd be entirely alone with her brother, and she decided to take advantage of it. She hated to put him on the spot, but the distance that was growing between them frightened her.

She cleared her throat and forced the difficult words out. "Tony, what can I do to make things easier between Sharon and me? You're all the family I've got, I love being with you, but I can sense that she's not relaxed with me around. Maybe if I knew what was wrong . . ."

Tony didn't answer for several moments, but when he did, he didn't try to pretend it was Paige's imagination.

"Ah, hell, it's lots of things, Paige." He sighed and squinted at the road, little more than a trail across the prairie. "Sharon feels a little inadequate around you, I guess." He thought that over and added, "More than a little. See, you're a career woman, a doctor, a specialist. You earn big money. Sharon graduated high school and then worked in the Safeway until we got married. She figures you lead this glamorous life, wear fancy clothes, buy the kids expensive stuff. She's gaining a bit of weight, you stay thin as a rail." A note of bitter sadness came into his voice. "And maybe it's not as great as she once figured it would be, married to me, stuck out on the farm with two kids and a pile of debts. Maybe she envies you your paycheck, your freedom. You know she was pregnant with Matthew before we were married. I guess she feels like she didn't really have much choice in the whole thing."

Tony's knuckles tightened on the steering wheel. "Shit. How do I know what goes on in women's heads? Why don't you try to talk to her about it yourself?"

The thought scared Paige to death, but if he thought she should . . . "Okay, I'll try. I've never been much good at making friends with other women; you know that. I'm okay with them as patients, but beyond that . . . well, I've just never had a close woman friend. But I'll do my best with Sharon."

She added thoughtfully, "Y'know, it's so ironic, her envying me. The truth is, I'd give a lot to have a husband and a couple of kids just like she has. I figured she knew that."

"How the hell would she know if you never said so?" Tony sounded exasperated. He was concentrating on the road and didn't look over at her, but Paige could tell he thought the problem was at least partly her fault, and it hurt.

She struggled to keep her voice steady and unemotional. "As far as being pregnant before you guys were married, she must know about me and Nick Morrison, that I was pregnant too before I got married."

Tony nodded. "Yeah, she knows." He turned and looked at her now. "That was a long time ago, sis. Water under the bridge by now. It doesn't still bother you, does it?"

Only when babies die. "No, like you say, it was a long time ago."

They'd crested a small hill, and Tony pointed down at the fields that stretched as far as the eye could see. "Over there, on your right. See the bare space in the wheat?"

Paige leaned forward and looked, but from this angle, it didn't look impressive at all, just a seemingly trampled area in the acres of surrounding grain.

"Here we are." Tony stopped the truck a few minutes later between two fields of wheat, ripe and heavy and deep gold, ready for harvest. Paige could see where a faint path had been formed into the wheat field on the right.

She felt a thread of anticipation and intense curiosity as Tony led the way single file, careful not to trample more of his crop than absolutely necessary. When he stopped abruptly, Paige moved to stand beside him, and her breath caught in her throat as she saw the circle.

It was much larger than it appeared from the road. Just as he'd described, it was perfectly round, as if a giant compass had circumscribed a ring from some invisible central position. The stalks of wheat lay flat in a concentric pattern inside it, all perfectly bent over at the same angle. Superimposed on the giant circle was a triangle, its three corners touching the circle in exact, equidistant points, the stalks of grain folded over as neatly as though some demented artist had painstakingly done the whole thing by hand.

"Strange, huh?" Tony stepped inside the circle, and Paige had to stop herself from reaching out and pulling him back. She was reluctant to step inside herself, but that was ridiculous. She forced herself to follow Tony, who was walking along tracing the triangle with his footsteps.

"Do you feel anything inside here, sis?"

She did. It was the same feeling she'd had once during a particularly violent thunder and lightning display, a feeling of unbearable tension, as if the very air were charged with static electricity. The tiny hairs on her arms and on the back of her neck were standing up, and her feeling of uneasiness grew as she moved further inside the triangular pattern.

"So what do you think, sis? Any idea what might have caused this?"

She couldn't think. She could only feel, and what she felt profoundly disturbed her, because it had no rational explanation.

They stood and looked at the bizarre formation in silence for a few minutes.

"I'm going to come down early tomorrow morning with the tractor and cut this whole damned field and rake it before anybody else has a chance to see it," Tony burst out. "I should have thought of doing that today, before anybody else got wind of it."

"Sounds like a good idea." But it didn't, for some inexplicable reason, although Paige didn't want to tell Tony that.

There was a mysterious force here, one that must have some purpose, and part of her felt it wouldn't be right to destroy it. But she understood how Tony felt.

She walked to the far side of the circle, where one of the triangular points met the circumference, and she noticed that the energy seemed to fade the further she got from the center. She moved further into the configuration, and the feeling intensified.

Tony's voice interrupted her before she reached the exact center. "Let's get the hell out of here, Paige. It's going to be dark soon, and I've still got chores to do."

They made their way to the truck in silence, and they didn't talk on the way home.

Back at the house, Sharon told them a reporter had called while they were out.

"What did you tell him?" Tony walked to the fridge and got himself a beer.

"I didn't tell him anything." Sharon sounded offended. "He said he'd heard we had a crop circle out here, and would we mind if he came out with a film crew and had a look. I just said he'd have to speak to you, and you weren't home. He's going to call back in an hour."

Tony swore and held the beer up. "You two want one?"

Both women refused, and he flipped the cap open and tilted it to his mouth, swallowing half the contents in one long draft. Then he walked deliberately over to the phone and unplugged the jack.

Sharon made a disgusted sound in her throat. "That's not going to solve anything. The thing is, Tony, I don't see what harm it can do to have a reporter just come out and look." Sharon's voice was petulant. "God knows there's little enough excitement around here, and he sounded like a nice guy."

Tony's face darkened with anger. "Nice guy, shit. I told you before, I'm not having reporters turn my farm into a three-ring circus. I've got a lot riding on this harvest, the bank's on my neck, and I don't have time or patience for this crap."

"It's always got to be what you want. Don't you ever think that I deserve some say in what goes on around here too? I work just as hard as you do." Sharon slammed open the dishwasher and began banging clean dishes out onto the counter.

"Nobody's arguing with that." Tony's voice had risen to match Sharon's strident tones.

The two of them didn't notice Paige get up and leave the room. She hurried upstairs, the sound of their angry voices echoing behind her. Stomach churning, she peeked in at her sleeping nephews and pulled their door shut, hoping they wouldn't be disturbed by the quarrel escalating downstairs.

She snatched up her housecoat and shower bag and hurried to the bathroom down the hall, turning on the water in the old-fashioned tub and letting it run as she stripped off her slacks and blouse and underwear. The running water muffled the sound of the angry voices.

She'd phone and change her reservations in the morning, she decided as she stepped into the bath. This wasn't a good time for a visit with her relatives, that was obvious.

Would there ever be a good time? She'd looked forward to these few days with Tony and his family so very much, deliberately using the promise of a holiday here as a shield against the despair and emptiness that had hovered close ever since the loss of the Jacksons' baby less than a week ago.

Tears slipped down her cheeks, and she angrily scrubbed them away with the washcloth.

In bed a short time later, she heard Tony and Sharon come upstairs. Their bedroom was next to her own, and she could hear them talking in quiet tones. Relief filled her. Perhaps they'd resolved their differences, and things would be better in the morning.

Soon afterward, she heard the unmistakable sounds of them making love. Paige tried not to listen, but the walls in the old house were thin. She pulled the pillow up around her ears, but she couldn't help but be aware of their passion, and it stirred strong conflicting emotions inside of her.

She told herself she was glad for them, pleased that their relationship was still a passionate one despite their problems, but the overheard intimacy also underlined for Paige as nothing else could the utter loneliness of her own existence.

Long after silence had fallen in the next room, she lay awake, painfully assessing her life.

It had been over two years since she'd had a lover, and even then, both of them were aware it was a transient thing. Her job had to come first in her life, and men couldn't seem to accept that.

Being a doctor ironically caused her to be party to the most private moments in other people's lives, while at the same time its demands on her time and energy made it impossible for her to have many private moments of her own.

Still, she knew other doctors who had husbands, wives,

and children, doctors who managed to balance out work and family.

She didn't even have any close women friends. What she'd told Tony was true; she found it hard to relate to women outside of the examining room.

Oh, she'd told herself that making friends took time, that when the clinic was prosperous enough, when she and Sam could hire another doctor to share the crushing workload, then there'd be time to make friends.

Well, maybe she was fooling herself; maybe she wasn't capable of true intimacy, either in friendship or in love.

She tossed and turned, kicking the sheet off and then tugging it back up again, hot and cold by turns and unable to sleep, marking the hours off on the wristwatch she'd placed on the bedside table.

She must have finally dozed off sometime after three, because she awoke with a start from a dream that disintegrated as soon as she opened her eyes. It wasn't dark any longer; the room was gray with early morning light, and she felt wide awake. She reached for her watch once again. It was four-thirty.

She knew she wasn't going to sleep any more. She got out of bed and rummaged until she found her running strip in the suitcase. She pulled on bra and panties, then her cheery red nylon shorts and matching tank top, and stealthily crept along the hall to the bathroom.

She washed her face in cool water and brushed her hair. The heat had turned it into a mass of uncontrollable curls, and she pulled a braided headband down over her forehead to keep it off her face. She'd have to see about getting it cut when she got home—it was easiest to manage when it was only a few inches long.

She stole down the stairs with her worn Nikes in her hand.

Outside, the early morning air was cool and there wasn't a breath of wind. It was a perfect fall day. The sky was clear, a wide canopy of denim blue, and in the east tinges of pink and purple foreshadowed a spectacular sunrise. The air smelled of hay.

The old dog, Amos, came trotting over and licked her face as she pulled her shoes on and tied them, and a rooster crowed from the chicken coop as she set off down the lane. Amos wagged his tail and followed for a few hundred yards, but soon he gave up and turned back.

She glanced around at the house once, still dark and silent behind her. Maybe by the time she got back, Tony would be up and they could have a cup of coffee together.

She hadn't changed her mind about leaving today; Tony and Sharon obviously needed privacy just now. She'd place a call to the clinic and then make up some story about an emergency that demanded her attention.

At the end of the long lane, there was no hesitation as to which direction she'd take.

She'd awakened knowing she had to see the crop circle again before Tony plowed it under, and she set off along the rutted road which they'd followed the evening before.

It was probably four or five miles to the field, and Paige paced herself carefully, enjoying the freshness of the morning, the sound of birds all around, the sense of being alone in a vast and open space.

It was further than she'd anticipated, and her shirt was stuck to her back with sweat by the time she came to the small hill above the field. She stopped there for a moment, puffing a little, staring down at the patterns in the wheat.

A shiver ran down her spine, and she started running again, down the hill and along to where the flattened pathway led into the field of waist-high grain. It was almost as though the circle were a magnet, pulling her toward itself.

Paige's heart hammered as she reached the periphery. She stood just outside its boundaries for some time, studying the exact and baffling configuration before she stepped inside.

She was immediately aware of the energy she'd felt the night before. This morning it was a deep, intense humming that seemed to resonate inside her body. It wasn't a sound, exactly. It was more a feeling, a sensation that intensified when she moved toward the center.

She stood in the epicenter, and the peculiar sensation became more and more pronounced. Light began to pour over her, but the sun hadn't yet cleared the horizon, and she stared up at the sky, puzzled.

Fear began to overcome curiosity, but by now she felt strangely light-headed and dizzy. She sank to her knees, aware of the prickly straw stubble on the bare skin of her legs, unable to rise to her feet.

Colors flashed in front of her eyes, brilliant red and purple and green hues that seemed to meld with the pervasive humming that was growing more and more intense.

It must be sunrise.

She really had to get up, get away, run. . . .

She was drawn into a brilliant, blinding maelstrom of color and sound and energy, a force so powerful there was no way of resisting.

She heard herself scream as the humming became unbearably loud, and then the world turned gray and formless.

Chapter Three

The summer of 1883 had been dry and hot in Saskatchewan, so dry that settlers' crops threatened to wither and die in the blistering prairie sun.

It was now late August, and still there was no rain. Each day seemed hotter and dryer than the last.

North West Mounted Police Sergeant Robert Bruce Cameron figured today would be no exception. The sun had barely cleared the horizon, and already he could feel its heat through the wool of his scarlet tunic. He wasn't sweating much yet, but he'd be soaked through long before noon. Military uniforms just weren't designed for comfort.

He'd been sent out four days before by his commanding officer to meet the Fletchers and conduct them safely to the Battleford Fort. Theodore Fletcher was a nephew to one of the North West Mounted Police officers in Ottawa, and word had come via the telegraph that they were to be met and escorted safely to Battleford, where they planned to homestead.

Rob had found them a gully the night before, a

sheltered place to camp where a stream used to run. A few willows gave a semblance of cover, and they'd been comfortable there.

This morning, he'd awakened them before dawn and helped Theodore harness the team, so they'd be on the trail as soon as they'd eaten. Rob wanted to get his charges to the fort at Battleford by evening, so they'd not have to spend another night on the trail. Clara Fletcher made him decidedly nervous.

Even to his bachelor's eye, it was clear that she was with child. The young Scot had no idea when the bairn might decide to put in an appearance, and he didn't want to waste any time out here on the bare prairie finding out. When Rob joined the North West Mounted Police three years before, he'd taken an oath to *"Maintein le Droit."* He was quite prepared to put his life on the line maintaining the right; delivering babies was something else entirely.

He rode beside the slow-moving wagon, trying to appear both reassuring and relaxed, answering Clara's eager questions about the settlement at Battleford while he prayed that the bouncing of the wagon wouldn't shake the bairn loose. He kept a weathered eye on the landscape as well.

There hadn't been any incidents lately with the Indians, but it paid to be alert.

"And tell me, Sgt. Cameron, is there a newspaper in Battleford?"

"Aye, there is, Mrs. Fletcher. Mr. Laurie publishes an issue of the Saskatchewan *Herald* every week. . . ."

From the corner of his eye, Rob caught a flash of bright red in the tall prairie grass off to his right. He reacted instantly, reigning Angus to a halt and putting himself and the horse between whatever he'd seen and Mrs. Fletcher.

"Climb in the back of the wagon and lie down," he ordered in a low voice, and she obeyed without question.

Theodore had caught the note of alarm in Rob's tone and he pulled the team to a halt. He jumped down, rifle in hand, and took shelter behind the covered wagon.

There was no sound and no movement from the dry grass, and Rob was pretty certain no self-respecting Indian would wear bright red if he were planning to ambush them. Nevertheless, he was not one for taking chances.

Colt revolver in hand, keeping low on Angus's neck, he rode cautiously over to see what it was that had alerted him.

As Angus drew near, Rob could hardly believe his eyes.

Sprawled on the ground was a woman, a nearly naked woman.

He stared down at her, shock and amazement mingling with admiration. She was well made.

Then it came to him that perhaps she was being used as a decoy, and he was in danger of ambush. He swung Angus around in a full circle, eyes squinted against the rising sun, studying every detail of the surrounding prairie. An undulating grassland stretched peacefully as far as he could see in every direction, with nothing nearby to hide behind except sagebrush or buffalo grass, and no sign of life but for the wagon and its occupants.

He slid to the ground and knelt down at her side, gingerly taking her wrist and searching for a pulse. It was there, slow and strong, and he breathed a sigh of relief.

She was in a faint, her face pale and her eyes shut. She was a right bonny lass, he concluded. She had shockingly short hair, black as coal and curly as ever he'd seen. She had long, dark lashes and some sort of headband over her forehead, the kind he'd seen Indian women wear, but she wasn't Indian.

It was her clothing—or rather, her lack of clothing—that

kept drawing his attention away from her face.

She wore brief red drawers that stopped high on shapely thighs, with a skimpy matching chemise that left her neck and arms bare. His gaze slid down her long naked legs to her feet, and he frowned.

She had on the strangest pair of short, thick-soled boots he'd ever seen, white with bright colors in stripes down the side. The laces were fiery orange, and he didn't think the boots themselves were even leather. They had a soft appearance, and he moved a bit in order to study them closer. They looked like some sort of canvas.

"Sgt. Cameron, are you all right? Do you need help?" Theodore Fletcher's bellow snapped Rob out of his reverie, and he stood up and waved a reassuring arm toward the wagon.

"No danger," he called. "I'll be there in a wee while."

His voice had disturbed her. She moved her arm and made a low sound in her throat, and Rob remembered his duty as a policeman. He knelt beside her again and conducted a quick examination, trying to be impersonal but all too aware of the softness of her skin and the rounded curves beneath the satin underwear.

She didn't appear to be injured, no broken bones or visible wounds.

In another moment or two she moved her head and opened her eyes, and Rob smiled down at her, hoping to reassure her as shock and puzzlement mingled in her expression and she struggled to sit up.

"Easy lass, take it slowly now. You're in no danger here. I'm Sgt. Rob Cameron, Battleford division of the North West Mounted. Are ye dizzy? Would ye like some water?" He got to his feet and retrieved his canteen from the saddlebag, unstoppered it, and then knelt beside her, holding it out.

41

She took it, sitting with one bare leg outstretched and the other tucked beneath her, totally unself-conscious of her state of undress. It was at that point that Rob concluded that she must be a whore. No decent woman would be that comfortable in her underwear, talking with a man in broad daylight.

It saddened him; she was a bonny lass, she wore no rings, and attractive single women were a rare and precious commodity in the West.

She gave him a tremulous smile.

"Thanks. I guess I must have run too far. Gosh, I fainted there for a moment. I've never fainted before in my life." Her deep, husky voice had a bit of a tremor in it, and she sipped at his canteen, wrinkling her nose and shuddering as she swallowed the brackish water.

"This stuff tastes godawful, but thank you, Mr. . . . what did you say your name was?"

"Cameron. Sgt. Rob Cameron."

She frowned at him. "Thanks, Sergeant. Rob. You're a policeman? A Mountie?"

He nodded. Her easy manner convinced him that what he'd first decided must be true; she was a fallen angel, no doubt about it.

"Are you from the Saskatoon detachment, Rob? Maybe you could give me a ride back to my brother's ranch. It's not far from here." She glanced around, puzzled. "At least, I don't think it is. I see you're on horseback, but could you maybe radio in for a car?"

Her words made no sense to him. He knew every settler in the area, and there was no ranch of any kind out here, and certainly no railway car.

He began to suspect that she was addled. He tried to sound as reassuring as possible, trying to keep her calm. The last thing he needed out here was a madwoman in hysterics.

"I'm from Battleford, lass. I'm conducting that wagon over there, Mr. and Mrs. Fletcher's wagon"—He pointed over to where the Fletchers were waiting—"in to the fort. We'd be pleased to have you accompany us." She seemed to be recovering now from her faint, so he dared to question her a little.

"Could ye tell me your name? And what were ye running from, lass? And how did ye come to be out here on the prairie all by yerself?"

In your red satin drawers, he added mentally, still having a difficult time keeping his eyes on her face where they belonged.

"I'm Paige Randolph." Her tone was confident. "I'm a doctor, a gynecologist, and I've been attending the midwifery conference in Saskatoon."

Rob managed to keep his expression neutral, but it was plain she was mad as a loon and gibbering.

"It ended on Saturday," she went on, "and I came out to visit my brother. Then I went for a jog early this morning, and I must have ended up with heat exhaustion or something. I got really dizzy, and . . ." She stared around again, frowning. "What the heck happened to the crop circle? I was in the middle of it when I passed out, and now it's gone."

"Crop? Circle? I'm sure I can't say." Lord, but she was daft. She wasn't dangerous, as far as he could determine, but it was perfectly obvious that her mind was unhinged. Most of what she said made absolutely no sense. He got to his feet and reached a hand down to help her up.

She was a bit unsteady, but she managed to stand. He was disappointed to find that she towered over him. She was a big lass, no mistake. She was thin, but all of five or six inches taller than his own five feet, four and a half inches. And standing, it seemed that even more of her was bare than before. Looking at her caused uncomfortable reactions in his lower regions that could prove embarrassing.

"Perhaps Mrs. Fletcher has some clothing ye could borrow, Miss Randolph. I'll ask her if ye like." He took Amos's reins in one hand and supported her elbow with the other as he led her toward the wagon. "We ought to be on our way soon. I'm keen to reach the fort by sunset today."

And when he got there, Senior Surgeon Baldwin wasn't going to be one bit pleased at having to deal with a lunatic, Rob concluded; not when he already had half the detachment and some of the townspeople down with fever. He was a fine doctor, was Baldwin, if a wee bit short on patience.

But what was Rob to do with this poor lass except take her back to the post and turn her over to the doctor? He couldn't leave her out here on the bald prairie, that was certain, all alone and unclothed as she was.

Where the devil had she come from? Puzzled, he looked around once again, searching for any sign of a wagon, or a horse, or even trampled grass that would indicate how she'd been transported to this spot.

There was nothing. Rob shook his head, confounded by the strangeness of it all. It was as if she'd dropped out of the sky.

He had to stifle a grin at his fancy. Falling from the sky would make her truly a fallen angel, would it not?

Paige was disoriented and more than a little frightened. When Rob hauled her to her feet, she was shocked to see that instead of miles of cultivated fields sown to grain, she was in the middle of an undulating prairie with no sign of roads—and a hundred yards away stood a covered wagon, of all things, pulled by two horses.

She closed her eyes and reopened them, in case she was hallucinating. The canvas-covered wagon was still there.

This young policeman was a mystery as well. He was much shorter than any Mountie she'd ever met. His head came just to her shoulder. He was gentle with her and courteous, but there were things about him that just weren't right.

He'd never heard of deodorant, for one thing. He had a pungent smell about him of sweat and dust and woodsmoke. And he was wearing red serge in this dreadful heat; the Mounties in British Columbia only wore red serge for formal occasions, certainly not for everyday. And there was the horse. What was a Mountie doing out here alone on a horse? Apart from posing for postcards, she didn't think they really used horses anymore.

Were they making a movie? Surely he'd have said so. And there weren't any sound trucks or other movie paraphernalia anywhere in sight.

Paige's head ached and she couldn't seem to get her thoughts in order.

Well, maybe the Mounties were different in Saskatchewan, she told herself. Lord knew she was no expert on Mounties, but the cut of his uniform seemed peculiar, the jacket much too tight and short. He wore a very large, clumsy-looking handgun in an open holster strapped to his hip. And he wasn't wearing a Stetson, either; instead, he had a queer little pillbox thing cocked at a jaunty angle on his head, with a wide strap holding it on under his chin.

He caught her looking at him and turned as red as his uniform. He wasn't handsome, but he had a wide, likable, sunburned face marred by a huge, rust-colored, swashbuckling mustache that didn't suit him at all. He was covered in freckles, with puppy-dog–friendly hazel eyes and a mop of sandy hair several shades lighter than the hair on his face.

He also had a pronounced Scots accent; she had to listen closely to decipher every word.

"Are you new to Canada, Rob?" Paige thought that must be it.

But he shook his head. "I've been here three years now. I joined the North West Mounted the moment I landed."

The North West Mounted? "But I thought you were all called RCMP now, Royal Canadian Mounted Police?"

He gave her that look again, that guarded, pitying look that annoyed her.

The puzzle of the Mountie faded to the back of her mind as they reached the canvas-covered wagon and he introduced her to the quaint man and woman standing beside it.

Paige smiled and extended her hand to each of them. They were extraordinarily formal, both calling her "Miss Randolph."

Paige realized they must be members of some strict religious clan, traveling by wagon this way; they looked to be in their midthirties or thereabouts, but they were dressed in the most old-fashioned clothing Paige had ever seen outside of a museum. The woman even wore a bonnet. Paige had never seen anyone but a baby wearing a bonnet before.

She tried to remember whether Tony had mentioned a Hutterite colony nearby, or a settlement of Amish people.

The woman, Clara, was pregnant, probably third trimester, and she could certainly have used a pair of maternity tights and a spacious T-shirt. Her dress was long and it looked hot and tight.

She had a plain, comfortable face, a shy, easy smile, straight, straw-colored hair peeping out from underneath the hat, and small round granny glasses perched on her upturned nose.

46

Her husband, Theodore, was big, both tall and wide, with gray-streaked brown hair down to his shoulders. He, like Rob, had a lavish mustache and a full beard. He also wore clothing that looked unsuitable for the occasion, a dark suit jacket that had seen better days, matching, worn pants and some kind of dress shirt. He swept off his battered brown felt hat when Rob introduced her, and then clamped it back on his head.

It was obvious the Fletchers were as shocked by Paige's running strip as she was by their clothing.

Clara took one horrified glance at Paige's legs and her round cheeks turned bright red. After that she kept her eyes carefully on Paige's face, although Paige caught Theodore shooting interested glances at her legs whenever he thought she wasn't looking.

Paige was exasperated. This was utterly insane; they acted as if they'd never seen a woman in shorts and a tank top before. They were making her self-conscious and uncomfortable.

Even the policeman seemed ill at ease, for heaven's sake.

"I told Miss Randolph you might have some clothing she could borrow, Mrs. Fletcher," he said. "Then we must be on our way."

"By all means," Clara agreed eagerly. "In my trunk in the back of the wagon, I'm sure there's something that will be suitable, Miss Randolph."

Paige was losing patience. "Really, there's no need for that, I'm staying not far from here and . . ." But before she could finish protesting, Clara had let down a small set of steps on the back end of the wagon and climbed inside, obviously intent on finding her some clothes.

Beginning to feel a little desperate, Paige turned to Rob Cameron. "Look, there must be some way you could get in touch with my brother. His number is 445-6226. If you'd just give him a call I know he'll drive over and get me."

Cameron didn't answer. He and Theodore exchanged a look that Paige didn't begin to understand.

This whole thing was making her really uneasy.

"Miss Randolph," Clara called from the back of the wagon. "There's a blouse and skirt here that I'm sure will fit you. Would you like to come and try them on?"

Paige blew out an exasperated breath and was about to refuse when Rob Cameron said in a pleading voice, "It might be the best thing, Miss Randolph. There's no way to contact your brother from out here. We'll have to proceed to the fort, there's a telegraph there, ye see, but it's a fair ways from here. That sun's hot; you'll burn without cover."

It was the first thing any of them had said that made sense to her. Of course she was conscious of the dangers of the sun, but she figured she'd never met such a bunch of prudes in her entire life.

She stomped around and climbed into the wagon. It was filled with trunks and wooden boxes and hopsack bags, with only a small central area to move around in. She had to stoop almost double, and it was so hot and airless inside she could hardly breathe. Flies buzzed and bounced against the canvas, and it smelled of turpentine or something else pungent.

Paige yanked off her terry headband and sweated and swore under her breath as she struggled into the white cotton blouse and long dark skirt Clara offered.

There was a stack of underwear which Paige ignored; she slipped her running top off and pulled the blouse on over her bra. The blouse had long, full sleeves and a neckline that buttoned right to the chin. Paige groaned and left the top four buttons undone, and shoved the sleeves up past her elbows.

She stripped off her running shorts and struggled with the skirt, a cumbersome deep green affair made of some stiff sort of fabric.

It was tight around the waist and came four inches from touching her ankles. Her Nikes looked ridiculous, sticking out the bottom.

Clara had busied herself folding things back into the trunk, turning only when Paige was dressed.

"I didn't know whether you'd care to use my under-garments," she said hesitantly, gathering up the underwear Paige hadn't bothered with and stuffing it into the trunk. "You're much taller than I am, Miss Randolph. I'm afraid that skirt's quite short on you. You're sure you don't want to try some stockings?"

Paige blew out an aggravated breath and shook her head.

The woman was nuts. It was already at least 80 degrees outside, and the stockings weren't even panty hose. In fact, they looked like hand-knitted wool, of all the godawful things.

"This is just fine, thanks." Paige thought with longing of the cool blue sundress back in her suitcase. "Lord, let's get out of here before we have heatstroke." Paige hiked the long skirt up and climbed down, Clara close behind her.

The men looked her over, their eyes lingering on her neck and ankles this time, but they didn't say anything.

Well, they were one and all a hell of a strange lot, Paige thought in disgust.

"Move along, now." Cameron climbed on his horse and Paige found herself sitting on the high wagon seat beside Clara as they rumbled off across the prairie.

Riding on the wagon was anything but smooth. They bounced and banged along, and Paige grabbed the side more than once for fear of falling off the high seat. Clara sat between Paige and Theodore, quite relaxed and obviously accustomed to the rough ride.

As they jolted along, Paige began to look around, and she seriously wondered if she could possibly still be unconscious and dreaming all this.

As far as she could see in every direction, there was still no sign of civilization. There were no houses, no power poles, no roads, no fences. There were no tractors pulling harvesting equipment, because there were no cultivated fields. There were just miles of undulating, open prairie with a few groves of trees here and there. She tipped her head back and stared up at the endless arc of blue sky, her eyes watering from the intensity of the sun.

Surely there ought to be an airplane or two up there, a jet stream dividing the heavens in half? There was nothing except a pillow of white cloud, floating along all alone at the edge of the horizon.

A sick feeling began to grow inside of her, a controlled panic. Where on earth was she? What had happened while she was unconscious? She'd obviously been out far longer than she'd thought, because somehow she'd been transported from Tony's field to here. Which was . . . where? And who had brought her? She wasn't anywhere near Tony's fields, so how had she arrived?

"Where are you from, Miss Randolph?" Clara's pleasant voice was a welcome relief, tamping down the hysteria building inside.

"Vancouver. I'm from Vancouver. And why not call me Paige? We're not very formal where I come from." She tried for a smile.

"Vancouver." Theodore sounded interested. "That's out on the West Coast, Clara." He raised his voice to be heard over the rumbling of the wagon. He held the horses' reins in one big fist, but the animals seemed to need little steering.

They plodded along at a steady, jolting gait, following Sgt. Cameron's lead.

"I've heard of Fort Vancouver," he stated. "It's quite some distance from here, with the Rocky Mountains between. Am I right, Miss Randolph? . . . Ah, Miss Paige?" He sounded pleased with himself, knowing where Vancouver was. They might have been talking of an obscure city in Asia, for lord's sake.

"On the West Coast, yes, that's right," Paige confirmed, growing more confused by the moment. "I've never heard it called Fort Vancouver, but I guess technically it did start as a fort. As for the Rockies, they're certainly between here and the coast, all right." She knew she sounded a trifle sarcastic, and she modified her tone. "I haven't personally driven through the mountains; I've only flown over them, but I understand they're breathtaking. I've never had time to drive. I've always been too busy." She was babbling, but it kept her from thinking things that brought that panic rising in her throat again.

"I'm a doctor, a gynecologist, actually." She wondered again where in heaven's name these peculiar people were from. Wherever it was, the twentieth century had certainly not reached out and touched them.

Both Clara and Theo stared at her and then exchanged long glances.

"A doctor? I've never heard of a woman doctor before," Clara said at last, uncertainty evident in her tone.

Now this was absolutely ludicrous. Where had they been living?

"Where are you and Theodore from, Clara?"

"Oh, we're Canadians."

Brilliant.

"We both grew up in Norwich, Oxford County."

Paige had never heard of it.

51

"Theo worked on his father's farm and I was a seam-stress," Clara went on, "but it was hard to get ahead. We decided to join a group of settlers heading out west to work in the coal mines in British Columbia, but when we reached Winnipeg, Theo fell in love with the wide-open country, didn't you, Theodore?" Clara smiled at her husband, and the look he gave her was caring and tender.

Paige was sorry she'd been critical. Here was love, and love was rare.

"So we decided to come out here and homestead," Clara continued. "Theo's uncle Lester is a Mounted Policeman in Ottawa, and he suggested this location, and Lester was kind enough to send word out to the fort that we were coming, and then Sgt. Cameron came to escort us in." She was rather breathless when she finished.

Well, it didn't sound as though they were part of any religious settlement, anyway. Paige was more puzzled than ever.

"My brother has a place near here," Paige remarked. "The price of land's dropped since Tony bought his farm, which will benefit you as buyers, but you should keep in mind that the price of wheat's fallen as well. Still, farming's a great way to live. It's a good place to raise children. Tony has two boys."

She thought wistfully of her nephews. Matthew and Jason would be wondering where she'd gotten to. And it was going to be too late by the time she got back today to change her reservations and fly out. Well, maybe tonight Sharon would change her mind and let Paige take them all out to supper. That might ease the tension a little. She'd have to talk to Sharon about it. She would, the moment she came to a place with a phone.

"That's what we thought," Clara was saying, excitement in her voice. "We just knew that the West would be a wonderful place for children to grow up." She turned toward Paige and said in a low, confiding tone, "I was concerned at first because of my condition—after all it's so isolated out here—but Sgt. Cameron assures me there's a doctor at Battleford, which is most fortunate."

Clara's round cheeks flushed at even this oblique reference to her pregnancy, and her voice dropped to a whisper. "You see, Mr. Fletcher and I married rather later in life than most, and because of my age, I'm a little worried."

"I'm sure there's a fine clinic and a first-class hospital as well in Battleford." Paige gave Clara a warm smile, pleased to be able to reassure this bashful, eccentric woman about something at which she was an expert. "Nowadays a lot more women are waiting until later in life to have babies," she went on. "You'd never believe how many of my mothers are already in their forties. I even had one mother two years ago who was fifty. But with the advances in medical science and the improvement in neonatal care, the risks are minimal. I deliver just as many older mothers as I do women in their twenties."

Clara's powder blue eyes were wide as she stared at Paige.

"Oh. I see. How . . . ummmm . . . how enlightening, Miss Paige."

It was obvious Clara found any discussion of childbirth disconcerting.

How on earth, Paige wondered, was the woman ever going to get through labor with a hang-up like that?

Discouraged, Paige gave up on conversation and silence fell, broken only by the sound of the wagon and the steady clip-clop of the horses. The sun rose higher in the sky, and the heat intensified. Even the breeze was hot, and Paige began to long for a cool drink. Her headache was getting worse, probably because she hadn't had anything to eat yet today. And even if there was a restaurant in sight, she thought dismally, she didn't have a credit card or a penny on her anyway.

At last, they did stop for a hurried lunch. The back of the wagon was on hinges, and it lifted down to form a convenient shelf for the contents of the wicker basket Clara produced.

Paige stared in disbelief at the food the other woman laid out on the clean red-checkered cloth. Even though she was hungry, the items looked anything but appetizing.

There were cold roasted potatoes, cold baked beans, and hard, round biscuits. There was some dry, roasted meat that Paige thought was beef until Clara told her it was antelope.

"Sgt. Cameron shot it two days ago. It was most fortunate because we were out of meat. I salted it down so it would keep."

Paige believed her. She took one bite and it was all she could do to swallow, the stuff was so stringy and salty.

There was no cheese, no butter, no salad, no cold soda or beer, no thermos of coffee—none of the things Paige had always assumed were standard fare for a picnic lunch.

These people were terribly poor, she concluded. How kind and generous they were, to share what they had with her.

The men ate with honest hunger. Paige had beans and a potato and chewed with determination on one of the biscuits, avoiding the heavily salted meat. She thought someone should tactfully explain to Clara the danger of so much salt in the diet, but Paige didn't want to hurt the other woman's feelings. In spite of her peculiar ways, Clara was warm and friendly, urging more food on everyone, particularly Paige.

Everyone shared cups from a canteen of the same

lukewarm, foul-tasting water that Sgt. Cameron had offered earlier, and Paige listened in disbelief to the conversation the men were having.

"Has there been much unrest among the Indians lately, Sgt. Cameron?" Theo was downing his second plate of food.

"Nothing too alarming. The Indian agent reported sixty braves had deserted a few weeks back from Poundmaker's reserve, but we followed them and managed to bring them back."

Paige couldn't believe what she was hearing. "That's disgusting," she burst out at last. "I thought the native people were free to come and go as they liked, just like any other Canadian citizens. I had no idea they were still confined to reservations out here. That's nothing short of barbaric."

The conversation came to an abrupt halt. Again, all three of them gave her that strange look and exchanged glances with each other that she didn't understand, and Paige lost her temper.

"Surely even you people have heard of aboriginal rights," she fumed. "No wonder there were all those problems a few years ago out in Quebec if this is your attitude toward natives."

Not one of them answered her. The men looked uncomfortable and embarrassed, and even Clara wouldn't look her in the eye.

After a few awkward, silent moments, Clara reached out and gently touched Paige's hand.

"Would you like to go for a little stroll with me, Miss Paige?"

It took a moment to figure out that Clara probably had to go to the bathroom. Paige did too, and they walked a discreet distance away from the wagon and shielded each other with their wide skirts as each woman took turns squatting in the grass.

Back at the wagon, Clara wiped off the plates and cutlery and then, to Paige's amazement, meticulously cleaned them with sand from the earth before packing them back into her basket, and the moment the back of the wagon was in place, Sergeant Cameron had them on their way again.

Paige gave up trying to figure things out. The afternoon was hot, a dry, blazing heat that absorbed every ounce of energy from mind and body, leaving her feeling lethargic and slightly sick to her stomach. The rolling, empty prairie stretched unbroken in every direction, and by late afternoon Paige had given up searching the horizon for power poles or cars or buildings.

She and Clara, stiff and bruised from the bumpy ride, climbed down from the wagon every now and then and walked beside it, but Sgt. Cameron soon urged them back up on the wide seat; he and the wagon would have to slow up so as not to leave the women behind, and he seemed obsessed with getting to Battleford.

The sun dropped with agonizing slowness toward the horizon, and a dusty haze seemed to settle over the prairie. Paige had sunk into an exhausted stupor, neither awake nor asleep, when Cameron's cheerful shout rang out.

"Battleford just ahead, Mr. Fletcher. We've arrived safely."

She sat up straight and strained her eyes, searching for the city, and her entire body began to tremble as the wagon crested a hill and the settlement came in sight.

It couldn't be. A wave of dizziness and nausea made Paige clutch the side of the wagon, and the uncertainty and strangeness she'd felt all day intensified until she thought she was about to pass out again.

Below them lay a deep, green valley situated between the

Saskatchewan and Battle rivers, the site of what Paige knew ought to be the bustling small city of Battleford. But there was no city. There were no lights, no welcoming billboards advertising motels and restaurants, there were no cars, there were no streets on which to drive them.

The modern community Paige had been expecting all day didn't exist; instead there was a Hudson's Bay Company store close to the river, a saloon, and a scattering of frame and log buildings. One building was impressive, a two-story structure up on a hillside.

"That's Government House," Rob explained when he saw her staring at it. "They transferred territorial government to Regina in eighty-two, so it's not in use now."

Paige didn't remember hearing a word about it, but she was too stunned by the entire vista to comment.

They bumped across a flimsy wooden structure that bridged the Battle River, and Sgt. Cameron led the way up a hill and into a large stockade made of posts set vertically into the ground. The heavy gate was open wide.

Inside, Paige could see a large two-story frame house constructed of hewn logs which Rob said was the residence of Inspector Morris, commanding officer of the fort. Numerous other buildings, made of logs as well but much less impressive, were built around the periphery of a large open area where at least 15 or 20 Indian tipis were erected. Figures in blankets and buckskin crouched around small cooking fires, and the dusk was full of the smell of roasting meat.

There seemed to be people everywhere, most of them male.

There were dozens of men in scarlet uniforms and black, shiny boots. Some were leading horses across the compound, and a group of them were lined up in perfect rows, doing some sort of drill.

The spectacle was straight out of one of the countless western movies Paige had gone to with Tony when they were little kids, and she found it difficult to believe that she was inside the scene rather than watching it on a movie screen.

Everyone stared at the newcomers, and a great many of the men smiled at Paige and bowed, lifting their caps.

She could hardly breathe. Her blood seemed to hammer in her ears and her thoughts were a confused jumble. What was going on here?

Rob Cameron climbed down from his horse with a flourish.

"Welcome to Fort Battleford," he said with a wide grin, reaching up an arm to help Paige down from the wagon.

She clutched at him, certain that without his support she wouldn't be able to stand. Her knees felt weak and rubbery, and she clung to his strong arm, barely remembering to turn and thank the Fletchers for having her along. She could hardly get the words out.

"It was our pleasure, Miss Paige," Clara declared. "It was lovely having another woman for company," she added with a warm smile. "Perhaps we'll meet before Mr. Fletcher and I venture off to look for land. If not, I do hope you'll come and visit me when we set up a homestead."

"Thank you," Paige managed again through the dryness in her throat. "I'll return your blouse and skirt as soon as I—as soon as I can locate my brother and get my suitcase."

"Gracious no, I wouldn't hear of it." Clara shook her head. "You keep them. They're of no use to me just now anyway. Please, Miss Paige, consider them your own."

Paige reached up and silently gripped Clara's hand. She was unable to say anything. The surrounding scene was frightening her more and more the longer she observed it.

There was something terribly wrong here. She'd known it all day, even though she'd struggled against admitting it to herself.

The scene before her was utterly incongruous, but all the pieces fit, as if she were looking at a carefully constructed historical jigsaw puzzle, a puzzle in which she was the only piece that didn't belong.

"Are you all right, Miss Randolph?" Cameron's solicitous voice seemed to come from a long way off. "This way, if you please."

She stumbled along beside him, gripping his arm as if it were her only connection to reality. He conducted her into a long, low building, so dimly lit that she could hardly see at first.

As her eyes adjusted, she realized it was some sort of hospital, that there were rows of occupied beds down each outer wall, as well as one in the middle. There was a strong smell of sickness and some sort of disinfectant and not enough fresh air, and she could hear several men coughing. There wasn't a single nurse in sight, but several policemen in uniform were moving along the rows, collecting bowls and cups from a recent meal.

She was aware of a tall, lean figure coming toward them, a wide-shouldered man who moved with peculiar grace despite his size.

"Rob Cameron, I do hope you're not going to tell me that the settlers you just brought in have fever, because I don't have even one more bed to put them in." He spoke in a deep, weary voice, his pronounced southern drawl making the words slow and musical.

Paige wasn't aware of Sgt. Cameron's answer. She'd caught sight of a calendar on the wall, and she found herself standing in front of it, staring at the date, frozen with horror.

August was the month displayed, and that was fine; she knew it was August.

What she couldn't believe was the year.

In large, bold numerals it read 1883.

Chapter Four

"That—that calendar," she heard herself stammer. She pointed a shaking finger toward it. "The date, the—the year. It's—it's preposterous." She scowled at the two men, now both studying her.

"This is all a joke, right? You're playing some kind of elaborate joke on me, aren't you?" She couldn't control the tremor in her voice, and it angered her. "I don't find this at all amusing, you know. It's childish, and—and outright ridiculous."

Sgt. Cameron cleared his throat and his ears turned as scarlet as his uniform. "Surgeon Baldwin, this is Miss Randolph," he began in an apologetic tone. "I found Miss Randolph unconscious in the middle of the prairie early this morning," he added, looking up at Baldwin, who towered over him. "I think perhaps the lass might have struck her head or had a wee bit too much sun, sir," he went on, obviously striving for diplomacy. He lowered his voice and leaned in close to the other man. "As you can hear for yourself, the poor thing seems just a wee bit addled,"

61

he said in a whisper. "She's no made a whole lot of sense in her speech all day, and she was most improperly dressed when I found her, sir." His face now matched his ears for color. "These wee bits of underwear were about all she had on."

Paige felt ridiculously betrayed as Rob pulled her nylon singlet and shorts out and handed them to the other man, who took the garments gingerly and studied them as if they were court exhibits.

"Those are mine, thank you." Paige snatched them from Baldwin's fingers and held them bunched in her fist as she glared at the two men. "These are standard jogging issue where I come from, not erotic devices," she snapped.

Baldwin moved closer to her and gave her a long, assessing stare, allowing his keen gray gaze to study with cool detachment first her face and then her figure. He paid special attention to her running shoes, evident beneath the ankle-length skirt, and it was a full minute before his eyes once again returned to her face.

Paige drew herself to her full height and stared back at him, giving him the same sort of arrogant appraisal he was giving her.

So he thought he'd intimidate her, did he? Well, she'd been subjected to just this sort of chauvinistic pomposity in medical school, and she'd learned to counter it with a challenging attitude of her own.

Insolently, she allowed her gaze to rove in slow motion over his face and physique. She hated to admit it, but he was an exceptionally good-looking man, fit and very muscular, probably a few years older than she. His thick, unruly hair was tawny gold and it curled a bit around his ears. Unlike most of the men she'd seen that day, he was clean-shaven except for long sideburns that seemed to emphasize the sculpted quality of his jaw and strong cleft chin.

The expression in his intelligent gray eyes was somber, his aristocratic features classically handsome, his tanned skin pulled taut over elegant cheekbones. There were fine wrinkles at the corners of both mouth and eyes that added character. His lips were narrow, tilted in a cynical half-smile as she met his gaze and held it, chin tilted high.

He smelled of cigars and some sort of strong carbolic soap.

"Are you able to recall your full name and where you're from, miss?"

"Oh, for God's sake. Spare me the psychological assessment, would you?" She blew out an exasperated breath.

He ignored her outburst. "Perhaps you can explain to me how you came to be unconscious, out in the middle of the prairie, dressed"—he waved a finger at the garments she held—"dressed only in those bits of satin?" His deep, slow voice was tinged with annoyance, his tone indicating to her that he was a busy man with no time or energy to coddle some woman.

Paige gave him a contemptuous look. "Of course I know who I am, you idiot. I'm a medical doctor just as you are, Mr. Baldwin, so you can stop speaking to me in that condescending manner. I live in Vancouver, in British Columbia; I'm sure even here you must have heard of it. I flew out to attend a conference on midwifery in Saskatoon. When it was over, I visited my brother's farm and got curious about"—her voice became less certain. "About a—ummm, a crop circle. Have you heard of crop circles?"

Apparently he hadn't. He shook his head, a look of exaggerated patience on his face.

She felt like smacking him one. "They're a bit difficult to explain. They're large circles that appear in farmer's fields for no known reason. Anyhow, I walked to the center of this thing, and there was this incredible energy and then—

then I passed out. I've never passed out before."

He was frowning at her, giving her an assessing look that told her more clearly than words that he considered her quite batty.

Her temper flared. "You can stop looking at me that way, Doctor. There's not a thing wrong with my memory, my intellect, or my reasoning ability. Or my sanity, for that matter. What's wrong is"—against her will her eyes flicked once again to the calendar on the wall and then surveyed the primitive conditions in the room.

She frowned and shook her head, confused and puzzled and deeply disturbed all over again. "There's a problem with the date," she finished in a voice much less assured than she'd have liked. "You see, yesterday it was August fourteen of nineteen hundred and ninety-four. And yet that calendar indicates . . ." Her voice trailed off and she swallowed hard. "It simply can't be right," she insisted, more to herself than to Baldwin. "There's some mistake, something here I'm missing."

"Did you suffer a blow to the head, Miss Randolph?"

Paige started to deny it, but then she stopped and thought about it. Could she have suffered a concussion? Was she having some kind of weird hallucinations? She could remember the peculiar sensations she'd experienced in the center of the crop circle, the energy and sound and color. Had someone—something—struck her on the head?

"I don't think anything hit my head, but I'm not entirely certain," she finally admitted. "I did lose consciousness; I'm not sure for how long."

Baldwin sighed, as if all this was a major inconvenience. "Well, you'd better come in here and let me have a look at you."

He took her forearm in an impatient grip and guided her into a small cubbyhole of an office, motioning her to sit on a straight-backed wooden chair while he donned the most outdated stethoscope Paige had ever seen.

She was acutely uneasy as his long-fingered hands deftly searched her scalp for signs of injury, and even more ill at ease when he used the ridiculous stethoscope to listen to her back and chest, even though to her profound relief he did so through the heavy cotton blouse she'd borrowed from Clara.

Doctor or not, she had no intention of taking off her clothing so that this man could examine her. He made her uncomfortable even fully clothed—more than fully clothed, she sighed to herself.

To her great relief, he didn't suggest it. After a cursory look at the pupils of her eyes, he stepped back and shrugged his shoulders. "As you said, you seem to be in perfect physical health, Miss Randolph."

The ever so slight emphasis on "physical" brought her to her feet. The last of her self-control was gone. She was exhausted, mentally and physically, and her life felt out of control.

"I've had just about enough of this," she exploded. "I don't know what kind of stupid game you're all playing here, but I don't find any of this the least bit amusing." She was aware that she was shouting at him, and she didn't give a damn. He was blocking the only exit from the tiny room, and all of a sudden she was desperate to leave.

"Get out of my way, you—you quack." She pushed him hard, wanting only to escape to somewhere sane. "Move, will you? I'm leaving, you can't keep me here, I'm not under arrest, I'm not one of your patients or prisoners."

It was like pushing a brick wall. His leanness gave no indication of how fit and strong he really was. He reached out and put restraining hands on each of her shoulders, his fingers like steel. His gray eyes were cold, his gentle southern accent at odds with his harsh words. "Get hold of yourself, woman. I have a hospital out there filled with sick men, and I'd suggest you lower your voice. I warn you, if you can't control your temper, madam, if you insist on continuing with this irrational behavior, I'll give you an injection and confine you to a cell." His speech became even slower, deliberate and menacing. "I will then have you transported to the Manitoba Asylum for the Insane at the earliest opportunity. I have neither the time nor the inclination to coddle a demented female."

Something in his tone convinced her he was in earnest, that he had the power and authority to do exactly what he threatened, and, given what she'd seen of this hospital, the concept of some medieval mental institution was horrible.

Trembling, heart thundering as though she'd just run up a steep hill, she made an effort to control herself. Wherever—whenever—this place was, it was the only reality she had at the moment, and she was going to have to find a way of dealing with it.

She forced herself to sit back down on the uncomfortable chair and held up both hands, palms out. "Sorry. Sorry, I apologize, I'm normally anything but a hysterical woman. I'll try to be as rational as possible from now on. I'll tell you what's bothering me, and perhaps you'll agree to answer some questions?"

He inclined his head, watching her carefully, folding his arms across his chest, and towering over her.

"Can you tell me what the date is, please? The real date? No playacting, no joking around?"

"August fifteenth. The year is eighteen hundred and eighty three."

Paige had to struggle with the icy fear his statement created. She swallowed hard, and groped for words that would make him understand, make him believe she was telling the truth, no matter how incongruous it sounded.

"Dr. Baldwin, something absolutely weird has happened to me today and I'm having trouble dealing with it," she began, staring into his eyes, willing him to believe her. "I seem to have somehow hit a time warp and ended up here, more than a hundred years in the past." Verbalizing it didn't help, and panic began to build all over again. "For God's sake, I wasn't even born until nineteen sixty." Her voice was high and thin. "I have a medical clinic and a busy obstetrical practice in Vancouver, I need to get back home. I don't want to be here. . . ." She heard her voice rising even more and noticed the wary look in his eye, the tensing in his posture.

Once again, Paige struggled for control.

Be practical, she cautioned herself. Maybe he'll understand practical. "Doctor, I have no money with me, no clothing of my own except these." She held out the jogging gear crumbled in her hand, and the enormity of her predicament hit her.

She had no credit cards. No shampoo, no toothpaste, no tampons, she listed silently. No medical bag, not even so much as an aspirin, and if ever she needed aspirin, it was right now.

"What you need, Miss Randolph, is some supper and a good night's rest. Things will undoubtedly look different in the morning."

He was humoring her, damn him.

She gave him a saccharine sweet smile. "Why, thank you so much for those comforting words, Doctor. I can't tell you how good they make me feel. Your bedside manner is so reassuring." Irony dripped from her voice.

Color rose in his face, and now it was he who seemed in danger of losing his temper. "What the hell do you expect from me, madam? You have no visible injuries, and as to your delusions, I am not equipped to deal with them. There's nothing more I can do for you. I'm a busy man and this fort is not the place for you to be. You can stay here overnight, but I shall instruct Sgt. Cameron to conduct you to the town of Battleford in the morning and help you find other, more suitable accommodation. As long as you manage to control yourself," he continued in a stern tone, "and not give in again to dementia."

Dementia, for God's sake. The term was about as antiquated as his stethoscope. Paige stood up and looked him squarely in the eye. "No problem, Doctor, I'll behave. I don't really fancy the idea of being drugged with God knows what dangerous concoction and hauled off at your discretion to some primitive loony bin."

His mouth tightened, but he didn't answer. He opened the door for her in silence and then led the way along a narrow corridor and up a steep, narrow staircase. At the top was another door. He took a key ring from his belt and located a key that opened the lock. He swept the door open, standing aside so she could enter.

It was dark inside the room, and Paige hesitated on the threshold. He brushed past her and lit a candle, setting its holder on a rickety table set against one wall.

Paige peered around in the flickering half-light, appalled at what she saw. The room was obviously being used for storage. Saddles were piled in one corner, and a stack of wooden crates filled the other. Various boxes and bags were slung here and there across the dusty board floor. A narrow unmade bed with an unappetizing mattress was wedged under the single small window, which was shuttered tight. It was hot, and the air smelled stale and musty. She could see cobwebs in the corners.

She wrinkled her nose in disgust. "It's filthy in here. You can't possibly expect me to sleep here."

"Because of the fever, the fort is seriously overcrowded. I'm afraid this is the only room available. I apologize for the dust. I'll send someone up with the necessities and some food."

"Where's the bathroom?"

He gave her one of the looks she was becoming all too familiar with, as if her perfectly natural questions were outrageous. "I'll make sure you get a basin and towels. Now, if you'll excuse me."

A basin and towels weren't exactly what she'd meant, but he was already closing the door behind him. To her utter horror, she heard the key turn in the lock once again—locking her inside.

Paige reached the door in two wild leaps, and the candle guttered dangerously from the wind her long skirt stirred up.

"You can't do this to me," she hollered. "Open this door! You can't lock me in here like—like some kind of animal." She heard his boots clatter down the bare wooden stairs, and she began to shriek at the top of her lungs and pummel the sturdy planks.

"Open the door, don't lock me in here, please don't lock me in here. . . ."

"Miss Randolph." The exasperated voice penetrated easily through both the planks and her shrieks. He must have come back up again, because he was just on the other side of the door. "Listen to me. This fort is full of men, both Indian and white, most of whom are eager at any time for a woman. I have my hands full with dozens of victims of mountain fever. I have no intention of dealing with the type of fever you would instill in the rest of the men. I'm not about to have a riot on my hands. This door is locked as much for your safety as my peace of mind."

"Then at least give me the key, damn you. I can lock

it just as well from inside. It's inhuman to lock me in like this."

There was a small silence, and then he said in his deep, soft voice, "Miss Randolph, in light of what Sgt. Cameron considered your profession, combined with what you were wearing when he found you, I consider it much safer for me to retain the key."

She'd never before considered murder a logical solution to anything, but she did now. "You—you miserable, stupid idiot of a man. I have to use the toilet." Her throat was sore from hollering at him.

"I said I'd supply the necessities, Miss Randolph. I intend to do so, the moment you stop wasting my time." Could there possibly be a hint of laughter in his voice? Was he finding all this amusing? Blood pounded in her temples, red dots danced in front of her eyes, and Paige wondered if she might have a seizure just from anger.

His boots thumped back down the stairs and she slumped against the door. Impotent rage washed over her in waves. She stood where she was for several minutes more, her head resting on the rough wood, her entire body trembling. She'd never thought of herself as anything but the most reasonable of women, and she couldn't remember a time when she'd lost her temper this completely at anyone. But neither had she ever been in a situation as strange and frustrating and outright frightening as this.

She made her way over to the bed and sat down—there was nowhere else to sit. Dust billowed up from the mattress.

She got up again and struggled with the thick shutters on the narrow window, but she couldn't get them to open.

She was a prisoner. In one short day, she'd gone from being a professional woman, highly respected in her field, to this. She made an effort to logically trace the path that had led her to where she was, going back to the moment when she'd walked to the center of the crop circle. It all came down to the incredible fact that she'd lost consciousness in one world, and awakened in another, 111 years in the past.

It seemed a long time before she again heard boots climbing the stairs. The key turned in the lock and Baldwin came in, his arms laden with sheets, blankets, towels. He had a lighted lantern slung over one arm, and the comparatively brighter light made the room marginally more cheerful.

A bearded, white-haired old man with a wrinkled face and mischievous black eyes puffed into the room behind Baldwin. He limped quite badly, and he was dressed in shiny black pants, a soiled white shirt, and a vest stretched so tight over his paunch it seemed the buttons would pop at any moment. He wore a bright red sash around his waist, and he carried a pitcher, an enamel washbasin, and an object with a lid that Paige recognized as a chamber pot.

"Bonjour, madame." He gave her a friendly nod, a grin, and a benevolent wink as he set the basin and pitcher on the table where Baldwin had placed the lantern. He then discreetly put the chamber pot in the far corner behind the stacked saddles.

"Armand LeClerc, this is Miss Randolph." Baldwin's introduction was brief. "Armand will be back with your dinner in half an hour. I think you have everything you need for now."

The doctor had given her only a cursory glance when he first came in, and he was already turning toward the door again as he spoke, ushering Armand out ahead of him.

"Wait, wait just a minute, please." Paige jumped to her feet. "Can you open that window at least? I'm going to smother in here unless I get some fresh air."

71

Baldwin went over to the window, unhooked the bars that held the shutters in place, and pulled them back. It was dark outside, but fresh, cool air seemed to pour in, dispelling the dusty closeness of the room. She heaved a huge sigh of relief, feeling that at least she could breathe.

The men left without another word, and Paige shoved the table against the door. She wasn't having them walk in on her, she told herself.

She first made use of the chamber pot. Then she stripped off her blouse and skirt and underwear, poured the lukewarm water from the pitcher into the basin, and gave herself an awkward but satisfying scrub from top to bottom. She ran her fingers through her tangled hair, wishing she had a brush. Back in Clara's clothing again but feeling refreshed, she tried to beat some dust out of the mattress before she made up the bed with the homespun sheets and rough wool blankets.

Tucked between the bedding was a long, quaint white nightshirt, hand-stitched and made of cotton so fine it felt like silk when she stroked it. Finely made, it was still distinctly masculine in style, and Paige marveled at the delicate handwork—the entire garment was hand-sewn, the stitches even and tiny. She held it against her and decided by the hem and the length of the sleeves that it probably belonged to Dr. Baldwin.

Well, that was a first; she'd never known a man who wore a nightshirt before.

She found herself wondering who'd made it, concluding that a man as undeniably good-looking as the good doctor probably had any number of women eager to sew their fingers into shreds for him.

A discreet tap at the door accompanied by the sound of the key turning announced the arrival of her dinner. Paige moved the table away to open the door, and Armand

LeClerc handed her a tray and set a steaming coffeepot on the table.

"Bon appetit, madame."

Paige had to smile. She'd heard the salutation in expensive Vancouver restaurants. To hear it here, in these circumstances, seemed the height of irony.

"Thanks, Armand." He grinned at her, and she tried to smile back. "Are you French? From Quebec?"

He laughed, a deep belly laugh that was good to hear. "No, no, I am Métis. You know what is Métis?"

History hadn't been her strongest area. "French and Indian heritage?" she suggested, her voice hesitant.

He nodded, pleased with her reply. "We call ourselves Bois-Brulees, the free people." He cackled at that, as if it were a joke. "Not so free anymore, since the government takes away our land and our buffalo."

"Do you live here at the fort, Armand?" She was dreading the moment when the key turned again in the lock, leaving her alone. Talking to Armand would delay it, at least for a while.

He shrugged, an eloquent gesture. "My horse, she falls on me one day when I am hunting. The *docteur,* he fix my old bones so I can walk again, and sometimes ride even. Then the fever comes and the *docteur,* he run all the day long, many people sick. So I stay a little while, help him maybe. When spring comes, I go back to my farm." He hesitated, and then moved closer to her, his brow furrowed, his black eyes curious. "I could not help but hear, before, when you and the good *docteur* speak to one another. You 'ave come from far away, yes, madame?"

Paige thought of the calendar and nodded, the fear rising in her once again. "Yes. From far away." She swallowed the lump that rose in her throat. "From—from another time."

73

Armand crossed himself. "It is a miracle, no? That you come here?"

Paige didn't know whether to laugh or cry. "No. More like a major accident, I'd say."

"But you are a *docteur,* also? This I heard you say."

"Yes. I am a doctor, a woman's specialist. I deliver babies, and help women when they have difficulties."

"But not men? You could not, say, fix the bones like the *docteur* did for me?"

"Of course I could. I mean, I'm no orthopedic specialist, but I could certainly set a broken arm. I studied general medicine before I specialized."

"Ahhhh." He looked at her with awe.

"Armand. Where the hell are those clean dressings that Doc needs for the morning?" The frantic male bellow echoed up the stairs and through the open door.

"I must go. And you must eat your dinner before it grows cold." He gave her a courtly little bow and hurried out.

He was careful to lock the door when he left, Paige noted.

Well, so much for polite dinner conversation.

There was no chair, so she dragged the small table over beside the bed and sat there to eat her dinner. The food was plain but plentiful: a lump of tough steak, boiled potatoes and gravy, turnips, a dollop of pickle, and a thick slab of brown bread with pale butter slathered across it. It was served on a tin plate with a rim. There was a smaller plate with an immense slab of black currant pie, and an entire enamel pot full of coffee.

Paige hadn't realized how hungry she was. She demolished most of the dinner and a fair portion of the pie, finishing her lonely meal with cup after cup of the hot, bitterly strong coffee. Caffeine had never kept her awake—in fact, it seemed to have the exact opposite effect.

74

The lamp cast shadows in the corners, but the soft light was soothing and warm. By the time she'd emptied her third cup of coffee, Paige could barely keep her eyes open. She had no idea what time it was, but the muffled sounds of male voices and trampling boots from downstairs had quieted, and there were stars in the sky when she peered out her window.

She moved the table back, stripped off her clothes, and tugged the nightshirt down over her head. It felt soft and welcoming against her skin.

A bit of experimenting taught her that by turning a knob on the side of the lamp, the light could be dimmed until it emitted only a faint glow.

Would Armand come back for the dishes tonight, or leave them till morning? She really didn't give a damn, she decided. She was far too tired to care.

Crawling between the sheets, she pulled the blankets up in a cocoon around her and closed her eyes.

Sleep was instantaneous, like a black and bottomless pit.

"Madame? Madame, it is morning, wake up."

The sound of Armand's cheerful voice and his loud rap on the door, followed by the click of the key in the lock, awakened her. Bitter disappointment brought tears to her eyes; some part of her had believed that she'd awaken back in the bedroom in her brother's house, back in her own place and time.

Instead, light and bird song spilled in through the open window, and on the table, the lantern sat beside the remains of her dinner. It must have burned up all its fuel and gone out at some time during the night.

Paige felt as though her limbs had turned to lead when she tried to move, a heavy lethargy that made sitting up an effort of will. The long trip across the prairie, the heat and dust and bouncing around on that cursed wagon had taken its toll, as well as the stress of finding out where and when she was.

"Come in," she croaked, although she felt more like snarling "Go away."

Armand had a pitcher of hot water in one hand and a fresh pot of coffee in the other.

"What time is it?"

"Six, madame," Armand informed her. He wished her a cheerful good morning, gathered up the dishes from the night before, and maneuvered out the door, balancing last night's tray. "I will bring food right away," he promised with a grin.

Like an old, arthritic woman, she dragged herself out of bed. The basin still held the water from the night before, so she carried it to the window and tipped it out. Just too bad for anyone standing underneath.

By the time she was washed and dressed, she felt marginally better, although she longed for a hot shower, a bottle of shampoo, a toothbrush, and a tube of Crest. Having to put on the same underwear and skirt and blouse again made her shudder. There was no mirror in the room, which was probably just as well. She could imagine what her mop of hair, unruly at the best of times, must look like by now.

She was going to have to do something about clothing and personal hygiene items and a spare set of underwear right away, that was certain. But how?

A bump at her door signaled breakfast. It wasn't Armand who brought it, however. Dr. Baldwin shouldered the door open and set the tray on the table. He turned without a word and gave her his now familiar assessing look, and Paige had to stop herself from nervously running her fingers through her uncombed hair.

For some reason, she hated having him see her creased and tousled looking. It put her at a disadvantage, she told herself, meeting his gaze with defiance and drawing herself up to her full height despite the fact that her feet were still bare.

"Good morning, Miss Randolph. I trust you slept well, and that you have everything you need?" His tone was brisk and impersonal.

"No, I don't have everything I need, thank you. Along with dozens of other basic necessities, I really need a hairbrush," she replied, and even to herself she sounded petulant.

He studied her hair for a long moment. "I do agree," he remarked without even a trace of a smile.

Her face burned and she gave him what she hoped was a scathing look.

"I'll send Armand up with one directly. And by the way, that nightshirt is yours if you want it. It won't fulfill your wardrobe requirements, but it's a beginning."

She opened her mouth to refuse, and then thought better of it. Galling as it was, she needed the damn thing. "Thank you."

He ignored her grudging response. "When you've finished your breakfast, come down and I'll have Sgt. Cameron escort you into town." He strode toward the door, and her temper got the better of her.

"I can't believe you intend to turn me loose on the unsuspecting citizens of Battleford, demented and immoral as I am," she snapped. "And with hair like this."

He stopped and turned to face her. This time his mouth tilted in the faintest semblance of a smile. "They'll just have to take their chances, won't they, Miss Randolph?"

*   *   *

Less than an hour later, Paige trudged along the main street of the town with Rob Cameron at her side and the small bundle that contained all she owned in the world under her arm. Billows of dust puffed up around her ankles with every step, and early as it was, the heat seemed already to penetrate her very skull. At least her hair was brushed; just as he'd promised, Dr. Baldwin had sent Armand up with a hairbrush and a comb as well.

When she'd come downstairs a short time later, it was to find Rob Cameron, in a well-brushed scarlet tunic and newly polished high boots, eagerly waiting for her. The doctor was nowhere in sight.

Paige told herself that was a blessing. If she never laid eyes on Baldwin again, it would suit her just fine.

The shock she'd experienced the previous day when she first caught sight of the frontier town wasn't as overwhelming this morning. Instead, she felt weary and rather numb as Rob chatted on about the various crude log buildings they were passing.

To Paige, the entire town of Battleford was nothing more than a cluster of the most primitive structures she'd ever seen, but Rob was vocal in his pride of the fledgling town.

"Yonder's our telegraph office," Rob announced, pointing to an unimposing log building. "John Little's superintendent and operator; he lives in the back. That's the Hudson's Bay Company store," he explained, motioning toward a large log building in the distance, close to the river, where several men were hitching horses to a rail in front, and a number of people, both native and white, were coming and going. "They stock a grand supply of almost everything a person could need."

Paige had a distinct feeling that her needs and those of

the general populace of Battleford had nothing in common. What she needed this morning were her old cut-off Levi's, a cotton halter, a pair of strappy sandals. . . .

A woman in a long dark dress, neck to wrist to ankles, was entering the store, and she turned and gave Paige a curious stare.

Rob gave her a polite salute. "Ye'll find everyone's wondering about ye, Miss Paige. It's a small town and when someone new arrives it's an event. There's a lot of talking goes on, but in the main, ye'll find the people friendly."

With any luck, Paige thought, she wouldn't be around long enough to find out whether people were friendly or not. Surely, somehow, there was a way to go back where she belonged, if she could only find it.

Rob was enjoying giving her a tour of the town. "Down this street's another general store kept by Mahoney and Macdonald. There's the mail station on the left, next to it's the printing office. Battleford has its own paper, the Saskatchewan *Herald*. That's the school, along there's still another store, kept by Peter Ballendine. And here's the boardinghouse I told you of. We'll just go in and have a wee talk with Lulu. Mrs. Leiberman."

Rob had generously offered to loan Paige some money, an amount he judged enough for a week's lodging and the toilet essentials she needed. She'd opened her mouth to ask for 50 just as he handed her six dollars. Speechless, she'd tucked the strange-looking money in the pocket of her skirt, grateful for his kindness, but six dollars? In Vancouver, it would hardly buy lunch, much less room and board and necessities.

The boardinghouse Rob indicated was two stories high and more substantial than most of the houses they'd passed. It was impressive compared to the smaller dwellings nearby.

The woman who came to the door at Rob's knock was younger than Paige expected; for some reason, she'd imagined a landlady to be matronly.

Instead, Lulu Leiberman was frankly sensual, short, plump, and young; Paige guessed her to be not much older than she was, maybe 34 or 35. She had big china doll–blue eyes, rosy cheeks, and thick masses of yellow-blonde hair wound around her head in braids like a coronet. Her breasts were spectacular, her waist minuscule, her hips impressive. Her lips had a pouty fullness, and when she saw who it was she beamed at Rob and swung the front door wide. Her rather shrill voice was both flirtatious and lilting.

"Why, Rob Cameron, you handsome thing, come on in, come right through into the kitchen and sit down. I've got fresh coffee cake just out of the oven." It was obvious she preferred men to women—beyond one dismissive glance, she ignored Paige.

They stepped inside and Rob removed his pillbox hat and introduced the two women.

"Miss Paige Randolph arrived in Battleford last night and she's in dire need of board and room, Lulu. I've told her this is the finest boardinghouse in all of Battleford," he said, smiling at the landlady.

Paige was sure he'd also said it was the only boardinghouse, but she kept quiet as Lulu led the way down a hallway and into a spacious kitchen, where various kettles and pots bubbled and simmered on a gigantic iron cookstove that crouched in one corner.

A skinny young girl with red braids was peeling a mountain of potatoes over a granite sink, and a long wooden table and numerous chairs occupied the middle of the room. The floor was bare boards, scrubbed almost white.

No modern conveniences here, Paige thought despairingly, envisioning refrigerators and microwaves and wall ovens and tiles.

"Sit down, Rob. You, Margaret," Lulu ordered in a bossy tone. "Leave that for now and go do the upstairs. And get a move on."

"Yes'm." The girl shot Lulu a frightened glance, dried her hands, and scuttled out.

Lulu set out thick china cups and cut delicious-looking slabs of cinnamon-topped cake. She poured Rob's coffee first and then turned to Paige.

"So you're looking for board and room?"

Her shrill voice was polite enough, but her cold blue eyes went over Paige inch by inch, paying special attention to the bare legs and ankles visible between the bottom of Clara's skirt and the Nikes Paige wore on her feet. Her contemptuous gaze flicked to the folded-up nightgown Paige had placed on the chair beside her. Inside it was her comb, brush, and running strip—all her worldly goods.

Without waiting for Paige to say anything, Lulu gave Rob a meaningful look, sniffed, and shook her head. Her tone was syrupy, but the words made Paige bristle. "I'm sorry, Rob, but I don't think my boardinghouse is the place for the likes of your Miss Randolph."

Paige opened her mouth to give Lulu a good piece of her mind, but a sharp kick on her ankle from Rob's heavy boot silenced her.

Rob had a story all prepared, and Paige listened in amazement as he manipulated Lulu Leiberman as smoothly as any con man.

Chapter Five

"Ye see, Lulu, Miss Paige was the unfortunate victim of vicious attack now under investigation," Rob improvised with a touch of pomposity Paige hadn't dreamed he was capable of. "The poor lass lost all her worldly goods and was left unconscious in the middle of the bare prairie."

Lulu clucked her tongue and shook her head, her blue eyes round with curiosity and avid with interest, her voice no more than an awed whisper. "Indians, Rob?"

"I'm afraid I'm not at liberty to say, Lulu. The matter is under investigation."

Even Paige was impressed with the somber and mysterious tone he used.

"Why, that's terrible," Lulu said, patting Paige's arm. "Of course you can board with me. I didn't understand the circumstances. You must tell me all about it."

But superficial sympathy didn't keep her from spelling out her rules and regulations, and Paige realized that Lulu might look soft and rounded, but inside there was a core as hard as steel.

"Now, as Rob knows, this is a decent establishment," she pronounced, "and there'll be no funny goings-on allowed in my house. Three dollars a week, payable in advance, fresh sheets every fortnight. Breakfast at seven, lunch at noon, dinner six sharp, no food served in between. No comings and goings after ten at night, and no male visitors allowed in the rooms—I'm very strict about that." Her chilly blue gaze and pursed mouth underlined her words. "You keep your own room neat and tidy. Margaret will do it out proper every Thursday."

A wave of agonizing homesickness for her own comfortable apartment nearly choked Paige. This sounded worse than a girl's dormitory, and unless Paige was mistaken, Lulu was a bitch.

And Paige also knew that right now she had no choice.

Still, it was a moment before she could nod and hand over three of the one dollar bills Rob had loaned her. She had to remember, she told herself, that she was as homeless as any bag lady on Cordova Street in Vancouver, with probably less money in her pocket.

As they ate cake and drank coffee in the immaculate kitchen, Rob told stories of chasing bank robbers and being chased by wolves, of bootleggers and con men and contrary horses, and Lulu oohed and aahed and hung on his every word.

At last Rob got to his feet and bowed to the women, settling his hat on his head at a jaunty angle and tugging down his scarlet tunic.

"I'm on patrol for the next few days, Miss Paige, but as soon as I'm back I'll look in on ye." He gave Lulu Leiberman a flirtatious wink, and she fluttered around him like an overstuffed pigeon.

"Yer coffee and cake are a treat, Lulu. I thank ye."

The moment the door closed behind him, Lulu reverted

to what Paige knew by now was her real self.

"I don't mind doing Rob a favor, but personally I prefer male boarders," she snapped as she led the way up the steep stairs to the second floor. "Men aren't always needing things the way women are."

A balding white-whiskered man with a sizable paunch stood to one side at the top of the stairs to let them pass. "Morning, Mrs. Leiberman." He dipped his head in a little bow to Paige and smiled, revealing two missing teeth. "Madam, good day."

"William Sweeney, this is Miss Randolph," Lulu said in curt introduction, and Sweeney held out his hand to Paige. "Pleased to make your acquaintance, Miss Randolph."

Paige shook his hand.

"If you need any help with your baggage, I'd be pleased to—"

"She hasn't any baggage, Mr. Sweeney. Not a scrap, except what she's carrying there. Indians attacked out on the prairie, made off with everything, left her for dead," Lulu told him with relish, already hustling Paige along the hallway.

"My goodness, what a terrible calamity." Sweeney's kindly face was full of sympathy. "If there's anything I can do, Miss Randolph—"

"Thanks," Paige said, smiling at him. He seemed both genuine and friendly, and after Lulu, that was reassuring.

"Come along, please, Miss Randolph, I have to get lunch on the table," Lulu snapped. She stopped at a door halfway down and flung it open, standing back so Paige could go in. "This here's your room."

The room was pleasant enough, large and sparkling clean, with a view of the river out the window and a big, soft-looking bed.

There was a washstand, with a rose-patterned pitcher and

a china bowl, and the inevitable chamber pot shut away in a cabinet at the bottom of the washstand. Lulu pointed it out and said the "necessary" was out the back, at the bottom of the garden, and that Margaret would empty the chamber pot each morning.

Poor Margaret.

"And where're you from, Miss Randolph?" Lulu Leiberman stood in the doorway of the bedroom, arms folded across her pouter-pigeon bosom, apparently having forgotten all about getting lunch on the table.

"Vancouver."

Lulu shook her head. "And where would that be, then?"

It was like being in a foreign country where they spoke a different language, Paige thought in despair. "It's out west, on the Pacific Ocean."

"That far away? Humph. That's a long and dangerous journey for a single woman. You are single, are you?"

"Yes, I am." Paige wished the landlady would leave, but Lulu seemed intent on lingering. She didn't make conversation so much as interrogate, Paige decided.

"Well, no need to be single long out here, dearie, unless it's your own choice." Lulu added in a coy voice, "I've had plenty of offers myself, but when you've got property, why, you just can't be too careful. But this is the place to come, if you're hunting a man."

"I'm not, Mrs. Leiberman." Paige tilted her chin up and gave Lulu a level stare. "I'm a doctor, and I assure you I'm not in the market for a husband."

The landlady's eyebrows shot up to her hairline, and her mouth dropped open. "A doctor, you say?" Her eyes went up and down Paige, taking in the ill-fitting skirt, the sweat-stained blouse, as if there ought to be some physical mark that proved Paige's claim. "And what kind of doctor would you be, then? I've never come across any women who were doctors before." The cold blue eyes were both suspicious and mocking.

"I'm an obstetrician." Lulu's blank look indicated her ignorance. "I specialize in pregnancy and childbirth."

"Oh, so you're not a real doctor, then." Lulu sounded smug. "You're a midwife, are you? Well, you want to step careful, because Mrs. Donald's the midwife around here. She's a nasty old battle-axe, and she might not take kindly to you moving in on her territory, so to speak." Lulu looked as if the prospect of a confrontation between Paige and the midwife delighted her.

Paige was irritated beyond belief by Lulu. There was no point, she told herself, in making an issue out of any of this with the landlady. But if it turned out she really was stuck here, if she couldn't find a way back, then she was going to have to find a way to make some money. The only thing she knew was medicine, and the response she'd received from almost everyone so far when she said she was a doctor was disbelief. It didn't make her optimistic about setting up a practice, that was certain.

"I need some things from the store. Can you tell me where I'm best to go?" Paige deliberately changed the subject. "I need a toothbrush, some underwear, shampoo." She paused, boggled by the list of things she was going to need to just exist. She only had three dollars left. Would it stretch to cover even some of the items? Did people even use such things as toothbrushes and shampoo in 1883?

Lulu shrugged, indifferent. "Hudson's Bay Company store stocks most everything." She went out the door. "Lunch will on the table at noon. Try not to keep everyone waiting."

Alone at last, Paige stripped off her clothes and had a thorough wash in the large china basin. Unable to face putting on her soiled underwear again, she pulled on her running shorts and tank top instead, using the basin to scrub out her bra and panties. She'd find a clothesline to hang them on when she went out; in the meantime, she hung them over the iron bedstead.

She hated having to put on the crushed and less than clean skirt and blouse, but it was that or go naked, and she figured Lulu wouldn't exactly approve of nudity.

Lunch was served by Margaret in the dining room, and there were only four boarders present: a round little man named Mr. Raven, Paige, William Sweeney, and, of course, Lulu.

Paige was the last to arrive, and it was clear that Lulu had already entertained the two men with her own embellishments on the story Rob had told about the "vicious attack."

"I hear you lost all you owned in that ambush, Miss Randolph," Mr. Raven said the moment Paige sat down. "What a frightful experience for you to endure. How many savages would you say there were?" He paused and waited expectantly, and Paige silently cursed Rob Cameron.

"I didn't get a chance to count them," she lied, and for the rest of the meal she had to sidestep curious questions and listen to grisly tales of Indian atrocities.

The food was both plentiful and heavy as lead: potatoes mashed with butter and cream, overcooked beef roast, gravy with fat floating on top, turnips, sauerkraut, and a raisin pudding with thick cream for dessert, all served with endless cups of hot, strong coffee. As one rich, substantial dish followed the next, Paige found herself longing for a salad with sprouts and avocado, served with a croissant.

"Mrs. Leiberman sets the best table in Battleford," Mr. Raven boasted after his second helping of pudding. He belched loudly behind his hand, and Lulu blushed and simpered while Paige wondered what the incidence of heart attack was among Lulu's boarders.

Paige excused herself as soon as she could. She went up to her room, intending to go to the Hudson's Bay Company store and see what she could buy with the money she had left.

She was trying to sponge a gravy stain off the front of her blouse when a timid tap sounded at her door.

William Sweeney stood there, looking embarrassed and determined. He was balancing two large boxes in his arms.

He cleared his throat twice. "Miss Randolph, I hope you won't be insulted, but my wife died some time ago and I haven't known what to do with her clothing. When I heard that you'd lost everything but the clothes on your back, I wondered if there might be some things here that would be useful." He shifted uncomfortably, his broad face and bald head flushing. "I think you and she were about the same size. I do hope you won't be insulted. I thought some of it might do till you get back on your feet, so to speak."

Paige was moved by his kindness. "Mr. Sweeney—William, how nice of you." She stood back and gestured him in. "Please call me Paige. And I'm very grateful for the clothes. I'm getting really sick of this skirt and blouse, I tell you." She sighed.

He beamed with pleasure. "They're yours, dear lady, do with them what you will." William set the boxes on the bed and immediately hurried back to the door. "If you can make use of them, I know my dear Letitia would be delighted. She hated waste of any sort. And I thought perhaps you might also like to know"—He blushed scarlet and ran a finger around the tight collar of his white shirt and cleared his throat—"Letitia always shopped for her—ummm, her more personal items, at Miss Rose Rafferty's Ladies' Emporium. She said she found the prices and selection better than at the Company store." He couldn't look at her, he was so embarrassed, and Paige suddenly had the urge to giggle.

These people made inhibition into a whole new science. She stifled her laughter and thanked William again. She was grateful and also touched by his generosity. "Sit down for a minute." She gestured at the high-backed chair by the window.

"Oh, my, no, thank you, Miss—umm, Miss Paige." His eyes darted from side to side, never quite meeting her gaze. "I must go. Mrs. Leiberman would be scandalized at my being in your room. It's against the rules, you know." He peered around the corner of the door as if he expected Lulu to leap out at him with a Bible in her hand and vengeance in her eye, and finding the coast clear, he scuttled off down the hallway.

Mystified by his actions, Paige closed the door behind him and then realized that he must have been looking at her underwear, draped in plain view across the end of the bed.

She did giggle then. Poor, dear William.

Still laughing, she opened one of the boxes, taking out a cotton dress, a voluminous green affair with long sleeves, a high neck, a lot of lace, and what could only be a bustle.

Paige groaned and turned the box upside down. A mound of similar garments spilled out. Paige looked them over, trying not to be horrified at the cumbersome long skirts, the awkward rows of endless buttons up the back of the dresses and the front of the blouses. It was all too obvious zippers hadn't been invented yet.

The clothes were all clean and in good repair: dark skirts, fussy white blouses, several gingham dresses, an elaborate black silk dress, a stack of slips—petticoats, Paige corrected, fingering the delicate embroidery on one of the voluminous items. There was a heavy winter coat, several pairs of sturdy high-laced boots, and a daintier pair of black high-heeled shoes. Paige looked at the shoes and shook her head. Women's feet must have grown much bigger in a hundred years or else Letitia Sweeney had awfully tiny feet for the rest of her.

There was a pervasive odor of mothballs about everything, but at least she had a wardrobe again.

In the second box, there was even a nightgown, plainer than the elaborate one Dr. Baldwin had given her, but serviceable all the same. There was also a pretty white satin wrapper to go over it, and with a pang, she thought of Letitia Sweeney, wearing these for her William. She hoped he'd overcome his reticence enough to strip them off a blushing Letitia at least once or twice.

Filled with gratitude, Paige took off Clara's skirt and blouse, grungy and smelling of sweat, and tried on some of her new secondhand clothes.

They fit pretty well, but God, how did women stand these confining sleeves, these high necks, these long skirts? She shuddered. She'd give anything for a pair of her well-worn Levi's and a T-shirt right about now.

Paige tugged on the coolest of the collection, a blue gingham dress that made her feel like an actress in a western movie, brushed her hair with the doctor's horsehair-bristled brush, and shoved her feet into her track shoes.

Then she grabbed her wet underwear and headed down the stairs and out of the house to look first for a clothesline and then for Miss Rose Rafferty's Ladies' Emporium.

Those first few days were pure culture shock for Paige, and she struggled through them in a fog of disbelief and denial and incredulity and occasionally helpless laughter.

Inconceivable as it was for Paige to accept, in 1883 Queen Victoria was still the reigning monarch of Great

Britain and Ireland, and even here in a small town in the middle of the vast Canadian prairies, the Victorian influence was strong. It seemed to Paige that the prudish and fussy women's clothing styles reflected a general attitude that put appearances above what she considered to be basic values and human comfort.

There was the whole matter of underwear, for instance.

That very first afternoon, she'd gotten a thorough tongue-lashing from Lulu Leiberman for something as innocent as pinning her bra and panties on the clothesline in the backyard. The landlady had been waiting for Paige when she came back from shopping. Paige's scanty ivory lace-trimmed bra and matching bikini panties dangled from Lulu's fingers as though they were contaminated.

"Miss Randolph, I shouldn't have to remind you that a lady never, ever hangs her unmentionables on the clothesline in plain view of the neighborhood. And these . . . these . . ." Lulu Leiberman sputtered and waved the garments at Paige and rolled her blue eyes as though words failed to convey just how obscene she found them.

After the harrowing hour she'd just spent learning what constituted underwear in this era, Paige did have some faint idea why Lulu would look askance at her bra and panty set.

At the emporium, in utter desperation, she'd had to buy a pair of the ridiculous pantaloons of the day, along with a garment that looked like a camisole—the nearest thing Rose Rafferty had to a bra. It seemed bras hadn't been invented yet.

Paige's bare ankles and uncorseted figure horrified the prim, elderly Rose Rafferty, so Paige had reluctantly added a pair of ribbed black stockings that hooked to an elaborate system of garters, which in turn attached to the camisole. She rejected a corset despite the shocked disapproval of

Rose and the other two elderly female clerks.

Just looking at the horrid stockings made her hot and uncomfortable, but the alternative—which she now understood to be instant classification as a whore by everyone she met—was even less desirable. The only good news was that all her purchases came to just two dollars and forty-three cents.

As each day passed, her hopes of somehow miraculously flipping back to the 1990s seemed less and less probable, and Paige had to face the prospect of staying where she was.

That brought her face-to-face with the whole problem of money.

She'd have to find a way of earning her living, and soon. Day followed day, and she was soon going to have to pay Mrs. Leiberman for another week's lodging.

Through talking to the other boarders, Paige determined that there wasn't any doctor in Battleford; the town relied on Dr. Baldwin, up at the fort.

Just walking around town showed her that a high percentage of the female population was pregnant, so surely there was a need for a highly trained obstetrician in the area.

There were a few little problems with setting up an office, however.

The first was that she had no way of proving she was a doctor. Her accreditation was with a university that wasn't in existence yet.

Second, she had no equipment, and no money to purchase any.

Third was probably the most difficult obstacle of all. Everyone she talked with had a major attitude problem toward the idea of a woman being a doctor.

It galled Paige, but women were very much second-class

citizens in this era. She was beginning to doubt that anyone in Battleford, male or female, would consider a woman doctor capable of treating them for so much as an ingrown toenail.

Well, she'd have to find some other way of earning a living, but it drove her nuts to have the expertise and training she had and not be able to use it. The thought of trying to find a job as a clerk or a housemaid—the only two jobs apparently open to women—depressed her, and she put it off from one day to the next.

The problem of employment became an obsession and she couldn't sleep. She tossed and turned until long past midnight and then was wide awake again at dawn.

Early one morning, unable to stand the confines of her room, she washed and dressed and crept down the stairs and out the back door. She walked to the river, following a faint path through the rough grass. She sat on a smooth stone and watched the sun come up over the eastern horizon, and after a while she made her way back to town.

It was still very early, but the town was slowly coming to life, smoke puffing out of chimneys as breakfasts were cooked, tousled figures slipping in and out of outhouses, roosters crowing in backyard coops.

Paige strolled down the street, enjoying the cool morning air. There were already a few Indians gathered around the Hudson's Bay Company store, waiting for it to open, and a heavy wagon pulled by two spirited horses was rumbling toward her down the wide street.

A small boy, five or six years old, was playing with a puppy in front of a log house.

Paige smiled at him as she passed. "Hi."

"Hi," he repeated the greeting and grinned back at her. The puppy slid out of his grasp and raced toward Paige. She bent over to catch the little animal but he veered off at the last moment into the roadway, and in a split second the quiet morning erupted into confusion.

The boy shouted, "Pal, come back here!"

The puppy ignored him, barking and darting this way and that, directly in the path of the approaching horses and the loaded wagon. The horses shied and reared.

"Pal, here Pal—"

"No, no, don't go after him!" Paige lunged for the child, but he was already dashing after his dog. Harnesses jangled, the horses snorted and threw themselves in the air, and the dog yelped in pain as a hoof caught him and tossed him high in the air.

"Pal, Pal!" the child screamed. He was directly under the horses' hooves. The driver cursed and hollered a warning, struggling to control his animals. One of the horses' hooves struck the boy's arm, and he screamed again, writhing in a twisted heap in the dust of the roadway.

Paige was already on her knees beside him as two men came bursting from nearby houses to grab the horses' bridles and move them away from the scene. The wagon had overturned, spilling sacks of grain everywhere. Some of the sacks burst and the golden contents oozed into the dirt. The puppy lay dead in the midst of the grain.

The boy was unconscious. With swift and gentle fingers, Paige examined him, checking his pulse, trying to determine whether or not there might be severe internal bleeding. The worst visible injury was what looked to be a compound fracture of the lower right arm. The arm was bent at a grotesque angle and the bone was protruding. Blood was pouring from the wound in a steady stream.

"I need a towel," Paige hollered. "Somebody get me a clean towel, fast."

Someone dashed into a house and came back with one,

and Paige pressed and held it directly on the wound to stanch the bleeding.

"Billy, oh Jesus, what's happened to my Billy?" A thin young woman in a stained blue dress came running down the street, shrieking and throwing herself down by the child, pressing her hand over her mouth when she saw the blood and the open wound.

"You're his mother?" Paige had her fingers on the boy's pulse again. It was rapid and weak. Shock was taking its toll.

The woman was becoming hysterical now, screaming and wringing her hands. "He's gonna die, ohmigod, Billy's gonna die—"

"Stop that noise, there's no time for that now," Paige snapped at her in a fierce tone that immediately brought the shrieks to a halt. "I'm a doctor and Billy's going to be fine as long as you do as I say."

The woman gulped and stared at Paige with wide, frightened, tear-soaked eyes. "What? Anything, just tell me what to do."

"We have to move him out of the street. We need a stretcher and it'll take too long to get him to the hospital at the fort—" Paige looked around, trying to think. Her own heart was hammering as though it were about to burst. She couldn't exactly have someone call 911.

"You," she called to a man hovering nearby. "Bring a plank, a flat piece of wood big enough to hold this child. And—what's your name?" Paige touched the mother's arm.

"Mary Wiggens, miss." Her lips were white-rimmed and trembling.

"Mary, I'm Dr. Paige Randolph. Be strong, now, Mary, I can't have you fainting on me. I want you to go and get me a clean blanket, and then clear off a table in your house to lay Billy on. Put it by a window where there's good light. And put pots of water on to boil."

But even if the boy were safely indoors, Paige realized she could do nothing without instruments. She caught sight of one of the young men who'd restrained the horses. "Hey, you. Hurry up to the fort, please, tell Dr. Baldwin what's happened and bring him back as fast as you can. Tell him to bring his instruments, bandages, antiseptic, and an anesthetic. We'll be in that house." She indicated where the boy lived. "Can you remember all that?"

"Yes, ma'am." He raced over to the Hudson's Bay Company store, leaped on one of the horses tied to the hitching rail, and thundered off in the direction of the fort.

Paige directed the men who brought the makeshift stretcher, making certain that Billy's arm was immobilized so no further damage would result from moving him. The direct pressure had stanched the flow of blood, and the boy regained consciousness, crying and struggling against the pain as she settled him on a clean sheet on the blanket-padded table in his mother's kitchen.

"Easy there, fellow, easy now, we're going to get you all fixed up. . . ." Paige kept up a soothing patter, but it was all she could do to stop her hands from trembling. She couldn't do a damn thing for this kid because she didn't have one scrap of equipment.

Damn you, Dr. Baldwin, get a move on. . . .

"Hello, Miss Randolph." The deep, drawling baritone acted like a tranquilizer on her nerves, and she was able to turn calmly toward Baldwin when he came in the back door.

He was wearing his scarlet tunic, but it had been thrown on hastily over a collarless white shirt. Instead of the small round pillbox that the other Mounties wore, he had on a wide-brimmed brown felt hat. He swept it off and shrugged out of his tunic, rolling the sleeves of his shirt above his elbows.

"Well, you young rascal, what have you been up to, hmmm?"

The man had presence. The small room seemed full of him as he bent over Billy, examining the wound with gentle fingers, and the terrified child quieted, reassured by his manner.

Baldwin hadn't washed before examining the wound, Paige realized in horror.

"There's hot water and soap over there by the washstand, doctor, and clean towels," she told him in a level voice. "The pans on the stove are also boiling; we can use them to sterilize your instruments. What do you use as a disinfectant? I'll see to them while you're scrubbing."

He gave her a measuring look, and for a moment she thought he was about to challenge her. But all he said was, "There's carbolic in the bag. Use that, Miss Randolph."

He turned to the washbasin and lathered his hands, and Paige unpacked his medical bag and lowered the supplies she thought they'd need into the boiling water. The instruments were recognizable to her, but so antiquated she felt they belonged in a museum.

In a low tone, she detailed what she felt the boy's injuries were. "Without an X ray, though, there's no way of telling what internal injuries he might have."

He was drying his hands and he gave her a narrow-eyed look.

"X ray? And what exactly is an X ray, Miss Randolph?"

With a sinking feeling in her stomach, Paige realized X rays hadn't been discovered yet. Flustered, she stammered, "I'll explain later."

She'd better find out exactly what the going treatment

was before she put her foot in it again. Meeting his cool gray eyes, she said, "What procedure do you suggest we follow in repairing Billy's arm, Doctor Baldwin?"

He gave her that assessing look again, but when he began to speak, it was obvious he'd had a great deal of experience with fractures of all types—certainly more than she'd had in ob-gyn, that was for sure. But apart from a few technicalities, it was pretty much what she'd have done by herself. The only major, and to Paige, distressing difference was sterile procedure.

Of course they had no gowns or gloves, and her efforts with scrubbing and boiling instruments were little more than token attempts at avoiding infection.

The only anesthetic he had was chloroform. The method of administering it was simple—at Baldwin's instruction, Paige dripped it onto a pad held over Billy's nose. Well aware of the dangers of even modern anesthetic, this barbaric technique left her horrified, but again, there was no alternative.

Doing her best to seem both coolheaded and professional, Paige gave the anesthetic and helped tie off vessels. She worked with Baldwin setting the bone, impressed by his obvious experience at this procedure. She helped suture the wound closed, longing all the while for an antibiotic that would prevent the infection she felt was inevitable. Baldwin casually sprinkled his nasty carbolic over the wound.

She had to admire the dexterity and skill of his gentle, long-fingered hands, however. He was as adept and as caring as any doctor she'd ever met, and his surgical technique was impressive.

When the plaster was at last in place, they moved Billy, still anesthetized, to his tiny bedroom off the hall at the back of the house.

Baldwin gave Billy's mother instructions about his care,

emphasizing the need for him to be kept quiet. Paige added strict instructions about absolute cleanliness in dealing with his injury. Mary Wiggens thanked them both tearfully, offering coffee and breakfast, which they both refused.

"I'm living just down the street at Mrs. Leiberman's. I'll come by and check on Billy this afternoon, and if he gets feverish or seems confused when he wakes up, come and get me right away," Paige instructed.

Out on the street, she squinted up at the sky and realized that several hours must have gone by while they worked; the sun was high, the day already airless and hot.

She ought to be exhausted after the morning's work, but instead she felt exhilarated, as if using her skills as a doctor again had infused her with new energy.

"I owe you an apology, Dr. Randolph." Baldwin's deep drawl came from behind her, and she turned to face him, hardly able to believe he'd actually addressed her as Doctor.

"You are indeed a physician, and a very capable one at that," he admitted. "Where did you train?"

He sounded curious, but there was also a trace of respect in his tone that pleased her. After the way he'd treated her at the fort, a little respect was quite welcome.

"At the University of British Columbia. I'm a gynecologist."

He shook his head, a perplexed frown creasing his brow. "I'm not familiar with that university, nor with your specialty."

Probably because the university didn't yet exist, and neither did the term gynecologist. It was maddening, this whole ridiculous problem with time. "How about you, Doctor?" she countered to deflect the awkwardness of again getting into a discussion of where and when she was from. "Where did you train?"

His gray eyes were remote. "University of South Carolina."

"Did you do a surgical residency?"

His glance flicked across her face and away, and his crooked smile was bitter. "I'm afraid my surgical residency was the war, Miss Randolph. There were adequate opportunities to practice surgery on the battlefield, I assure you."

She shook her head, perplexed. What war was he talking about? History was anything but her strong suit, and her mind went blank.

"Sorry, you've lost me. What war?"

His eyebrows shot up and he said in his soft southern drawl, "The War Between the States, Dr. Randolph. Surely you've heard of it?"

Lord. He was talking about the American Civil War. Shock vibrated through her. She was actually standing here, talking to a man who'd been on the battlefields of the Civil War.

"But—wasn't that—it was quite a while ago, wasn't it?" She struggled for a date. "Eighteen sixty, about?"

"Sixty-one to sixty-five. Four endless years, Dr. Randolph."

"And were you—were you involved, that whole time? As a doctor, I mean?" Her curiosity overcame the animosity she felt toward him. She wondered again how old he was. If he'd been old enough to take part in the Civil War, that would make him older than she'd estimated.

He seemed to choose his words with care when he answered her. His voice was devoid of inflection, as though he were reciting from a factual document.

"My father was a career officer in the Confederate army. He insisted I finish medical school when the war broke out. I graduated in the spring of sixty-three and volunteered immediately for active duty. I was involved, as you put it, from then until the end." As if he'd guessed what she'd been thinking, he added, "I was twenty-four years old when it was finally over."

So he was—Paige added swiftly—42 now. Eight years older than she, give or take a few hundred years or so. She stared at him, aware once again of how attractive he was. He'd replaced his tunic and settled the broad-brimmed hat on his head, and the hair that escaped from under it was golden in the sunshine.

The nurses at Grace would have labeled Dr. Baldwin a hunk.

"Here's your horse, sir." A boy of about 12 hurried up to them, holding a spirited horse by the reins. "I watered Major and gave him some hay over at the livery stable." The boy obviously hero-worshiped the doctor.

"Thank you, Freddie." Baldwin smiled and gave Paige a formal little bow. He handed the boy a coin and tousled his hair, and then swung easily into the saddle. "I'm due back at the fort. Afternoon, Dr. Randolph, it's been a pleasure. I'm sure we'll meet soon again."

He nodded down at her, expertly turned the horse, and cantered off down the street.

As soon as he was out of her view, however, Myles Baldwin turned Major away from the route that would have led to the fort.

He urged the powerful animal into a furious gallop, tracing the river's path along the valley floor for a mile or so, and then urging the horse to climb the embankment.

They followed a faint trail that led across rolling hills in an easterly direction across the prairie, the ever-present wind forcing Myles to tighten the cord on his hat and bend low over Major's back.

He pushed himself and his mount at a pace that demanded

absolute concentration, trying to outdistance the chaotic emotions that filled him, the memories that haunted him.

It didn't work; it never did. After a while he slowed, letting the animal choose its own gait, holding the reins loosely.

He couldn't outrun the past. He'd learned that long before.

Today, however, mixed in with his memories were new and disturbing images. Against the canvas of the endless prairie and the blue canopy of sky, he could see Paige Randolph as she'd looked that first moment he'd seen her at the hospital, her huge green eyes frightened and defiant, her outrageous hair curling like an aura around her head.

He saw her as she'd looked today, working beside him, her beautiful, high-cheekboned face intent on their patient, her slender body brushing against him from time to time, rousing his desire, angering him because it took his attention from the task at hand.

Where had she come from, this annoying, disturbing, mysterious woman? How long would she stay in Battleford?

He hoped not long. She was headstrong and assured, outspoken in a way he wasn't accustomed to in a woman. There was the mystery surrounding her that puzzled him, the mystery of where she'd really come from, how she'd ended up as she had on the bare prairie. He'd called Cameron in and had him go over and over the details, but there seemed no rational explanation of how she'd come to be where the sergeant had found her.

Of course, her version of the incident was totally ridiculous.

Except that today's events had convinced him that she was a talented, highly trained doctor, and so that portion of her hysterical rambling the other night was the truth.

She'd exhibited a knowledge and skill today that impressed him—several suggestions she'd made during the operation they'd performed had been brilliant, and one of the techniques she'd used during the surgery was unknown to him.

As to the rest of who and what she was—he shook his head. The story Paige Randolph told of coming from the future was, of course, preposterous.

Chapter Six

Major's steady gait and the hot, windy peace of the prairie afternoon eventually lulled him.

The gut-wrenching pain that always gripped him when he thought about his home, his family, his former life, began to ease.

He'd imagined lately that he was beginning to forget; he'd fooled himself into believing that the memories were starting to fade.

He'd even begun to hope that somewhere in the future there might be a time when he could sleep through the night without jerking awake in a panic, heart pumping, body soaked with sweat, ears ringing with the screams of dying men . . . or, infinitely worse, the agonizing moans of a dying woman.

He ought to get back to the fort, he reminded himself. He had dozens of patients to attend to at the hospital, and the young constables assigned to him on ward duty weren't competent to deal with anything but the most superficial of problems.

But he felt restless, reluctant to hurry back to the stuffy confines of the hospital ward, the demands of his patients.

His good friend, Dennis Quinlan, lived not many miles away. Myles hadn't seen Dennis or his wife for some time now.

The hospital could manage without him for another hour or two. He urged his horse in the direction of Quinlan's cabin.

"Myles, you old son of a gun, am I glad to see you." Dennis mopped sweat from his forehead and grinned up at his friend, his white teeth gleaming through the layer of grime on his face and neck. "I was praying something'd come along to drag me away from this confounded job." Dennis was digging stumps out of a field, tying a rope to them, and then urging his horse to uproot them.

"Farming's rotten, backbreaking work, Myles. You're a smart man to stay with broken arms and carbuncles."

Myles grinned. "Seems to agree with you, though. No trace left of that paunch you were developing before you quit the force."

Dennis laughed and unhooked the rope he'd attached to his horse's harness. In one graceful leap he mounted the animal and led the way toward a log cabin surrounded by willow trees a short distance from a stream.

"Let's go see if Tahny's got any coffee brewin'. She'll be delighted to see you; I know she gets fed up with lookin' at my ugly mug all the time." He winked at Myles, his irrepressible grin flashing. "Not that yours is all that appetizing either, Dr. Baldwin. But at least it's a change for the poor girl."

Two years ago, Dennis, an officer in the NWMP, had fallen in love with and married a beautiful Indian woman, a highborn member of the Cree nation, and brought her with him to live at the fort.

It soon became apparent that the other officers' wives would never accept Tahnancoa, and worse, were going out of their way to make things difficult for her.

Dennis was enraged. He resigned his position in the force and homesteaded this isolated piece of land, planning to buy stock and raise beef to supply to the fort and Battleford.

"Honey, look who's here." Dennis ushered Myles into the modest cabin.

"Myles Baldwin, welcome." Tahnancoa came hurrying to greet him, her oval face glowing with pleasure, her soft, dark eyes and her beautiful smile conveying how pleased she was to see him.

He was one of their few white visitors, and Tahnancoa greeted him like a brother, taking his hand in hers and leading him to the hand-hewn pine table in the middle of the cabin's large, multipurpose main room. She poured Myles and Dennis mugs of coffee, placing a jar of strawberry preserves and gigantic slabs of fresh corn bread in front of each of them.

Myles watched her as she moved from stove to table and back again. He was convinced that Tahnancoa's startling beauty was the primary reason many of the officers' wives were cruel to her.

Tall and slender, she moved like a proud forest animal. Her long, shining black hair hung in thick braids which reached past her waist. She often wore her traditional native buckskin, but now she had on a red cotton housedress that set off her smooth brown skin and huge, liquid, dark eyes.

She gave her husband and Myles a wide, bashful smile, and he saw the way Dennis's gaze followed her.

They were very much in love.

For some reason, Myles found himself thinking again of Paige Randolph.

Paige, too, was a beautiful woman. Her dark hair was only a few shades lighter than Tahnancoa's ebony tresses, wildly curly instead of satin smooth, cropped short.

Paige's creamy skin was lightly tanned, with a few freckles scattered across her nose. She, like Tahnancoa, was also tall and slender and graceful. He'd noticed her hands today particularly, long-fingered, amazingly strong, adept at her tasks.

And, Myles concluded, that's where any similarity between Dennis's wife and Paige ended—with physical appearance.

Tahny was gentle, sweet-natured, shy, soft-spoken.

Paige Randolph was loud, brassy, and ornery. She was stubborn as a mule, and he'd bet he'd already been in more fights with her in the few days he'd known her than Dennis and Tahnancoa had ever endured.

"So, my friend, what's new at the fort?" Dennis interrupted his musings, and Myles was relieved.

"Eighteen new cases of malarial fever, if you want the medical report. Apart from that, not much out of the usual. Jenson and Jerry Potts caught the bandits who robbed that mail shipment last month—a couple of escaped jailbirds from the east." He paused, and to his chagrin, Paige Randolph was again in his thoughts.

"A peculiar thing occurred a week ago," he said slowly. He realized that he wanted to talk about Paige; he wanted his friends' reactions to the whole story.

"Rob Cameron was escorting some settlers in to the fort, and he came across a young woman unconscious on the prairie." He told Dennis and Tahny how Paige had reacted when she arrived at the fort, and her outrageous story about being a medical doctor from another time. "I have to admit

107

the doctor part was true," Myles went on, describing what had happened that morning. "No one could have done what she did unless they'd had extensive medical knowledge."

Tahnancoa had sat down at the table with the men, and she was paying close attention as Myles talked. There was a silence when he finished.

"Where does she say her home is, this woman?" Tahnancoa inquired. "Besides another time, what place does she say she's from?"

"From the Pacific province of British Columbia," Myles said. "A town called Vancouver."

"I hear this new province is threatening to join the United States if Sir John doesn't make good his promise of a railroad that links them with Ontario and the maritimes." Dennis loved discussing politics.

For the next half-hour, the men talked about the proposed railroad and the ensuing fight over land expropriation that had already caused hardship and bad feelings between the Métis, their relatives, the Indians, and the government of Canada.

Myles and the Quinlans were in total agreement about the matter; they knew that the native people had been unfairly treated by the government, their land stolen from them, and with it, their livelihood. In addition, the settlers that swarmed across the prairies had all but destroyed the buffalo, which the natives had relied on for food and clothing and shelter.

The trouble was, none of them knew what to do to rectify the injustice.

After several more cups of coffee and two huge slabs of Tahnancoa's corn bread spread with homemade strawberry preserves, Myles reluctantly said good-bye and rode back to the fort.

The demons of memory and pain that tormented him were

quiet now and he could enjoy the still, hot ride across the rolling meadows. He thought of the Randolph woman only once, when a scarlet jay started and took flight in front of his horse.

The bird's plumage was the same dramatic color as the scraps of clothing she'd been wearing when Cameron found her.

Myles was exasperated when he realized that he'd spent several miles imagining just how she'd look in those skimpy garments.

His arousal had nothing whatsoever to do with any particular woman, he told himself. It was biological, plain and simple. It had been too long a time since he'd lain with a woman.

"Please, ma'am, my husband said I was to give it to you, to pay for Billy's operation and all. The police doctor gets paid by the government, but if it hadn't been for you, our Billy mighta died. And my Jim don't want to be beholden to anybody, ye see." Mary Wiggens pressed the crumpled five-dollar bill into Paige's hand.

It was the day after the accident, and Paige was relieved and delighted to find that Billy's arm seemed to be healing nicely, without the redness and swelling she'd been afraid would indicate infection. Perhaps Baldwin's dreadful carbolic had done the job after all; certainly there was no faulting the neat and efficient job they'd both done on the reconstruction of the arm itself.

Paige didn't want to take the money from Mary Wiggens; it was obvious from their house and threadbare clothing that the family didn't have money to spare.

But there was also the matter of pride; she could see it was important for these people to feel they'd paid their debts. And Lord knew, Paige needed the money; Lulu Leiberman hadn't yet asked for the next week's rent, but she certainly would any moment now.

"Thank you, but my fee is three dollars, Mary, not five," she improvised, trading the five-dollar bill for three equally crumpled singles.

Three dollars would pay for the next week's board and room at Leiberman's, and Paige knew from the relief on Mary's face that the family would put the two dollars' change to good use.

Guess what, Sam Harris? she silently addressed her partner at the clinic who was a stickler for proper bookkeeping and billing procedures. I just billed three whole dollars for an emergency operation and who knows how many home visits, what'ya think of that?

The thought of Sam brought a heavy sadness that seemed to lodge in her chest like a rock, and she forced herself back to here and now. As the days slid by, her chances of going home seemed to become more and more flimsy.

Last night, however, she'd had an idea that just might allow her to earn a living wage for a few weeks—at least, she hoped it might. It would depend on the North West Mounted Police and their attitude toward hiring women.

"It's very irregular, Chief Surgeon Baldwin. The force doesn't hire females in any capacity, you know that, and a woman who claims to be a doctor? Absurd. Questionable moral character, if you ask me, a woman even wanting to be a doctor. I feel quite certain the commissioner wouldn't approve." Inspector Morris frowned at Myles and twirled the ends of his handlebar mustache.

Myles stood his ground. "I'm satisfied that Dr. Randolph's a good physician, sir, and the fact is I need trained help immediately and she's available. Considering the fact that I've sent two urgent requisitions to headquarters for an assistant surgeon at this post and had no reply, it seems I must take matters into my own hands." Myles had fully expected the inspector to object to his suggestion that the force hire Dr. Randolph to assist him during the fever outbreak that was now threatening to become an epidemic.

Myles would never have considered it himself if he weren't exhausted from tending day and night to the ever-increasing numbers of victims from both the post and the town.

The truth was, he'd never thought of it at all if Dr. Randolph hadn't brazenly proposed it to him. And once she had, he couldn't see any reason it shouldn't work.

"Do you have any objection to me personally taking Dr. Randolph on for the duration of this outbreak, Inspector? I'll pay her salary out of my own wages, of course. If that's not acceptable, sir, then I must insist you spare me another four men immediately to act as ward attendants."

Inspector Morris's bushy eyebrows shot to his hairline. "Four more men—now, Surgeon Baldwin, be reasonable. As you well know, the epidemic has left me seriously shorthanded. I've had to cancel several patrols, and the work on the new barracks has been postponed until God knows when"—His voice rose to a bellow—"and every day there's more blasted men on sick parade."

He slammed his hand down on the desk, making papers flutter. "Assigning another four of my able-bodied men to hospital duty is quite out of the question. Quite out of the question."

"Then I take it you suggest I should make a private arrangement with Dr. Randolph, is that right, sir? The fever is spreading rapidly to the civilian population, and I must have help."

Morris's face was purple. Myles thought the old boy

might be going to have a stroke one day soon, considering his temper.

"Do what you feel you must do, Surgeon Baldwin, and don't bother me with the details," he finally sputtered.

Myles snapped off a salute and concealed a weary but triumphant smile. "Thank you, sir. Good day to you, sir."

There'd been three new cases of fever among the enlisted men yesterday, and this morning another four showed up at sick parade. He had another dozen patients sick in their homes in the town, whom he had to visit.

The young constables who'd been assigned hospital duty were next to useless around sick men.

"You can't possibly give adequate medical attention to all the patients by yourself," Miss Randolph had pronounced in that irritating tone of hers. "I suggest you give serious thought to hiring me, Dr. Baldwin. I'm an absolute bargain."

Her green eyes had sparkled with sarcastic amusement. "My fee is eight dollars per week, based on an eight-hour day, which for a doctor with my experience is a joke. However, I need the job as much as you need my help. You can reach me at Mrs. Leiberman's."

The woman's insufferable attitude infuriated him, but after he'd spent most of last night tending to chronically sick patients, he had to admit, albeit grudgingly, that her suggestion made sense.

As soon as he left the inspector's office, Myles sent a boy with a curt note agreeing to her terms and telling her to come to the infirmary as soon as possible.

Within a single hour of her arrival, however, he was sorry he'd ever been desperate enough to hire her.

"First of all, open every window in this building," she instructed Armand LeClerc and two constables. "And after that, we'll begin scrubbing every single thing in the room with that nasty carbolic solution you people use as a disinfectant. I can't believe you're putting new cases in beds that haven't been disinfected. The men's blankets will have to be laundered and hung out in the sunshine to dry. And each one of you is to scrub your hands thoroughly every single time you touch one of these patients."

Myles swore under his breath and strode over to where she was already preparing a basin of carbolic solution.

"What I wouldn't give for some decent antiseptic and a few dozen vials of ampicillin," she was muttering. "Not to mention some trained nurses and a couple of decent orderlies and"—She glanced over her shoulder at Myles, interpreted the look on his face, and whirled around to face him, arms folded across her chest, chin high, ready for battle.

"Madam," he began, clenching his teeth against the outrage he felt at her peremptory takeover of his hospital, "Madam, I don't believe you fully understand the nature of this particular fever."

He hadn't intended to sound quite so pompous, but the devil take the woman, she brought out the very worst in him. "We're very familiar with this malady, Dr. Randolph. We call it mountain fever, or malarial typhoid. We believe it to be noncontagious. It's caused by bad air from the low level of water in the river, which accounts for our keeping the windows and doors firmly closed. We treat it with quinine, medical comforts, stimulants, beef tea and milk, and—"

"And it's spreading like wildfire." Her hands were on her hips now, and her green eyes flashed defiantly. "Spare me the outdated medical hogwash, Doctor. Typhoid, if I remember correctly, is caused by bacteria and usually transmitted by insects, water, food, or carriers. Without antibiotics to cure it, the best thing we can do is try to prevent its spread. We boil all the water before drinking it, scrub everything, most especially our hands, in this blasted, stinking, harsh carbolic, and we allow fresh air and sunshine into this dungeon. Quinine's okay, I guess, but I'd cut out the milk—milk makes diarrhea worse, and we certainly don't need that, do we?" She gave him a saccharine smile.

Myles glared at her. "Madam, may I remind you that I'm the surgeon in charge here—"

"How many deaths have you had from this fever, Dr. Baldwin?"

He scowled at her, but she wouldn't back down. "Five in two months," he snapped. "Which is minimal considering—"

"Which is ridiculous, considering that hygiene and some fresh air and sunshine might just work wonders and prevent any more."

They stood, green eyes challenging gray, and neither would back down.

Finally, she heaved a sigh and said in a more conciliatory tone, "Look, your methods haven't worked all that well. Why not give mine a try? Washing everything down and letting some air in here isn't exactly insurrection, Doctor." She gazed around the room and rolled her eyes. "It's bloody hard work, is what it is, considering the lack of every modern convenience, such as washing machines and dishwashers and sterilizers." She gave him a challenging look. "Don't tell me you're afraid of a little hard work, Doctor?"

Hard work didn't begin to describe the controlled chaos that ensued during the following week. Soon there were row after row of clotheslines out back of the hospital strung with wet blankets, and the constables on laundry duty complained bitterly about their raw hands and the dozens more blankets waiting to be washed.

From daybreak until after dark, cauldrons of water stood steaming over open fires, and the pervasive smell of carbolic made everyone's eyes stream. All the constables on hospital duty had come in for tongue-lashings from Paige for neglecting to wash their hands after touching patients, and all had complained at length to Myles, outraged at having to take orders from a female.

The only person besides the patients who accepted Paige without reservation was Armand LeClerc, which infuriated Myles, because Armand had always been his own staunchest supporter.

Having the old Métis change allegiance was unsettling.

During the first week she worked at the fort, there was one new case of fever. The second week saw no new cases, and by the third, many of the sick had recovered. There were no more deaths.

Paige arrived at the fort at dawn and often it was past dark by the time she left again, usually escorted back to the boardinghouse by Rob Cameron; it seemed decent women didn't walk the streets of Battleford alone after dark. Aching with weariness, she crept up to her room, washed in icy water, slid the nightshirt Myles had given her over her head, and fell into bed.

During those first hectic days, the two doctors worked nonstop, taking little time even to eat. They clashed with monotonous regularity on the finer points of patient care, but soon they were both too tired to even argue with much energy, and they began to work together as a team.

By the end of the second week, however, things had slowed enough so that even an occasional regular mealtime was possible. Armand rigged a makeshift table out on the small back porch and served them their meals there.

Myles Baldwin, Paige found during those breaks, was

scrupulously formal and unfailingly polite, with the exquisite manners of a southern gentleman—as long as the two of them didn't get into some heated argument about medical techniques.

He was also remote and impersonal; his conversation mostly centered around the weather and the patients, until she rebelled one evening over a hasty dinner they were sharing.

Paige swallowed a mouthful of turnip and plunged straight in. "So, Dr. Baldwin, whatever made you decide to come all the way from Charleston to Canada and join the North West Mounted Police?"

For an instant, she thought she saw pain in his expression, but it was gone before she could be sure. His gray eyes flitted across her face and settled on the endless clotheslines filled with laundry that formed a backdrop to the small screened porch.

It was several moments before he answered, and then his voice was noncommittal. "Why does anyone join the Mounted, Miss Randolph? We're all seeking adventure in the great North West, aren't we?"

He wasn't getting off that easily. "I'd have thought being in the Civil War would provide adventure enough for a lifetime. And you're a long way from home. Don't you miss your family?"

Memories of her own brother and her nephews, of Sam and the clinic, of the patients she'd left behind haunted her. Surely he must be lonely too? Did he ever visit the South? He was fortunate—at least his relatives were inhabitants of the same century.

"I have no living family, Miss Randolph." His tone was cool and dismissive, and she couldn't detect any hint of emotion on his handsome features. "Most of them died as a result of the war."

She felt like a nosy child who'd had her knuckles rapped.

"I'm sorry." Her voice was soft, apologetic. "That must have been a horrible experience for you." She knew she probably shouldn't go any further, but for some reason she needed to know about him, so she threw caution to the winds. "Were you married? Did you have children?"

She thought he wasn't going to answer. A long, charged silence hung between them, and his spare features seemed carved from stone. When he spoke, his voice was taut, controlled, but she could sense the grief behind the abrupt, choppy sentences.

"I was married once, yes. My wife's name was Beth. I'd known her all my life. We married after the war." He drew in a ragged breath and expelled it. "We'd been married five years when she became pregnant for the first time." He cleared his throat and lifted his water glass to his lips, swallowing before he went on. "It ended in miscarriage, and Beth hemorrhaged to death. Our baby boy died with her."

She felt the utter horror of it in the blank spaces between his words, saw the effort the words cost him in the bleak, flat pain in his gray eyes, the careful stillness of his features.

"I'm sorry. I shouldn't have pried." Her own eyes filled with tears and she reached across the table blindly to take his long, surgeon's hand in her own. His skin was icy cold, and she could feel the bunched muscles in his arm.

"I'm a nosy bitch. I am sorry."

His faint smile held no humor, and he didn't reply.

After a moment, she withdrew her hand from his, bending her head over her dinner, becoming self-conscious and busy with her knife and fork.

"And you, Miss Randolph?"

His cultured, drawling voice slid into the silence that had fallen between them. She looked up at him, surprised. He was in control again, turning the tables on her.

"Do you have a family waiting for you back there on the West Coast? A husband? Children, perhaps? Or maybe just a beau? Or do women still have beaus in your time?" His cool gray gaze was fixed on her face, watching her closely, waiting for her answer.

She knew he was thinking of that first night, when she'd told him where she'd come from. They hadn't discussed it again, but now he wanted to know if she'd tell the same story. He was testing her. This time she was careful in her choice of words.

"No significant others, which is what beaus have become in my time, Doctor. And as for family, I have only one brother, Tony, living out here in Saskatchewan. He's married, with two little boys. He's younger than I am by a couple of years. He has a farm, quite a large one."

He nodded, still watching her with an intensity she refused to let bother her. "And will you be joining him and his family on their homestead in the near future, Miss Randolph?"

She felt tears rising again in her throat, and she fought them. If he could be this cool and detached after talking about his lost family, then damn it, so could she.

"I don't believe so, no," she drawled. "At least, not right away. Not—not in the foreseeable future, anyway." She looked straight into those inscrutable gray eyes. "You must realize there doesn't seem to be any way for me to get back to where I came from. At least, no way I can think of."

It hurt in every fiber of her being to admit it.

He didn't question her further, and it was a relief.

"You're planning on staying in Battleford, then."

"Yes, I am." It dawned on her that he actually thought she had a choice. The incongruity of that might have been

118

funny, but she didn't feel like laughing.

He'd paid her for two weeks the day he hired her, 16 dollars that had felt like riches to her. She now had six dollars left, after paying Lulu and buying a few absolute necessities.

Six dollars didn't really leave her a hell of a lot of choice about staying in Battleford, she mused with a bitter taste in her throat. And anyway, wherever she did go, she'd still be trapped in the wrong century, wouldn't she?

"Have you considered setting up a medical office in the town, Miss Randolph?"

"Of course I have." His polite question both surprised and irked her, because it was one she'd pondered again and again without arriving at any solution. She was furious with him all of a sudden.

"Look, I'm sick to death of this Miss Randolph thing. Can't you break down and call me Paige? And surely you have a first name as well, don't you, Doctor? Where I come from, we just aren't this formal, and it makes me crazy."

One eyebrow raised again, and he gave her that long, enigmatic look. Finally he cleared his throat. "I do have a given name, as a matter of fact. It's Myles."

"Well, what a relief. Now, Myles, here's the problem with me considering setting up a medical office in the town." She deliberately mimicked his formal, dry tone of voice. "There's a few little things I haven't quite figured out what to do about. First, I have no office, no instruments, and very little money. Second, I have no idea what medicines are prescribed or even available at this precise point in history, having learned my trade in a foreign land, so to speak." She stopped for a moment and added in a different tone, "And finally, judging by the reactions I get from most people, being a woman in this era and establishing a medical practice are mutually exclusive."

"Not necessarily." His gaze was earnest. "You could treat only women, Paige. Some of them come to me, but I'm sure they'd be more comfortable consulting a woman doctor. And as to medications, I could give you guidance."

Before Paige could answer, one of the constables on ward duty stuck his head out the door, eyes popping and face faintly green.

"Come quick, sir. Abbot's throwing up and having convulsions at the same time. And there's shit all over them blankets we just changed—"

Myles swore and hurried after the constable. Paige followed at a slower pace, thinking about his surprising suggestion and his generous offer to teach her about medications.

Every time she thought she understood him, Myles Baldwin managed to surprise her.

And for the first time, he'd called her Paige.

Six days later, Lulu Leiberman looked down her perky nose at the rent money Paige was proffering, but she didn't reach out and take it. Instead there was malicious satisfaction in her shrill voice. "Sorry, Miss Randolph, but I don't think this arrangement's suitable any longer. You'll have to find another place to live."

Paige gaped at her. "Another place to live? What on earth are you talking about? I don't understand." She tried to figure out which of Lulu's strict rules she might have broken, but for the past weeks, she'd hardly been around the boardinghouse except to bathe and sleep. Now, however, the epidemic was over; Myles had told her last evening that he no longer needed her help.

She'd been expecting it; there were only three patients left in the hospital, and no new cases of fever had occurred for days. Still, it was a letdown; she hadn't realized how much she'd enjoyed the backbreaking work until it was over.

She'd awakened this morning without the sense of purpose that work at the fort had provided, but at least she had enough money to give her some breathing space. Myles had been more than generous, insisting on paying her a bonus.

"You have to leave," Lulu declared. "That's all there is to it. I run a respectable place here, and I can't afford to have my good name compromised. Mr. Raven has twice seen you escorted home after dark by different policemen. Now whatever's going on up at the fort is your own business and none of mine—I wasn't one ever to meddle in other people's affairs—but there's talk. And I've got my living to earn."

"Talk about what, for God's sake?" Paige had the most overwhelming urge to reach out and slap the smirk from Lulu's plump face.

Lulu was enjoying herself. "Well, they're saying around town that you're a scarlet woman, Miss Randolph. Up at the fort every day with all those men, and you claiming to be single and all, and then not home till after dark. Two of the townsmen saw you up there, said it was a disgrace, you in the hospital with all those half-dressed men. It's not proper." Lulu's lips pursed into a tight, prim little knot.

"But I told you in the beginning that I was a doctor, and you know about the epidemic. I explained that I was working with Dr. Baldwin. Would you like me to bring him down here and have him explain our work to you, perhaps?"

Paige was being sarcastic. She'd die before she dragged Myles Baldwin into this.

"Don't you get snippy with me, Miss Randolph," Lulu snapped. "I told you in the beginning I didn't stand for goings-on."

"Goings-on? I was working my ass off to make enough money for rent. Look at my hands, for God's sake, they're wrecked from that cursed carbolic. Damn it all, this is ridiculous."

"Such language, Miss Randolph." Lulu pretended shock and horror at Paige's profanity.

"Language, hell. It's unfair of you, tossing me out without notice." Paige suddenly had a flash of inspiration. "Well, Lulu, I'm certainly going to mention to Rob Cameron that you threw me out without so much as a week's notice. And he thinks so highly of you too."

As she'd hoped it would, mentioning Rob had an immediate effect on Lulu. Paige suspected Lulu had plans for herself and Sgt. Cameron—plans Paige was fairly certain poor old Rob knew nothing about.

"Now, you hold on, Miss Randolph. This is business between you and me," Lulu sputtered. "No need to involve Sgt. Cameron." With great reluctance, using the tips of her fingers, the landlady reached out and took the three dollars Paige still held. "I'll give you one week's notice, Miss Randolph, but that's that. I can't afford to lose my good name; even you must understand that."

Paige ignored the insult, even though she felt as though she were about to explode with frustration and rage.

"One week and I'll be gone. You can count on it." She turned on her heel and strode out of the kitchen, her hands aching to take Lulu Leiberman and shake her until every tooth rattled in her nasty head.

Chapter Seven

The persistent knocking finally sifted through the heavy cloud of sleep holding Paige prisoner.

"Miss Randolph? Miss Randolph, wake up in there." Lulu's shrill voice was muffled by the door, but the thumping of her fist echoed through the dark room. "Open this door, Miss Randolph."

Paige's long nightshirt had tangled around her legs, and she struggled with it as she rolled out of bed and staggered toward the door.

She groped for the doorknob and remembered it was locked. She turned the key and swung it open.

Lulu stood gripping a sputtering candle, her blonde braids hanging down her back and her robe clutched around her neck.

"There's some man at the door who says his wife needs you, which sounds a likely story to me," she snapped.

It was obvious that Lulu was not amused.

"It's three in the morning; I hope you're aware of that."

The landlady's eyes were puffy with sleep, and her tone was nasty.

"Two more days're all you've got left here, and the end of the week can't come any too soon for me, let me tell you."

She turned and huffed her way down the stairs. Paige snatched up a shawl and followed.

"This is scandalous," Lulu was griping. "Strange men banging my door down, waking all the boarders in the middle of the night."

"Just put a sock in it, would you, Lulu?" Paige ignored the landlady's *hmph* of outrage and stared at the man waiting at the foot of the stairs, his battered brown hat clutched in his hand, his eyes filled with stark terror.

"Theodore Fletcher, what is it? What's the matter?"

Paige hadn't seen the Fletchers since that fateful first day on the prairie, but she'd kept in touch with Clara through Rob Cameron. Rob visited the Fletchers whenever his regular patrols took him near the area where they'd chosen to homestead, a choice tract of grain-growing farmland about 20 miles west of Battleford.

"I'll take ye out to visit them on my day off," Rob had suggested, and Paige had been planning to accept his offer. Then she'd started working at the fort and hadn't had time.

"Miss Paige," Theo said now, his voice hoarse with emotion, his words tumbling out one on top of the other.

"Miss Paige, Armand LeClerc at the fort sent me here. He said you'd be able to help my Clara. She's been took bad for almost two days now; the midwife says she needs a doctor bad. The baby—" He gulped and struggled for control. "The baby won't come. Clara's sufferin' somethin' awful. I couldn't stand it anymore. I came for Dr. Baldwin but he's been gone since yesterday afternoon. Appears a

124

man shot himself in the leg over at Bresaylor settlement."
Theo sounded close to panic, and Paige put her hand out
and squeezed his arm in sympathy.

Theo swallowed hard and added, "LeClerc sent a rider
right away to tell the doc to come to my homestead, but
it's certain he won't make it in time."

A feeling of awful helplessness overwhelmed Paige.
What could she possibly do for Clara without medicines,
an operating room, instruments?

"Will you come, Miss Randolph? Please? I've got a team
and a wagon outside."

She couldn't refuse. "Of course I'll come. Just let me get
dressed. I won't be a minute." She tried her best to sound
reassuring, but inside she was sick with dread.

The ride in the wagon across the dark prairie was
frightening; Theo urged the horses to trot, and the wagon
rocked and swayed dangerously in the darkness. Dawn was
beginning to color the horizon purple and pink by the time
they finally sighted the far-off lantern light shining from the
Fletchers' window. A big black dog came running toward
them, barking ferociously.

"Quiet, Barney. You go on in, Miss Paige; the midwife's
there. I'll unharness the team."

Paige could tell by his voice that Theo was terrified
of what might have happened since he'd left. She was
apprehensive herself as she stepped down from the wagon
and hurried toward the door of the rough log cabin.

Several lanterns were lit inside, their glow making
shadows in the corners. Paige shut the door after herself
and took stock of the single room. The corner opposite the
door was curtained off, obviously as a bedroom. An iron
cookstove was sending off palpable waves of heat, and a
cauldron of water and two kettles bubbled on its lid, as
well as an immense white enamel coffeepot.

The interior walls were papered with newspaper. Round, hand-hooked rag rugs made pools of color on the bare wooden floor. A rocking chair stood near the stove, and under a lace-curtained window was a sturdy kitchen table and four chairs. Paige's breath caught when she noticed a beautiful wooden cradle, made up to receive a baby, standing empty in one corner. Several packing boxes used as cupboards comprised the rest of the furnishings.

A ramrod-straight little woman in an immaculate starched white apron came hurrying out from behind the curtain, her iron gray hair caught back in a tight bun, sweat standing out in droplets on her forehead.

"And who might you be, dear?" Her chocolate brown eyes behind wire-rimmed spectacles were both intelligent and wary. "I thought Mr. Fletcher was bringing the doctor."

Paige drew a deep breath and let it go slowly. "I'm Dr. Paige Randolph. There's been an emergency and Dr. Baldwin's not available, so I'm here in his stead."

"You, a doctor?" The woman studied Paige with a narrow-eyed gaze and then slowly nodded. "Ah, yes, the lady doctor from up at the fort. I know who you are now. You're boarding with Lulu Leiberman." She gave Paige a calculating look and then added, "My name's Abigail Donald."

A frenzied moaning rose and fell from behind the curtain.

Paige hurried over and stepped behind it, forcing a note of confidence into her voice that she was a long way from feeling.

"Clara? How are you, love? It's Paige. I've come to help you get this baby born."

At first there was no response. Clara lay on tumbled sheets, her eyes shut, her face alarmingly pale and still.

The mound of her belly rose like a small mountain beneath bloodstained linen. Slowly her eyes opened, and she looked up at Paige, her glance filled with entreaty.

"Paige . . . remember, you said . . . babies . . . lots of women my age—" Her face contorted as another pain began and she couldn't finish the sentence. Her head began to move back and forth on the sweat-drenched pillow as the pain intensified, and a low, guttural moaning that accelerated into an agonized scream filled the room as the violent contraction gripped her.

Paige reached for Clara's wrist, monitoring her pulse. Mrs. Donald was holding Clara's other hand in one of hers and massaging her swollen stomach with the other.

"How close together are the contractions, Mrs. Donald?"

"Four minutes. Been the same now for over fifteen hours. Water broke a long time ago, but she's got no urge to push. The baby's in the wrong position, crosswise, sort of, and I can't turn it." She patted Clara's hand. "She won't relax her muscles enough for me to get my arm in, poor thing. Can't relax, what with the pain. I've tried several times."

Mrs. Donald studied Paige with bird-bright eyes. "Forgive me for saying so, but if you're a real doctor, where's your bag? A little bit of that chloroform Dr. Baldwin uses and the pain would ease; then it would be easier to turn the baby around so she could deliver. I've seen Dr. Baldwin use chloroform in cases like this before."

For a moment, Paige knew utter, cold panic. Mrs. Donald was right. With anesthetic, turning the baby would be a simple matter. Without it . . . she fought the terror threatening to consume her.

She had no instruments, no medications of any kind. She had nothing to alleviate Clara's agony; she had no way of knowing whether the baby was dead or alive. Panic began to overwhelm her, and she felt dizzy and sick.

The midwife was watching her. She couldn't let this woman see how helpless she felt.

Get hold of yourself, Doctor, she lectured sternly. This feels like a nightmare, but there must be something you can do. Find out what it is, and do it.

The answer came in a rush. She had knowledge, Paige realized. She had hundreds of successful deliveries behind her; she had strength, and experience, and the desire to pull Clara and her baby through this. With or without instruments and medication, she was a doctor, and that was what mattered here.

She drew the midwife out of earshot of Clara's bed and her quiet voice was full of confidence. "I assure you, Mrs. Donald, I've delivered a great many babies. Delivering babies is my specialty, the type of medicine I'm most familiar with. Unfortunately, I haven't any instruments or medication, so we'll just have to use our wits here, won't we?" She had to win the midwife's trust. "I'll need your help. I know you're very experienced at this, and that you want this baby to be delivered safely just as much as I do."

Mrs. Donald didn't answer. She glanced over at Clara and back at Paige, and then her eyes rested on the cradle in the corner.

"Will you trust me? Will you help me?" Paige stared into the other woman's brown eyes.

Mrs. Donald still looked undecided, but then she gave a hesitant nod. "Don't have a lot of choice, do I?"

"Neither one of us has much choice, when it comes down to it. We have to get this baby born or we'll lose both of them."

Mrs. Donald nodded again. "Right you are. Let's get to it."

Paige heaved a sigh of relief. "If you'll keep an eye on

her, Mrs. Donald, I'll scrub up now. I don't suppose you have any disinfectant?"

"Plenty. Carbolic, in that brown bottle on the washstand. Dr. Baldwin keeps me supplied."

Under other circumstances, Paige would have smiled at that. Myles and his carbolic.

As she scrubbed, the acrid smell was somehow comforting, as if he were sending her reassurance.

There was a stack of threadbare but snowy clean towels folded under the washstand, and she dried herself on one and tied another around her as an apron. She noticed that Mrs. Donald had already set some of the boiling water aside to cool, to use for washing Clara and the baby. The midwife was both clean and efficient, for which Paige was grateful.

Next, Paige folded the sheet up and did a quick vaginal examination. What Mrs. Donald said was basically correct; the baby was lodged at the top of the birth canal. Fortunately, the umbilical cord hadn't prolapsed, and there was no unusual bleeding yet.

Without even a stethoscope, there was no way for Paige to know if the baby was still alive.

Well, she'd just assume that it was, Paige vowed. A familiar sense of absolute determination filled her, the sensation she always experienced when confronted with a difficult birth.

She'd do whatever was necessary. She'd use every ounce of knowledge, expertise and gut intuition. She'd do whatever it took to get this baby born safely.

Again, she drew the midwife away from the bed and in a low voice she outlined the technique she was going to try, and again she asked for any help she might need. Mrs. Donald was obviously an intelligent woman, although she was skeptical.

"I never heard of anything like that, but if there's a chance of it working, I'll help you," she assured Paige.

When Clara was between contractions, Paige made an effort to rouse her from the exhausted stupor she'd fallen into.

"Clara, listen to me. Wake up and listen. We're going to get this baby safely born, but I need your help." Paige's voice, deliberately reassuring and filled with confidence and energy she didn't feel, brought Clara's eyes fluttering open.

"I want you to listen closely and try your very best to do what I say," Paige instructed. "This baby of yours needs to be turned around before it can get out, and in order to do that, you have to relax the muscles in the birth canal. You can learn to do that, Clara, with your mind and your will. Can we work together here? Will you try?"

Clara's tortured eyes filled with tears. "Can't," she whispered. "Hurts too much. Tired . . ."

"Clara, I promise that if you try what I'm going to show you, it'll start to hurt less. And your baby will get born. You want this baby healthy, don't you? Clara, you know how Theodore's counting on this baby. Give it a shot for him, won't you?"

It was a form of blackmail, the only thing Paige could think of that might be powerful enough to motivate her patient.

Clara's lips trembled. "All right, I'll try," she whispered.

Paige had used hypnosis during childbirth many times before, but always there'd been hours of preparation for the mother, with at least five practice sessions that made the hypnotic state easier to induce when the actual birthing began. She had no idea whether Clara would be able to summon the discipline necessary to relax enough so that

Paige could turn the baby, but, Paige concluded grimly, there weren't a hell of a lot of other options at the moment.

Another contraction began, and Paige and the midwife massaged Clara's belly and thighs in an effort to ease the pain. Mrs. Donald followed Paige's lead, and was quick to adapt the advanced massage techniques Paige had learned from talented nurse-midwives she'd worked with in the twentieth century.

The instant the pain faded, Paige began talking in a quiet, soothing tone, gesturing to Mrs. Donald to go on with the massaging.

"I want you to close your eyes, Clara. Breathe deeply, and direct your awareness to your eyelids. Cause your eyelids to relax. Relax each muscle so that your eyelids become completely relaxed." Knowing how short a time she had before the next contraction began, Paige's natural instinct was to hurry the process, but she forced herself to speak in a slow, reassuring manner, directing Clara's attention to each group of muscles in turn, in a prolonged, slow journey that began at her head and continued down her entire body.

Paige went right on talking during the contractions, instructing Clara to relax as much as she could, to stop fighting against the pain and simply go with it to a place deep inside where the pain couldn't reach.

At first, Paige's suggestions seemed to have no effect. Clara writhed and moaned, but gradually, her thrashing eased, at first imperceptibly, and then more noticeably until, bit by bit, she began to breathe more rhythmically.

Paige lost all track of time, concentrating every scrap of her attention on Clara, endlessly repeating her singsong suggestions.

Theodore came in and put wood on the fire and went out again, closing the door softly behind him. Somewhere out on the prairie, coyotes yipped in an eerie chorus. Birds began to twitter and dawn light filtered through the small windows of the cabin, but inside the tiny curtained area, it was as if time stood still.

By some miracle, Clara proved to be an excellent subject for hypnotic suggestion. When Paige judged her to be as relaxed as it was possible to hope, she told Clara she was going to turn the baby, reminding her over and over that she would experience only pressure without pain.

It was horrific for Paige to have to slip her hand into Clara without the protection of surgical gloves, but she closed her mind to the dangers of infection. The main thing right now, the only thing, was to turn the baby so it could be delivered.

Clara managed to remain relaxed just long enough for Paige to do what was necessary. With Mrs. Donald's help, she managed to flip the slippery baby around so the head was in the birth canal. At the last instant, Clara lost control and screamed and bucked in agony, but by then it was done.

With the very next contraction, Clara had the urge to push, and within a half-hour, a tiny, blood-streaked baby girl appeared.

She was alarmingly small, and her skin was deep blue. She wasn't breathing. Using a clean piece of cloth, Paige swiftly wiped out the baby's mouth, held her aloft, tapped the minuscule buttocks.

C'mon, baby . . . please, baby . . . breathe, damn it.
Nothing.

Familiar dread gripped Paige. Praying hard, she put her mouth over the little face and puffed gentle bursts of air into the tiny girl, one, two—and after the third puff, the baby made a choking sound and her limbs jerked spasmodically. She drew in one and then another short, gasping breath and then she began squalling, weak at first but gaining in volume with every breath.

"Thank the Lord," Mrs. Donald whispered. Paige glanced at the midwife and saw remnants of her own white-lipped fear mirrored on the older woman's face.

To their delight, the baby went on crying, gaining in volume, the short, angry wails of the healthy newborn, and soon even her microscopic fingers and toes were turning a healthy pink. Paige mentally checked off color, breathing pattern, muscle tone.

"You know, I think this kid's going to be just fine," she murmured. She severed the cord and tied it off, using Mrs. Donald's equipment.

"That cry's music to the ears! Just look at the little beauty," Mrs. Donald crowed. She and Paige grinned at one another as they laid the baby on Clara's abdomen.

"My glasses," Clara begged, cradling her daughter. "So I can see her."

"She's a beauty. Gonna take after her mommy," Paige assured her, locating the round spectacles and perching them on Clara's upturned nose. Clara gazed in absolute wonder at her child.

"You've got the lady doctor to thank for this little bundle," Mrs. Donald said in her forthright fashion to Clara. "What she did was nigh on a miracle, in my book. Never seen anything like it."

The afterbirth had arrived in normal fashion, and the moment she was certain that Clara was out of danger, Paige hurried over to the door. Mrs. Donald, efficient and quick, had already cleared away the bloody sheets and sponged and diapered the baby, wrapping her in a soft blanket and laying her in Clara's arms.

"Theo," Paige called, her voice filled with joy. "Come in here and meet your new daughter."

He was leaning against the wall of the makeshift barn, head down, hands clenched at his sides.

At the sound of Paige's voice his head snapped up and he came running over, hope and fear mingling on his weather-beaten features. "Clara?" he gulped. "Is she—?"

"She's fine, and you've got a gorgeous daughter. Come in and say hello to her." Paige couldn't stop grinning. She drew in a deep lungful of the crisp morning air, wondering how long it had been since she'd last taken a deep breath. She was amazed to find that the sun was already well over the horizon, the day fresh and already warm, promising to be hot by afternoon.

Theo hastily pulled off his boots and went in his stocking feet toward the curtain, hesitant about moving it aside as if he still wasn't certain what awaited him there. Then he caught sight of Clara, a beatific smile on her weary face, cradling his baby.

"Look, Theo. Just look at how beautiful our girl is," she whispered, and the big man's face crumpled. Sobs shook him and tears coursed down his face. Wordlessly, he knelt beside the bed and wrapped his arms around his family.

Clara stroked his hair, but her weary eyes were on Paige.

"I bless the day we met you, Paige Randolph, out on that bald prairie," she said, a tremor in her weak voice. "We're going to name her Ellie, after Theo's mother, but her second name will be Randolph, after you, Dr. Paige, if you don't mind. Ellie Randolph Fletcher."

"I'm flattered, but she's liable to hate it," Paige said with a grin, unable to hide her pleasure.

The two women left the little family alone then, pulling the curtain across the opening to give Ellie and Theo some privacy.

Mrs. Donald splashed fresh water in the basin. "You wash up first," she suggested.

The hot water felt good on Paige's face, and she did her best to smooth her hair down. She emptied the basin in a slop bucket and refilled it for Mrs. Donald.

The midwife removed her glasses and scrubbed and then suggested, "Let's make some tea for the new mother, shall we, dearie?"

Paige noted the affectionate term and felt pleased. It was gratifying to be accepted by the midwife.

"I could surely stand a cuppa myself right about now, as I'm sure you could as well," Mrs. Donald remarked. "And maybe some breakfast all around, how does that sound?" She bustled around Clara's immaculate kitchen, unearthing bacon and a loaf of fresh bread and oats for porridge as easily as if she'd put them away herself.

Exhaustion was claiming Paige. She tried to help, slicing bread for toast, pouring boiling water into the huge brown teapot, but her hands were trembling. She marveled at the older woman's energy.

They took a tray to the new parents, but Theo insisted he wasn't hungry. "Have to do the chores," he mumbled as he pulled on his boots and bolted out the door. Paige could see tears still trickling down his cheeks. It was obvious he needed some time to collect himself, away from women.

Clara, sponged and in a fresh nightgown, ate a little and then fell into an exhausted slumber.

The baby, dressed in the exquisite handmade garments Clara had fashioned for her, was tucked into the hand-carved cradle and placed close beside the bed. Bright sunlight filtered through the lace curtain at the window, and a deep and satisfying peace filled the cabin as Paige and Mrs. Donald finally sat down to breakfast.

For a few moments, they ate in silence. With the first mouthful of porridge and fresh rich cream, Paige realized how hungry she was. By the time she'd worked her way through eggs and bacon and toast, she was feeling revived, and the two women chatted about babies and pregnancy and difficult births, finding common ground in their shared interest.

"You know, Doctor," Mrs. Donald said after they'd talked for some time, "Lulu Leiberman's been spreading nasty tales around town about you. Believe you me, I'm going to set her straight on a few things next time I see her. She's a jealous lot, that one, and she's no better than she should be, either. She's got eyes for the men, I always noted that."

"Thanks for your support." It was splendid to have an ally.

Mrs. Donald poured them each another cup of the strong tea, and they sat back in their chairs, sipping the hot liquid.

Then Mrs. Donald tilted her head to the side and gave Paige a long, considering look. "Would you mind telling me, dearie, how it is you came to be a doctor in the first place?" She reached across and touched Paige's hand. "I sound like a nosy parker, but there's a reason for me asking. See, I've only ever heard of one other woman who was a real doctor. My sister Lizzie lives in Toronto, and she was having female problems. Well, she heard of this woman doctor, this Dr. Emily Stowe. She went to her and Dr. Stowe fixed her right up. But she's the only woman doctor I ever heard of, till you came along."

Paige thought about how best to answer. Mrs. Donald seemed to have accepted her, and that acceptance meant a great deal to Paige.

The midwife was warm and friendly, and God knew, Paige needed a friend. She wouldn't get into the incredible story of how she came to be here, she decided. She'd stick to the emotional reasons for becoming a doctor.

"I was married when I was very young. My husband was a medical student, and I became interested in medicine. When my baby died at birth, I decided to study medicine myself and specialize in childbirth."

"And where's your husband now, dearie?"

"We divorced."

Mrs. Donald shook her head and clucked her tongue. "He couldn't accept having a bluestocking for a wife, I suppose."

Paige smiled noncommittally and sipped her tea. The truth was, Nick Morrison couldn't accept having a wife, bluestocking or not.

"That's how it goes with some men," Mrs. Donald remarked. "My man went off looking for gold twelve summers ago, never heard from him since."

"That must have been hard for you. Did you have children?"

Mrs. Donald shook her head. "Never could, though I wanted them bad. Guess that's how I come to be delivering other folk's babies. And speaking of babies . . ." She got up and checked on Clara and the baby, and then sat down again. "Are you planning on doctoring in Battleford, Miss Randolph?"

The question was meant to sound casual, but Paige was aware of its ramifications. Mrs. Donald earned her living as the local midwife; she was understandably concerned about having a lady doctor in Battleford who specialized in delivering babies.

Paige thought fast, but when the words came out of her mouth, her own audacity astonished her.

"Yes, I am. I'm going to specialize in women's problems. I'd like to set up an office, and if I do, I wonder if you'd consider coming to work for me, Mrs. Donald?"

Good God, what was she thinking of? She didn't have

money, instruments, patients, or, as of this Friday, even a place to live—and here she was, hiring an assistant for a practice she didn't have either. The damn crop circle must have weakened her brain as well as shooting her across time.

Mrs. Donald looked flabbergasted at first. Then she tilted her head to the side and gave Paige a long, considering look. "I couldn't promise right off the bat," she said slowly. "I'd have to think about it. But it's kind of you to offer, Miss Randolph."

"Please, call me Paige. And kindness has nothing to do with it." She gestured toward the curtain where Clara and her baby slept. "I couldn't have managed that without you. I'm most impressed with your knowledge and ability."

The midwife's wrinkled cheeks flushed with pleasure. "Dr. Baldwin from up at the fort has taught me a great deal," she said modestly. "You know him, of course?"

"We've worked together. He's a good doctor, and an excellent surgeon."

Mrs. Donald surprised Paige by giving a mischievous wink. "He's a well-made man, that one. If I were younger, I'd say he could put his shoes under my bed anytime."

Paige grinned and felt herself blushing. She had to admit she'd had her own lascivious thoughts about Myles Baldwin.

Mrs. Donald's laugh was young and delightful, a high, chortling giggle that was contagious. "I see you've had similar thoughts. Well, dearie, if I had your looks, I'd do more than think about setting my cap for Dr. Baldwin." She poured them more tea. "My name's Abigail. You don't mind if I call you Dr. Paige, do you?"

"Just Paige is fine with me."

They spent the next hour cleaning up, heating up water, and then washing out the sheets from the birth and hanging them outside in the sunshine, picking and washing and cutting up carrots and turnips and potatoes from Clara's kitchen garden to make a hearty soup. Abigail would stay with the Fletchers until Clara was feeling stronger. Theo had offered to drive Paige back into town after lunch.

It was almost noon when the dog's frantic barking announced the arrival of a horse and rider.

Paige glanced out the window in time to see Myles swing down from his mount.

Theo hurried over and the men spoke, and then Myles smiled and shook Theo's hand, obviously congratulating him on his daughter.

A few moments later, they came in. Myles's high black boots and brown breeches were dusty from riding, and there were lines of weariness around his mouth and eyes. He was smiling, however, and his broad-shouldered, tall form suddenly made the small cabin seem even smaller.

"Good day, ladies." He swept his broad-brimmed felt hat from his head and gave them each a courtly bow. "Theo tells me you did a fine job of delivering his daughter. My congratulations to you both." His remark was directed at the two of them, but his gray eyes lingered on Paige, and there was respect and admiration in his gaze.

There was the hint of something more as well, and she felt herself flush under his scrutiny.

In the weeks they'd worked together, a bond had formed between them, the bond of two doctors fighting a common cause, doing their best to safeguard the health of their patients.

At this moment, however, in the Fletchers' little cabin, Paige was suddenly and shockingly aware that what she was feeling for Myles Baldwin wasn't simply the camaraderie of one medical person for the other.

Her heart was hammering, the blood pounding in her veins. She felt breathless, and she couldn't seem to tear her eyes away from him.

She couldn't possibly be falling in love with Myles Baldwin, could she?

Chapter Eight

The seat of the buggy was so narrow Paige could feel Myles's strong thigh pressed against hers. Frequently, one of the large wheels hit a depression in the earth, and then the buggy tilted precariously to one side or the other, forcing even closer contact between the occupants.

When Myles offered to take Paige back to Battleford with him, Theo had insisted they borrow his buggy.

So she and Myles were bouncing across the uneven prairie in this small, unstable-feeling conveyance, with an enormous lunch that Abigail Donald had insisted on packing them in a canvas bag at their feet.

Myles's saddle horse, Major, trotted along beside them, and Paige couldn't help but feel that the aristocratic animal looked at his master with an expression of contempt for riding in a lowly buggy.

In the pocket of Paige's skirt was the ten-dollar bill Theo had insisted she take as payment for the delivery. Paige had tried to refuse, but it was clear that to Theo it was a matter of pride to pay her, and so she'd gracefully accepted.

As soon as they were away from the cabin, Myles had wanted to know the details of Clara's delivery. Paige, both exhausted and euphoric, told him about using hypnosis.

Myles's eyebrows shot up, and he turned to give her an astounded look. "I've heard of mesmerism," he said. "In a medical journal, I once read about a professor of neurology in Paris, Charcot is his name. He uses mesmerism to treat hysteria. But I've never heard of anyone using such a technique during childbirth."

"Oh, it's very common in my time," Paige explained. "There are drugs we use during childbirth as well, but hypnosis is noninvasive, which to me is wonderful. Whenever any of my patients expresses an interest, I use it. It usually takes more preparation than Clara had; it was just plain old luck that she was so responsive to it."

She went on to tell him about ultrasound, and fetal monitors, and birthing underwater, and the use of soft music and dim lights in some delivery rooms. She told him of difficult deliveries she'd made, and she even poured out the story of the last, tragic delivery she'd done in her own time, detailing the cesarean section and then the awful death of Dave and Liz Jackson's baby son. It seemed so long ago now, and to her surprise she could talk about it without reliving the nausea and guilt that she'd experienced at the time.

The trouble was, she couldn't seem to stop talking. She gave him an abbreviated history of medicine's major breakthroughs from 1883 to the late nineteen hundreds, beginning with the development of X rays and antibiotics and finishing with organ transplants, genetic engineering, operations performed by laser.

"Surgeons have even begun operating on the fetus long before it's ready to be born, while it's in its mother's womb. It's still experimental, but in several cases they've removed tumors from the unborn baby's body that would kill the baby before it had a chance to be born. The child isn't removed from the mother's body—it's still partially inside the womb during the operation. Then it's put back inside, and with luck, it has a chance to heal and grow into a full-size fetus before delivery."

Myles hadn't said anything during Paige's monologue. She knew he'd been listening closely because of the distracted way he managed the horse.

"Paige, please describe for me the exact steps in this cesarean operation you mentioned," he finally said, and Paige did, pretending in her mind she was actually performing the technique, describing for him every small detail of the procedure, painting a word picture of the modern operating room, the smells, the sounds, the reasons for the cesarean.

She described how she'd prepare the mother, why she preferred one anesthesiologist over another, the nurses she most enjoyed working with, the advanced technology of the instruments she would be using.

For a few enchanted moments she was there, in her mind's eye, back in the familiar surroundings of a 1990s hospital, doing what she did best. She described every minute detail, even adding a description of the type of sutures she'd use to close the incision, and the special attention the baby would receive from specialists in the operating room.

It took a long time, and when she finished, the only sound was the steady clop of the horses' hooves and the sound of the buggy's wheels. There was a constant humming and chirping, the melody of grasshoppers, gophers, and birds that surrounded them on the undulating prairie.

As if she were awakening from a dream, she looked around. The afternoon was hot, the air was still, the sky stretched like a blue tent from one horizon to another with only a few fluffy white clouds scudding across to the west. The rolling hills and scattered, sparse trees stretched around them, unbroken by any trace of civilization.

No planes, no power lines, no roads.

It was 1883, and even penicillin hadn't yet been invented, she reminded herself. The scene she'd just described was lost to her, perhaps forever.

The lack of sleep, the strain she'd been under delivering Clara's baby, all the difficult realities of her situation overwhelmed her quite suddenly, and without any warning, she started to sob.

"Paige, my dear. What is it?" Myles's concerned voice, the tender endearment, made her cry even harder.

Damn, she had no handkerchief. She mopped at her streaming eyes with her palms, sniffling, trying to control the sobs that seemed to originate in the toes of the high-top boots she'd finally purchased.

Myles pulled the horse to a stop and dug in his pocket, producing a snowy square of white linen. He didn't give it to her; instead he turned on the narrow seat and, with gentle care, blotted her eyes and her cheeks until at last the storm of tears slowed.

Finally he handed her the handkerchief. "Now blow your nose and tell me what brought that on," he instructed.

She blew, and then she said, "I-I just realized how much my life has changed, and how much I took for granted, before. Until a short while ago, I had money, I was good at my job, I had my own clinic and a small fortune in equipment." She gulped. "And last night, with Clara, I had to deliver a baby without so much as a stethoscope. It was the purest luck that everything went as well as it did, because I had nothing to use if it didn't, no forceps, no anesthetic,

144

nothing to stop Clara from hemorrhaging. I was scared to death."

She drew a shaky breath, trying to stop the new flood of tears that threatened. "Back in my own time, I had a lovely apartment, with a view of English Bay. By the end of the week here in Battleford, I won't even have a place to live. Lulu Leiberman's tossing me out on my ear."

Myles frowned. "Why's that?"

Paige felt a hysterical urge to giggle. "Thanks to Lulu's gossiping, I gather the local women think I'm a prostitute. Apparently, she hinted that's what I was doing at the fort during the fever epidemic. My God, I should give it some consideration; just think of how much money I'd have made during those weeks. As it is, all I ended up with was dishpan hands from that lousy carbolic of yours."

Myles was torn between the urge to laugh at her outrageous words and the desire to shake her hard for her suggestion that she should even consider becoming a prostitute.

It embarrassed him to remember that he'd thought so himself in the beginning.

The smartest thing to do, he decided, would be change the subject fast, before Paige remembered those first conversations they'd had and reminded him of them.

"You're tired, and probably hungry as well," he suggested. "Abigail packed us a substantial dinner." He squinted out across the rolling landscape. "There's a grove of willows over there; let's head over that way and eat." He clicked his tongue at the horse, and the buggy jolted its way toward the sparse shade.

He tethered the horses and Paige used the seat of the buggy to spread the food out on the clean cloth it was wrapped in.

There were thick slabs of homemade bread, spread with

butter Clara must have churned before her labor pains began. There were pieces of fried salt pork and rhubarb pickles to eat with the bread. There was water in Myles's canteen as well as a stone bottle of buttermilk, still cool and refreshing, and two generous slabs of the dried apple pie Mrs. Donald had made and served at lunch.

Myles was hungry, and for a while they chewed and swallowed without saying much. Paige perched on the running board of the buggy in what meager shade the conveyance provided, and Myles leaned against the side.

"You were right, I was starving. This food tastes wonderful," Paige said with a sigh, reaching for another slice of bread and piling it with pork and pickles. She'd casually hiked her long skirt up almost to her knees, and her legs were shapely and slender in their lisle stockings.

"You know," she went on, "that first day when Rob found me, we stopped for lunch and Clara put out what she had. I was used to such different food, I didn't appreciate what she served."

"Even the food is different where you come from?" Myles felt a combination of curiosity and ambivalence about this other world of hers.

She nodded. "Yup, it sure is. We have stuff like packaged lunch meats, and turkey rolls that only contain white meat, and soda pop in cans. And microwaves to heat food in, and dishwashers to do the dishes afterward." She described them as well as she could and then thought for a moment.

"And then there's Pop-Tarts, and TV dinners, and instant coffee, and containers of ice cream." She chewed on the bread for a moment. "God, sometimes I miss chocolate ice cream worse than anything else. Well, almost."

A feeling was slowly building inside of Myles as he listened to her talking about her other world, a confused mixture of anger and resentment and something he couldn't

146

identify at first—he'd had little experience till now with jealousy.

He didn't know yet if he believed absolutely in the things she spoke of; they were too farfetched to even imagine, some of them.

But he didn't disbelieve her either; he didn't think anyone, regardless of how disturbed they might be or how great their imagination, could possibly invent the incredible things Paige spoke of with such authority.

He only knew he didn't want to hear any more about them just now. He wanted her instead to look around and really see the magnificent wide prairies, the blue sky, the autumn beauty of this wild and open land.

He wanted her to see him, to be here, now, not obsessed with these magic lantern slides of some other time and place that brought that expression of yearning to her lovely features.

They finished their meal with long drafts from Myles's canteen. As she'd done before the meal, Paige again used a small amount of the water to clean her hands. This time she washed her face as well, cleaning away the silver traces of dried tears, drying her face on a corner of her skirt.

She removed the straw hat Clara had insisted she borrow and, taking the brush he'd given her from the small bag she'd brought, did her best to smooth down her rebellious mop of coal-dark curly hair. It shone in the sunshine, and the curls sprang back up the instant the brush had smoothed them, as if they had an obstinate life of their own.

He had an overwhelming urge to reach out and stroke those curls, learn their texture, bury his nose in them and memorize the faint perfume his nostrils detected as she leaned close to him.

Myles watched her fuss, intently aware that the two of them were totally alone out here.

147

Her cheeks and nose were sunburned despite the hat, and scattered with freckles. Her tall, lithe body beneath the long dark skirt and patterned cotton blouse was slender— naturally slender, without the artificial aid of whalebone. He'd noted long before that she didn't wear the constricting stays most other women did. It was a bold and sensual thing to do, to allow her body to fill out her clothing without barriers.

He remembered the red silken garments she'd worn when Cameron found her. He wondered now what had become of them.

She lifted her arms to settle the wide-brimmed hat on her head. Her rounded breasts thrust against the fabric of the patterned blouse, and she was aware suddenly of his eyes on her.

She became still, her arms up for an instant, her clear green eyes startled. Then his hands were on her shoulders, drawing her toward him. He could feel her warm skin against his palms through the thin fabric of the blouse.

"Paige, come here to me. . . ." His voice was a choked whisper.

She gasped aloud when he slid his hands down her back, pulling her into his arms, and then she tilted her head back so that she could look into his eyes, her own a deep and thrilling green against the tan of her skin. There was a question in those eyes, and a challenge.

Her hat fell off, and her arms went around him.

He found her mouth, the full lips soft and sensual beneath his own, and abandoning all restraint, he kissed her, exploring, experimenting, nipping, licking, parting her lips with his tongue and showing her with lips and tongue and teeth the near violence of the desire that raged in him.

And with each new caress, she answered in kind.

His hands stroked her back, then slid down to her

148

buttocks, thrilling to the feel of her body, unrestricted and soft beneath his touch.

The kiss went on and on, and his body, hard as stone and screaming for fulfillment, surged against her. He pulled her even closer, spreading his legs slightly and urging her into the hollow.

She moaned and her hips rocked to the rhythm he'd begun.

He stroked her, his palms aching to touch naked flesh, moving restlessly from her hips up to her breasts, cupping their soft fullness, his thumbs flicking across hard nipples.

It had been so long, so long since he'd allowed himself to make love to a woman—and even then, it was a woman he'd bought and paid for.

He was more lonely than he could bear to admit. He wanted this woman; he'd wanted her since that very first night, when she'd worn his nightshirt and cursed at him for locking her up. But the habits of years, the hard-won peace that had come from locking his emotions away and tossing out the key, were too deeply ingrained to overcome with just a kiss.

In some silent, simultaneous agreement, they moved apart, their breathing loud and uneven in the stillness of the afternoon.

He still held her, his hands lightly on her waist now, her fingers spread on his chest. He could see a pulse hammering in her throat, could feel with his palms the force of the heartbeat shaking her body.

"I apologize, Paige," he said when he could speak at all. His voice was thick, barely in control. "This is not a good idea."

She drew back, her wide green gaze suddenly wary. "Oh? Why's that? It felt pretty darned good to me."

It had felt more than just good to him, but he had to

explain somehow, make up an excuse that would allow her her dignity. It was difficult when all he wanted to do was tumble her to the grass, strip off her pantaloons . . .

"Because it wouldn't stop just with today, Paige. It couldn't. For me, today would only be a beginning."

Her lips were swollen and bruised-looking, and he rubbed a trembling finger across them, aware of their moistness, their warmth. He racked his brain for a reasonable explanation.

"The last thing I want is to cause still more trouble for you in Battleford," he finally said. "What you must do now is convince the town and its gossips that you're a talented medical doctor. In order to do that, you must safeguard your character. There are no secrets in a town that size, and becoming my mistress would destroy your reputation beyond redemption."

She'd pulled completely away now. She was straightening her clothing, not looking at him. "You're right, of course." She sounded almost flippant. "Besides, the last thing I want is to become emotionally involved with anyone from around here. From this era, I mean. I have to find a way back, sooner or later. To my own life, my own time."

It hurt more than he could have imagined, having her brush him off so lightly, as if—as if that blasted other life of hers was real, and here and now nothing more than a fantasy.

He harnessed the horse to the buggy and helped her in without a word. The remainder of the drive was made in almost total silence, and they each took care not to touch the other.

Back at the fort that evening, Myles couldn't sleep. His emotions were in a turmoil, the memory of that one kiss burning in him like a fever. Cursing his own weakness, he finally got up and lit a candle at his writing desk.

He composed an urgent telegram to a medical supply house he was familiar with in Toronto, requesting that they send him as quickly as possible a fully equipped medical bag, complete with the most modern of French forceps and the newest of stethoscopes, and a generous supply of medicines as well.

Early the next morning, he saw to it that the telegram was sent. He spent the day writing the interminable reports the NWMP demanded and dealing with the usual parade of sick policemen and ailing Battleford residents.

One of the civilians was a newcomer from Ontario, Jimmy Gillespie, a middle-aged man who'd been transferred to Battleford to work as a bookkeeper at the Hudson's Bay Company store. Jimmy came into Myles's office in the afternoon, his face white as paper, leaning heavily on a crude makeshift crutch. His right foot was swollen to twice its normal size.

"Good day, Doc. Had a bit of an accident this noon. One of the clerks dropped a barrel of molasses on my foot. Clumsy young oaf." He grimaced as Myles removed the bloody rag tied around it.

The foot was broken in several places, with a deep cut on the instep as well that required several stitches to close.

When he'd done all he could to repair the damage and set the bone, Myles wrapped the foot in a plaster soaked in carbolic and said, "You'll have to stay off this for several weeks, Mr. Gillespie, if you want it to heal."

Sweat stood out on the older man's forehead, and he nodded. "If it ain't one thing, it's another," he said with a sigh. "My wife's been sickly ever since we moved here. I've been takin' care of her, and now this."

"What's the matter with your wife?" Myles was sure that Mrs. Gillespie hadn't consulted him.

Jimmy shook his head. "Female troubles of one sort and another. Nerves, she puts it down to, but it worries me. She's not one to lay about like this, is my Helen. I've told her to come on up here and see you, but she won't hear of it. Can't talk about such things to a strange man, she says. Always been a bashful lass. Mighta gotten over it if we'd had young 'uns, but we never did."

"There's a new female doctor in the village," Myles said slowly. "Dr. Randolph is her name. I can personally vouch for her expertise as a physician. Perhaps your wife would feel more at ease talking to a woman doctor?"

Gillespie thought it over and his narrow face brightened. "Might be you're right, Doc. Where's she located, this lady doc?"

"She's at Mrs. Leiberman's boardinghouse at the moment, but only for another day or two. She's looking for a place to rent, somewhere with enough room so she could set up an office. You don't know of anywhere, I suppose?"

Gillespie thought for a moment. "Well, there's that house the factor's mother lived in, up on the hillside. During the flood in eighty-two her house got ruined, so Walker built her a place away from the flats. House ain't very big, though. And it's not right in town, neither. Old lady only lived there six months before she up and died, y'know. He hasn't rented it out yet; it's full of her things still. Walker said the missus and I could rent it if we liked. We looked at it when we came but we got all our own furniture, and Helen didn't want to be that distant from the town, so to speak. Walker's a bachelor; he don't want to live up there either. He's got the little place the company built for him, close in to the trading post, suits him fine."

"I'm sure Dr. Randolph would be a good tenant. And she doesn't have any furniture of her own, so she'd be pleased to rent the place furnished."

"I'll ask him about it, Doc, straightaway. Got to go back to the store right now anyhow and finish the day's entries. How much do I owe you?" Gillespie struggled up and balanced precariously on his crutch, reaching for his wallet. "Lucky thing my work is done sitting down. Things'd be in a fine fix if I lost my job over a keg of molasses."

"There's no charge, Mr. Gillespie. The Mounted's purpose is to serve the community."

"Thanks, Doc. Much obliged to you."

And I to you, Myles thought as the man clumped away on his crutch. This would take care of the problem of where Paige would live.

Maybe he could get some badly needed sleep tonight, Myles reflected, knowing he'd now done everything he could for her.

Why in blazes did he feel responsible for the woman, anyway?

As it had repeatedly, the vivid memory of the kiss they'd shared flashed into his mind. It had been a rash and stupid thing for him to do, allowing himself to be overcome by sexual desire for Paige Randolph.

He assured himself that's all it had been—the normal sexual response of a healthy man to an attractive woman.

There was no more to it than that. How could there be? Apart from a shared interest in medicine, they had absolutely nothing in common.

Well, he'd done his best to atone for the kiss, and now he could get back to normal. He'd write her a note, telling her of the house, mentioning that Mrs. Gillespie might appear as a patient, and then he'd put her firmly out of his mind.

He sat down at his desk, quill in hand, and began to write one note after the next and then tear it up.

*   *   *

The envelope was actually sealed with wax, and the paper was heavy vellum. In the upper left corner was the distinctive crest of the NWMP, with Dr. Myles Baldwin's name stamped beneath.

Classy. Formal. Paige studied the letter, mesmerized by the strong, dramatic strokes that slashed her name across the front in black ink that had no relationship whatsoever to ballpoint.

"Should I wait for an answer, miss?" The young boy who'd hand-delivered the envelope stood at Mrs. Leiberman's back door, shifting from one foot to the other.

"Hold on a minute and I'll see." She ripped the envelope open.

"Miss Randolph," the note began.

Her temper rose. God almighty, the man was impossible. How the hell could he address her as Miss Randolph after kissing her senseless the way he had?

She snorted and read on. "It has come to my attention that the factor at the Hudson's Bay Company store, Mr. Walker, has a small house which he might be pleased to rent to you. Also, the wife of his clerk, a Mrs. Gillespie, will perhaps be consulting with you about a female complaint. I trust this is acceptable to you. I have the honor to be, very respectfully yrs., Myles Baldwin, Senior Surgeon."

She read the stiff and formal words again, and now her face relaxed into a smile.

He had to be the most uptight, formal man she'd ever met, in spite of his astounding proficiency at kissing, and it was obvious from this caricature of a friendly note that he was concerned about her welfare. He was trying to find her a place to live, and he'd also referred a patient.

Warmth filled her, a mixture of gratitude and relief and

154

tenderness for the complex man who'd written the note—
and a wave of desperate longing for the passionate man
who'd kissed her.

Oh, Myles, thank you.

"No answer just at the moment," she told the boy, and
he hurried off.

Paige flew up the stairs, tidied her hair, and grabbed her
bag. Moments later, she was hurrying down the street in
the direction of the Hudson's Bay Company store.

Chapter Nine

That afternoon Charlie Walker, factor at the store, took Paige to view what had been his mother's house.

It was situated high on a plateau between the rivers that converged at Battleford. It was away from the town, but still close enough that Paige would have no problem walking to town for supplies.

The house was low and rambling. There was a porch at the front, then a hall with a parlor on one side and a sitting room on the other. Further back was a large kitchen and two small bedrooms.

Paige looked at the parlor and sitting room with an eye to a reception area and an examining room. More than three patients at a time would cause a traffic jam, but what the heck. She should be so lucky as to have three patients at a time, she pondered with wry humor.

"All the windows have glass. As you can see it's a well-built house; I built it meself," Mr. Walker stated with pride.

Paige had learned that glass was hard to come by in

Battleford, and many houses had factory cotton nailed across openings, which allowed some light in but did nothing to stop the cold. The windows Walker was so proud of were not more than a foot square. She thought of her apartment, its one entire gigantic wall entirely window, and she could have wept.

"You won't need a thing; it's fully furnished," Walker bragged.

The place was claustrophobic, so stuffed with bric-a-brac and furniture and plain old junk it was difficult to move from one room to another. Every available surface had an embroidered or crocheted or knitted cover, and there were afghans in drab shades of blue and gray and brown draped across every sofa back and armchair. "She liked to keep busy, Mother did, always had a bit of handiwork on the go," Walker explained.

Paige nodded. She'd have to clear a ton of junk out. She'd also have to learn to light and care for the coal oil lamps.

God, for an electric switch . . . Why hadn't she ever thought about the miracle of electricity when it was available? And bathrooms—the "necessary," Walker mumbled, was just out the back.

On the plus side, the house was clean, apart from a liberal coating of dust. All the interior walls were whitewashed, and wilted lace curtains covered every window.

"Won't have no problems heating her this winter," her landlord bragged. "There's a stack of firewood in the shed out back, and you can get the McKenzie boys from down in town to bring you more when needed for a reasonable price."

Paige looked at the stoves with trepidation. She'd need plenty of wood, all right; she'd heard how cold it could get here in the winter, and already the nights were frosty.

There was no central heating, of course. There was a

fireplace in the room Walker labeled the parlor, and a formidable gleaming cookstove in the kitchen. There was even a tiny wood heater in one of the bedrooms—for times when the thermometer dropped down to 40 below, Walker explained without batting an eye.

Paige shivered at the thought.

The house was well equipped. There were quilts, pillows, sheets, towels, cutlery, dishes, cooking pots, and kettles. There was a barrel for collecting rainwater outside the back door, and a contraption built into the kitchen wall called a "cold locker," a screened box open to the air which Walker insisted would keep her perishables fresh—as long as they didn't freeze first, he guffawed.

Out back was a neglected garden that Walker assured her still had potatoes and turnips in the ground if she cared to dig them. There was a shed where the old lady had kept a goat and a larger building that had been used to house chickens and a pig.

Paige wasn't about to start raising livestock, she told Walker when he confided he could find her a few chickens.

"Good investment, chickens. It wasn't long ago eggs sold for twenty cents apiece, chickens were that scarce hereabouts."

Paige considered going into the poultry business and quickly decided against it. Her previous experience with chickens was pretty much limited to neat, labeled portions in plastic wrap at the supermarket, and eggs labeled large and medium.

"I'll take the house, Mr. Walker, if you'll be good enough to show me how all these lamps and stoves work."

Paige shoved nostalgic thoughts of automatic thermostats out of her head and paid her new landlord a month's rent, relieved that thanks to the Fletchers, she'd have enough money left for a few supplies. She was getting used to how far a dollar stretched in these days—as well as how difficult it was to earn those precious dollars.

Filled with excitement, she rode back into town in Walker's buggy, shopped for necessities at the store, gathered together her few belongings at Leiberman's, and said good-bye to William Sweeney, the only real friend she'd made at the boardinghouse.

Lulu was out somewhere, so Paige wrote her a note, thanking her for her kindness and hospitality, certain that the landlady would never recognize sarcasm.

"Come and visit me sometime, William." Paige smiled at the portly man, anticipating the crimson blush that stained his face and bald head.

"I'll do that, Miss Paige. And best of luck to you. If I can be of assistance in any way, let me know."

Paige would miss him. The only sign he'd ever given of recognizing his wife's clothing on Paige was a polite, "You look charming today, Miss Paige." But apart from William, leaving Lulu's boardinghouse behind was a blessed relief.

She'd hired a trap at the livery stable to carry her things, and it didn't take long to unload.

At last she was alone in the little house. She lit one of the coal oil lamps the way Walker had showed her and hung it on the hook over the kitchen table. She struggled to light the kitchen range as well, but she couldn't manage to make the flame burn hot enough to even boil a kettle. There was something tricky called a damper, and she couldn't remember what she was supposed to do with the stupid thing.

She settled for bread and cheese and apples for supper, with water as a chaser.

In the gentle glow of the lamp, she munched her simple meal and thought about this new development in her life.

Inconvenient as the little house was, at least she'd have privacy; she'd have a place of her own again. She could hang her underwear on the clothesline when she chose, by God, and if someone needed her in the middle of the night, there was no one to complain.

But Lord, it was lonely. At Leiberman's, there was always the knowledge that there were people down the hall, just as there'd been in her apartment in Vancouver. Living alone in a house was another whole new experience—as if she hadn't had enough of those lately.

As darkness fell she wrapped one of Letitia's shawls around her shoulders and stepped out on her tiny porch, watching the lanterns from the town pierce the gloom. It wasn't exactly like seeing the lights come on in Vancouver's west end, she mused with a lump in her throat. Lately, that far-off city and what she'd come to think of as her past life had begun to seem like a pleasant dream from which she'd awakened into this harsh reality.

Her new house wasn't far from the fort, but the stockade wall blocked any lantern light she might have seen. She thought wistfully of Myles.

Was he ever lonely? He seemed so remote, so self-assured, it was hard to imagine him aching inside the way she was for something or someone. And yet, there had been that break in his composure the day she'd asked him about his family, his home.

There'd been that kiss, out on the prairie.

And he'd helped her. She had him to thank for this house. She'd write him a note in the morning and tell him how grateful she was. She'd invite him up here to have coffee with her.

Damn it all, maybe she'd even seduce the honorable Myles Baldwin. She remembered Abigail's raunchy comments about him and grinned, imagining his shock if he knew that the prim midwife thought he was sexy.

She looked up at the sky, at the billions of stars that shone in the cool, crisp air. The nights were growing much colder, and people were remarking on the fact that there wasn't any snow yet. Autumn was almost over, and all too soon snow and icy temperatures would plummet the prairies into winter.

She shivered, imagining long, bleak days when the wind would howl and snow pile up around her porch. She'd have to buy some warmer clothing, a heavy coat, a scarf, mittens—long underwear, for heaven's sake—for which she'd need money.

With a sigh, she went back inside to the bed she'd made up with fresh sheets and a warm patchwork quilt. Shivering in the chilly bedroom, she put on Myles's long nightshirt, lit one of the candles she'd bought, and resolutely turned out the lantern.

Climbing into bed, she took a deep breath and blew out the candle. Inky blackness settled over the small room. The window was open a little, and she could feel the breeze on her face.

Outside, owls hooted and coyotes yapped in eerie chorus. Dogs howled. The house creaked, the huge clock on the dresser ticked like a time bomb. Paige had never felt more isolated and alone in her life.

It was a long, tense time before she slept.

The next afternoon, Rob Cameron arrived leading a dappled gray horse behind his own mount.

Paige was once again out on the porch, sipping a cup of tea and taking a breather from the massive housecleaning she'd been doing since early that morning. She'd carted load after load to the cellar, and it was now possible to move easily from room to room.

"Rob, you're my very first visitor," she called to him when he rode up. "Welcome to my new home."

He dismounted, his wide, sunburned face creased in a pleased grin. "I've brought ye a wee housewarming gift from the force," he announced, gesturing to the horse. "Her name's Minnie, and she's a nice, gentle thing."

Paige gaped at him. "Rob, I can't possibly accept a horse—"

"Hush," he ordered, waving a dismissive hand at her. "Minnie was abandoned at the fort because she was lame, puir wee thing, and Surgeon Baldwin had a look at her and now she's fine again, but he says she'll never make a police mount, she's no hardy enough. So she needs a good home, says he, and you need a horse, if ye're dead set on livin' up here all by yerself." He gestured at the open fields around Paige's house. "There's plenty of grazing for her before the snow comes; all ye need do is tether her and she'll be fine. And if there's a wee shed or something out back . . ." He ducked around the back of the house and reappeared in a moment, looking delighted. "Why, there's a barn back there ready-made where she'll be snug and dry come winter. I'll make her a stall, and bring over a bag of oats."

Paige understood and appreciated that a horse was this era's equivalent of a car, and as such, represented mobility. Horses were both expensive and valued, just as automobiles were in her time. Rob's generosity brought tears to her eyes, and she thanked him.

"Surgeon Baldwin was the one suggested it."

Myles again. A torrent of emotions welled up inside her.

"Ye can ride, can ye not? I'll try to find a sidesaddle—"

"My brother taught me to ride, but forget the sidesaddle. I'll ride astride. And don't look so shocked, Robert Cameron. Did I ever tell you there are women in my time who're Mounties?"

The look on his mustached face was priceless. Paige giggled. "Come and sit down and have a cup of tea before you faint. Well, maybe you'd better show me first what I'm doing wrong with that blasted cookstove, or I'll never get the water to the boiling point."

A week passed. Paige spent three more of her precious dollars at the Hudson's Bay Company store on a pair of men's denim pants, which she wore on her blissful early morning rides on Minnie. The pants didn't fit as well as her designer jeans had, but they weren't bad. They were fine through the hips and bottom, and she rolled the cuffs and threaded a belt through the waist to cinch it in.

She tried to stay busy so she wouldn't notice that she was alone most of the time.

Rob came twice. He made a stall for Minnie on his first visit, and the next time he brought her a saddle which he explained was on unofficial loan from the quartermaster's stores at the fort. He also brought two sacks of oats, and Paige thought it wise not to ask if the oats were on loan as well.

Rob took her riding, teaching her how to figure out direction on the open prairie by using the sun and the wind.

When he saw her in her pants the first time, he didn't say anything. He gulped and swallowed hard and then made a point of looking only at her face, for all the world as if she'd forgotten to wear clothes below the waist. Paige couldn't resist teasing the bashful young policeman a little.

"Believe it or not, Rob, where I come from, women wear pants like these all the time, twice as tight as mine are." She did a slow turn, and he looked scandalized. But then he caught her amused glance and rolled his hazel eyes. "Best not wear them to church," he advised with a straight face and a twinkle in his eye.

163

Paige had transformed the two front rooms of her house into a comfortable waiting room and a starkly furnished examining room which at the moment contained only two chairs and a cupboard she'd had Rob bring in from the kitchen. It would hold her medicines and instruments, she decided, telling herself she was an incurable optimist. You'd be better off asking if they need a clerk down at Rose Rafferty's Ladies Emporium, she chided herself. You could die of starvation up here waiting for nonexistent patients to examine with your nonexistent instruments.

One morning after her ride, Paige sat down with a calendar and a cup of coffee and added up the weeks since that fateful day in August when she'd jogged down to Tony's field to have a look at the crop circle.

It was now the fifth of October. She'd been in Battleford six weeks. Outside, a few snowflakes were drifting down. Thanks to Rob's patient instruction, she now knew all the secrets of the cantankerous stoves, and it was warm and cozy in her house—as long as she remembered to constantly stoke the voracious things with wood.

Also thanks to Rob, she'd mastered some basic pioneer cooking abilities. He'd shown her, amid much laughter and mess, how to concoct basic bean soups, make oatmeal porridge, and stir up a batch of bannock. She'd even conquered biscuits, which took a bit more skill—and expanded her limited diet somewhat.

She felt more at peace at this moment than she had at any time during those six weeks, except for the ever-present concern about money.

She was broke. There was no point fooling herself any longer; she was going to have to go out and look for a job, any job. She thought of the social programs of her own time, and a wry grin came and went.

She'd paid enormous taxes that helped support those

social programs, and now when she needed assistance, welfare wasn't yet a glimmer in a politician's eye.

A sharp rap at the front door made her jump.

She hurried along the hall and opened it, and her heart began to hammer.

Myles stood on the porch, his red tunic and wide-brimmed felt hat covered with snowflakes. He had a medical bag in one hand and another huge lumpy canvas sack clamped in the other.

"Myles, come in, it's great to see you."

On some level, she'd been waiting for him. She'd expressly invited him to visit in the thank-you letter she'd written, but now that he was here, she was flustered. All she could think of when she looked at him was the way his lips felt, moving over hers.

Get a grip, Randolph.

"It's great to see you again. Come on in, I've got some coffee on if you'd like a cup." She was suddenly short of breath, and an unreasonable delight spilled through her at the sight of him, tall and elegant, smiling at her.

He ducked his head to avoid hitting it on the door frame, and once inside he made the hall seem even smaller than usual. He set his things down and took his hat and gloves off. She reached for them.

"This place was designed for little people," she said as she tucked the leather gloves inside the hat and then hung them on the coat tree she'd put in the hallway. "Be careful or you'll brain yourself on the doorways; even I have to duck through a couple of them." She led the way down the short hallway and into the kitchen. The palms of her hands were damp.

"Sit down," she urged, taking a cup from the shelf and filling it with coffee from the enamel pot on the back of the stove. "This stuff's still fresh, you're lucky. By afternoon it's industrial-strength, powerful enough to strip paint—"

She turned from the stove and put the cup on the table in front of him, the rest of whatever she'd been saying wiped from her head. "What?"

He was staring at her blue denim–clad hips and legs. She'd grown so used to wearing denim pants in the house that she'd forgotten all about them.

"Damn, I keep forgetting women don't wear pants yet," she said in an exasperated tone. "Why on earth not, I'll never know. Those stupid long skirts and petticoats are cumbersome and clumsy."

He was still looking at her, gray eyes narrowed, expression inscrutable, and now she grew exasperated. "For God's sake, Myles, surely it must have dawned on you that women have legs under all that crap they bury their lower bodies in."

His gaze lifted until he was looking into her eyes, and to her amazement, she could see that he was angry.

Furious, in fact. It simmered in his eyes and underlined his polite, southern drawl with cold steel. "You're living alone here, Paige, some distance out of town. You're young and beautiful."

It wasn't a compliment the way he said it. It sounded more like an accusation. "Whether you know it or not, this is still the frontier. Why, half the men in town would take the way you're dressed as an open invitation to rape." His gray eyes glittered like ice, and she felt heat rising up her neck and flowing over her cheeks. She opened her mouth to blast him, but he didn't give her a chance to say anything. "I warn you, if you hope to set up any sort of medical practice here, you are going to have to obey the conventions of the town. Just by being female and a doctor, you've already defied what people consider right and proper for a woman."

He took a long, slow breath and let it out again. "If you

insist on traipsing around in those—those trousers, madam, I guarantee you won't ever have the opportunity to treat a single patient. You'll be totally ostracized by the women, and you'll be in grave danger from a large portion of the male population."

Paige snorted in exasperation. "God, I can't believe this," she exploded. "I wear these pants to ride my horse, for God's sake, not to parade around on the main drag in downtown Battleford."

Her temper sizzled even though a rational part of her recognized the logic in what he was saying.

Logic, hell. Every liberated bone in her body screamed in outrage at the unfairness of his attack. "I wear what I choose in the privacy of my own home." Her voice rose, and she leaned on the table, glaring over at him. "And why shouldn't a woman be free to wear whatever the hell she wants, I'd like to know?"

He studied her with narrowed eyes, his mouth compressed into a thin, tight line, his cheekbones tinged with angry color. "Women should be free to do as they please, in an ideal world. Unfortunately, this isn't ideal."

He got to his feet in one quick motion, steadying the chair that almost tipped over behind him. "Now, madam, if you'll excuse me, I must get back to the fort."

Paige's anger gave way to bitter disappointment. He was leaving, and they hadn't talked at all. She'd wanted so much to sit here with him, here in her cozy kitchen for an hour or two, talking about everything and nothing, laughing together.

She missed him. Why in God's name did they argue so much?

But she'd be damned if she'd beg him to stay. She stood straight and tall, defiant in her close-fitting jeans. She even stuck her hands in her rear pockets, flaunting the offending pants, realizing she was being childish and not caring.

He gave her a long, silent look and then nodded stiffly. He strode down the hall, retrieved his hat and gloves, and was closing the door behind him before she realized he'd left his things on the scatter rug beside the door.

Some demon in her whispered, Let him go. He'll have to come back for them, won't he?

She hesitated, swore, and then reached down and grabbed up the bag and the canvas sack. It took her a fumbling moment to get the door open.

Myles was already on his horse.

"Wait," she called. "Myles, hold it a minute. You forgot your things." She held up the medical bag.

He reined the huge black horse around and raised one hand to his hat brim in a stiff salute.

"They're yours, Paige. May they bring you good luck." He touched his spurs to Major's flanks and rode off without a backward glance, seeming to disappear into the whirling white snowflakes.

Stunned, she watched him until she couldn't make him out anymore, and then she slowly shut the door. She knelt on the hall carpet and, with shaking fingers, opened the medical bag. One by one, she lifted out the contents.

A gleaming stethoscope, a grooved speculum, a silver disk she identified as a primitive curette, a set of forceps, various rolls of bandage, dressings, a thermometer, even several pairs of short rubber gloves—the equipment was archaic when compared with what she was accustomed to, but she knew the bag was lavishly equipped by the standards of the 1880s.

The canvas bag contained a sturdy box, inside which Myles had painstakingly packaged and labeled commonly used drugs of the day: quinine, laudanum, chloroform, herbal preparations she'd never heard of—and a huge, ugly bottle of carbolic.

"Oh, Myles," she whispered as a lump rose in her throat.

He'd included a black book with gold lettering called *Physicians' Standard Modern Medical Practice*. She flipped through it, having to smile at the antiquated terminology, but relieved to find that it gave explicit dosages for the medications, detailed directions for administering chloroform to patients of different weights, instructions for using the instruments.

Hot tears dripped down into the bottles and vials and boxes as she fingered the treasure trove Myles had given her, and she sniffled and rubbed her nose on a sleeve.

Here were all the raw materials she so desperately needed to earn a living, the tools she had no way of buying for herself, the medical information that would allow her to use the current methods and treatments of the day.

His gift was the most thoughtful she'd ever received. And, she realized with a sinking feeling in her chest, they'd gotten into a lousy fight before he'd even had the chance to present it to her in person.

She knotted her fists in frustration and banged them on her knees.

God damn you, Myles Baldwin, for being a stiff-necked, opinionated, stubborn, cantankerous, old-fashioned . . . Her hands relaxed and her shoulders slumped. *Extravagant, considerate, kind, handsome gentleman.*

And sexy, she reminded herself with painful honesty. Don't forget sexy. Damn it to hell, Myles Baldwin was as sexy as any man she'd ever laid eyes on, in any century. Why couldn't she have met him—She closed her eyes and shook her head at her own stupidity.

There wasn't any way she could have met Myles Baldwin

back in the time where she belonged. He'd been dead a good many years before she was even born.

Myles gave Major his head, letting the stallion pick his way across the snowy landscape.

Below them, steam was rising from the river in a silvery cloud. Myles drew in a deep breath and let it out again. The air was cold in his lungs, but he felt as if a raging fever was burning its way through his body.

Paige. Paige Randolph.

He was on fire, wanting her. Right now, he could see in his mind's eye the exact contours of her slender hips, the way the top of those confounded trousers nipped in and hugged her slender waist, the way his hands might span her if he held her. . . .

He saw again her buttocks, swelling in tantalizing mounds, outlined only by a thin layer of denim cloth. His palms tingled, imagining how he'd cup her, draw her into him, feel those long legs twine around his own as he—

Damn her, she roused him to the point of madness.

The very next afternoon, there was a banging on Paige's front door.

She'd spent a delicious morning sterilizing and arranging her instruments and medications in the cabinet in the front room she'd come to think of as her office.

She'd moved a long, narrow table in, padding it with a blanket, then stretching a snowy sheet over the top, thinking it would do as an examining table—if the time ever came when a real live human person needed to be examined by her, which she was beginning to seriously doubt.

She was stirring a pot of bean soup on the kitchen range

when the knock came, and her first thought was of Myles. Her heart leapt with excitement.

He'd come back; she'd known he would. Her hands went to her hair, trying to smooth the obstinate curls. She undid the apron she'd tied around her waist and chucked it on a chair. She checked her blouse for stains, patted at the wrinkles in her skirt.

She grinned down at herself. At least she was wearing a skirt today; that should please the old prude.

She flew down the hall to the door and swung it open, a welcoming smile on her lips.

Chapter Ten

There was a buggy hitched to the gatepost. On Paige's porch stood a man balancing on a crutch, his right foot in plaster, with a pale little woman huddled at his side. Her hands were encased in a furry muff. She wore a large brown hat with a veil that came down over her eyes and overwhelmed her thin features.

"Dr. Randolph?"

Paige nodded. The man looked uncertain, the woman terrified. Her thin lips were trembling.

"Dr. Baldwin up at the fort said to come see you. My name's Gillespie. This here's my wife, Helen."

The name rang a bell in Paige's mind. This was the referral, the "female complaint" that Myles had mentioned in his letter.

Elation swept through her. Here was her first office patient.

She smiled in welcome. "Come in, why don't you? It's cold out here."

Paige settled them in the tiny waiting room, taking a chair

herself, searching for and finding her professional manner as she said, "Now, how can I help you?"

"You're sure you're a doctor, miss? You look awful young to me," Mr. Gillespie began, uncertainty in his voice.

It was so much like the reaction her modern-day patients had shown to her appearance that Paige had to grin, even though she was painfully conscious of the lack of any framed diplomas on the walls here to reinforce her right to practice medicine.

"I'm cursed with eternal youth," she joked, just as she'd done in her other office. "I assure you, I'm well on my way to forty, and I've been a practicing physician for nearly ten years now." It was stretching the truth a little, but it seemed to reassure them.

"Now, what seems to be the problem?" She directed the question to Helen Gillespie, but again, it was her husband who answered.

"Helen's been having female troubles. She fainted clean away yesterday afternoon, ain't the first time either. I told her she either came willingly today, or I'd hog-tie her and bring her that way."

Paige studied what she could see of Helen, which wasn't much. Her hands were still thrust into the muff, she was bundled from neck to toe in clothing, and the hat shaded her face.

"Perhaps you'd feel more comfortable talking to me in private, Helen," she suggested, getting to her feet. "Come in here, why don't you? And let me take your coat and hat," she added.

Divested of her coat, hat, and muff and seated in the examining room, Helen was a fragile wisp of a woman. She seemed on the verge of tears. Fading blonde hair puffed around her head like fluff on a molting dandelion, and her

173

skin was gray-white and pasty-looking.

Anemia, Paige guessed, leaning over and taking the woman's narrow hand in hers, glancing at the colorless fingertips and nails.

"Are you having menstrual problems, Helen?"

The woman's eyes filled with tears and she gulped and nodded. She looked down at her hands and whispered, "Trouble with my monthlies, yes. They won't stop, see, they go on and on, right from one month to the next."

"How old are you, Helen?"

"Forty-seven. I know it's just the change, but it leaves me so weak and sick-feeling. . . ."

For the next few minutes, Paige questioned Helen, gently but persistently, trying to establish whether or not the problem was actually one of periomenopause, or whether there was reason to suspect a malignancy or some other problem.

It became clear to Paige that Helen had only the most rudimentary understanding of her own body and how it functioned. Paige got a pad of paper and with a pencil, she drew a feminine outline, sketching in the female internal organs.

"These are your ovaries, and this is what happens to us women each month," Paige explained. "Here's what occurs during ovulation—" Paige sketched and described her drawing in simple terms. "Now, during menopause, the lining of your uterus . . ."

As Paige talked Helen relaxed by degrees, fascinated by the lesson, eventually even asking shy questions that illustrated how little she understood about what was really happening to her.

"There's absolutely no need to feel embarrassed or self-conscious about any of this," Paige reassured her. "It's a perfectly normal process, one which we all experience."

It still took a great deal of coaxing before Helen finally agreed to remove her pantaloons and climb up on the makeshift table so Paige could examine her. She was bleeding heavily, but as far as Paige could determine, there weren't any obvious tumors or abnormalities. The elementary procedures available to examine and treat Helen's problem made Paige grit her teeth in utter frustration.

No Pap smears, no ultrasound, no hormone replacement therapy, no blood or urine analysis. Certainly no hospital available where a hysterectomy could be performed if it was needed.

If the bleeding persisted, all she could do was attempt a D and C.

Was dilation and curettage a procedure even in use at this time, she wondered?

Well, if it wasn't, she was about to introduce it, Paige decided with grim determination. Helen was becoming seriously anemic from blood loss, and it was quite conceivable that she could die from it, because iron replacement by intravenous methods wasn't yet an option. What the hell was used to treat anemia in these times, anyhow?

Paige explained to Helen the dangers of hemorrhaging. "I want you to come back and see me in two days, Helen. I'm going to perform a very minor operation to stop the bleeding." She explained to Helen as simply and clearly as she could what the procedure consisted of.

The thought of performing a D and C here in her tiny office was daunting, but it could be done. She'd need help, though.

Paige thought of Abigail Gordon. She'd ask her to assist.

Helen agreed to come back, but she looked frightened. Well, Paige mused, she had a right; Paige was scared half to death herself, but there wasn't any other option that she could see.

As Helen finished dressing, an idea came to Paige about the problem of anemia.

"I want you to take a tablespoon of blackstrap molasses in a cup of hot water every morning and evening," Paige instructed. Molasses was high in iron, and also readily available here. "And do you have iron cookware?"

Helen nodded. "It's so heavy, though, that I've been using enamel lately."

"Use the iron. It'll put significant amounts of usable iron in your system."

The moment the Gillespies left, Paige scribbled a hasty note to Abigail Gordon, asking for her assistance. The second note took much longer, and she tore up three pieces of paper before she finally settled on what to say.

"Dear Myles," she finally wrote, "From the bottom of my heart, I thank you for this treasure trove you've given me. Also thanks to you, I've just seen my first patient, Helen Gillespie. I'm sorry we quarreled the other day— I miss you and value your friendship. Hope to see you soon—Paige."

She shoved more wood on her fires, grabbed a coat, and went off in search of a boy to deliver her mail, hoping that Myles would recognize and accept her attempt at making peace between them.

Two days later, Paige could feel the sweat collecting on her forehead as she bent over Helen Gillespie's unconscious form.

It would have helped so much to have stirrups, and a proper table—this one was much too low. Her back felt as if it were breaking.

She'd brought three lanterns in and hung them above the

table, so at least the light wasn't bad. The trouble was, the heat from the lanterns made the tiny room into an oven, and the fumes from the ether even more powerful.

Both Abigail and Paige were sweltering. They were swathed in enveloping aprons that Paige had cut from linen sheets and then sterilized in the oven to approximate operating-room gowns, and they both wore the masks Paige had improvised from gauze.

"Watch her breathing, Abigail. We need to keep her nicely under so she doesn't struggle," she said now. "And try to keep her legs steady for me if you can. They seem to weigh a ton when a patient's unconscious."

Abigail Gordon was a godsend. Steady and utterly reliable, she seemed to instinctively know what Paige required of her, monitoring the patient's pulse, handing Paige sponges when they were needed.

Paige's eyes were glued to the slight undulations of Helen's abdomen as she blindly guided the curette inside the uterus. In her mind's eye, she visualized the technique she'd performed so many times before, praying that it would be successful under these difficult conditions.

There was no point in agonizing over what she didn't have—she had to work with what was available here, Paige reminded herself for the thousandth time that morning.

She had to forget that there was no drip in Helen's arm to administer drugs if they were needed, no crew of nurses, no anesthetist, not even a tray of tapered dilators when she needed them.

She didn't dare think of hemorrhage, or heart failure, or the dozens of other life-threatening things that could happen here this morning.

There was just her, and Helen, and Abigail—three women, dealing with women's problems as best they could in a stifling little room lit by gas lanterns.

"That's about got it." Paige sighed in relief. "Now, we can use that sterile cotton to swab with, and then we're done."

"How do you know when it's enough, Doctor? The scraping, I mean. When you can't see what you're doing." Abigail had paid rapt attention to the entire procedure.

"You continue scraping until there's a gritty feeling to the entire lining of the uterus. It's called the 'cry of the uterus.' It's something you learn by experience."

Abigail nodded. "I see. There's lots of things has to be learned by experience, aren't there, Doctor? That's how I learned about midwifery, too."

Together, they removed the sterile cloths Paige had draped around her patient's hips and thighs.

"Bleeding's stopped already," Abigail confirmed. "You figure her monthlies will stop altogether now, and the poor woman will start feeling better?" Abigail was helping Paige with their patient, making her tidy and comfortable.

"It often happens that way after a D and C." Paige didn't add that no one was really sure why; it was one of medicine's unexplained mysteries. The important thing was that it worked in a great percentage of cases.

Helen was still deeply asleep, breathing in heavy sighs, and Paige put her stethoscope to her patient's chest, reassured by the steady, strong beat of Helen's heart.

Ether used as anesthetic scared her spitless. She'd spent half the previous night checking and rechecking all the information she had on how to use it to anesthetize a patient. When she'd memorized every bit of information she could find, she found herself wishing desperately, at two in the morning, that she could consult with Myles.

The two women washed again in carbolic solution and then stripped off their voluminous aprons, watching the patient closely.

178

"There we are, she's starting to come around now," Abigail announced several moments later as Helen moaned and muttered something unintelligible.

Thank God. Oh, thank you, God. Paige felt overwhelming relief as Helen's eyelashes fluttered.

"If you don't need me here, Doctor, I'll go and make us all a cup of strong tea," Abigail said, bustling out the door. "We could all use one. I expect that poor Mr. Gillespie's let the kitchen range out by now; he was beside himself when he brought Mrs. Gillespie in this morning—he sure won't remember to put wood on the fire. I'll just go tell him his wife's right as rain and get him to chop some kindling, should I, Doctor?"

Paige grinned at Abigail. "Get him to chop a lot while he's in a good mood. Tell him Helen's right as rain, for sure," she confirmed, feeling jubilant.

Helen stirred just then and Paige took her hand, smiling at her as she struggled to regain full consciousness.

"Everything went well, Helen. I think you're going to be just fine from now on. We'll move you in a few minutes to a more comfortable bed in the spare room, and by tomorrow morning you should feel well enough to go home."

Helen rewarded her with a weak smile. "Thank you, Doctor," she whispered, and Paige felt the familiar rush she always experienced after a successful treatment.

Lord, she'd missed this so much, this job she'd chosen as her life's work. She suddenly wished that telephones were in use.

She'd love to pick one up and call Myles this instant, and tell him her first operation was a smashing success. She imagined herself describing the procedure in detail, the questions she'd ask him about medications.

Damn it, she missed him.

*   *   *

Two days later Paige was coming out of the Hudson's Bay Company store, her arms loaded with supplies. An icy wind was blowing, and Walker had just warned her that they were in for a bad snowstorm—the Indians had told him, he said, and they were never wrong.

"Paige, good afternoon."

The deep, slow drawl rippled through her every nerve ending, and she felt considerably warmer than she had a moment before.

"Hello, Myles." He'd hitched his horse to the railing in front of the store, and now he came over to stand beside her, a smile tilting his long mouth upward.

She hoped he noted that she was wearing a skirt today.

"Can I be of help with those packages?"

"Thanks. I'm going to try to fit them all in Minnie's saddlebags."

He took the heaviest of them, a bag of flour, and followed her over to where she'd tied the horse. Together, they stowed the groceries away.

She felt tongue-tied all of a sudden. What the hell was wrong with her? She'd spent hours having imaginary conversations with this man, and now that she was with him, she couldn't think of anything to say.

"It's going to snow," she blurted out.

Brilliant, Randolph.

He nodded. "Usually happens about this time of year."

She felt a hysterical urge to giggle. Either they fought like cats and dogs, or they were as polite as bankers to one another.

Unless, of course, he was kissing her. She stole a glance at him. Did he even remember that day out on the prairie?

"Mrs. Gillespie came to consult me. I performed a minor

operation, and I think she's going to be fine. I appreciate the referral, Myles."

He nodded his head. "I'm pleased it turned out well. You charged a fair sum, I hope?"

She grinned. "Actually, Mr. Gillespie paid me on the spot, without me having to bill. Twenty dollars, which is how I come to be at the store, buying them out of supplies. I feel rich."

"That sounds about right."

"I hope it is. I'm afraid I really don't have much idea what to charge."

She was hoping he'd offer to come home with her so they could talk about it, but he didn't.

She stood a moment longer, racking her brain for something else to say, her heart sinking as the moments dragged on in silence. "Well, I really should be getting back home or my fires will all be out. . . ."

"Would you care to come for a ride with me some afternoon when the weather's a bit warmer, Paige?"

The brusque invitation took her by surprise.

"Sure," she stammered. "Yes, anytime. Yes, I'd like that."

He untied Minnie's reins from the hitching post and stroked the horse's nose. Minnie whinnied and snuffled at his pocket. It was obvious she knew him well.

"No apples today, old girl, sorry." His smile was directed at Paige as well as the horse. "I have friends who live a few miles out of town. I'd like you to meet them. They don't get much company, especially this time of year." He steadied the animal as Paige stepped into the stirrup and up, curling her leg around the saddle horn and arranging the clumsy bulk of material in her skirt in what she hoped was a suitably modest manner.

As soon as she was away from the town, of course, she'd

ride astride, but she wanted him to see that she'd taken his warning to heart. There was no point in alienating people for no good reason, even though this awkward riding position put her in danger of breaking her damned neck.

"As soon as this coming storm dies down, I'll come by," he promised, giving her that little salute of his.

Paige rode demurely through the town, nodding at several people she passed. When there was no one to see her, she slipped her leg over Minnie's back and into the stirrup, giving a whoop of joy that startled the poor horse.

"Minnie, you won't believe this, but I've actually got what amounts to a date with our elusive Dr. Baldwin," she crowed.

The mare's ears flicked, and she danced and picked up her hooves as if Paige's excitement were contagious.

The storm lasted three days, cold winds and icy snow blowing against the windows and howling down the chimney. Paige was grateful for the generous woodpile Walker had provided. She kept her fires stoked—she'd learned the hard way to get up in the night and put more wood on the stoves so the house would stay warm.

The fourth morning, Paige awoke to brilliant white light streaming through the small window in her bedroom. The storm was over, and blinding sunshine had turned the snowy world outside into silver brilliance.

She hurried into her jeans and warm coat and went out to give Minnie hay and a cupful of oats, pausing to look out over the town below.

Smoke rose from chimneys, curling up like commas against the intense blue of the winter sky. Everything looked virginal, blanketed with snow. Paige loaded wood into a basket and carried it into the house, going back outside to pump a pail of water from the well.

Her outside chores done, she stoked her fires and had her morning bath in front of the stove, a procedure involving two basins: one for washing, one for rinsing. She dressed in long underwear and then a skirt and plain shirtwaist blouse, with a shawl over her shoulders, and made porridge for breakfast, remembering with a pang of nostalgia electric toasters and boxes of cold cereal.

She was washing the sticky pot in a basin of hot water when Myles appeared at the back door, stamping snow from his high boots, knocking his wide-brimmed hat against his leg when she opened the door.

His thick golden hair was flat where the brim of his hat had been. He wore a buffalo coat over his uniform, and it made him look immense. The fine wrinkles around his gray eyes deepened when he smiled at her.

"'Morning, Paige. It's a fine day, cold but clear. Care to come visiting with me?"

"I'd love to." She couldn't seem to stop smiling.

"Good. I'll go out and saddle Minnie for you while you get ready."

The ride out along the riverbank and then along a trail that cut across the frozen prairie was breathtaking. Everything shimmered, jewellike, in the sunshine, and the clear, cold bite of the winter air in Paige's lungs was exhilarating. It was slow going; the horses often had to struggle to break a trail through the snow. Myles was quiet for the first part of the ride, but as they grew nearer to their destination he told Paige a little about Dennis Quinlan and his Indian wife, Tahnancoa, the young couple they were going to visit.

"Dennis was the youngest son of a well-to-do banker in Toronto, and he told me his entire family was horrified when he joined the North West Mounted rather than making banking his career," Myles began. "Dennis was an exceptional policeman and he soon was made a sergeant in the force.

183

Two years ago, he was investigating a murder that involved one of the young Indians from Poundmaker's reserve, and that's how he met Tahnancoa. She's Poundmaker's niece. Dennis fell in love with her, and they married."

"I'll bet that caused a near riot." Paige knew enough about the strict and narrow moral code of the times to guess at the reaction to intermarriage.

"Actually, the North West Mounted didn't object," Myles said. "Dennis was an officer, free to marry whomever he chose, and the force is well aware of the scarcity of young white women in the West. It was Tahnancoa's people who put up the most resistance. You see, the native people are losing respect for the whites. There's growing discontent with the promises made to the Indians by politicians in Ottawa. Those promises are never kept, and the Indians feel betrayed."

How little things had really changed between her own decade and this one, Paige mused. In her own time, it wasn't only the native people who felt betrayed by politics—the entire populace of the nineties was disillusioned with politicians and their unkept promises.

"Dennis and Tahnancoa lived at the fort at first," Myles was saying, "in married officers' quarters. But the other officers' wives and some of the good women of Battleford made Tahnancoa's life miserable."

Paige felt a rush of sympathy for the young woman. She knew from personal experience how it felt to be lonely.

"Dennis resigned from the force and bought a section of land out here. He bought cattle, and he's trying to establish a business supplying beef to the North West Mounted and to the town."

"Is he making a living at it?"

"I believe so. Dennis is a hard worker, and Tahnancoa

works right along beside him. She's a fine woman. Good-
looking, too."

"They sound like great people. I can't wait to meet
them."

Tahnancoa had just finished rolling biscuits to go with the
soup she'd made for lunch when the dog began barking.

Dennis was still out in the barn, shoveling hay from the
loft down to the cattle. Curious, Tahnancoa went to the
window, astounded to see Myles helping a woman wearing
a blue coat and a woolen hat down from her horse. The
woman was smiling at Myles, and his hands were around
her waist.

Tahnancoa could feel nervous apprehension turn her
stomach sour.

A white woman. How could Myles Baldwin bring a
white woman here, to Tahnancoa's home? A woman from
the town, with a smile on her lips and contempt in her eyes
for Dennis Quinlan's Indian wife.

They were walking across the yard now, toward the
house.

Tahnancoa stepped back from the window, her heart
thumping. If there'd been a back door, she would have
slipped out, leapt on the back of her pony, and ridden
far away.

But there was no back door. She peeped out the window
again, relieved to see Dennis loping across the yard now
from the barn.

He called something to Myles, and Tahnancoa watched
through the narrow window as Myles and the woman
paused, waiting until Dennis was near. There were smiles
and nods and handshakes, and then all three of them turned
once more toward the house.

There was no escape. Tahnancoa raised trembling hands

and smoothed the single black braid that hung down her back. She took off her apron, brushing flour from her checkered blouse, her plain dark skirt, and took a deep breath, straightening her spine and standing tall and still, chin tilted high, as the door opened.

She was the niece of a great chief, she reminded herself, forcing her features into an expression of calm dignity.

She was of Poundmaker's blood.

She was Dennis Quinlan's wife.

This woman—she looked at Paige and swallowed—this beautiful white woman was a visitor in her home, brought here by the man her husband thought of as a brother.

Therefore, Tahnancoa would treat the woman with respect, offer her food, hide the burning resentment she felt for all women like this, women with white skin and disdainful eyes and a certainty that Tahnancoa and all her people were nothing more than dirt beneath their feet.

They'd finished the delicious soup and hot biscuits a silent Tahnancoa set before them, followed by enamel mugs of steaming coffee and slabs of dried apple pie.

"Myles, I'd appreciate it if you'd come on out to the barn with me," Dennis said. "There's a heifer I'd like you to have a look at. She's not eating and I'm afraid I may lose her."

Paige felt a surge of panic as the cabin door closed behind the men, leaving her alone with the aloof Indian woman.

Tahnancoa hadn't said one unnecessary word to Paige since they'd arrived, more than two hours ago now. Apart from hello, and would you like more coffee, she hadn't once addressed Paige directly or even looked her way.

Twice, Paige tried to start a conversation, asking about a beautifully tanned fur rug on the floor, and complimenting Tahnancoa on the apple pie, asking how she'd made it, but both times Tahnancoa gave only the briefest of answers and then busied herself at the far end of the room.

The men seemed unaware of any undercurrents, but to Paige the tension in the room and the silence were part of a graphically clear message.

Tahnancoa resented her presence here. It was obvious Dennis's wife didn't want her around, and had no intentions whatsoever of being friendly. Uncomfortable, Paige sat at the table, wondering how many aeons it would be before Myles and Dennis finally reappeared.

The logs in the stove shifted; the silence seemed to stretch like taut elastic.

"I'll help you with these dishes." In desperation Paige got to her feet and started scraping them.

"I will clean them." The quiet words were more of a command than a suggestion.

It was now or never. Paige went over to the other woman and laid her hand on her sleeve, trying to put into her smile all the warmth she could muster. "Please, Tahnancoa, let me help. See, where I come from, there's a golden rule— the person who cooks doesn't clean up the dishes."

Tahnancoa's huge, dark eyes studied Paige for what seemed a long time, and then a ghost of a smile flitted across her classically beautiful features.

"And do the men of your tribe agree to this rule?"

Paige grinned. "Actually, I think they were the ones who dreamed it up, after the women started making them do the cooking."

"The men cook?"

Paige could see the incredulity on Tahnancoa's face.

"Sometimes they do. Well, they did. I came from a very different place." She was getting into deep water here. "Far away." Each time she had to explain some difference between her time and this one, she felt herself

187

grow tense, anticipating the look on people's faces, that wary, disbelieving skepticism.

"The customs were totally different where I came from. I lived in a city, and men's and women's work weren't as clearly defined as they are here. I was—am—a doctor. Many women in my time are doctors, lawyers, businesspeople. Policemen, even. Women have much more freedom than they do here." Paige waved a hand in frustration, talking more to herself now than to Tahnancoa.

"Darn, it's so difficult to even explain how much time changed everything, when no one even knows what the heck I'm talking about when I mention a car or an airplane."

Tahnancoa had listened in silence. She was studying Paige intently, and now she nodded. Her voice was warmer when she spoke, the stiff formality gone. "I think you are the woman Myles told of once, the one who walked between the worlds. Is that so? Are you this person?"

A shiver squirreled its way down Paige's spine. "Yes. Yes, I guess I am." Haltingly, she explained what had happened to her on that fall morning that now seemed so long ago and far away.

Tahnancoa nodded when Paige finished. "So you traveled from then to now," she said.

It was an accurate and poetic description of exactly what had happened to Paige. More than that, Tahnancoa seemed to accept without question that such a thing could happen.

Paige could only stare at this beautiful Indian woman, stupefied by her calm acceptance. Without any elaborate explanations, without the details everyone else who'd heard her story had demanded and then rejected, Tahnancoa simply believed.

Tears of gratitude welled up in Paige's eyes.

"Oh, Tahnancoa, yes," she said when she could swallow the lump in her throat enough to speak at all. She was trembling with excitement, and overwhelming gratitude welled up in her. It was so good to be believed, to have what happened to her verified and accepted. "Yes, I did exactly that, I walked between the worlds, from then to now. God, you're the very first person I've met who doesn't think I'm a total lunatic." She reached out and grasped Tahnancoa's hand between both of hers and squeezed it, trying to convey some of what she felt and couldn't express.

Tahnancoa nodded again, her expression calm and accepting. Her fingers curled around Paige's.

"Sometimes my people, too, walk between the worlds, Paige Randolph. Chosen ones, only."

It took a long moment for Paige to absorb what Tahnancoa had said. It sunk in slowly, the fact that there were others who knew about the phenomenon that had happened to her—who perhaps had even experienced it, as she had. She wasn't alone, she wasn't some kind of freak after all.

But it sounded as if Tahnancoa's people did it at will.

Paige's heart began to thunder against the wall of her chest as the ramifications slowly dawned on her.

If someone knew how to get from now to then . . . then maybe. . . . oh, God . . . maybe . . .

Maybe there was a way for her to go back.

Chapter Eleven

"Myles, Tahnancoa said that some of her tribe have actually experienced what I did, this time-travel thing. It's like a miracle, meeting someone who's actually heard of this happening before."

They were on their way back to Battleford, and Paige's excited voice echoed like a bell across the frozen landscape.

The early winter twilight cast blue shadows on the snow. A wolf howled somewhere far away. That, and the jingle of the horses' harnesses and creaking of the saddles were the only sounds to break the silence, apart from Paige's monologue.

With part of his mind, Myles noted the tracks of a jackrabbit, the marks of a coyote chasing it.

He turned from the tracks to look at the woman riding beside him. Paige's wild dark curls were escaping from beneath the blue woolen toque she'd pulled carelessly over them. She had a red scarf wound around her neck, and her face was pink from the frosty air. Her green eyes looked almost turquoise in this half-light, shining like gemstones against the creamy paleness of her skin.

She looked so very alive, so full of energy, vital and arresting against the frozen landscape. She rode carelessly astride, her skirt hiked up almost to her knees, an expanse of shapely, slender leg encased in thick black stocking showing between the top of her boots and the hem of her skirt.

She was totally unaware of his eyes on her. Her voice rose and fell, the words bubbling out of her like a stream, irrepressible.

"We didn't get much time to discuss any of it in detail, because you and Dennis came in just then, but it formed the basis for a friendship. Tahnancoa invited me to ride out and see her soon again, Myles, and I'm going to. I'm sure I can find my way back out here alone."

Alarm bells went off in his head. "Let me know when you want to come, and either I'll bring you, or if I'm busy I'll arrange for an escort. It's not safe for a woman to ride out here alone."

"Oh, phooey." She sounded disgusted. "What on earth could happen to me between Battleford and the Quinlans? The trail is deserted; it doesn't even take an hour to get out there. I certainly don't need a bodyguard just to ride across a few miles of deserted prairie."

"It's exactly because this trail's deserted that I'm concerned. There are dangers here you're not aware of. For instance, there's still a number of renegade Indians around," Myles warned.

"Oh, for heaven's sake, Myles. Indians aren't going to bother scalping a woman riding out to visit her friend."

"There are also wild animals, Paige, and white men who are anything but civilized." Myles was losing patience. "You know nothing about defending yourself, you don't have a gun, and neither do you know how to shoot.

Therefore, you need someone with you if you intend to travel alone in country like this."

He was doing his best to be reasonable, to hold on to his temper. Why did she always argue with him? He was an officer in the North West Mounted; he was accustomed to being obeyed. He ran his hospital wards with an iron hand—none of the men assigned to him would ever defy him the way she did constantly.

"But I don't want anyone with me," she insisted, her chin jutting out. "I want to be able to visit Tahnancoa by myself. I want to talk to her alone, so we can both relax and get to know one another. I want to learn about her people and their customs. I need to know about this traveling between the worlds. Don't you see, Myles? This could be my only chance to get back to the nineties, where I belong. This could be a way for me to go home."

He felt a sinking sensation inside. Finally, he understood her excitement. He hadn't realized till right now where all this talk about Tahnancoa and some obscure ceremony her tribe performed was leading.

He should have understood right away, but he hadn't. He hadn't wanted to, he admitted to himself, because he didn't want to think about that part of Paige, the peculiar mystery that surrounded her background, the unimaginable place and time she insisted she'd come from.

The cold air seemed suddenly to turn his blood to ice, and a shiver ran through him. He didn't want her to try to return to wherever it was she came from. He didn't see her often, but on a subconscious level he was aware every moment of every day that she was nearby, that if he chose to, he could climb on Major and be at her door in ten minutes.

He didn't want to lose her before he'd had a chance to really know her.

* * *

"Myles, thank you so much for taking me today. It's been wonderful. I don't know when I've enjoyed a day more." They'd reached her house. It was almost full dark now, the short winter twilight fading quickly into night. A few stars were already out, and yellow lanterns shone in windows. Paige's house looked cold and empty, its windows dark, its chimney without smoke.

She'd thought for the last half-hour of inviting him in for a makeshift supper, but it would take her a good hour just to get the stove lit and a kettle boiling. There was some soup leftover from last night's supper, and half a loaf of bread, but not much else.

He got down from his horse and caught her as she slid from Minnie's back. It had been a long ride, and her legs were a trifle unsteady. She leaned on his strong frame for a delicious moment, taking a little longer than was absolutely necessary before she reluctantly straightened.

He smelled wonderful, of wet wool and tobacco and fresh air. His breath held a hint of the hot rum drink Dennis had given him just before they left.

"Go ahead in," he ordered, as if they came home together like this every evening. "I'll tend to the horses and then bring some wood in and get the stove lit for you."

She lit the candle she'd learned to keep by the door, and in a few moments she had the gas lantern glowing. It was a relief to find that it wasn't too cold in the house; the fires she'd banked must have burned for most of the day.

Myles chopped an armload of kindling and soon had her kitchen range and the fireplace sending out waves of heat. It felt both strange and exciting to have this tall, broad-shouldered man in his red serge tunic making himself at home in her kitchen.

"I've got a pot of barley soup," Paige suggested. "Want to stay and have some with me?"

"Thanks. Soup sounds good."

"Don't get too excited," she warned with a wry grin. "I'm not much of a cook. You're in luck, though—this is the first pot of soup I haven't scorched."

Paige heated the soup and put it on a tray along with bread and a lump of cheese, and they ate the simple meal in front of the fireplace in the parlor. They talked easily, of Dennis and his farm, of the small surgery Paige had set up in the other room.

She'd given Myles what she called a guided tour, and she'd been elated when he approved of what she'd done to make her surgery both efficient and comfortable.

Now, Myles sat in an armchair, and Paige, in her stocking feet, pulled her legs up on the settee, covered them with a crocheted afghan, and folded her arms on her bent knees. The lantern light spilled a soft incandescent glow over the room, an intimate glow. Sparks shot up the chimney from the logs Myles occasionally stirred with the poker, and the old clock on the mantel seemed to tick in slow motion.

"So now that I've given you every detail of Helen Gillespie's D and C, tell me what's been going on up at the hospital."

Myles recited a list of the injuries he'd treated in the past week: horse bites, frostbitten lips from blowing the bugle in below-zero temperatures, old gunshot wounds, tapeworms, lumbago, removing a constable's toenails after he'd been stepped on by a horse.

Paige couldn't help it—she dissolved in giggles at the ailments he listed.

"I don't quite see why you find such matters entertaining," Myles teased, giving her a quizzical smile. "The poor patients certainly didn't find them at all amusing."

"I know, and I shouldn't laugh. It's just that I get a mental picture of a modern clinic in Vancouver being presented with a man suffering from, say, horse bites," she tried to explain. "My God, Sam's eyes would fall out of his head."

"Sam?" Myles's voice was carefully casual.

"Doctor Sam Harris, my partner." Paige stared into the flames, her head resting on her bent knees. "Well, he used to be my partner. I suppose by now he's taken legal steps to take over the clinic. It's what I would have done, if he'd disappeared like I have." Her voice was nostalgic, but she was surprised to find she didn't feel dismal when she thought about the clinic and Sam. It was just too comfortable here with Myles tonight to miss that other life as much as she usually did.

"And was he in love with you, this Sam Harris?"

Paige turned from studying the flames to look at Myles. He was staring into his empty coffee cup as if it held all the answers to the universe.

"Yes, I suppose he was."

"And you? Were you in love with him, Paige?" He looked at her now, his gray eyes inscrutable in the firelight.

She shook her head, feeling her riotous mass of curls tickle against her neck. "Nope. I often wished I could have been, though. Sam was—is—a great guy; he'd have made a wonderful husband. But I didn't love him."

Because he wasn't you, she wanted to blurt out. I never felt this giddy, delicious sense of excitement with Sam, this awful desire to be in his arms, this need to have him know me, to know him, through and through, the way I do with you.

She wanted Myles to understand who and what she was. She wanted honesty and truth between them.

"I've only fallen in love once before in my life," she

began, unaware of what she'd just confessed. "I was seventeen, in my first year of university."

She could feel Myles's eyes on her, but she didn't look at him. It was easier to stare into the flames.

"He was a dashing medical student six years older than I was, named Nick Morrison, and neither of us knew much about birth control, because within two months I was pregnant with his baby. He wanted me to get an abortion, but I couldn't do it. A baby—" She swallowed and tried again. "God, I just couldn't destroy my baby. She was already a person to me. Nick was furious. I guess he was scared too."

Even after all the years, it was difficult to tell the story. Paige cleared her throat, still avoiding Myles's eyes.

"I confided in a friend who knew Nick. She called his parents, and then things got messy. They were very moral people; they pressured him into marrying me by threatening to cut off their financial support. He needed it; he wanted to be a doctor. I was too scared, too young, and too much in love to realize what a mistake it all was. All I could think of was that we could work it out, that at least our baby would have a family."

Paige remembered the agony of loving Nick, the sleepless nights when he didn't call or come home, the terrible day she'd seen him kissing another student in the library, the lace panties she found in the pocket of his tweed jacket. She was wearing enormous maternity briefs herself by that time. The panties had been pink, extra small.

"I soon realized he didn't love me. My life began to center around my baby."

She remembered the night her labor began, and even after all these years, she shuddered. As usual, Nick was nowhere around, and even those first pains were agony, with hardly a minute between.

She'd managed to call a cab, stagger out to meet it. The entire thing was a nightmare. Her obstetrician was out of town, and the young doctor who attended her was inexperienced.

"They couldn't locate Nick that night. My pelvis was small, and my labor went on and on. The baby was finally delivered by emergency c-section. I was unconscious. When I came to, they told me she was stillborn, a perfectly formed little girl who just couldn't seem to—to breathe. I screamed and carried on until they let me see her, hold her for a minute or two. She was an exceptionally big baby, which is why I had so much trouble. She would have been so beautiful." Paige hadn't cried for her daughter in a long time, but tears came now. "I still remember exactly how she looked. Oh, Myles, even for those few moments I loved her so."

She was aware of Myles moving, coming to sit beside her on the narrow settee. His muscular arm came around her shoulders, dragging her close to him, and it was infinitely comforting to rest her cheek against the rough wool of his scarlet tunic.

"There were complications during the operation, and infection afterward. They told me it was unlikely I would ever bear another child."

She felt the sound he made, a wordless murmur of understanding and comfort, and it soothed her.

It was hours after they'd taken her baby away before Nick appeared at her bedside. He'd been drinking. Paige could smell both Scotch and a sweet, pungent perfume when he leaned over and pressed his lips to her forehead.

She'd looked up at his wicked, handsome face, his curly black hair, and he might have been a stranger. Any feelings she'd had for him had died with the death of her baby.

"We divorced." Paige remembered the appalling emptiness of her body, the agony of mourning the baby. She'd felt at times that she was losing her mind, and that was when she'd started using textbooks to distract her, to draw her thoughts away from the mental picture of her naked blue baby, forcing herself to memorize whatever was between the pages of whatever textbook she happened to pick up. Always a good student, she'd become an exceptional one. The textbooks gradually became medical tomes, and when the time came she was able to qualify easily for the faculty of medicine.

"I was probably wrong, but I had a feeling that if she'd had better medical care, she might have lived," Paige confided softly. "So I became an obstetrician."

The medical training was gruesomely difficult. Chauvinism was alive and well in the faculty of medicine. She'd learned to survive, to be tough, to ignore the blatant sexism. She'd graduated with the offer of a residency at Grace Hospital, renowned for its obstetrical care.

"I met Sam during my residency, and we were friends from the start. We set up a practice together, and eventually opened our own clinic."

A log shifted in the fireplace. The coal oil in the lantern had burned low, and now the soft light flickered and went out.

Paige moved her leg, planning to get up and tend to the lamp, but Myles's arm around her shoulders held her firm.

His deep voice was quiet and slow, his lips so close to her ear she could feel his breath.

"You said something earlier, Paige. You said, 'I've only fallen in love once before.' What did you mean by that? Before what?"

Her mouth fell open in horror, and she was grateful for the darkness of the room, because her face felt as though the sparks in the fireplace had set fire to her skin.

"Paige?"

He wasn't going to let it pass, she knew that. She knew him. Under the quiet southern-gentleman exterior was tempered steel, a stubborn nature that more than matched her own.

God, why had she let her mouth run off with her like that? Talk about a Freudian slip . . .

Well, she was no coy Victorian damsel, he was well aware of that by now. And if he was too thick to figure it out on his own, she'd damned well spell it out for him. She took a deep breath and swallowed.

"I meant that I've somehow managed to fall in love with you, Myles Baldwin." My God, she'd actually said it. She gulped and tried once again to get up.

She had to move away from him; she was sure he could feel the thundering of her heart. She had a lump in her chest that seemed to be moving into her throat, threatening to choke her.

But he held her against him, effortlessly preventing her from moving. A long, shuddering sigh went through him.

"I thought perhaps that might be what you meant, Miss Randolph." There was a slight tremor in his voice. Then he was turning her toward him, lifting her across him so she was cradled in his arms, her breasts tight against his chest, her bottom resting in his lap.

"I hoped that's what you meant, dear Paige. Because I think I've been in love with you from the first moment I saw you."

Before she could fully absorb the words, his mouth came down on hers, his lips at first soft against her own, almost gentle.

Soon, though, the gentleness changed to urgency. Paige felt as though the heat from the fire had entered her pores. She was melting inside, a wave of volcanic lava flowing downward, slow and sweet, in response to his mouth, his tongue, his strong hands stroking her body.

"I want you, Paige." His voice was hoarse, urgent. "Day and night, you're all I think about. You're driving me mad."

His fingers trembled at her neck, fumbling at the dozens of buttons that held her blouse closed. Impatient, she raised her hand and deftly undid the closures for him, forgetting for a moment that she was still wearing the long underwear she'd put on that morning.

He made short work of those larger buttons, however, stripping cotton shirtwaist and flannel long johns away from her shoulders and off her arms, revealing her lacy bra.

He gave an exclamation of surprise, cupping her aching breasts in his palms, studying the bra a moment before his lips trailed down her throat, his tongue testing the pulse at the nape, then tracing a path to first one nipple and then the other.

She gasped as his mouth closed over her, sending burning heat and dampness through the delicate lace and shooting downward to her core.

A growl of frustration came from his throat as he tried to find the closure to her bra.

"What the hell is this infernal contraption," he cursed, and she laughed, a shaky laugh, showing him the hidden front closure and then allowing the scrap of lace to slide slowly, provocatively, down her arms and off.

Then his lips were tugging at her breast in earnest, expertly teasing, nipping, and soothing, his teeth making her gasp with pleasure, his tongue sending those delicious licks of flame shooting down her body. His hands were adept at finding the fastening of her skirt, and in one impatient motion he stripped off her petticoats and underwear, leaving her bare.

"Not fair," she whispered. "I'm naked and you're not."

Swiftly, he lifted her off of him and stood up, his clothing joining hers in a pile on the floor. He eased her back on the settee, kneeling beside it, caressing her with those long-fingered hands.

Her breath caught in wonder as the firelight played over his aroused, naked body. He was a magnificent man, long-limbed, broad-shouldered, slender-hipped, his chest matted with curls that gleamed golden in the flickering light of the fire. His gray eyes glowed, filled with admiration as he studied her naked body, taking his time, tracing her shape with a gaze so intense it sent shivers of delight coursing through her.

A smile played across his lips. "I have a good imagination, but it fell far short of the real thing this time," he breathed. "You are ravishing, my love."

And then his lips followed the path his eyes had traveled a moment earlier, tracing a burning path across her breasts, down her abdomen, his strong hands gently rearranging her, urging her legs apart.

She gasped as his tongue touched, teased. Her eyes closed as silver ripples of delight coursed through her. Her hands clutched at his hair as the ripples became waves she could barely endure.

His mouth was hot and sweet, and his tongue—God, his tongue . . .

Her body convulsed, and a cry erupted from her throat as heat centered, exploded, consumed her in a wash of ecstasy.

"Paige, come here to me."

His voice sounded strangled. Impatient now, panting with need, he spread the afghan and lifted her in one swooping motion down to the carpet. She cried out again as he entered her and immediately began to move, a cry of joy, of triumph, of thanksgiving.

She was exactly where she longed to be, in his arms, pinioned by his long, strong body.

There was nothing gentle about this joining. He drove into her with savage abandon, his body and her own soon wet with sweat.

She wrapped herself around him, arms and legs locking him in place, her body trembling uncontrollably as the waves began again, building slowly at first, and then, with his guttural cry resounding through every pore, her own shuddering climax slammed through her, fading slowly into a delicious, warm stillness, a lethargic peace so encompassing she wondered if she could ever move again.

He collapsed on the carpet at her side, his hair-roughened legs still entwined with hers, his arms holding her, his eyes closed. He tipped his head and nuzzled her jaw in lazy contentment.

"You smell like roses."

"Ummm." Her voice was languid, lazy. "I bought rose water. I used to have this rose-based perfume I loved, and I miss it."

They were quiet, and then she said, "You're very good at this, you know." Her breathing was slowly returning to normal, but aftershocks of pleasure were still shooting through her nerve endings. "You've obviously had much more practice at it than I have." The thought of him with other women sent a distinct twinge of jealousy through her.

"I devoutly hope so." He adjusted his body so her head rested more comfortably on his shoulder. "Women are not expected to have a wealth of experience at such things."

"Decent unmarried women of this era, you mean."

She felt him nod. "Decent unmarried women, I mean."

Curiosity was getting the best of her. "So I suppose you

practiced a lot with the other kind, the women considered not so decent?"

His voice was thick and sleepy. "A gentleman doesn't discuss such things with a lady."

She made a rude noise. "The last thing I want to be is a lady. From what I can see, ladies in this day and age don't have a whole lot of fun."

"They don't wear this kind of underwear, either." She could tell he was smiling. "If that's a fair sampling of the undergarments from your time, I'd say the world must have progressed rather nicely."

Paige thought over what he'd just said. She propped herself on an elbow so she could see him. His eyes were closed, and she noticed that he had incredibly long, golden-tipped eyelashes.

She trailed a finger down his face, loving the high cheekbones, carved hollows, and strong jawline, the slight roughness of his skin where his beard had grown since he'd shaved that morning.

"You believe me now, don't you, Myles? That I came here from the nineteen nineties?" She wasn't certain why it should be so, but it meant everything to her, to have him believe her.

He opened his eyes and looked up at her, his contentment obvious, his love for her just as obvious. "Yes, my dear, I do. I think I've believed you for some time now, even though I was skeptical." He closed his eyes again. "But ever since I saw you in those damn trousers of yours, I knew that all the things you said were real and true."

She frowned, puzzled. "My jeans? But I don't understand why my jeans'd convince you when there's so much other stuff I've told you about that I couldn't possibly have made up, about medical science, and microwaves and dishwashers and—well, just everything."

He grasped her shoulders and rolled her over onto his body so she was resting full-length on top of him, and he took her head in his hands, threading his fingers through her wild curls, locking her green gaze with eyes that shone silver in the firelight.

"You were totally comfortable in those outrageous pants, Paige. You didn't even remember you were wearing them until I pointed it out."

She still didn't understand. "Of course I was comfortable. Why shouldn't I be? I used to wear them all the time, they were my favorite casual clothing."

He smiled, and she thought it was a sad smile.

"Exactly. When I got over the shock of seeing you in them and thought it over, I realized that you must have worn them often before, to be so at ease in them, and you couldn't possibly have done that unless you were from some other era, just as you kept insisting you were. Women here just don't wear denim trousers."

"Saved by the seat of my pants," she sighed, making a joke of it all because she was perilously close to tears.

His hands cupped her buttocks, and she could feel him growing hard against her belly. "I absolutely forbid you to wear those pants around anyone but me," he growled. "I've had nightmares about you and those damnable garments. Give me your word, Paige."

She grinned against his chest, rubbing her cheek against the soft mat of hair, feeling desire uncurl like a sleepy cat inside her stomach.

"What do I get if I promise?"

He made an impatient sound and captured her mouth in a kiss that became urgent. He moved against her in a way she couldn't misinterpret.

"Okay," she gasped. "You win. You have my word."

She lifted her hips and took him inside her, familiar and

yet so new and strange, resting her hands on his chest, tipping her head back, closing her eyes, rocking in age-old rhythm as their hunger built to unbearable heights.

She heard him growl, "I love you, Paige," and she wanted to reply, but passion had stolen away her ability to form words.

So she showed him, with her body and her soul, crying out a moment before him, falling forward on his chest exhausted, filled with profound peace. There was the strangest sensation inside of her, one it took a while to decipher.

Gradually, she realized that for the first time in years—perhaps for the first time in her entire adult life—she wasn't lonely anymore.

Chapter Twelve

"That fire's going to go out unless I put more wood on it. And I have to get back to the fort."

They'd lain entwined on the carpet, half asleep, while the flames died to embers and a chill crept into the room.

Myles stirred now, getting to his feet and then lifting her to the settee, wrapping the afghan around her when she shivered. He pulled on his long underwear, socks, and pants, and then stoked the fire.

"I wish you could stay," she sighed. It would be heaven to wake up beside him in the morning, to lie cuddled close and warm in his arms.

He laid a small log on the glowing embers and waited until it caught before he turned to smile at her. "I do too, darling, but the entire fort and then the whole town would know that I came riding in from your house during the small hours of the morning."

A frown creased his brow. "We're going to have to be discreet, Paige. That is, of course, if you want to attract patients and become known as a respectable woman's doctor in this town. Being known as my mistress would affect me very little, and you a great deal."

It went against every instinct, but she knew he was right.

Treating Helen Gillespie had shown her how much she wanted to practice her profession, and she was all too aware of the rigid moral code of the times.

When he was dressed, Myles swept her up in his arms and carried her along the hallway to her bedroom. He found her nightshirt—his nightshirt—and put it on her.

"Who made this for you?" She'd always wondered.

"My mother." His voice was tender. "She was beautiful, just as you are."

"But I can't sew anything except incisions."

He laughed, tucking her under the sheets and quilts as if she were a child. The kiss he gave her was anything but fatherly, however.

"Sleep well, my lady. I'll be back to see you soon."

Exhausted from lovemaking as well as the long ride the day before, Paige was still in bed when Rob Cameron arrived at her door the next forenoon.

Only half awake, she leapt up when the knocking began, scrabbling for a robe to put on over her nightgown. The bedroom was warm; Myles had lit the small heater before he left, and stoked the other fires as well.

Unable to find a robe, Paige wrapped a huge shawl around her shoulders and staggered to the door, feeling as if she were drugged.

"Rob. Good morning." Half blinded by the brilliance of the sunshine, she squinted at the stocky policeman. "Lord, what time is it?"

"My apologies, Paige." His already ruddy face had flushed brick red at the sight of her nightgown. "I'm sorry to get ye out of bed. I was sure ye'd be up and about by now. I came by because I thought ye might fancy a bit of fresh meat. I shot a deer out on patrol yesterday." He held up a canvas-wrapped parcel. "I'll just put it in the cold locker and be on me way."

He looked so disappointed, like a small boy promised a treat and then deprived of it, that Paige felt guilty.

"No, no. Don't hurry away, Rob. Just give me a few moments to wash and dress and put a pot of coffee on, and then you can come in and share breakfast with me."

Hell. She closed the door and scowled. She didn't feel like company this morning. She wanted to laze her way through her chores and review last night, scene by delicious, X-rated scene.

Which reminded her. She dashed in to check the parlor for odd bits of clothing, grabbing up her bra and panties, her long underwear and petticoat, strewn across the rug.

Half an hour later, Rob sat at her kitchen table, a steaming mug of coffee cupped in his broad, chapped hands.

"I'm getting pretty good at making porridge," she bragged, scooping two generous helpings into bowls. "In fact, I'm not doing too badly at making soup and biscuits, either, thanks to you."

She smiled across at him, thinking how much she valued his friendship. "You're a good teacher, Rob." She set the bowls on the table and slid into her chair. "You're a good friend."

Abruptly, Rob set his cup down, and Paige noticed that his hands were trembling. Sweat stood out on his forehead, and he smoothed his mustache with two fingers. Then he got to his feet, shoulders back, standing at attention, hands curled into tight fists at his sides. His face had turned as scarlet as his tunic, his freckles invisible in the strong wash of color.

Paige stared at him, astonished. "Good grief. What the heck's the matter, Rob? Is it the porridge?"

He took three quick steps and dropped to one knee at her side.

"Paige, I've fallen in love with ye. Would ye do me the great honor of becoming me wife?"

The words tumbled over one another, Rob's Scots accent more pronounced than she'd ever heard it, his broad, earnest face contorted as though he were in pain.

She was speechless for long, endless moments. His ruddy face was only a foot from her own. She stared at him, unable to think of a single thing to say.

Rob cleared his throat. "I realize this is most improper, Paige. I've wanted to find the right moment to ask ye, but somehow it never seems to come."

Paige was wishing frantically that she'd stayed in bed. She wasn't up to this this morning, of all mornings. But the sight of Rob's earnest, open face turned her thoughts from her own discomfort to what he must be feeling.

She reached out a hesitant hand and touched his cheek. It was burning hot, as though he had a fever. "Oh, dear Rob. Oh, my God. Rob please, get up, sit back down at the table, let's—let's talk about this, okay?"

He got to his feet and, stiff as a marionette, sat down in his chair, his hazel eyes pinned on her face, assessing her reactions, a nervous stream of words pouring from him like sweat.

"I ken that it's too soon. I realize ye'll need time to consider this, Paige. I know I haven't properly courted ye, walking out with ye the way I ought to have done. I'll make it up to ye, we'll go out together proper, there's a sleigh ride planned next week, will ye go with me? Ye will go with me, will ye not?"

First, he'd proposed. Now, he was asking her for a date.

The incongruity of the whole thing made her head spin, and a hysterical giggle rose in her throat. She suppressed it, because it was dawning on her that she had to be very cautious and tactful here, or she'd hurt Rob and lose a friendship she very much valued.

A disturbing thought struck her. Had he heard something about her and Myles? How could he have done? Gossip traveled fast in this town, but between midnight last night and this morning?

Nevertheless, she felt herself blushing like a guilty schoolgirl. Good God, the mores of the day were really getting to her.

"Rob. What I don't understand is—" she stammered. "Has anything happened to—this is such a surprise, I don't—" She silently cursed herself for hedging this way. "Rob, what made you decide to ask me now, this morning, to—to marry you? Because it is a complete surprise to me."

His gaze dropped and she could see his Adam's apple bob as he swallowed, once, twice. "It seems my visits here have compromised yer reputation," he finally choked out. "I was planning on asking ye soon anyway, when I felt the time was right. Then I happened to see Lulu, and something she said made me realize—"

Lulu Leiberman again. Paige felt like marching over to the boardinghouse and planting a punch right in Lulu's busy mouth.

"Look, Rob." She tried to map out what to say, and finally just told him the truth—as gently as she knew how.

"I can't marry you." If she'd thought his proposal was for anything but love, she knew better by the devastated expression on his face and in his soft hazel eyes. She hated hurting him, but there were no other options—she had to set him straight, here and now.

"It's marvelous of you to ask me, and I'm terrified that now I'm going to lose you as my best friend, but the truth is—" She was running out of breath. She gulped and went on. "The truth is I'm involved with someone else." Involved. Damn, no one said involved yet, she was certain of it. But whatever the going expression, it was beyond her at the moment.

"Betrothed?" His shock made the word sound like a cough. "You're already betrothed to someone else?"

This was getting worse by the minute. She shook her head. "No, not engaged. Not betrothed," she corrected. How to explain to this simple, wonderful man the complexities between her and Myles? "But I am in love with him," she said in a firm tone. Even in these circumstances, her heart soared as she added, "And he loves me."

Rob's face was as pale now as it had been red before, his freckles standing out like drops of paint. "Who?" he choked out. "Who the hell is he?" His good manners reasserted themselves, and he added hastily, "Forgive me, Paige, that was rude of me." His feelings got the better of him once more, and he burst out again, "But tell me who he is, damn it all."

"You have the right to know, Rob. It's—it's Myles, Myles Baldwin. But we'd rather no one else knew just yet."

"Surgeon Baldwin?" Rob was in shock. He couldn't have sounded more astonished or disbelieving if she'd said she was in love with Chief Poundmaker. Paige felt a twinge of irritation with him. Why should it be so inconceivable that she and Myles were in love, for heaven's sake?

"I thought—I mean, the two of you—well, ye fight like cats and dogs. And it's well known that Surgeon Baldwin keeps to himself, he's no one for the ladies. I mean, a lot of the women hereabouts have tried, but—" Rob suddenly realized what he was saying and shut his mouth.

It was a relief to Paige to know that Myles wasn't romancing half the town, but Paige couldn't think of a single thing to say to Rob.

There was a long, painful silence. At last Rob got to his feet again, and Paige stood up too, feeling helpless to remedy the situation.

"Rob, can't we please stay friends? I enjoy your visits, I look forward to them. I'd miss you so much if this caused problems between us."

There was a touching dignity to the way he donned his heavy coat and tugged the muskrat cap down over his ears. He met her anxious gaze with a sad, crooked smile that touched her heart.

"Aye, we'll stay friends, Paige, never fear. I just need some time to get used to all this." He gave her a half-salute with his gloved hand and went out the back door, closing it quietly behind him.

When he was gone, Paige poured another cup of coffee with hands that shook and collapsed in her chair, unsure whether she wanted to laugh or cry. In the space of 24 hours, she'd declared her love for one man and been proposed to by another.

She'd never had anything like that happen back in what she'd begun to call her "other life."

She'd once heard someone remark back in the nineties that things must have been much simpler before technology took the world by storm.

They'd overlooked the simple truth that people were people, and emotions stayed the same regardless of the calendar.

Her medical practice began to flourish.

To Paige it seemed a miracle when women needing

medical attention began appearing at her front door.

It seemed that Helen Gillespie and Clara Fletcher had spread the word among the women of Battleford that there was a woman doctor who'd saved their lives, but it was really Abigail Donald who did the most for Paige's reputation and her business.

Abigail was lavish in her praise of Paige's expertise as a woman's doctor and a surgeon, and through her work as a midwife, she began to send women with gynecological problems to Paige, who established regular office hours, Monday, Wednesday, and Friday, ten to four.

Women began to appear in her waiting room on the appointed days. Paige scheduled her minor operations for whenever Abigail could come in and assist her. Anything complex was dealt with at the hospital at the fort, with Myles scrubbing in with her.

Having office hours three days a week was a perfect situation for Paige—she had ample time to shop and tend to her chores.

Abigail came to help when Paige needed her, and the easygoing agreement between them worked well.

Most of the conditions Paige encountered would have been simple enough to deal with in the twentieth century; many of the patients she began to see had simply had too many pregnancies, too close together.

Birth control was obviously the answer, but in this day and age, it was almost nonexistent. Just like Helen Gillespie, Paige found that most of the women had only the vaguest concept of their own anatomy. A portion of her work was educational, and frustrating as well; many of the women rejected any talk of pregnancy prevention, insisting that interfering with what they labeled "nature's way" was a sin.

For the others, the ones who came to her wanting and

needing birth control, Paige did the best she could. She consulted with Myles, ordered a supply of sponges, and taught women how to tie a string around them and insert them, using a vinegar solution as a spermicide.

Paige had just completed that ritual one cold December morning. "Good-bye, Mrs. Todd. Come see me again in two weeks."

"But that's right on Christmas, Doctor."

Paige glanced at her calendar, surprised to see that the woman was right. "It is, too. Make it three then, Mrs. Todd, but no longer."

Paige opened the door of her examining room to usher Mrs. Todd out and found Clara Fletcher just entering the parlor, a white-wrapped bundle in her arms.

"Clara!" Paige was delighted. "Hey, hello there, Clara Fletcher, what a wonderful surprise. How great to see you." Paige hurried over and wrapped both Clara and baby Ellie in a huge hug. "Hi, young Ellie Randolph, how you doing, anyway?"

Paige had seen the baby only once since Ellie's birth, and then only for a few moments. The Fletchers had come to town for supplies a few weeks before and dropped in for a moment, but because of a threatening storm, they had to get back home quickly.

"Come here to me, love, while Mommy gets the frost off her glasses." Paige eagerly took the baby in her arms and undid some of her wrappings, smiling down at her tiny namesake as she appeared from the blanket cocoon Clara had devised to keep her warm.

"Abigail's not here this morning. She's going to be furious when she finds out she missed seeing you—" Paige halted the excited flow of words. "Clara, what is it?" She'd glanced up and seen stark terror on Clara's round face.

"Come in here and sit down," she ordered, leading the

way into her examining room. She motioned Clara to a chair and laid the baby on the table, swiftly undoing the rest of the blankets.

"Now, what's the problem?"

"She had some kind of convulsion," Clara stammered out. "A bad one, her eyes rolled back and if Theo hadn't put his finger in her mouth and grabbed her tongue, I think she might have choked. Oh, Paige, it seemed to go on forever. It was early this morning, about five. We got ready and brought her straight here."

Clara was obviously distraught and close to tears.

Ellie was awake, but very quiet; she seemed sleepy and lethargic. She had huge blue eyes in a triangular face, a lovely little rosebud of a mouth, and an incongruous scrap of peach-colored fuzz on the very top of her tiny skull. She was sluggish at responding to the stimuli Paige used to test her.

Paige questioned Clara closely while performing as intensive an examination of the baby as possible.

"She was a little cranky last night, didn't want to nurse the way she usually does," Clara explained. "But she didn't have a fever or anything. We thought maybe she was starting to teethe, or maybe coming down with a little cold." The tears that had threatened now began trickling down Clara's round cheeks.

"It was awful; her whole little body jerked for what seemed hours. What—what do you think is wrong with her, Paige?"

Paige had unfastened Ellie's diaper in order to examine her, and now she bent over the baby, repinning the safety pins, tying up ribbons, wrestling the tiny limbs into sleeves, unwilling to turn just yet and face Clara in case the awful frustration she was feeling showed on her face.

Damn it all, she just didn't know. She needed blood tests,

brain scans, an EEG, all the aid of the sophisticated modern equipment she didn't have in order to properly diagnose baby Ellie Randolph Fletcher.

Without them, the best Paige could do was guess, and even her guesses were anything but reassuring.

A convulsion was a symptom rather than a disease.

Birth injury? There had certainly been complications enough to make that a possibility. Congenital defect of the brain? There was no way to tell, except to wait and see how Ellie developed.

Anoxia, intercranial hemorrhage, infection of the central nervous system—some progressive degenerative disease? Subdural hematoma? Paige examined the small skull minutely for signs of swelling, but there were none.

The list of possibilities seemed endless, and none of them were good. And even if she could correctly diagnose the baby, what could she do about the problem? Abdominal surgery in this day and age was all but unheard of, never mind brain surgery. Paige felt sick.

But she made certain she had a reassuring smile on her face when she finally turned and put the baby gently back in Clara's arms.

"She's a bit listless just now, but that's natural after a severe convulsion such as you describe," Paige said. "Other than that, she seems fine. Her eyes are focusing quite well, and her temp's normal. I can't hazard even a guess as to what caused the convulsion; all we can do is pray there won't be another one. But don't worry yourself into a state about this—about seven in every hundred babies have convulsions, Clara, and few of them suffer permanent damage."

It was a small white lie, because Paige had absolutely nothing else to offer, no medication, no further testing. She couldn't even keep the baby here for observation—the

Fletchers had to go back to their farm and their livestock, and anyway, testing would be fruitless without treatment to back it up.

"I want to know if and when it happens again."

There were no other patients that morning, and when Theo came in from tending the horses Paige took the Fletchers into her warm kitchen and gave them sandwiches and bowls of the ongoing pot of soup she kept simmering on the back of the range.

Paige managed to remain cheerful and upbeat until the Fletchers, reassured by her attitude, climbed in their sleigh and waved to her later that afternoon.

As the sound of the harness and the squeak of the sleigh runners faded into the distance, Paige could at last stop smiling, close the door, and then rest her head against the wood and swear in a steady stream, every foul word she'd ever heard.

What good was all her book learning, her years of experience, if she couldn't use it to help one tiny little girl?

All her knowledge seemed bitter mockery at times like this.

She was slumped at the kitchen table, her uneaten dinner from hours before still not cleared away, when Myles slipped in the back door late that night.

She was still in her jeans—she'd changed into them to do the outdoor chores, bringing in wood and water, cleaning Minnie's stall and putting down fresh straw for her in the stable, trying to work off the sense of gloom that hung over her like a storm cloud.

She'd given up hoping Myles would be able to come tonight, damning as always the lack of a telephone, which meant that she never knew if or when he'd arrive.

"Myles. God, Myles, I'm glad to see you."

She flew into his arms before he could shuck off his

heavy buffalo coat, ignoring the dusting of snow that clung to the fur.

"I see you dressed especially for me." His gloved hand patted her rump, snugly encased in denim. He hugged her tight and kissed her hard, then held her away while he took off his coat, hat, and mitts. He sat down on a chair and unlaced his buckskin moccasins, pulling her down on his lap for a more thorough kiss when he was done.

That kiss went on until he stood up and lifted her into his arms. Within moments, they were in her bedroom, and he'd tossed her jeans haphazardly to the floor along with his wool breeches.

He didn't bother removing the rest of her clothing, or his own; Paige made it clear she neither wanted or needed preliminary caresses. They tumbled in a frenzy onto the bed, and their mutual hunger sent them spiraling out of control the moment Myles entered her.

Afterward, folded in one another's arms, comforted by his presence, Paige told him about Ellie. "It makes me half-crazy when there's nothing I can do," she whispered. "It's unlikely Clara and Theo will ever have another child, because Clara's near menopause. And now if they should lose Ellie . . ." She shuddered, and he drew her tighter against him.

"None of us are gods, my darling. And one convulsion isn't a death sentence. Just as you told Clara, some babies have them, for reasons unknown. They often grow out of them."

"Do you ever get a feeling about patients, Myles? Just a sense in your gut that something's not right, even though you can't detect any problem?"

She felt him nod. "I know it well. It's a sixth sense some doctors develop."

"Well, I've got that bad feeling about baby Ellie." She

sighed, a frustrated sigh. "Damn it all, Myles, if I were a drinking woman, I'd have gotten wasted tonight."

He stroked her hair in silence for a while, and then he said in his slow drawl, "After Beth died, I took to drinking."

"Beth . . . Your wife?" Paige took his hand in hers and threaded her fingers between his, curious about his past.

"Elizabeth, but she was called Beth. You know, Paige, when she started to hemorrhage, I felt I should have been able to save her." He made a sound that could have been either a laugh or a sob. "Still feel that way some days, and it's been over nine years now."

"Can you tell me what it was like when you were young, Myles? Tell me about your family?"

He drew in a deep breath and let it out again. "My daddy, General James Frances Baldwin, was a career officer in the Confederate army. He was a stern man, the general. Had strict ideas about how things ought to be, what his sons should amount to." His voice softened. "Mama, now, she was a belle. I was always told she was one of the prettiest girls in the county when daddy and she were married. We had a good life, plenty of everything. We lived on a cotton plantation outside of Charleston; the land had been in our family for generations."

Paige remembered watching *Gone With The Wind* and an incredible thought struck her, sending chills up her spine.

"Your family didn't have slaves, did they, Myles?"

"Of course." He sounded astonished that she would even ask. "Everyone we knew had slaves; it was part of our culture. Why, my brothers and I were raised by Mandy, our black nurse. It was a way of life in the South. A few of them stayed on after the war, till after Beth died."

"How many brothers and sisters did you have?"

"Two brothers, no living sisters. Ma had six babies in

all, we three boys and also two girls and a boy that didn't
live past babyhood. I was the middle one. We were the
apples of our mama's eye, and Pa wasn't home a lot, so
we ran pretty wild when we were growing up."

Paige could tell from his voice he was smiling.

"All the old ladies thereabouts called us rakes and warned
their granddaughters not to speak to those wild Baldwin
boys, which seemed to bring the girls flocking."

Paige smiled at pictures his soft drawl conjured.

"I remember one summer especially, before the war
came. Chance was two years older than me, he was
home from college, he was studying law. I was heading
back for medical school in Charleston in the fall. Beau,
two years my junior, was still in prep school. It was hot,
seemed it never rained that whole summer. Pa was away.
We were full of the dickens. We gambled, fought some,
stole Pa's best bourbon, went fishin', tore around on fast
horses, romanced the neighbor girls." He laughed, a deep
rumble in his chest. "Poor Mama was at her wit's end all
that summer." He paused, and Paige waited.

"Then the war came." Myles's voice changed, becoming
flat and toneless. "Chance died at Manassas. Beau got
typhoid in a federal prison camp and died there three
months before the war ended. Pa was killed at Gettysburg.
Mama wasn't really a strong woman; she'd always been
pampered, had her servants and her menfolk to protect and
care for her. She retreated into a kind of dreamworld after
the war, couldn't face up to the way things really were."

He shifted to his back, settling her head more squarely on
his shoulder. "I tried to get the plantation back to some kind
of working order when I came home, but it was pretty well
hopeless. Part of the house was still standing, but the fields
were ruined, and I didn't have the time, the money, or the
inclination to set it right. I was busy; there was a shortage

of doctors after the war. Ma never got over losing Pa and the boys and the plantation. She died of heart failure the year after Beth and I were married." His voice sounded weary.

"We'd about given up on the idea of a family by the time Beth got pregnant, and she was happier than I'd ever seen her when she found out she was carrying our baby. To me, that baby seemed like a fresh start, a new generation of Baldwins, something good in the aftermath of all that horror."

He was silent so long Paige thought perhaps he'd drifted off to sleep, but after a long while he began to speak again. "I haven't ever really talked about this to anyone but you. It's hard to put into words. After Beth was gone, it seemed that everything in me died too. Nothing seemed important anymore. I didn't bother going to the hospital each day the way I'd always done. I started drinking to stop the pain, and liquor became my reason for getting up in the morning. For months, I kept a bottle of bourbon always within reach. Then one afternoon I was called on to treat a neighbor, an old man I'd known all my life. He'd cut his foot nearly off with a scythe. I tried, but I was simply too drunk, couldn't even apply a tourniquet to control the bleeding. He came near to death before they could transport him to the hospital."

Paige winced, aware of the self-loathing in his voice.

"And that's when you stopped drinking?"

"Yes, ma'am. I looked in a mirror and saw myself and what I'd become, and I didn't like it much. I sold the land and left Charleston, traveling west, nowhere in particular. I wanted to get as far away from the South as I could."

"How did you start to practice medicine again?"

He raised her fingers to his lips and kissed them. "As you know so well, darling, work usually finds a doctor. I treated frontiersmen and settlers in one small settlement after another. Eventually I heard of the formation of the

North West Mounted in Canada, and I volunteered my services as a surgeon. The Canadian frontier and the nomadic life of a mounted policeman suit me fine."

"It must seem like another world, all this snow and ice, and the Indians." She was thinking of what it had been like for her, the total culture shock she'd experienced.

But Myles disagreed. "It's not as different as you might think," he insisted. "People get sick, accidents happen, and I find people everywhere are basically alike, good and bad, weak and strong."

He seemed to make a conscious effort to shrug off the somber mood that had sprung up between them, rolling over all of a sudden and covering her with his body, his voice teasing.

"And the women are warm and willing. . . ."

She punched him in the ribs, and they ended up in a wrestling match which ended, inevitably, with loving. She never did get around to telling him about Rob's proposal of marriage.

The Christmas season in Battleford was a lighthearted time, a time for parties, sleigh rides, dances, and concerts, many of which were organized by the men at the Mounted Police post and held at the fort. Attendance wasn't by invitation; it was simply expected that every single resident who could possibly manage it would turn up at these festivities—and almost everyone always did.

Feeling affluent with the income from her patients, Paige splurged and bought herself two new dresses from the emporium, one in a green shade that matched her eyes, and the other a deep, dramatic crimson. For the first time, she found herself actually thinking that the voluminous, fussy styles of the day were romantic and very feminine—as long as she could trade them for her jeans when the party ended.

She was almost embarrassingly popular at these events. Myles escorted her to many, but Paige insisted on going by herself to others, to avoid the very wagging tongues he'd warned against.

The first time Myles became visibly jealous when she danced once too often with some handsome policeman, Paige was astonished, and although it embarrassed her to admit it, she was also flattered.

No one had ever been jealous of her before; but then, she'd never been the belle of the ball before, either. She reminded herself sternly that her popularity had everything to do with the shortage of available women in Battleford, and the numbers of single young policemen and settlers.

The one person who didn't ask her to dance at any of the functions was Rob Cameron. He greeted her with stiff politeness when they happened to meet, but he kept his distance.

Paige tried several times to talk to him, to recapture the easy camaraderie they'd shared, but it was clear that Rob wasn't comfortable in her presence. She finally gave up trying, sorry to lose his friendship.

For Christmas, Myles presented her with an elaborately scrolled hand-carved sign for her front door that read, Paige Randolph, M.D., Specialty Women's Medicine. Another, smaller notice, said Walk In on one side and a firm Closed, Come Again on the other. He also gave her a bottle of exquisite rose-scented perfume with a French label.

She presented him with Levi's that matched her own.

At six one morning, near the end of January, Paige was shoveling out Minnie's stall before she put fresh hay down. Myles had spent the evening and a good part of the night— whenever his duties allowed, they were together, and this morning her body ached pleasantly from their loving the night before.

Puffing with exertion, she went to the stable door to clear her nose of the acrid smell of horse dung and urine.

It had been cold and overcast for several days, but this morning the sky was clear, a few stars still showing on the eastern horizon. She drew in deep gulps of cold air, relishing the way her lungs burned a little.

Down in the town there were lanterns lit and smoke pouring from chimneys as housewives got fires stirred up and breakfasts going.

From the direction of the fort came the sound of a bugle playing reveille, the clear, haunting notes floating, pure and sweet, in the frosty air.

An unfamiliar feeling crept over Paige, a tightness in her chest that brought tears to her eyes. There was a sense of lightness in her body and in her mind, a sense of being one with her surroundings.

It took several moments to figure out just what the strange sensation was, and when she identified it, it amazed her.

The feeling was happiness, a deep and total happiness and contentment with herself and her life that she couldn't ever remember feeling before.

She examined it, putting together the pieces as if they were a puzzle.

She was doing work she enjoyed, she had a house of her own, she was financially secure, she was madly in love with a man who loved her equally as much, and for the first time in her life she had women friends—Clara, Abigail— and she'd promised herself she was also going to get to know Tahnancoa Quinlan.

She'd thought of Tahnancoa often since the day she and Myles had visited, but she hadn't yet gone out by herself to visit, the way she'd planned to.

Myles was leaving the following day, Friday, to inspect two outposts where there'd been consistent reports of illness. He'd be gone the better part of a week.

She'd miss him, but she decided that she'd also take advantage of his absence to ride out alone on Sunday to visit Tahnancoa.

Chapter Thirteen

Paige left home early Sunday morning, and the solitary ride across the half-frozen prairie was exhilarating.

When she rode into the Quinlans' yard, Tahnancoa came running out of the cabin to greet her.

Paige slid down from Minnie's back, put her arms around the other woman, and gave her an impetuous hug. "Hi, Tahnancoa. Hope you don't mind me dropping in this way; there wasn't any way to let you know I was coming."

"You are welcome, Paige Randolph." Tahnancoa's black eyes sparkled, her smile just as wide as Paige's own. "Come inside. Dennis is off hunting a wolf that's made off with one of our calves. He won't be back until late tonight, and I'm making soap. It's a perfect time for us to talk."

Paige had never seen anyone make soap, although she knew most of the settler women made their own supply. The process provided for easy conversation with Tahnancoa; Paige asked endless questions, and Tahnancoa described the process for her.

"The ashes from poplar fires are best. I collect them all

summer. Then I boil them, stirring all the time. I did that yesterday. This morning I strained the liquid, which is very powerful; it burns if it gets on your skin. I mixed it with fat—I raised some geese, we ate them at Christmas, and I saved their grease—that kind of fat is best for the soap we use on our skin—and now I'm boiling it all down again."

Paige helped by stirring the smelly concoction with a wooden paddle. When Tahnancoa considered it done, the women carried the soap kettle into the lean-to attached to the back of the cabin, and carefully poured it into shallow wooden molds Dennis had made for this purpose.

"When it's cool, I'll cut it into bars, and we'll have enough soap for the rest of the winter," Tahnancoa said with satisfaction. "Thank you for helping."

Paige admired a row of small woven baskets lined up on a long shelf, and Tahnancoa opened several to show Paige a collection of dried herbs.

"My grandmother, Lame Owl, is a mighty shaman among our people," she explained. "Before Dennis and I married, I was her apprentice." A shadow passed over Tahnancoa's face. "She's angry with me for leaving my tribe, for marrying Dennis. She's refused to continue with the training, but I keep hoping she'll change her mind. From the time I was a small child, she taught me to gather and use the medicines from the earth."

Paige was entranced. Myles had given her some of his favorite native remedies, but most of them were useful only for such things as gunshot wounds or infection; he'd admitted he didn't know of many for women's ailments.

"What's this one for?" Paige touched a finger to a dark, shredded mass inside a straw basket.

"Headache, or aching limbs. It's the bark from the willow tree. I steep it and then make a tea."

"And this?" Paige touched another.

"Wild black cherry. For the pain of childbirth, or in a smaller dose, to ease women's monthly cramps."

Paige questioned Tahnancoa at length, determining that the herbal remedies had been in use for centuries among the Indians, and their effectiveness, proven many times over, was now taken for granted. She grew more and more excited as she examined one basket after another.

"This, Tahnancoa?"

"I don't know the English word for that. When it's mixed into a paste and put on burns, the burn heals quickly without blistering. Also, we use it on the rash babies get." Tahnancoa put a few dried red berries on Paige's palm. "These are wild rose hips. Made into tea, they soothe colds or winter flu."

Of course, the original source of vitamin C. Paige was fascinated. As she examined each basket, Tahnancoa listed the uses of the herbal concoction within.

Wild wintergreen, for colds. Catnip leaves, for colic. White pine bark, for coughs.

Paige was totally intrigued; the medicines that Myles had supplied her with were woefully inadequate for many of the common problems her female patients and their children complained of. Paige felt these remedies would be every bit as trustworthy and effective as some of the medications currently in use by the medical profession.

"I don't suppose you could sell me some of these herbal remedies to treat my patients?" Paige asked tentatively. "Many of them dose themselves with patent medicines, like Lydia Pinkham's, and this stuff called Perry Davis Vegetable Pain Killer—God, it's almost pure alcohol, with staggering amounts of opium added. What d'you think, could you sell me a stock of your medications and instruct me in how to use them?"

Tahnancoa was surprised, and flattered as well. She

readily agreed to supply Paige with some of the herbal preparations. "A few I don't have a good supply of," she explained. "And others will need careful instruction in how to prepare them, but I can teach you. In the spring and summer, I will gather and prepare a good supply, if you find them effective."

Deftly, she packaged a number of the remedies she had, and Paige carefully labeled them along with the dosages and instructions Tahnancoa gave her. Pricing was difficult; they worked out a system that took into account the availability of the herb and the ease of gathering it.

Tahnancoa was excited at the prospect of earning some money of her own. "There is a special knife Dennis has wanted, a skinning knife. I will save this money and surprise him," she confided.

Paige smiled at her new friend, aware of how deep the bond was between this extraordinary couple, grateful that she'd found a similar bond with Myles.

As they worked with the herbs, Tahnancoa was eager to know about Paige's work as a doctor, both now and what she called simply "before."

She asked intelligent questions about how Paige treated certain ailments, explaining how her grandmother might deal with a similar problem.

As they talked, Paige expressed some of the concerns she had for the patients she treated, needing to vent some of her frustrations to another woman.

"This horrible practice of putting on a corset and lacing it up so tight breathing is nearly impossible and all the inner organs are compressed is one of the reasons women are having the problems they do with childbirth and menstruation. It's a barbaric custom."

Tahnancoa nodded. "When I lived at the fort with Dennis, one of the other wives told me I must wear a corset and lace it tight, that it was considered indecent not to. I tried, but it made me sick. I burned it."

"Smart move." Paige told Tahnancoa of her first visit to the ladies' emporium, and the pandemonium she'd created by refusing to wear one. They giggled together, and the bond between them grew stronger. At last Paige felt comfortable enough to ask Tahnancoa about the ceremony she'd mentioned, when her people walked between the worlds.

"Only special female shamans are allowed to do this thing," Tahnancoa explained. "They are caretakers for the earth spirits, special guardians appointed to make certain no lasting harm comes to Mother Earth because of man."

Paige thought of the environmental devastation in her own time. She asked Tahnancoa what these travelers might make of it.

"They travel into the Beyond and look, and when they come back again they make powerful magic to counteract any damage they have seen."

Paige had a million questions. "Can they pick a certain time, a certain year in the future, for instance, and go there?"

"I don't know. There are many things I don't know about this ceremony; it's very secret, even among the shamans. I was never allowed to be present. There are few shamans now who even know the ritual—the old ways are dying out. Lame Owl is one of the last who have the special knowledge. That is why she was so disappointed in me; she wanted me to learn all that she knows so I too could help the guardians on their way and bring them back again."

"Does your grandmother conduct these ceremonies often?"

Tahnancoa shook her head. "I don't think so. I haven't seen her for many months now, but when the weather is better, I will visit."

"When you do, could you ask her if there's any chance of me traveling in this way, back to my own time?"

"I will ask, but I doubt that she will answer. She is a very obstinate old woman."

It sounded as though the chances were slim, Paige mused, surprised that it bothered her as little as it did. She really ought to be feeling more discouraged about it.

Falling in love with Myles had changed her, no doubt about it.

Tahnancoa served dinner early in the afternoon, a stew made from prairie chicken and freshly made bannock. The conversation skipped along, from medicine to clothing to food.

Paige amused Tahnancoa with tales of modern-day fast food, burgers and pizzas and milkshakes, and how people had adopted food of different cultures: Chinese, Greek, Italian.

"There was even a very famous restaurant in Vancouver that served traditional West Coast Indian food: bannock— not half as good as yours—smoked salmon, saskatoon pie," she recalled. She listed the prices that were charged for the dishes, and Tahnancoa's jaw dropped in astonishment. She pressed both hands to her lips and giggled. "I will remember this each time I cook, how much my food is worth. It will make it easier at times when I don't feel like cooking at all."

Curious, Paige questioned Tahnancoa about the traditional food her Indian people had eaten before the coming of the white man. Tahnancoa listed an impressive array of natural dishes: wild rice, bush cranberries, wild strawberries, a tuberous root she called prairie turnip, and of course, most important, the buffalo.

"My people are deeply troubled now because the buffalo are disappearing," she told Paige, her lovely face sobering.

"Why is this happening?" Myles had mentioned the same problem, but Paige hadn't paid much attention at the time.

"My people hunted for many years with bow and arrow," Tahnancoa explained, "killing only what they needed to eat. With the coming of the white man and rapid-fire guns, buffalo began to be slaughtered by the thousands, for sport instead of for food. Now there aren't enough left for us to hunt, and the problem is serious, because to us, the buffalo isn't only food—we use the hides for clothing, for sleeping robes, and for our tipis; we sew hides into sacks to carry pemmican; the bones we crush and cook to extract marrow fat, which is stored in the buffalo's bladder after we clean it and blow it up to dry. The sinews are used for sewing; the horns are hollowed out to carry powder."

Paige nodded. "I see what you mean." She reached across and took Tahnancoa's hand in her own. "I'm sorry, Tahnancoa." What else could she say? She felt both angry and embarrassed for her white-skinned race—and ashamed when she thought of how little they'd learned even during the next hundred years.

Their conversation shifted to other things, and soon it was time for Paige to ride home, before the winter afternoon turned to twilight and then darkness.

She'd taken her boots off, and now she struggled her way back into them. Tahnancoa handed her the package of herbs.

"Good-bye, Paige. I hope you will soon come again."

"I will," Paige promised. "The next time you and Dennis come in for supplies, come and visit me. I'd like to show you my office."

A shadow flitted across Tahnancoa's face. "I don't go with Dennis for supplies to the town. I tell him what I need, and he buys everything for me."

Paige understood, but she felt outraged that Tahnancoa

should have to live in a sort of exile. "Come and spend the day with me next time. Dennis can drop you off and then pick you up again when he's finished shopping. You need to get away from here sometimes too, Tahny. It must get lonely for you."

"I go to visit my own people, at Poundmaker's reserve, when Dennis is away. But perhaps I will come to you. I would like to see where you live."

They parted with a hug.

On the way home, Paige urged Minnie into a trot whenever the ground was clear, and she found herself humming under her breath the whole way home.

"I thought I told you not to ride out to the Quinlans' alone, Paige." Myles's steely gray eyes were narrowed on her, his jaw clenched, his voice iron hard. "What in damnation are you trying to do, get yourself killed? When I give you a direct order, I expect you to obey it."

Paige could hardly believe she was hearing him correctly. "Obey? You expect me to *obey* you?" Her voice shrilled into the upper register. "I'm not one of your constables, Myles Baldwin, to order around as you choose. I don't take orders from you or anyone else."

Anger and bitter disappointment added to her vehemence. It was Friday, and he'd been gone a full week. He'd arrived at her back door less than half an hour ago, and she'd flown into his arms, aware of how alone she'd felt without him, telling him with her kiss how ridiculously pleased she was that he was back.

She'd missed their passionate lovemaking, the intimate conversations, the simple and intense pleasure of having a best friend to whom she could confide all the happenings of her day.

And instead of swooping her up into his arms and

carrying her into bed the way he ought to be doing, this impossible man was standing, hands low on his hips, glaring at her as if she were a child who'd misbehaved.

She'd asked about his trip, and he'd asked what she'd done while he was away, and of course she'd told him about the visit to Tahnancoa. The warmth of his expression had instantly faded, replaced by this grim scowl.

"Damn you, Paige, don't be so contrary. I warned you about marauding Indians, and wolves, and—and white men who aren't any better than animals. Even the weather can change in an hour at this time of year; a blizzard could come and you'd be lost in a snowstorm."

"Myles, listen to yourself, you're being unreasonable. All I did was take a little ride out to visit a friend, for God's sake."

He gave her an icy look. "You didn't tell a living soul where you were going or when you might be back, did you? There are rules that have to be adhered to if you're going to travel alone in this country." His face was hard. "Rules, Paige, do you hear?" He lowered his voice, but there was nothing gentle in his tone. "I won't have you ignoring everything I tell you, putting your life in danger the moment my back is turned. I simply won't have it. Have you no common sense at all?"

The sarcastic question pushed her over the edge, and she lost her temper completely. She swore and bashed her fist down on the table, making the sugar bowl jump and the spoons rattle.

"Common sense, phooey. Don't be so melodramatic, Myles Baldwin. I'm a grown woman, and I'm used to going wherever I choose, when I choose to go. Why, I used to travel all over a huge city by myself, at all hours of the day and night. I used to—"

To her amazement, Myles reached out and took her

shoulders in his strong hands, fury in his eyes. "Forget what the hell you used to do," he gritted out between clenched teeth, punctuating each word with a shake that jerked her forward and shoved her back again. "Forget it, do you hear, Paige? I'm sick to death of hearing about your perfect other life."

"Myles—Myles, stop it, you're hurting me." His fingers were digging into the soft flesh of her shoulders.

He let her go so fast she almost tumbled backward. He reached out quickly and steadied her, his touch gentle again, and she could see that he was as shocked by his actions as she.

They stared at one another for a moment, and then, trembling, she threw herself at him, wrapping her arms around his middle and holding on tight until his arms slowly came up and enfolded her.

"My God, I'm sorry, Paige." His voice was ragged, filled with remorse. "I'm truly sorry. I can't think what came over me."

But she knew what had happened, if he didn't. Like a bolt from the blue, she'd suddenly understood his anger, and her own had evaporated.

"I'm sorry too, Myles."

It was so obvious, she ought to have seen it before. He was afraid of losing her. His life had been filled with loss, and by loving her, he'd left himself open and vulnerable all over again. Her heart ached for him, and the enormity of her love brought tears to her eyes.

Much later, her naked body snuggled against his, she whispered, "Myles?"

Nearly asleep, he mumbled a response.

"You know that perfect other life of mine that you're so sick of hearing about?"

She knew by the tensing of his muscles that her words

had awakened him, but he didn't say anything.

"It really wasn't perfect at all, not even close. I'm much happier here than I ever was there. And there was nothing to compare with what we have together."

The muscular arm that molded her to his body relaxed, and she felt his contented sigh, warm on her neck.

"Nothing like this—or this." She wriggled her bottom a bit, just enough to tease him, and her hand slid down his body and cupped him. She felt his response, immediate and urgent, and heard his quick intake of breath.

"Now this is perfection, Myles Baldwin," she whispered as he rolled her beneath him.

Myles said no more about Paige riding out alone to visit Tahnancoa—instead, he gave her a gun and taught her to shoot it.

He urged her to carry the weapon, and some emergency rations as well, if she was going to ride out alone. Reluctant to even touch the gun at first, Paige found Myles an excellent teacher and soon she was a good shot. She did as he asked the next time she visited the Quinlans alone.

During February and March, she rode out as often as weather permitted to visit Tahnancoa, often with Myles, sometimes by herself. It was partly business; Paige needed to constantly restock her supplies of herbal remedies, which she was now using with great success on her patients.

Besides the business, however, strong bonds of affection and friendship grew ever stronger between the two women.

They simply liked one another. They shared a deep interest in healing, and they laughed at the same things. During the visits, they talked nonstop about everything and anything. Their backgrounds were so diverse that each found the other's reminiscences fascinating—eventually, as they came to trust one another implicitly, they talked about more intimate matters, about the two men they loved.

One afternoon, a cold Sunday when Dennis and Myles had gone ice fishing on the river, Paige told Tahnancoa the story of her unhappy marriage, the stillbirth of her daughter, the physical damage from that tragic birth that meant she wouldn't have any more children, and the way the experience had affected her.

"I poured all my time and energy into my work back then, and I was afraid to even dream that I'd meet someone who'd love me as Myles does," she said thoughtfully, recognizing the truth of her words only as she spoke them. "It makes me sad, though, to know that I can't have his child."

As she listened, tears began to slide down Tahnancoa's tawny cheeks. "I too wish to bear Dennis's child," she burst out, her voice choked with sobs. "Oh, Paige, more than anything else, I long to give Dennis the son he dreams of having, but in three years of marriage, I haven't conceived, and I doubt I ever will." She wiped the tears away with her palms. "Dennis says it doesn't matter to him whether we have a child or not, but I know better. A man needs sons to carry on his name. I see the longing in his eyes when he watches other men with their children." A sob caught in her throat.

"I've told him he should divorce me, that a man shouldn't stay with a wife who is barren. In my culture, there's no shame in divorcing a barren wife, but Dennis gets angry when I say such things, and then we quarrel." New tears formed and trickled down her face.

Paige reached out and took the other woman's hands in both of hers, appalled by the depths of Tahnancoa's misery. "Dennis is right to get angry when you talk of divorce, Tahny; you know how much he loves you," she said in a gentle tone. "I'm quite sure you're all that matters to him. And you shouldn't blame yourself anyway," she protested. "What if it's Dennis's fault that you can't have children?"

Tahnancoa shook her head. "There was a girl, long ago, when he was very young. She became pregnant, but she lost the child. He told me this once when we quarreled."

Paige was silent, not knowing what else to say. Obviously, this was a serious problem in the Quinlans' marriage.

"I've tried all the things I know," Tahnancoa said in a desolate voice. "All the things Lame Owl taught me to do when a woman wants to conceive, all the things I've ever heard of from other shamans. None of them work for me."

Paige had wondered, once or twice, what Tahnancoa used as a birth control measure. She'd thought perhaps the Quinlans might be worried about having a child of mixed blood, and were choosing to wait. Now, seeing the anguish on her friend's face, hearing the desperation in her voice, Paige realized how wrong she'd been.

"Tahnancoa, maybe there's nothing that can be done, but why don't you come in to the office and let me examine you?" Paige found a handkerchief and handed it to Tahnancoa. "I used to see a great many women who wanted babies and were having difficulty getting pregnant. Sometimes there was a simple solution, just some tiny thing that needed to be corrected. There are several things we can try."

Tahnancoa blew her nose. "I think it's hopeless for me, but perhaps I will come. I will think about it."

Paige tried to press her, get her to set a date, but Tahnancoa wouldn't make a definite appointment.

"I will think about it," was all she would say.

*   *   *

Early one stormy morning in late March, when the snow was blowing and the long winter seemed to have taken on new strength just when it should be spring, Clara and Theo again brought baby Ellie to Paige.

The baby had seizures on a fairly regular basis, Clara admitted, but they were usually mild. The ones in the past few days had been extreme, terrifying Clara and Theo and leaving Ellie exhausted.

Paige examined the tiny girl, and all the bad feelings she'd had the last time she'd seen the baby came back in a sickening rush. It was now more obvious than ever that Ellie was not developing the way she should.

According to Clara, the baby slept a lot. She seemed too lethargic, and she was small and weak, not gaining weight the way she should, even though Clara nursed her almost constantly. She was a touchingly happy baby in spite of her health—every time Ellie smiled at her, the winsome baby almost broke Paige's heart.

Clara, formerly plump and strong, had grown thin and gaunt from worry. She had a persistent cough, and Paige made her tea of Tahnancoa's white pine bark. Ellie was seldom out of her mother's arms, and Theo seemed to have grown morose and silent.

Feeling utterly helpless, Paige prescribed several tonics for Ellie, harmless preparations she knew contained vitamins and minerals, but ones which she also knew wouldn't cure whatever was wrong.

Paige insisted the Fletchers stay for dinner and spend the night with her. Besides enjoying the chance to visit with these first friends, Paige wanted to observe Ellie over a period of time.

Myles came by later that evening as Paige had hoped he might, and he and Theo sat in the small parlor and discussed politics while Paige and Clara washed and dried the supper dishes and talked.

Ellie was asleep, and when she awakened, Paige asked Myles to have a look at her. They took her into Paige's examining room and laid her on the table. Theo and Clara hovered in the doorway.

Myles smiled tenderly down at the baby and murmured nonsense phrases. Ellie was naked except for her diaper, but she didn't fuss. She cooed back at Myles, and flirted enchantingly.

When he finished his examination and looked up, Paige's heart sank. She could read in his eyes the same stark fear and hopelessness she herself felt for this delicate baby. He was hearty in his reassurance to Clara and Theo, however, and they seemed to relax a little after he talked with them.

Myles left shortly afterward, and Paige grabbed a shawl and slipped out after him. He was waiting for her in the shadow of the barn.

"You'll catch pneumonia," he chided, opening his buffalo hide coat and wrapping her inside of it. He kissed her hard. "And what will the Fletchers think, you chasing after me this way, Dr. Randolph?"

"Clara knows about us; she told me over dishes she's happy we've found each other." She nestled against his warmth. "What about Ellie, Myles?"

He hesitated too long, his arms tight around her.

"I've seen cases before that seem hopeless, and then the patients get well again," he finally said. "Children are tougher than they look."

"But not this baby, right?" Paige whispered softly, and then had to fight back tears when he sighed and shook his head.

"No. I don't think Ellie's going to make it, my darling."

In bed that night, alone and lonely with the Fletchers snug in her spare bedroom and Myles back at the fort, Paige silently raged against the limitations of the medical profession as it existed in the 1880s.

She fantasized about all the tests she'd have ordered for Ellie in her own time, all the specialists she'd have called in on the case, which treatments she'd have ordered for each of the unknown problems the little girl might have.

After what seemed like hours of futile imaginary diagnosis and treatment, Paige lay wide-eyed as one last realization came over her, and with it came a measure of peace.

Even in the twentieth century, babies died.

It might not make one bit of difference whether Ellie had been born then or now.

Myles had summed it up. We're not God, he'd told her once.

He was right. Finally, she was able to let go. Her body relaxed and she fell asleep.

In the middle of May, Tahnancoa came to Paige.

It was a blustery spring day, with a chill wind blowing down from the north. There was still snow on the ground, but it was fast turning to mud, and when the sun came out, it held the promise of summer warmth soon to come.

Tahnancoa arrived early in the morning; it was barely nine o'clock when she slipped timidly through the front door.

The two women embraced, and then Paige led the way to the kitchen where a fresh pot of coffee was waiting.

They chatted for a while, and then Tahnancoa set her cup down and looked at Paige, her expression somber. "I have decided that if I can't bear a child for Dennis this year, I will leave him. I will go back to my people. But first, I will try your medicine."

241

It was obvious she'd made up her mind. Paige choked back all the arguments that came to mind. "Come into the office and I'll examine you," she said.

She could only pray that her knowledge would be helpful. If it wasn't, her friend's marriage was doomed, which was tragic—Paige had seldom seen two people more in love than Tahnancoa and Dennis—unless it was herself and Myles.

Selfishly, Paige suspected that if Tahnancoa went back to her people, she herself would lose contact with a friend she'd come to cherish.

She'd never been there, but she didn't think Pound-maker's reserve was a place she'd feel comfortable about riding out to visit.

Explaining to Tahnancoa exactly what she was going to do, and then donning her gloves and one of the sterile gowns she'd improvised, Paige sent up a quick prayer to the fickle god of fecundity.

There really didn't seem to be any balance in the universe, she concluded as she smiled into Tahnancoa's frightened eyes and began a thorough vaginal examination.

The major percentage of her patients were worn out with having too many babies, and here was Tahnancoa, desperate to get pregnant.

Chapter Fourteen

"From what I can tell, Tahny, there's no physical reason for you not to conceive."

Paige chose to ignore the fact that her examination had, of necessity, been limited compared to what she'd have done if the tools and times were different.

She'd have liked to have performed a tubal insufflation to ascertain that the Fallopian tubes were open, but she needed carbon dioxide for the test. She'd have liked a thyroid test, but Battleford was noticeably lacking any facility that could test anything, unless it was a loose horseshoe.

What the heck, she was getting used to having to rely on her own eyes and ears and conclusions a lot more than she'd had to when fancy tests were available.

"What we're going to do is figure out when you're ovulating by having you take your temperature first thing when you wake up in the morning, before you lift your head off the pillow."

Paige had drawn and pinned to the wall of the examining room a diagram of a woman's female organs, and she used it now to help explain the reasons for what she was asking Tahny to do. She demonstrated how the thermometer registered body temperature, and then she said, "When your temperature's elevated, it means your body's ovulating, and that's when you can become pregnant. So when that happens, you must corner Dennis and get him to make love to you right away, as many times as possible during the period of ovulation."

Tahnancoa's eyes widened, and for the first time all morning, she held a hand over her mouth and giggled.

Paige laughed too. "I know it sounds pretty crazy, but there's a good chance that it'll work. Will you give it a try?"

The bleakness that had been in Tahnancoa's eyes all morning returned, and she nodded. "I said I would try your medicine, Paige, and I will, even though I doubt that it will work." The ghost of a twinkle came and went in her eyes. "Some of Lame Owl's remedies were a lot worse-tasting than this one."

When she left, equipped with a thermometer, Paige wondered how Dennis would react when Tahnancoa started coming on to him at odd hours of the day and night.

She imagined herself and Myles in the same situation, and a wistful grin came and went on her face. If Dennis was anything like Myles, it wouldn't be a problem at all.

June came, and summer with it. Almost overnight, the prairies were dotted with buttercups and dandelions, and men and women worked in backyard gardens.

When Paige went out to feed Minnie one morning, she found Armand LeClerc in her backyard, shovel in hand, digging and planting a stack of seeds and bulbs.

"Armand, how are you?" Pleased and surprised, Paige walked over to shake the old man's grubby hand. "This is really nice of you, but I have to warn you, I know zilch about taking care of a garden."

"So?" His bushy white eyebrows lifted over mischievous black eyes. "Armand will care for your garden, madame."

"But I thought you told me once that when spring came you were going back to your farm."

He shook his head. "I 'ave no farm. The government has taken the land, *madame la docteur.*"

"But how can they do that, Armand?"

He shrugged, his old face set in bitter lines. "We Métis, we 'ave the land from our fathers, no papers to say we own it."

Paige was outraged. "But that's terrible. Isn't there something you can do?"

He didn't answer. He picked up the shovel and began to dig again. "Here, we will put the potato, yes? And here, carrots, and spinach here."

Armand came every day. When the vegetables were planted, he brought flower bulbs and cuttings, and soon hollyhocks, poppies, daisies, and sunflowers were growing in neat beds at the front of the little white house.

Paige tried to pay the old man, but he refused.

"You come from far away, *madame la docteur.* I think you bring magic along with you."

Puzzled, Paige asked Myles what the old man meant.

"The Métis are very superstitious, darling, and very religious. Armand was there the day you arrived, and he heard your story and believed it. He thinks it was a miracle." He kissed her. "Sometimes I think so too," he added, only half joking.

The third week in June, Myles had to ride out to treat an officer at an outpost who'd suffered a gunshot wound to the leg, and he invited Paige to come along. The trip would only take a day, and the route was near Clara and Theo's homestead. Paige could visit there until Myles returned.

Clara was delighted at the unexpected visit, but it took all Paige's self-control to hide the shock she felt when she saw Ellie.

The baby had deteriorated in the weeks since Paige had last seen her. Now nine months old, Ellie's huge blue eyes seemed too large for her tiny, pinched face. She was still not sitting upright or trying to crawl. She was, however, starting to talk, illustrating clearly to Paige that the little girl's problem was physical rather than mental.

It hurt to hear the little piping voice identify Mommy and Daddy and dog and baby. As always, Ellie's nature was exceptionally sweet and agreeable, and she played pat-a-cake and hide-the-baby with Paige, smiling her angelic smile, but she tired quickly and slept a great deal of the time.

"She has convulsions about every third day now," Clara said, a dreadful weariness in her eyes and voice. "Usually not the bad ones, just little ones. I keep hoping she'll grow out of them, like Dr. Baldwin thought might happen."

Paige could hear the entreaty in Clara's voice, begging her for reassurance, but Paige couldn't bring herself to tell Clara what she knew to be an outright lie—that Ellie would get better with time.

Ellie wasn't going to grow out of anything. It was obvious to Paige that the baby was dying.

The ride home later that evening with Myles should have been carefree. Instead, Paige couldn't shake the depression that had been growing ever since she'd laid eyes on Ellie that morning. She talked to Myles about it as the horses picked their way across the uneven prairie.

"Next week, Clara and Theo are going to be coming in

on Tuesday to pick up more of those tonics I prescribed for Ellie, and I feel like such a fraud, Myles. That damned stuff isn't going to help, other than getting some vitamins into her."

A few moments before, the sun had set in waves of spectacular color in the western sky. The ever-present wind had died, and the prairie stretched before them, calm and serene, broken here and there by clumps of stunted pine, studded with sagebrush and wild roses in full bloom, but Paige didn't see the beauty that surrounded her. She was obsessed with Ellie.

"Myles," she begged, "in all your wandering, or maybe in your experience as a doctor in the war, can you think of anything that might help Ellie? Anything, Myles, no matter how farfetched or unlikely. Anything you've ever heard about that we could do to help her?" Paige moved restlessly in the saddle. "If she was your own baby, Myles, what would you do?"

Myles reigned Major to a stop, and Paige pulled Minnie up beside him. Myles sat, staring thoughtfully out over the prairie.

"A few years back, darling, I read an article published in the *Virginia Medical Monthly,* by a Dr. Jacob M. Toner," he began. "Never had the pleasure of meeting the gentleman myself, but his article stuck in my mind." Major whinnied and pranced, and it took Myles a moment to settle him.

"This article was an address Dr. Toner had given back in seventy-seven, to the Rocky Mountain Medical Association. In it, he praised Indian medical practitioners for their use of syringes, sutures, the enema, their knowledge of anatomy, their childbirth practices. He went so far as to say the Indian shamans have treatments for things we western-trained physicians consider hopeless. Lots of doctors laugh at Indian medicine, dismiss it as savage hocus-pocus."

Myles looked at her, his handsome face solemn. "I don't, Paige. I've seen wounds that should have killed a man, healed by the Indians. If Ellie was my child, I'd take her to a shaman." He clucked to Major, and the big horse started off again, the jingle of the horses' bridles and the creaking of the leather saddles combining pleasantly with the songs of meadowlarks and the whispering of the slight breeze that heralded the coming night.

"Trouble is," Myles went on, "it might be impossible to get the Fletchers to trust an Indian shaman with their daughter. It's unfortunate, but settlers' feelings run high against the Indians in these parts, and about the last thing they'd be likely to do is ask for help for Ellie from people they fear and look down on."

"Maybe they won't, but I damned well intend to," Paige declared, her jaw set and her mind made up.

Tahnancoa had been taught the healing techniques of the Indian shamans. Tahnancoa and Clara were her friends, although the two of them had never met. Both of them loved babies as much as Paige did.

All she had to do, Paige schemed as she rode beside Myles, was figure out a way to get the two of them together. Soon.

That part, at least, wasn't difficult. Dennis made deliveries of beef to the fort every week. Paige wrote an urgent note to Tahnancoa, telling her she needed to see her on the Tuesday that Clara would be there. She gave the note to Myles to pass on to Dennis, hoping against hope that Tahnancoa would come.

She did, and so did Clara.

They sat like stone effigies on either side of Paige's kitchen table, and the strained silence was broken only by the increasingly desperate sound of Paige's voice, making ridiculous small talk.

Ellie was sleeping on the bed in the spare room, and Paige had struggled through a half-hour in which neither woman had volunteered a blessed thing to the conversation she was trying to kindle.

"More tea, Clara? Tahnancoa?"

Damn it, she felt like pouring it over their respective heads.

Awakening from her nap, Ellie started fussing, and Clara sprang to her feet and went hurrying off to collect her daughter.

Tahnancoa got to her feet, her face set in stern, inapproachable dignity. "I will go now, Paige Randolph."

"No, you won't go," Paige hissed, scowling at her friend. "Sit down. Right now," she ordered between gritted teeth. "I need you here."

Tahnancoa looked shocked, but she sat down again, staring at Paige as if she'd taken leave of her senses.

Clara, a freshly diapered and immaculate Ellie on her arm, came back into the room and took her place at the table.

Paige watched as Tahnancoa's eyes gravitated to the baby. She saw the sudden understanding on Tahnancoa's face when Ellie's fragility and thinness fully registered.

"Ellie Randolph, come here and see your Auntie Paige." The agreeable little girl grinned and held out her arms.

Paige took the slight body and knelt with her at Tahnancoa's knee. "Say hi to another auntie," she cooed, ignoring the expression on Clara's face. "This is Tahny, can you say hi to her, Ellie?"

The baby babbled something, and then reached out and took a handful of the bright red skirt Tahnancoa was wearing and tried to cram it into her mouth. Tahnancoa smiled and reached out a finger, stroking the velvet skin on Ellie's sunken little cheek.

Paige promptly lifted the baby into Tahnancoa's lap, and Ellie transferred her attention to a beaded necklace Tahnancoa wore.

The ruse worked like magic. Tahnancoa relaxed for the first time all morning and cradled Ellie, bending to sniff at the sweet baby fragrance of her tufts of golden hair.

"What a beautiful girl you are, small one," Tahnancoa murmured softly, and Clara's face softened and lit up with motherly pride.

The three women were drawn into a circle now with the baby at its center. When Tahnancoa said, "How old is she?" it was Clara who answered, and only Paige caught the slight frown that flitted across Tahnancoa's face. Ellie, because of her size and fragility, seemed much younger than she actually was.

"She's starting to talk quite a lot now," Clara offered. "Just the other day, she put two words together. Theo was outside, and when he opened the door, Ellie laughed and said, "Da Da come.""

Paige and Tahnancoa made appropriate admiring noises, and Paige was beginning to really relax when suddenly Ellie made a strange noise in her throat. Her spine stiffened and then bent backward, and her eyes rolled up until only the whites showed. Her body began to twitch and then to jerk spasmodically.

"Oh, Lord help us, she's having one of her convulsions," Clara cried, rushing over to Tahnancoa. She tried to take the baby, but it was impossible to transfer the wildly jerking child from Tahnancoa's arms.

Clara began sobbing, a high-pitched, despairing sound that mingled with the choking noises that now came from Ellie's throat.

Paige snatched up a spoon to insert in Ellie's mouth so she wouldn't swallow her tongue, but Tahnancoa already had her finger between the tiny, clenched lips.

Paige swept the dishes from the table and grabbed up several clean tablecloths to pad the surface so they could lay the baby there.

Tahnancoa rested the small body gently on the table, and Clara, still sobbing, loosened her daughter's clothing so she could breathe freely.

Paige ran for her medical bag. There was an injection she could give if the convulsion showed signs of worsening, but by the time she returned, bag in hand, the seizure was already disappearing.

Tahnancoa, her finger still clamped tight in Ellie's mouth, made soft, crooning sounds over the baby as the thrashing of the small limbs gradually slowed and then stopped. Ellie's mouth became slack.

Tahnancoa removed her finger, which was bleeding a little from the force of Ellie's clamped teeth, and after what seemed an eternity, the baby stirred. She opened glazed eyes and stared listlessly at the ceiling. Her mouth quivered and pulled down, and she gave two huge, shuddering sobs.

Tahnancoa gently transferred the baby to Clara's arms, and with an effort, Clara stopped crying and tried to smile down into the thin little face. "There, there, love, Mommy's here." Her voice trembled, and the arms that held Ellie were quivering as though she too were convulsing. "Everything's fine, Mommy's right here."

"She has done this before," Tahnancoa said. It was a statement rather than a question, and Clara nodded.

"They're—they're getting more frequent all the time," she whispered, tears once more trickling down her cheeks. "She's—she's not growing the way she ought."

Suddenly, as if a dam had broken, Clara's face twisted

with agony and she choked out, "I'm scared, I'm scared all the time now. I see the way people look at her, compare her to their own babies. I'm so afraid she's—she's going to—to die." She turned on Paige, her face a mask of helpless fury, her arms clasping Ellie so tight that the baby too began to sob.

"You're a doctor, you say you're a doctor. Can't you do something to stop this?" Unable now to stifle the gasping sobs that shook her body, Clara thrust Ellie blindly at Tahnancoa and ran from the room.

Tahnancoa soothed the crying baby. She met Paige's eyes in silent question.

"My medicine is useless in this case, Tahnancoa," Paige said with a sigh. "This is why I wanted you here today. Do you think there's anything you can do for Ellie?"

Tahnancoa didn't answer right away. She hugged the baby to her, rocking her and singing a lullaby in her own language, a lilting song that sounded like a brook trickling across pebbles.

At last, she looked at Paige and gave a single nod. "There is a healing ceremony. I saw Lame Owl use it on a child like this one."

Clara came back just then, her nose and eyes red, a handkerchief clutched in her hand. "I'm sorry," she stammered. "I spoke out of turn." She took Paige's hand in hers and said again, "I apologize, Paige. I didn't mean to lash out at you. I know you're doing all you can, but sometimes I feel so helpless. So hopeless."

Paige took her in her arms and hugged her. "Forget it, Clara. God knows I feel that way myself. Now, let's make a fresh pot of tea," she suggested, wondering how many women in the history of the world had used tea to ease their pain and mend their hearts.

Tahnancoa went on holding the sleeping baby. Clara

made no attempt to take Ellie. Instead, she touched Tahnancoa's finger, still bleeding from the bite of Ellie's teeth.

"I'm grateful to you, Tahnancoa." It was the first time Clara had used her name. "You thought fast, putting your finger in her mouth that way." She touched one of her daughter's curls. "She trusts you; look at how she's sleeping on your shoulder."

Paige seized the opportunity. "Tahny's a healer, Clara. Her grandmother is a famous shaman, an Indian healer, and she's taught Tahnancoa to be one as well."

Paige felt her heart begin to knock against her ribs, knowing that either woman—or both—could refuse what she was about to suggest.

"Clara, there's nothing I or any other medical doctor I know of can do for Ellie," she stated. "Just as you said, she's getting worse." There was no longer any point in pretense. "There's a ceremony that Tahnancoa knows of, a healing ceremony that might help Ellie. If Tahnancoa would agree to try it . . ."

Paige gave Tahnancoa a beseeching look, and the dark-haired woman hesitated a heart-stopping second before nodding assent.

Paige looked at Clara, holding her breath. But Clara was looking at her baby, cradled lovingly in Tahnancoa's arms.

"Would you try?" Clara's words were humble. "Please, Tahnancoa, would you try to help her?"

Tahnancoa looked down at Ellie. "I will try. But there are no promises," she warned. "If the Great Spirit wishes to take her, he must be obeyed. But if I can bring the darkness out and make her well, I will do that too. You will bring her to my cabin tomorrow morning just after sunrise. Paige will show you the way."

* * *

Theo, surprisingly, was in full agreement when Clara told him.

"Way I see it, we gotta try anything we can," he said, smiling tenderly at his daughter as she pulled at his beard.

He loaded them all in the wagon the next morning before dawn, and Paige directed him along the trail to the Quinlans' cabin.

Dennis and Theo didn't know one another, but they were both farmers, and they soon were deep in a discussion of livestock and crops. They wandered off in the direction of the barn, and Tahnancoa led Paige and Clara inside the cabin.

Tahnancoa was in native dress today, the first time Paige had seen her in her native costume. Her buckskin dress and leggings were finely made, intricately beaded with patterns of birds and flowers, the background a soft dove gray that suited her natural duskiness and huge dark eyes.

She seemed a stranger, however; Paige felt a remoteness in her friend.

As soon as they were inside the cabin, Tahnancoa took Ellie in her arms and from a cup, spooned some herbal preparation she'd prepared into Ellie's mouth.

It must have tasted vile, because Ellie made a face and shivered. The women smiled, and Tahnancoa persevered, coaxing the baby to swallow another spoonful, and then another.

When Ellie refused to swallow any more, Tahnancoa spread a tanned buffalo hide on the floor with a blanket over it, and she laid Ellie on it.

"Clara, you will sit here at her feet, Paige, over there at her other side," Tahnancoa instructed.

Tahnancoa knelt near the baby's head, and Clara and

Paige awkwardly settled themselves in the appointed places. Paige felt a stab of apprehension, wondering just exactly what procedure Tahny had in mind.

Tahnancoa now sipped at some concoction herself, drinking from a hollowed buffalo horn, her eyes closed, seeming to pray or meditate. After a time, she withdrew a small stone, several feathers, and a piece of shiny quartz from a buckskin bag at her side. She placed the objects at equal intervals around the baby who lay, quiet and good-natured, observing the proceedings with curious eyes. From time to time, Ellie patted her hands together or waved and babbled to her mother, but she seemed content to stay where she was.

Paige's apprehension grew as Tahnancoa began a strange, rhythmic chant, a hypnotic sound punctuated by the shaking of a rattle she took from her bag. Using an eagle feather, she began a repetitive sweeping motion over the passive baby, always accompanied by the chanting.

As the ritual went on and on, Paige was unable to look across at Clara. She felt mortified by the whole ceremony. She could feel the hot color her embarrassment brought to her cheeks. She was certain that at any moment, Clara would snatch Ellie from the blanket and insist they leave, but when Paige dared a glance, Clara seemed intent on what was happening and not as skeptical as Paige.

Now Tahnancoa discarded the feather, but the chanting became even louder, demanding, invasive. She was crouching over Ellie and she seemed to be drawing something out of the baby's head, something invisible but strong.

Paige stared, unable to make sense out of what was happening.

Tahnancoa was perspiring with effort, pulling at what seemed an invisible rope that came from the center of Ellie's skull.

Ellie was absolutely still. Her eyes had the glazed expression she'd worn the day before, after the convulsion. Suddenly, her body jerked spasmodically, her arms and legs thrashing.

"She's having a convulsion." Alarmed, Paige made a move, about to get to her feet, but Clara reached across and touched her arm, shaking her head, her finger at her lips signaling silence.

Soon Paige realized, just as Clara must have, that Ellie wasn't convulsing this time—this was something different. The baby's fragile body moved four or five more times, violently, and then she was still, her wide eyes clear now and fastened on Tahnancoa.

The moment the baby was still, Tahnancoa's eerie chanting stopped abruptly, and as the sound died away, Ellie began to gag.

Tahnancoa lifted her into her arms and held her over a small basin as the baby vomited up a strange, dark liquid.

Clara, clearly frightened now, quavered, "She's sick, what's made her so sick?"

Tahnancoa, however, smiled at Clara reassuringly. "She will vomit several more times, and her bowels, too, will loosen. She is getting rid of evil spirits that have made her sick. She will be better after today."

For the next two hours, Ellie alternated between violent diarrhea and severe vomiting. Paige was concerned about dehydration, but Tahnancoa seemed to view the purging as a positive sign and insisted Ellie was to have nothing to drink.

Clara was kept busy changing diapers, washing them out, and pegging them on the line to dry.

Tahnancoa seemed to sense exactly when the violent purging was done. When two hours had passed and Ellie, her tiny face more pinched and pale than ever, lay exhausted in Paige's arms, Tahnancoa put a small pinch of some herb in a cupful of tepid water and again coaxed the baby to sip it from a spoon.

"The worst is over," Tahnancoa declared when the baby swallowed several spoonfuls. "She will sleep now. We will prepare some lunch; the men will be coming soon." Tahnancoa laid the baby on a pallet of furs and covered her warmly. "For the next two days, she must be quiet and have nothing but your milk, Clara," she instructed.

Then, as if the entire morning's proceedings had been as ordinary as a ladies' sewing circle, Tahnancoa whisked away the buckskin bag, washed her hands at the basin in the corner, and set about rolling out biscuits and stirring a stew bubbling on the back of the range.

The Fletchers, anxious to get back to their homestead, dropped Paige off at her house late that afternoon and set off immediately for home. Ellie had slept most of the day, waking only to suck eagerly at Clara's breast several times. The milk stayed down, and the baby seemed no worse than she'd been before the morning's ordeal.

"But the big question is, will she be any better?"

Paige and Myles, unwilling to stay inside on the warm summer's night, were strolling along the riverbank the following evening. Paige had told Myles in graphic detail what had taken place with Ellie. He'd listened without saying much.

"God, Myles, I was embarrassed by all that mumbo jumbo Tahny went through," Paige confessed, her hand tight in his.

"I guess I thought she'd just give Ellie some medicine or other, and that would be that. Instead, there was all that stuff with rattles and chanting and evil spirits. I've never

257

seen that side of Tahnancoa before, and it shocked me."

Myles smiled at her. "The first time you witness it, it's pretty strange. All the same, it seems to work, not all the time, but often enough. The Indian people believe disease is caused by possession by evil spirits. I've watched many shamans at work, and it seems to me that the mental effect of the ceremony on the patient is just as important as the herbal concoctions they use."

"Psychology, and the placebo effect," Paige agreed. She explained what she meant. "But the weirdest thing was when Tahnancoa seemed to actually pull something from Ellie's head," she added. "I can see her using the ritual to impress Clara with the fact that the baby was being cured, but why did it seem so real to me when she was heaving on—on whatever it was?"

"Maybe she was actually taking something bad out of Ellie's head, who really knows? A great many things exist in spite of the fact that we can't see them," Myles said in a reasonable tone, and when Paige began to laugh, he looked at her and frowned. "What's so funny?"

"Nothing. Everything. See, I'm the one that should be telling you about all the stuff that we can't see, you crazy, wonderful man. I'm the one that knows about atoms, and electron microscopes, and viruses, and still I need you to remind me not to be narrow-minded. Oh, Myles, you're far ahead of your time, you know that?"

He reached out and drew her into his arms. "I don't want to be ahead of my time," he declared, his slow drawl giving emphasis to the words. "All I want is you, here in my arms right now, my darling Paige."

"Me too." She lifted her head for his kiss, amazed

that it was true. That other time, the future time from which she'd come, had begun to seem hazy and far away.

At what point had she stopped dreaming of finding a way to go back?

Chapter Fifteen

"May I have a word with you, sir? In private? It's a personal matter." Rob Cameron stood formally at attention, and Myles shot him a questioning look. Cameron didn't meet his eye.

"All right, Sergeant." Myles glanced at the other men waiting in line on early morning sick parade and gestured to his office door.

"In here." He ushered Rob in and shut the door, hoping this wouldn't take too long. "Now, what's the problem, Rob?"

The young constable's face grew as deep a red as his scarlet tunic, and Myles sighed, certain that he knew what Rob was about to tell him.

Myles had treated four other men in the past week for a particularly nasty strain of venereal infection no doubt contracted from one of the local prostitutes, and here, he felt certain, was a fifth.

He'd already paid a call on Jeannie, the madam who ran the local house, and insisted her girls come in for treatment before all the young men at the fort came down with the clap. But Jeannie had insisted her girls were clean, and when Myles examined them, he'd been forced to agree. Where, then, were these young men contracting the infection? He'd asked each of them, but none would admit who they'd been with.

"Yes, Rob?" It was difficult for these young constables to describe their symptoms. Myles was sympathetic, but he was also aware of all the men outside still waiting for a consultation. He was about to order Rob to drop his pants when the sergeant swallowed hard and burst out, "It's Miss Randolph, sir."

Paige? Myles frowned. What the hell could Paige have to do with Rob's problem?

"There's talk among the men. They're saying she's your mistress." Rob spat the words out, and Myles was taken aback.

He'd realized there'd be gossip among the men when it became clear he was spending a great many of his nights away from his quarters, but there was little he could do except ignore it.

"I've waited to hear of your betrothal to her, but it's obvious your intentions are no honorable," Rob went on in a scathing voice. "It's a crime to ruin her reputation in this way." Rob's voice was quavering with the intensity of his feelings. "The lass has neither father nor brother to protect her honor, so I'm calling you out, Surgeon Baldwin."

Myles was speechless and stunned. At last, he recovered enough to say, "Do I understand this correctly? You're challenging me to a duel?"

"Aye. Yes, sir, I am that." Rob, his back ramrod straight, glared up at Myles with both pain and determination in his eyes.

Dumbfounded, Myles rested one hip on the examining

261

table and gestured at the room's only wooden chair. "Sit down, Rob. We need to talk about this."

Rob refused with a shake of his head. "I've said all I'm going to." His mustache bristled and his chin jutted with stubborn resolve.

"You're in love with her too, aren't you, Sergeant?" The question was unnecessary—the answer was written plainly on Rob's face.

His shoulders seemed to slump, and he looked away from Myles. At last, he nodded, one abrupt dip of his head. "I love her, aye, I do that. But I'd never take advantage of her the way you're doing," he accused hotly. "I already asked her would she marry me—"

Aware of what he'd just said, he stopped and gulped.

Myles felt a harsh stab of raw jealousy and possessiveness, and then his heart went out to the younger man.

"I take it she refused your proposal," he said as gently as he could.

Miserable, Rob bobbed his head again. "Aye. She told me she—she was in love with you. That was last November, and it seemed she expected . . . she thought . . . well, I've waited for the banns to be posted, but it's never happened, has it? And I've seen you riding off to her house, and coming back all hours of the night."

"Is it true the other men are talking about her?"

Rob hesitated, and then shook his head. "I'd brain any man who whispered a word about her. There's some talk about you, that's all." He tapped his chest with a forefinger. "It's me that's concerned about her. I didn't want to say it was Paige told me about the two of you."

It was a tremendous relief to Myles to know that her name wasn't being bandied slyly about the fort. But what was he going to do about this situation with Rob? Perhaps the truth would help, he decided.

262

"I'm in love with her, Rob. Deeply in love," he admitted, feeling his own face flush. His feelings weren't something he was accustomed to talking about with another man. "I can only tell you that I won't hurt her in any way, ever. Nor will I allow anyone else to do so." His voice hardened. "But the arrangements we make between the two of us are private and personal, you must see that."

"But you are going to marry her, Surgeon Baldwin? Do I have your word on it?"

Damn, did this stubborn young Scot never give up?

"Yes, God damn it, I'm going to marry her." Myles speared Cameron with a scathing look that had sent lesser men scuttling, but the Scot held his ground, and Myles felt grudging respect.

"You have my word, Sergeant. And I've no intention of fighting any duel with you over the matter. Now get the hell out of here, will you? I have sick men to see to."

"Sir." Rob snapped off a salute and slammed the door behind him.

Myles wiped cold sweat from his forehead, aware that underneath his exasperation was a nagging suspicion that Cameron was right: he should marry Paige; it was unforgivable of him to risk her reputation this way.

The truth was, he'd started to think more and more often lately of being married to her, but each time he considered it, the fear was there, on many levels, the terrible fear of losing her, of trusting fate again and losing what remained of himself when it was over.

He'd almost convinced himself that when the time came, it would be easier to say good-bye if they weren't married, if there were no legal bond between them.

Because he had no doubts that sooner or later he'd lose her. Although she hadn't mentioned it recently, the matter of her going back to where she'd come from was always a possibility, if the means presented itself. If there was a way, Myles was certain she'd attempt it.

If that happened, he'd be alone again, more alone than ever before. What he shared with Paige was unlike anything he'd had in his life, even with Beth. This was physical, emotional, and mental, this connection with Paige that consumed him. Even labeling what he felt for her simply as love seemed woefully inadequate.

And losing her, he realized, would be agonizing, whether she was his wife or his mistress.

Well, he concluded, running a hand through his hair and straightening his tunic before he called the man next in line, the matter was now out of his hands.

He'd given Cameron his word, and his word was his bond. He'd propose to Paige at the first opportunity.

That Wednesday morning, Paige's first patient was Helen Gillespie. Helen's health had been excellent ever since the D and C. To her delight, her periods had entirely stopped, and the anemia improved as a result—she looked almost pretty today. She'd come in for a new supply of the herbal preparations Paige had recommended for hot flashes, and as she was leaving, Paige opened the waiting room door to greet the next patient.

"Would you step in—Lulu?" Paige could hardly believe her own eyes. Lulu Leiberman, waiting to see her?

Paige knew she sounded as astonished as she felt at finding her former landlady sitting stiffly in an armchair in her parlor.

"Come in, Lulu." Paige led the way into the office and shut the door behind her, wondering what on earth would bring Lulu here.

It wasn't easy to hide the emotions that seeing the woman again generated in her—the harsh memories of her first, difficult weeks in Battleford all came rushing back, along with the urge to confront this malicious woman with some of her lies.

Instead, Paige summoned her most professional, detached manner. "What seems to be the problem, Lulu? I assume you're here for a medical reason?"

Lulu's fair skin flushed a mottled red, and she avoided Paige's eyes. "I think I might have caught the pox from using the same privy as the boarders," she said, her shrill voice trembling. "I just want you to give me a potion to cure it."

Paige insisted on an examination, and after an intense argument, Lulu finally agreed.

Paige was appalled by what she found. Without testing, it was impossible to determine the exact strain, but it was plain that Lulu had some virulent form of venereal disease. It wasn't impossible, but Paige would have bet her prized stethoscope that pious Lulu hadn't contracted this mess from any toilet seat—it was quite obviously the result of sexual activity.

However tempting it was to challenge Lulu with the facts, confronting her on this score would undoubtedly result in outraged denial followed by her storming out without any treatment.

Paige's professional sense of responsibility prevailed. Knowing the woman as she did, the smartest thing to do was to go along with the flimsy pretense that Lulu was an unknowing victim.

Paige did so, barely able to contain a knowing grin when the plump woman sanctimoniously castigated the "filthy beasts who'd give a thing like this to an innocent woman."

Treatment was a problem. Not for the first time, Paige wished for antibiotics.

Fortunately, she'd had a long discussion one day with Myles about venereal disease among the troops—it was a common enough situation, according to Myles.

The currently accepted medical treatment, he'd told her, was ineffectual as well as dangerous in his opinion—hers too, when he reminded her what it was. She'd forgotten that nineteenth-century doctors injected syphilitic patients with a macabre dosage of arsenic and gold.

Myles had explained that he used instead a decoction of prickly ash and a drink made from boiled thistle roots, an effective two-barreled treatment he'd learned from an elderly doctor he'd worked with in the Civil War. He'd assured Paige the combination seemed to cure almost all the cases he treated.

Paige didn't have a stock of the remedies in her cabinet; this was the first case of venereal disease she'd encountered.

She arranged to send an errand boy to the boardinghouse with the medications later that afternoon, and she sold Lulu some salve Tahnancoa had made that would ease the chronic pain she was in from the open sores and burning of her pubic area.

"Absolutely no sexual contact until this is cleared up," Paige warned. "You'll infect your partner." Her reward was a filthy look.

Unable to forget how Lulu had deliberately spread malicious rumors and all but kicked her out on the street, Paige didn't blink an eye about charging double her ordinary fee, and Lulu paid without comment.

When the woman left, Paige sat for a moment, remembering something her partner, Sam Harris, had been fond of saying. "What goes around, comes around."

Lulu's nastiness had rebounded back to her, Paige reflected—in spades.

* * *

Myles surprised her on Sunday by packing a lunch and taking her on a picnic to a secluded spot miles up the river where a quiet backwater ringed by willow trees formed a natural swimming pool.

He'd thought of everything. He brought a blanket, a stone bottle filled with cold lemonade, and a canvas sack with enough lunch to feed a battalion.

On the ride out, they talked about Lulu. Myles had been as astounded as Paige when he learned who it was that needed his pox remedy—which, he'd explained, was already being used in abundance at the fort by the four young constables.

And all the while, he'd been blaming Jeannie's girls for the infection.

"I'll call each of the gentlemen in separately and have a talk with them," he'd declared the evening of Lulu's visit.

The results were fascinating, and Myles related them as they rode.

"It seems that our Madam Leiberman is a talented actress," he explained. "Each of the young men believed they were blessed and unique, the only ones enjoying her favors, and each believed her to be wildly in love with only him. When the infection began, she turned on floods of hysterical tears and told each the story about the unscrupulous boarder and the outhouse, and the gullible young fools were ready to defend her honor and die for her rather than reveal to me where they'd become infected. It seems she's been enjoying all four of them for quite some time, and of course there must be a fifth who gave her the pox in the first place. She must be quite voracious, our Lulu."

"Well, I just hope Rob Cameron isn't one of them," Paige exclaimed, and bristled when Myles gave her an inscrutable

Bobby Hutchinson

look. "She had her eye on Rob. And he's so innocent and honest, I'd be furious if she deceived him that way."

"Put your mind at rest, Paige. Innocent Rob Cameron is quite safe," Myles said in a dry tone.

They forgot about Lulu and Rob as well as they spread their blanket and set out the ample lunch Myles had cajoled the cook at the barracks into preparing.

It was a blistering hot July day, and Paige was sweating from the long ride. "Myles, are you coming swimming? That water's too good to waste."

"Of course I am." He began to unbutton his tunic.

"Great. Last one in's a rotten egg." She shucked off her blouse and within moments, the rest of her clothing lay in a heap on the grass.

It felt delicious to be naked in the open air. She ran and dived, squealing when she hit the cold water. Myles was only seconds behind her, half-drowning her with his shallow dive, grabbing her and ducking her under the water, and then kissing her before she could surface.

"I hope you realize I'm breaking regulations by being out of uniform and away from my weapon," he joked.

"I won't tell if you won't."

They played like children and their laughter and teasing voices filled the quiet air.

Paige had been swimming on her back. She flopped over, glanced toward the horses, and gave a little scream.

Four Indians, all men, were sitting quietly astride their horses, watching the goings-on in the pool. They were only yards from the tumbled heaps of clothing—and from Myles's handgun and rifle.

"Easy, Paige." Myles had seen them too. He kept his body between the Indians and Paige.

"My God, Myles, what are we going to do? They're right beside our clothes. And—and there's four of them." Paige

268

knew she sounded hysterical and didn't care. "Are they—are they going to—"

Visions of rape and murder made her shudder. "Myles, I'm scared."

"Let me handle it." Myles called out to them in their guttural language, and one of the men answered at some length.

"They're not a war party; I don't think they mean us any harm," he said when the conversation ended. "They've been out hunting, and heard us carrying on. I think they're just curious."

He was doing his best to reassure her, but Paige saw how intently he watched as the men hobbled their ponies and dismounted, squatting on their heels on the grass.

"Curious, hell. They're—they're bloody perverts." Her teeth had started to chatter from both fear and the icy water. "Can't you just tell them to go away? Or turn their backs while I get out?"

She was stark naked and the four men didn't look as though they were going to be polite and ride into the sunset just so she could get out of the water with her modesty intact.

"Myles, can't you do something to get rid of them?"

"We're not in the best of bargaining positions, darling." There was irony in his voice. "We're just going to have to brazen this out. I'll get out of the water and put on my breeches and holster. Then I'll hold up the blanket and you make a run for it."

Paige had never felt more alone than she did during the next few moments. Myles did as he'd said, not hurrying, walking out of the water casually, nodding and saying something to the men as he pulled on his pants and buckled on his sidearm.

She saw him move the food to one side and lift the

269

blanket. She swam to the shallows, aware of four pairs of eyes on her. Myles waded into the water and shielded her with his body as she stood.

"Smile and be polite, my love," Myles said in a low tone as he wrapped the blanket around her and guided her up on the grass. "I'm afraid we're about to have company for lunch."

Paige didn't feel at all like smiling. She gave the Indians a dirty look, snatched her clothing up, and went behind a clump of bushes to struggle into it. When she came out, the Indians were wolfing down the food, talking to Myles in long, staccato bursts as the cold roast beef sandwiches, apples, and cookies disappeared in rapid succession.

They paid no attention to her, but they consumed every scrap of the lunch, and Paige grew increasingly hungry and bored as the afternoon wore on and the Indians showed no signs of leaving. Their conversation with Myles went on and on, and Paige moved some distance away and slumped down with her back against a poplar.

In the late afternoon, the air became heavy and suffocating, and the sky to the north turned a muddy brown color. Thunder rolled ominously, and a few drops of rain landed on Paige's face.

As if it were a signal, the Indians suddenly got up, mounted their ponies, each raising a hand in farewell to Myles, and rode off.

"Thank God," Paige sighed, trying to struggle to her feet. "My rear end's asleep," she complained. "I thought they were going to be with us the rest of our lives. And they ate every last scrap of food, and I'm starving. And now it's going to rain." She knew she sounded petulant, but their day together had been thoroughly ruined, and she was disappointed. "What on earth were you talking about with them all that time?"

Myles came over and took her hands, hauling her to her feet. "I'm sorry, but there was nothing else to do but hear them out. They're Cree, from Big Bear's reserve." He frowned and shook his head, his voice both angry and sad. "They were telling me the same story all the Indians tell these days, about the lack of buffalo, the shame of being trapped on a reserve instead of roaming free and hunting the way they've always done, and now the pain and anger of watching their families starve because the white man's government doesn't keep its promises to feed and clothe them. It's a bad business, there's going to be rebellion—"

A loud clap of thunder and a dramatic flash of lightning made Paige yelp and sent her scurrying into his arms. An instant later, rain came sheeting down in torrents, and Myles grabbed the blanket and raced with her for the dubious shelter of the poplars. They were both soaked to the skin even before they reached the trees.

Myles draped the blanket around them and cradled her in his arms, trying to protect her from the worst of the deluge. "We'll just have to wait this out too. God damn it to hell." He swore, a long, steady stream of curses that amazed her— he hardly ever swore in front of her. "I wanted things to be perfect today, and instead, you're cold and wet and hungry, and we're still two hours' ride from home." His voice was dejected.

"Well, it could be worse," she said, trying for optimism. Her arms were wrapped around his comforting warmth, and being held close against him wasn't really hardship. "They could have taken our clothes, you know."

The mental image of riding back to Battleford like Lady Godiva suddenly made her giggle. A similar thought must have occurred to Myles, because he started laughing as well.

A moment later he bent his head and kissed her, and

after a time, they slid down to the grass. Somehow his pants became undone, and her underwear slid off, and the blanket stayed wrapped snugly around them. The rain stopped, but they didn't notice.

The storm rolled off to the west at last, and they started the long ride home.

Damp, thoroughly disheveled, bone tired, and famished, Paige tried to take her mind off the immediate physical discomfort and forget exactly how far she was going to have to ride to get home tonight.

Instead, she thought about the things that had happened that day, about the Indians and the way they'd talked for hours to Myles, about how they were being treated, about the stupidity of the government and what Myles had said about trouble brewing. She remembered Armand's face when he told her his land was gone.

She thought of the news broadcasts on television in her other life, the more sophisticated but still similar problems the native people had complained of, and she felt guilty, remembering how little attention she'd paid to any of it. She hadn't known any Indians in those days, or any Métis either.

Since coming here, she'd heard talk of the trouble the railroad was causing as it invaded the native people's lands, and Tahny had made reference to the problems her people were having on the reserves, but again, Paige had been caught up with her own struggles and hadn't really paid all that much attention.

Myles had said it would come to rebellion.

A long-ago history lesson filtered into her consciousness, and she suddenly reined Minnie in so unexpectedly the little mare reared, almost unseating Paige.

"What is it?" Myles scanned the landscape, hand on his gun, anticipating trouble.

"The rebellion. God, Myles, I-I just remembered, I can't believe I didn't think of this before." She stared at him, wide-eyed. "It's because I was always so bad at history, and I've stopped paying attention to the date anyway." Her words tumbled out, and she stammered with the need to warn him.

"Myles, it happened just the way you said. There was a rebellion, a huge fight, the Indians and the Métis against the whites. It was about the same things those Indians today were talking about, lack of food, their land being taken over, the government not keeping its promises. It was led by a man named Louis Riel, a great folk hero."

"Riel?" Myles was holding Major in check, close beside her. He frowned at her. "I know of Riel; he led an insurrection at Red River in 1869, long before I joined the force. You're sure that skirmish isn't what you're thinking of?"

Paige wasn't sure. Her recollection of dates and events was atrocious. "Was there a battle at a place called Batoche at that time? I remember something about a battle of Batoche, led by Riel."

Myles stared at her. "There's been no battle at Batoche. Batoche is a Métis village, built along the Saskatchewan River, about a hundred miles east of Battleford."

Paige clucked to Minnie, and they set off again. "I know he was hanged for his part in the rebellion," she remarked.

"Who was hanged?" Myles was riding close beside her.

"Louis Riel. He was hanged as a traitor, but in later years he became a Canadian hero." She was racking her brain, trying to remember more details, but they eluded her. "There was a stamp with his picture on it."

"Riel is very much alive, Paige. He's spent the last few

years in Beauport Asylum, near Montreal. His mind is deranged."

"I remember that he was thought to be schizophrenic; there was something about him riding around naked on a white horse in the midst of the battle." She thought for a moment. "But if he's still alive, then that couldn't have been the rebellion I'm talking about, that one at Red River, could it? Because I know for sure that he was hanged after the rebellion. They named it the Riel Rebellion, after him."

"When, Paige? What was the date of this rebellion?"

She tried to remember and couldn't. "I think it was in the spring," she said vaguely. "In the 1800s, in the spring."

Exasperated, Myles swore under his breath. "It would help if you'd paid more attention in class."

Paige scowled at the acerbic note in his voice. "Come off it, Myles, it was history, for God's sake," she snapped. "It was boring as hell, all those dates and battles. I memorized enough to pass the exam and then forgot it all. Why, even in my worst nightmares, I never dreamed I'd end up back here living through it."

Myles mouth tightened. "So that's all this is to you? A nightmare, Paige? Some kind of living hell?"

She was tired, hungry, and out of sorts. "There are definitely times like right now when it feels like it, yes," she said flippantly.

He reached over and grabbed Minnie's bridle, yanking both horses to a stop. Paige almost fell off again, and when she regained her balance she stared at him, her eyes narrowing when she realized how angry he was.

"I'm a stupid fool. I'd begun to believe you lately, insisting you were happy and content here, that you no longer dreamed of going back." His eyes were cold, his voice almost sneering. "I'd actually planned today to ask you to marry me. It's a very good thing the opportunity didn't present itself, isn't it, Paige? Because if this is all a nightmare, what does that make me? Where does it leave me when you wake up some fine morning back where you want to be?"

She gaped at him, stupefied. Then the day's frustrations overcame her, and she yelled, "It makes you a chauvinist, that's what it makes you. So you were going to do me the favor of a lifetime and propose, were you? Do the right thing, make an honest woman out of me, well how bloody noble. How unnecessary, because weird as it may seem, I don't want to get married, Myles Baldwin."

She knew she was being unfair, but she couldn't stop once she'd begun.

"I won't marry you or anyone else. Every single day in my office, I see what marriage is like for women in this era, and believe me, that's a *real* nightmare."

She was sorry the moment the words were out. Damn, she hadn't meant to blast at him like that. It was just that his sarcasm had stung, and her legs ached like fire, and she wanted to get down from this blasted horse. She wanted a hot bath in a big tub, and a TV dinner, and a huge bowl of chocolate ice cream.

He'd been going to propose, he'd said.

How many times had she fantasized lately about what it would be like to be married to him?

Well, it was a cinch she'd never get the chance to find out now.

She felt faintly ill, and she had to struggle to stop the tears that threatened, but she managed.

The rest of the ride was long and silent and dreary.

Chapter Sixteen

With icy politeness, Myles saw Paige to her door that night and returned to the fort, seething with frustration.

Dinner in the mess hall was long over. Myles settled for several apples and a slab of bread and cheese, and stomped off with them to his room.

He yanked off his boots and removed his tunic, giving it a shake to dislodge some of the dust from the ride. He washed at the basin in the corner and sat down in an armchair, propping his feet on a wooden box and staring at the plate that held his meager dinner.

Damnation. He slammed a fist down on the desk, and the plate with his food tumbled to the floor, the apples rolling off under the bed.

What the hell, he wasn't the least bit hungry anyway.

How could the day he'd planned with all the care of a delicate surgical procedure have turned into such an unmitigated disaster?

He was disgusted and furious with himself for a great many things: his carelessness, for one. What had possessed him, cavorting buck naked in the pool with his weapons nowhere within reach? He shuddered at his own stupidity.

If the Indians had been warlike, the scene would have had dire consequences. He thought about what could have happened to Paige and felt his stomach grow nauseous.

Curse the woman, she had the ability to make him lose his reason. She drove him mad with lust, she infuriated him with her stubbornness and her temper. He'd almost been angry enough tonight to ride off and leave her on the godforsaken prairie.

His mouth twisted in a mocking half-grin. What made him think he could ride off and leave Paige Randolph anywhere? She'd just follow him with that dogged determination of hers and give him holy hell when she caught him.

His thoughts strayed to the passion they'd shared that afternoon in the pouring rain, the way her wide-open eyes had looked straight into his in the dim shadow of the blanket, holding only primitive need and the clear, pure message of her love for him. Even the memory made his body clench again with need of her.

But, he reminded himself bitterly, the only time she was truly his was when she was in his arms, when he was thrusting into her, when her memory was gone and only wild, immediate desire remained.

Never in her worst nightmares had she thought of coming back to this time. Her words had been devastating. Even now, they twisted his gut into knots. He got to his feet, violently shucked off the rest of his clothing, blew out the lantern, and climbed into his narrow bed.

The far future, the time she came from, was so unbelievable it didn't particularly surprise him anymore when she told him of the curiosities she'd known, these automobiles, airplanes, televisions she talked about.

But she'd surprised him tonight with her talk of Riel, because only a few days ago, Armand had told Myles that Louis Riel was now back in Batoche with his wife, his infant son, and his daughter. The Métis had asked him for help with their land claims, Armand had confided.

Myles doubted that even Inspector Morris knew about Riel's return.

What Paige had related about a coming rebellion made perfect sense. The Indians and the Métis needed a hero, and Myles had heard many reports of Riel's ability as an orator able to stir fire in the blood of his passionate people.

So a bloody rebellion was coming.

Myles had seen more than enough of battles, of war, and the thought of another sickened him. But foreknowledge might allow for preparation.

If only Paige could remember exactly when it would happen.

September was hot, far hotter than even July or August had been. Old-timers told Paige it was the hottest September they ever remembered, and she believed them, irritably wondering why the hell she'd never really studied the inner workings of an air-conditioning unit when she'd had the chance.

Her house was worse than an oven, and she pitied the poor patients in their long dresses and corsets almost as much as she pitied herself.

She and Myles had each apologized after that fateful Sunday in June, and although at first everything seemed fine between them, Paige was painfully aware that he never mentioned marriage again.

As the weeks went by, she realized that there were other things too that they didn't talk about; Paige avoided referring to anything that related to her past. They'd never discussed Riel again. There were long silences between them, awkward silences.

Worse, their lovemaking suffered. What had been wild and free was now constrained. Well, she told herself in disgust, when you closed off communication in one area, it put a strain on everything.

Two things occurred that September which took her mind off both the blistering heat and her relationship with Myles.

The first was Ellie Randolph Fletcher, and the second was Tahnancoa Quinlan.

Clara and Theo arrived at her office with Ellie late one afternoon.

"Theo broke a blade on the plow, so we had to make a rush trip in, and we just wanted you to have a look at Ellie," Clara declared, her broad face wreathed in smiles. "Say hello to your Auntie Paige, sweetheart," she instructed.

Paige reached out and Ellie, exquisitely dressed as always in one of Clara's hand-embroidered creations, came willingly into her arms.

"How you doing, pumpkin?" Paige noted that the baby was gaining weight, that the sick pallor of her skin had taken on a tanned, rosy hue. The huge blue eyes with their long lashes were no longer sunken and weary-looking.

Paige couldn't believe her eyes. Ellie grinned at her, displaying two new teeth. She reached out and patted Paige's cheek, and at a prompt from Clara, put her lips to Paige's skin and planted a wet, openmouthed kiss. Then she laughed and clapped her hands. "Goo baby," she lisped.

"Clara, she looks absolutely wonderful," Paige said, amazed at the change in the baby.

Ellie squirmed and demanded to be set down, and

when Paige released her on the rug, Ellie began heading energetically toward a basket of bright flowers.

"My God, she's crawling." In vivid detail, Paige remembered the last time she'd seen this baby, pale and immobile in her mother's arms, barely able to hold her head up, much less crawl.

"She's never had another convulsion," Clara said. "She's eating most everything we eat, although I'm still nursing her like Tahnancoa said to do." Clara's plain face was suffused with pride and love and gratitude. "Tahnancoa cured her that day, Paige. She gave our baby back to us." Her voice was thick with tears. "We'll be grateful to her the rest of our lives, and to you as well, for arranging that we meet." She glanced at her daughter and moved quickly after her. "Ellie, you rascal, don't touch that."

The baby was gleefully destroying the floral arrangement in the basket, and Paige thought she'd never seen anything as wonderful.

"We're going to go see Tahnancoa ourselves," Clara said, scooping her daughter into her arms, "soon as the harvesting is over, but in the meantime I want you to give her this parcel." She handed Paige a large, brown-wrapped bundle. "Tahnancoa wouldn't let us pay her any money that day, so these are just some things I made for her, to say thank you."

Ellie squirmed like a little eel, wanting to get down again, and Clara added softly, "Not that we ever could. Thank her properly, I mean. How do you thank someone for giving you back your heart?"

Paige hadn't seen Tahnancoa for some time, so toward the end of the month, she used the parcel as an excuse to ride out early one morning for a visit.

Wanting to avoid the heat, Paige left home before

dawn, worrying that she'd arrive and find the Quinlans still in bed.

But Dennis was already out in the field cutting hay when she rode up. He pulled the team to a halt and waved a greeting.

"Tahny's making breakfast. Go along in; she's gonna be mighty happy to see you," he hollered, his rugged features creased into a wide grin.

The cabin door was open wide. "Tahny, it's me. Where are you?" Paige rapped her knuckles against the thick wood, but Tahnancoa was nowhere to be seen.

Inside, a pot of oats was foaming over the lip of an iron saucepan on the hot range lid. Paige stirred it down and turned some salt pork, sizzling to a frazzle in the frying pan. Fresh eggs sat on the apron of the stove, waiting to be cracked and fried. Bread was sliced for toasting. It looked as if Tahnancoa had had to leave in a hurry.

"Paige Randolph, how good to see you."

Paige turned with a smile to greet her friend, but the smile faded when she noticed the pronounced greenish cast to Tahnancoa's dusky skin and the heavy shadows beneath the liquid dark eyes.

"Hey, Tahny, you're sick, you look terrible," she said, reaching out a hand to feel Tahnancoa's forehead for fever.

"Only in the mornings, when I have to cook this salt pork for Dennis's breakfast." Tahny shuddered, but then her face broke into a radiant smile. "I'm pregnant, Paige Randolph. I think a little over two months now."

Paige let out a delighted whoop and wrapped her arms around Tahny, giving her a joyous hug. "It worked, I'm so glad, I was afraid to even hope."

"At first, when I explained what you said we must do, Dennis was sure I'd gone loco, but"—Tahnancoa shot Paige a sidelong glance and rolled her eyes—"soon he decided he liked your medicine very well. It's fortunate that we don't have a lot of visitors."

They giggled, and then Paige took over cooking the rest of breakfast. Tahny sipped a cup of her own soothing herbal tea to settle her stomach.

"I went to the reservation as soon as I was sure," she told Paige, "to see Lame Owl and tell her about the baby. I told her that it was your magic that cured me. She wants me to bring you to see her. I told her that you are a powerful shaman who has walked between the worlds."

"Sounds like it's going to be hard to live up to my own PR," Paige muttered. When Tahnancoa shot her a puzzled look, Paige added quickly, "I can't wait to meet your grandmother. When shall we go?"

"Soon, while the weather holds. This hot weather could change to cold and snow in the space of a day."

"Maybe it's not such a good idea for you to ride right now, in the early stages of your pregnancy," Paige worried, but Tahnancoa laughed at her concern.

"I ride all the time. I've already been out to the reserve since I became pregnant," she reminded Paige. "The women of my tribe consider pregnancy a natural condition, and a normal amount of exercise necessary and healthy. We have few miscarriages, and little trouble delivering our children."

It could have been a lecture Paige herself had delivered to her pregnant patients many times. It was ironic that Tahnancoa should lecture her, practically in her own words.

"Then how about this Thursday?" Paige would put a notice in the weekly paper, she decided, saying that her office would be closed Friday.

They agreed on the date and called Dennis in for breakfast.

When the meal was over and Dennis had gone back outside again, Paige produced the package Clara had given her and told Tahnancoa about Ellie.

"I still don't know what you did or how you did it, but it's nothing short of a miracle. The Fletchers are grateful to you."

Tahnancoa unwrapped the package. Inside were two beautiful blouses of fine white lawn, with inset lace in a floral pattern on the bodice and tiny pearl buttons down the front and on the cuffs.

Both women exclaimed over the exquisite workmanship—the blouses obviously represented untold hours of loving effort. There was a small piece of paper with the gift, in Clara's flowery handwriting. It read, "For Tahnancoa, from your devoted friend, Clara Fletcher. Bless you for what you did for our daughter. Please come and visit us soon."

Tahnancoa looked at the note for a long time, and then carefully folded it up and tucked it away in one of her baskets with the same care she gave the blouses.

"I came to hate white women when I lived at the fort," she mused in a thoughtful tone. "And I was angry with Myles Baldwin the first time he brought you here, Paige Randolph. I thought I wanted nothing to do with white women ever again. And now I have two friends, and both are white."

"Go figure," Paige said with a tender smile.

Tahnancoa nodded and solemnly repeated, "Go figure" in her softly accented voice, just as if she'd been using the phrase all her life.

The weather held, and Thursday morning, escorted by both Dennis and Myles, the women rode off to Poundmaker's reserve.

"I'm looking forward to meeting Lame Owl," Paige had

283

explained to Myles when she suggested he come along on the trip. "From what Tahnancoa's told me, Lame Owl's a doctor among her people, just as you and I are among ours. There must be a ton of stuff I could learn from her."

She was scrupulously careful not to mention the mysterious ceremony that allowed travel through time, even though she knew it must be what Myles was thinking about when she mentioned Lame Owl. It was certainly on her mind.

She suddenly wished with all her heart that he'd say something about it, that the awful constraint between them would somehow be shattered—even if they fought, it would be better than this polite avoidance. But Myles didn't say anything, and she couldn't find the courage to either.

"I'd like to have a talk with Poundmaker myself," he commented instead. "It's been a while since I was out at the reserve."

The journey turned into a delightful outing. The women talked nonstop, and several times Tahnancoa called a halt so she could gather some medicinal flower or plant, at the same time instructing Paige in its preparation and use.

They had a leisurely lunch in the shade of a poplar grove, and while the women rested, Dennis and Myles hunted deer to take as a gift to the Indian encampment. They shot two and skinned them, packing the meat in canvas bags Myles had brought along for that purpose.

The rest of the ride was short. It wasn't long before the tipis and lean-tos that made up Poundmaker's reserve came in sight. Several young braves rode out to meet them and escort them into camp, followed by a horde of excited, noisy children.

Paige's heart was hammering with excitement and nervousness. The dusty Indian village looked exactly like the ones depicted in every Western movie she'd ever seen— she wouldn't have been at all surprised to see a Hollywood director pop out of nowhere and start giving orders.

There were dogs barking and women gathered around smoky cooking fires. Small children staggered around, falling in the dirt, and curious dusky faces peeped out at them from folded back flaps on the buffalo-hide tipis.

A tall, fierce-looking man with a blanket wrapped around his shoulders came striding out of a tipi and marched over to greet them.

"My uncle, Chief Poundmaker," Tahnancoa whispered to Paige.

Poundmaker was a physically powerful man, about six feet tall, very broad and muscular, wearing buckskins. Paige thought him handsome; he had overwhelming presence, a dignity that commanded respect, chiseled features, and piercing dark eyes under hooded brows.

Myles and Dennis dismounted and walked forward to meet him, and the men shook hands. Myles said something in the Cree language to which Poundmaker responded at some length. The women dismounted and joined the group, and Tahnancoa introduced Paige to the chief.

"My niece has told me of your powerful magic," he said in English in his guttural voice. His black eyes were hypnotic. "You are a welcome guest in my village."

He turned back to Myles and Dennis and lapsed back into Cree, and the women were ignored as the men talked on and on.

Tahnancoa gestured to two young boys hovering nearby, and they came and took charge of the horses, leading them off to a corral.

"Come, I'll introduce you to the women." Tahnancoa led the way to where a group of women, young and old, were gathered.

She spoke to them in Cree for some time, and when she was done, each of them came up to Paige and took her hand, smiling and saying their name and hers.

Some of them spoke a little English, and those who did proudly tried it out on her.

"How you are?" one said.

"Good to meet," another offered.

They giggled and brought tea and food, dried fruit and a sweet-tasting stew that Tahnancoa explained was made from bear meat.

Paige admired the babies, beautiful, smiling little creatures strapped to elaborately painted buckskin cradles, carried on their mothers' backs or propped casually against the sides of tipis.

They all looked remarkably healthy and happy. She watched one young mother unstrap her baby and change the dried and sterilized moss that was used for his diapers. Paige held him for a moment, a plump, naked cherub who smelled of woodsmoke and some sweet oil his mother used on his delicate baby skin. She cuddled his wriggling body and pressed her lips to his fuzzy head. The appeal of babies was universal—and so were their habits. Paige laughed with the others when the baby's tiny penis sprayed urine all over her.

"Come now and meet my grandmother," Tahnancoa said.

It was the moment Paige had been waiting for and dreading, a chance to meet the woman who might hold the key to a doorway that led to the future.

A wave of panic came over her for a moment as she followed Tahnancoa through the maze of tipis. What would she really do if Lame Owl agreed to let her attend the ceremony that might open that door? If the opportunity presented itself, would she choose to go—or would she stay? She thought of Myles, of the love they shared.

Would she be able to leave him?

She no longer knew the answer, but she'd like to have a choice, to know there was a way to make the journey back.

Feeling a mixture of fear and anticipation, Paige ducked after Tahny through the low opening of a tipi.

Inside, buffalo hides covered the floor, and the air was pungent with smoke and the smell of hides curing. Cooking utensils and sleeping robes were arranged neatly around the walls, and from the tent poles hung strips of drying meat, gourds, and intricately woven baskets.

At first glance, Lame Owl was not an imposing figure. She was tiny and toothless, her brown skin stretched so tight across her cheeks and jutting nose that she reminded Paige of a wild bird.

Her still-dark hair was so thin her scalp showed through the braids wound around her head. She was smoking a pipe, and small puffs of white erupted from her nostrils at regular intervals. She huddled in front of a small fire with a blanket wrapped around her shoulders despite the heat of the afternoon. Her black shoe-button eyes were bright and alert, however, and she studied Paige, her expression unreadable.

Respectfully, Tahnancoa bowed to the old woman and then knelt at her side, talking to her in Cree, gesturing at Paige.

Myles had advised Paige to bring Lame Owl a gift. Tahnancoa suggested tobacco—her grandmother, she said, was addicted to her pipe.

Paige handed the old woman the package. She'd added a pretty necklace she'd bought at the store and a package of sugar, and Lame Owl seemed pleased with the gifts. She made a long speech to Tahnancoa, her toothless mouth sending spittle flying.

"She welcomes you and thanks you for the gifts. She

wishes to know what magic you used to start the baby growing within me," Tahnancoa interpreted. "She asks if you were a great shaman in your own land, before you walked between the worlds."

Still nervous in the presence of this mysterious old woman, Paige wondered how on earth to respond. In spite of the flattery, Paige had the feeling Lame Owl was wily, that she was testing her, making her own judgment about how powerful this strange white woman's medicine might be or how truthful her stories.

Paige decided to begin by explaining in simple terms, as she had so often, the functions of a woman's organs and how conception worked.

Lame Owl listened, nodding, her expression noncommittal.

On impulse, Paige then launched into a vivid description of in vitro fertilization, fertility drugs, artificial insemination—all the strange and wonderful techniques that medical science had developed to aid in conception.

Tahnancoa stumbled over the words that were difficult to translate, but now Lame Owl was visibly intrigued. She leaned forward, listening intently, forgetting even to puff at her pipe.

Through Tahny, she asked questions, intelligent questions, and Paige answered.

Soon, Paige felt secure enough to ask some questions of her own, about special techniques Tahnancoa had told Paige her grandmother had used for difficult births, about herbal preparations for specific problems Paige had encountered with her patients for which the medical profession of the day had no medications.

The dialogue went back and forth until Tahny, weary with the effort of translating, called a halt for tea. Paige and Lame Owl sipped the strong, sweet brew Tahnancoa offered, and the old woman nodded and smiled at Paige.

Paige drank her tea, and when Lame Owl noisily sipped the last of hers, Paige decided it was now or never. She had to ask about the ceremony that sent people through time, or the opportunity would be lost. She told Tahnancoa what she wanted to know, adding, "Ask her if I could be there the next time the ceremony is held, please."

She knew as soon as Tahnancoa turned the question into Cree that it was a mistake. Lame Owl interrupted before Tahnancoa was finished speaking. She shook her head and gesticulated with her hands. Her words were vehement, almost angry, and they went on for some time. Paige's heart sank.

When Lame Owl was finished speaking, she scrambled to her feet and walked out the door of the tipi without another word, without so much as a glance at Paige.

Tahnancoa sighed and shook her head. "My grandmother is old and set in her ways. You must excuse her."

"I'm sorry, Tahnancoa. I've made her angry."

Tahnancoa shrugged. "She has strong feelings, my grandmother. She thinks the white people have taken much from the Indian—their buffalo, their freedom—and given too little back. You are one of the few whites she's ever even spoken to. Some of our knowledge she will share with you, she says, because you have helped me become pregnant, and you too are a healer—but our ceremonies are all we have left that the white man hasn't taken from us. Therefore she will not speak of them with you."

"I can understand how she feels." Paige remembered what the Indians had told Myles, the Sunday of the picnic, about promises made and broken, a way of life forever lost. Sadness filled her, and a sense of futility.

"It's getting late. The women were preparing a feast with the fresh meat we brought; it'll be ready soon,"

Tahnancoa said, making a determined effort to lighten the mood. "There's a creek nearby where we can wash. And I'll show you where you will sleep."

Outside, it was already twilight. Tahnancoa pointed out the small tipi where Paige's things had already been piled beside Myles's saddlebags and bedroll.

So it was taken for granted here that she was Myles Baldwin's woman, that she'd sleep beside him in this buffalo-skin shelter. It was a freedom they didn't have back in Battleford. They'd never had the chance to sleep together all night long.

Paige located her towel, a bar of soap, her hairbrush, and then, with a wry grin at herself for playing the part of the dutiful female, she unfastened the bedrolls and spread them close together on the soft buffalo rugs that covered the floor.

Maybe here, she thought wistfully, in one another's arms in an Indian camp on a night when the harvest moon promised to turn the prairie molten silver, maybe here she and Myles could somehow mend whatever it was that had gone so wrong between them.

Chapter Seventeen

Hesitantly, Paige approached the noisy gathering grouped around the cooking fires.

While she and Tahny had been talking with Lame Owl, two other visitors had arrived at Poundmaker's village. They were dark-skinned, long-haired men in buckskin trousers, each wearing the distinctive red sash around their middles that labeled them Métis.

They were passing around a bottle of whiskey, and their laughter was raucous and bold.

Feeling shy, Paige stayed on the outskirts of the group until Myles noticed her. He came and led her near the fire, close beside him, his arm looped protectively around her shoulder.

"Ahhh, *le docteur,* he 'as found himself a beautiful woman," one of the Métis men called out in a good-natured fashion. He was a good-looking young man, tall and dark-haired, with startling light blue eyes. He came toward Paige, bowing in a courtly fashion and holding out the whiskey bottle. "A little drink, madam?"

Paige smiled and shook her head. "I think I'll stick to tea, thanks." She felt Myles's hand on her shoulder, drawing her closer to his side as the man looked at her with admiration in his sparkling silver-blue eyes.

"Introduce me to this so charming lady, *Monsieur Docteur* Baldwin. Or do you keep her all to yourself, eh?" The handsome man's tone was teasing, and he gave Paige a huge wink. He was flirting outrageously, and Paige couldn't help smiling back at him.

"Pierre Delorme, Dr. Paige Randolph." Myles's voice was curt and cold.

The blue eyes widened in surprised recognition, and he stretched out a hand in greeting. "Ahh, so you are the *bonne femme* from far away that Armand LeClerc has spoken of." Paige put her hand in his, and with a courtly bow, Pierre brushed his lips across the back of it.

"Armand LeClerc is my cousin, madame, and because of him, your fame has spread across the land. It is indeed an honor to meet you." He turned and hollered at his friend, still talking and laughing with the group of braves nearby, "Gabriel, come over here."

The other man, shorter and much stockier than Pierre, extricated himself from the Indians and came walking toward them.

In the rapid-fire burst of French that followed, Paige understood only her name and the repeated *docteur*. Her high-school French was sadly lacking, but it was obvious Pierre was telling the other man all he knew about her.

"*Madame la docteur,* this is Gabriel Dumont, mightiest of our Métis buffalo hunters," Pierre introduced proudly. "We call him Prince of the Braves."

Prince or not, Paige felt that Dumont had none of Pierre's physical charm. He was shorter than Paige, about five seven. He was thickset and heavy-chested, with high Indian cheekbones, a full beard, stern dark eyes, and rather thick lips. He made no move to shake her hand, only nodding his head in acknowledgment when she said hello, studying her with his intent dark gaze.

Paige, in turn, stared at him. She was certain they'd never met before, and yet there was something familiar about Gabriel Dumont.

Myles spoke to him. "Hello, Gabriel. How are things at Batoche?"

Dumont shrugged his massive shoulders. "We survive," he said, his baritone voice heavily accented. "Da crops, dey 'ave been poor dis year. And you know well"—He fixed Myles with an accusing look—"dere are no more buffalo. Maybe a few only, but the mighty herds we knew, dey are gone forever. And now our farms, even, are in danger of being taken from us. You know of this, yes?"

Myles nodded. "Armand tells me things are bad for you. I'm sorry."

Myles knew all too well about the Métis problems. Sir John A. Macdonald, Canada's prime minister, envisioned a railroad linking the Atlantic to the Pacific, and he was ruthlessly pursuing that dream. The railroad was pushing ever further westward, and the strip farms the Métis depended upon for survival were being conscripted by Eastern land speculators. The Métis, like the Indians, had also depended heavily on the buffalo herds to feed their families.

"It's a bad business," Myles said.

Paige was aware of the tension in his body, although his voice was relaxed and friendly. "I understand your people have sent a petition to Ottawa."

Dumont snorted. "A waste of time. What do politicians care about us ignorant Métis?" He gestured at the noisy crowd surrounding the fire, and there was bitterness and resentment on his bearded face. "Or about our brodders, de Indians? Dey, too, are hungry now. No longer do dey 'ave freedom to travel where dey like, or buffalo to eat."

"I wish you luck with your petition, you and all your people," Myles said in a quiet tone.

Dumont frowned at him, trying to sense, Paige thought, whether or not Myles was sincere. At last he nodded again, turning back without another word to the fire where his friend Pierre was laughing and joking at the center of a noisy group of young braves.

After that, the party seemed to go on for hours. Everyone ate, drums pounded, and both men and women danced in the firelight.

Paige sat beside Myles, and soon she had to struggle to stay awake. The scene became surreal as she slipped in and out of dreams, and at some point, Myles took her hand and together they slipped away from the boisterous scene, making their way by moonlight to their tipi.

Inside, it was musky-smelling and still hot from the sun. Myles knelt and undid her boots and tugged them off, then gently unbuttoned her clothing and stripped it away along with his own.

Sleepy and limp, her body deliciously naked, Paige sank down into the welcoming softness of the bedrolls she'd arranged earlier, and Myles's strong arms encircled her.

At first, his lovemaking was gentle, and the remoteness that bothered her was still there. Half dozing, she returned his kisses, passive as his lips and tongue touched and teased.

Her muscles were lax, her thoughts unfocused. She could hear the drums, and it took a long, slow time before they became part of her own heartbeat.

Gradually, her skin became sensitive, her breasts aching for Myles's caress. Her pulse skittered, her hips undulated as his fingers searched for and found all the right, familiar places.

He was still going slow, holding back. She could feel his restraint in each labored breath, in the muscles that quivered at her slightest touch, and something deep within her wanted him to let go of whatever constraint there was between them. She wanted him to possess her, to claim her as his own.

His kisses were deeper now, hot and wet, drugging her. She shuddered as pleasure coursed through her. Suddenly she was greedy for him. Her hands slid along his body, her lips following, down his chest and across the flat planes of his stomach.

She took him in her mouth, and the drums became part of her, thundering in her blood.

At last, when he could bear no more, he pulled her up, covering her with his body, his bare skin with its rough patches of hair enveloping her in the darkness, teasing but not yet fulfilling.

He was breathing hard, as if he'd been running, but still he waited.

She moved beneath him. "Myles, please, I want—"

"What? Tell me what it is you really want." His voice, thick and slow and sweet, choked with need, was still insistent. "Tell me, Paige."

"I want you—I need you—to love me," she gasped.

"Why?" There was something remorseless in his tone, something he needed from her before he would go on.

"Because I love you. Because I'll always love you," she breathed. "Forever, now, always—"

"My darling." The last of his control fled then, and with a low cry, he parted her thighs and entered her at the same instant his mouth came down and swallowed her cry of fulfillment.

And their joining was the way she remembered, wild and passionate and free. Relief mingled with rapture.

She must have slept for some time, afterward. It was still black dark when she came out of a floating dream, aware that he was awake and still holding her close to his body.

"Myles? What time is it?" She was groggy, and it seemed important to know the time. "Why aren't you sleeping?"

"It's about three. The party finally died down an hour ago and everyone's gone to bed."

"The Métis must have finally run out of whiskey," she mused, turning a little so she rested more comfortably against his side.

She closed her eyes again, floating, thinking of the scene around the campfire, and somewhere between waking and sleeping an image stole into her mind, of a long-ago class on some hot afternoon at the university. She heard the instructor's voice droning on, she saw a blurred photograph in a textbook, and without any further effort on her part, she suddenly knew where she'd met Gabriel Dumont.

"Oh my God, that's it. That's him." She shot bolt upright.

"What?" Alarmed, Myles propped himself on an elbow, his hand straying toward his gun, close to his pillow. "What's the matter?"

She shivered. It was chilly in the tipi in the predawn morning, but it wasn't the cold that made her shiver. "That Métis man you spoke to tonight. Gabriel Dumont? Well, I just realized who he is."

Myles lay back down. His voice seemed to come from far away. "And who is he, Paige? What do you know about Gabriel Dumont?"

"He's Riel's general. He was Riel's general," she corrected. "He masterminded the battles that were fought in the rebellion. He came very near defeating an entire

British army with only a handful of soldiers. I remember Professor Wood going on and on about it, how this one man was a genius at tactical warfare. And I know his name was Gabriel Dumont. It was very sad, because after the rebellion he escaped to the United States, and ended up in Buffalo Bill's Wild West Show. That's what stuck in my mind; I remember thinking that it must have been humiliating for a man like him to end up as a sideshow attraction. There was a picture of him."

"Come here, lie down beside me." Myles reached for her and drew her down into the warmth of the bedrolls. "You're trembling. Your shoulders are freezing."

"Myles, do you believe me?" She was suddenly terrified that once again her traitorous memories would cause problems between them.

He sighed. "Yes, I believe you. And it doesn't surprise me at all that Dumont would be the one in charge of Riel's battles. Gabriel's illiterate, he can't talk English worth a damn, but he's a brilliant man all the same, a leader of his people." Myles was quiet for some time, and then he added, his voice somber, "He's here tonight for a purpose, Paige. Dumont and Riel are uniting the Indian tribes, rallying them behind the Métis cause, which is really the Indians' cause as well."

"But I thought you told me Riel was in a mental hospital."

Myles nodded. "He was, for a time. When he got out, he went to Montana and got work there as a schoolteacher. Around the fort, rumor has it that Dumont went down to Montana this summer and asked him to come home and be the political voice for the Métis people. He agreed. He's been at Batoche for several months now."

Frustration and anger were both evident in his voice. "I don't blame the Métis. There's no question their demands

297

are legitimate. But damn it all, Paige, there's a bloody uprising in the making, and those idiots in Ottawa are paying not one single bit of attention."

She felt like saying I told you so, but good sense prevailed. Instead, she asked softly, "Is that why you can't sleep?" She cuddled against him, aware of the tension in his long, strong body.

"That's why. I keep feeling that I should be able to do something to prevent it."

She sighed, her hand stroking the familiar contours of his chest. "I don't think it's possible to change history, Myles." She thought for a moment. "When I first got here, I used to rage about things: the lack of conveniences, the fact that there weren't the medications I used to use. I used to think, there's a better way than this, I know there is, I've seen it. But as time went by, I started thinking differently. Now is now, and the things that happen here, the way people are, that's how it's meant to be now."

"There still must be something we can do."

She noticed that he'd gone from I to we. He was including her in his plans, and it made her irrationally happy, in spite of the circumstances.

"We can prepare, I guess. We can stock up on medical supplies, get extra food, blankets, clothing stored at the fort."

"You think this rebellion happened in the spring?"

She'd given it a great deal of thought. "In the spring of eighteen eighty-five. I'm almost certain."

"About five months from now."

They talked on and on. The constraint that had been between them was gone.

Most of it, anyway. Paige was aware that Myles still didn't mention marriage, but perhaps that would come with time. She didn't bring up the conversation with Lame Owl, either. Why rock the boat just when she'd gotten it back in the water?

It was almost dawn before they slept, curled in one another's arms.

Summer became winter that year with no slow transition between the seasons. Barely a week after the trip to Poundmaker's reserve, the unusual September heat changed to icy rain from one day to the next, and shortly after that, to snow.

The sudden change brought flu, a virulent strain that kept both Paige and Myles so busy tending to its victims all through October that they had little time to spend with one another.

November came, and the flu epidemic still raged through the community and the surrounding countryside. Several old people and two young children died from the disease.

Hardly a day passed without more snow falling, and Paige had trouble keeping her house even moderately warm—she was called out night and day to tend to those who were ill, and her fires had a tiresome habit of going out while she wasn't there to shove more wood on them.

Then, in the middle of December, both the snow and the flu subsided almost overnight. A warm wind began to blow, a chinook, and a substantial amount of snow melted in a single day. The wind continued, and soon the weather was almost balmy.

Two days, and then three, went by without an urgent call to someone's bedside, and Paige woke up one morning feeling rested for the first time in weeks. She looked at a calendar and realized that Christmas was only ten days away.

It was her second Christmas in Battleford, and on impulse, she decided to celebrate by having all her friends for Christmas dinner.

Before she could change her mind, she scribbled notes to the Fletchers and the Quinlans and Abigail Donald, inviting them for Christmas Day—as long as the weather held, of course. She told Myles to invite Armand as well.

Eight people, plus baby Ellie. That number of bodies would stretch her tiny house until it was bursting at the seams, but after all, she told herself, that was what Christmas was all about.

Between patients, she spent the remaining time cleaning the house, planning the dinner, and wrapping gifts. Her own cooking was still hit-and-miss, so she bought whatever was available.

She ordered a large ham from the butcher. A small bakery had opened recently in town, and from the plump woman who owned it she ordered fragrant loaves of rye bread and a savory meat pie as well as mince and pumpkin pies.

From the Hudson's Bay Company store, she splurged on dried fruit and nuts and fresh oranges—a rarity in Battleford. She bought a bottle of sherry, and another of whiskey for the men, and more small gifts for everyone.

By Christmas Eve she was a nervous wreck, aware of just how much cooking she'd still have to do to feed eight people. She'd somehow overlooked the fact that she'd never in her life cooked an entire meal from scratch for a large group.

Nervous about cooking the ham, she decided to have a turkey as well. No one in the area raised turkeys, so she bought a goose—fortunately, the farmer agreed to chop the bird's head off, and for a small fee, his wife plucked and cleaned it. But now Paige was faced with the daunting task of stuffing the huge, ugly carcass—Abigail had offered, but Paige stubbornly insisted she'd manage on her own.

The evening before the big day, she cursed herself for being an optimistic fool. Sitting at the kitchen table with the corpse of the goose spread-eagled beside her, she was trying to figure out the vague instructions Abigail had written out for her when Myles arrived.

He came in, stamping his feet on the rag rug at the back door.

"Thank God you're here." Paige leaped to her feet and kissed him, brandishing the stuffing directions in one hand. "Take off your coat and help me with this, Myles. Removing somebody's gall bladder has to be a cinch compared with this procedure," she moaned. "How many onions do you figure qualify as a few?"

"About six, maybe?" Myles was as confused as Paige. Together, they studied the recipe and did their best to follow it. Soon, the table was littered with utensils and dishes and spices.

Myles went out for wood and restocked the fire, and the cookstove turned the kitchen into an oven.

He stripped his tunic off, revealing gray underwear and wide suspenders. Sweating, swearing under his breath, he chopped onions and wiped his eyes with the dishtowel.

It seemed to Paige that every time she turned her back, the concoction they'd put on the stove to "fry lightly" started to burn.

By the time they finally had the goose stuffed, trussed, and ready to go in the oven, both Paige and Myles were exhausted.

"God, I smell like a fried onion," Paige complained. "We both do. I've got to get someone to put a bathroom in this house with a shower. When the hell were showers invented, anyhow? Oh, Myles, I hope we didn't go overboard on the pepper."

Myles was washing a stack of dishes in the dishbasin, his underwear sleeves rolled to his elbows. "It said a good quantity of pepper, we added a good quantity. Don't fuss about it, love. It'll taste fine."

"Did your mother ever stuff a goose, Myles? Can you remember if this is the way it ought to look?" Paige frowned at the trussed bird.

Myles turned and smiled at her. "My mama would've been scandalized at the very thought of stuffing a goose herself. We had slaves who tended to such matters. I only remember the goose arriving at the table, golden brown and ready to eat." He scrubbed at a saucepan. "What was Christmas like when you were a little girl, Paige?"

She glanced at him in surprise. He'd never asked much about her childhood—it belonged to that other reality that caused such friction between them.

"Christmas? Oh, not much fun." She picked up a dishtowel and began to dry the dishes. "Nothing about my childhood was much fun. My mother died when I was five, and dad remarried a year later. Joan, her name was." Paige shook her head. "Talk about your wicked stepmothers, that woman wrote the book. She was mean as hell to Tony and me when she was alone with us, and if we tried to tell Dad on her she insisted we were liars. We were just little kids; we couldn't outwit her."

"You and your brother were close." It was a statement, and Paige nodded.

"Yeah, we really were. We grew apart as we got older, but as little kids we were inseparable." She grinned, polishing a glass until it shone. "If I was sick and couldn't go to school, Tony wouldn't go either. Joan would spank him until her hand nearly dropped off, but he just wouldn't go without me."

"You must miss him."

Paige nodded. "I do. My nephews too." She described the boys, the way she remembered them. "They must be getting big. They used to be so excited on Christmas Eve," she said in a wistful tone. "But I'll bet Jason doesn't even believe in Santa anymore." She thought about it and shook her head. "Heck no, he wouldn't, he's almost eight by now. And Matthew is nine, going on ten. They're too old to believe in Santa."

Myles tipped the dishwater into the slop pail under the counter and wiped his hands on a towel, changing the subject abruptly. "I never did ask you if Lame Owl said anything about the ceremony that you wanted to know about, the one that lets people travel through time." His voice was carefully casual.

"Oh, I asked her, all right. She got mad at me and walked out."

"Will you try to talk to her about it again?"

Paige frowned and tossed the dishtowel across a chair back to dry. She understood that the conversation wasn't casual any longer. "I don't think so, Myles." She struggled to find words that would convey what she felt. "Sure, I miss my brother and the kids terribly at times, and there's things I really miss about that other life in Vancouver, but—well, I've made a place for myself here. I have friends, and a practice, and patients I feel responsible for." She met his eyes squarely. "I have you, that's the big thing. I never had anyone like you back there. I'd never experienced this—this fantastic thing we have together." She reached out a finger and traced the line of his jaw, frowning with the effort to express what she felt, to get it right.

"I guess it's a bit like the way you feel about your home in Charleston, and the people you knew back there. It'll always be your home, and you'll always miss it, but it's gone. You've got a different life now, right?" She looked square into his eyes, and the words were easy and honest. "I'm happy here, Myles. I don't want to go back."

He coughed, as if something were stuck in his throat. "This isn't the time or place I'd planned to say this, Paige, in your kitchen over a pile of dishes with a damn stuffed goose looking on." A rueful smile came and went. "Although come to think of it, when I planned it, it didn't work very well either."

His voice deepened until it rumbled in her ears. "I love you, Paige, more than I've loved anyone or anything in my life. If you're planning to stay here, then I think we should get married, my darling."

She'd waited so long to hear him say it again, and now that he had, it caught her unawares.

"You really think so?" She drew in a shivery breath and let the words spill out. "Oh, Myles, so do I. I think we should too."

He drew her into his arms, and the kiss he gave her was chaste, as if this were a whole new beginning.

He turned and searched the pocket of his tunic, drawing out a blue velvet ring case. Opening it, he withdrew the diamond-and-emerald ring inside and slipped it on her finger. It was a little tight on her knuckle, but once it was on, it felt fine. It felt marvelous. It felt as if she'd never take it off again.

The gems flashed in the lamplight. "It's gorgeous," she breathed. It was beautiful—and it looked very expensive.

"It was my mama's. She'd want you to have it."

"Thank you." She looked up at him, knowing her eyes were glistening with unshed tears. "When—" She cleared her throat. "So, Doctor, when do you want us to get married?"

"As soon as possible. It's past time I made an honest woman of you, love. I'll send off a memorandum tomorrow to the commissioner, requesting permission to marry."

Her eyes widened. "You actually have to ask the commissioner's permission to marry me?"

"Yes, ma'am. The North West Mounted is based on formal British Army tradition."

"And what if this commissioner of yours says no?"

A glint of humor appeared in his gray eyes. "Then I turn you loose on him. I doubt he'd last long in a skirmish."

She put her hands on her hips, eyes flashing. "Just say the word."

He laughed and turned down the lamp, and then scooped her up in his arms. "Bedtime. The word is bedtime, my darling." He carried her down the hall.

There was a difference in their loving that night. Slowly and infinitely gently, Myles worshiped her body.

The next day, each of the women brought something to contribute to the dinner, which eased some of the terror Paige was feeling about there being enough to eat.

Tahny and Dennis were the first to arrive, and Tahnancoa contributed a delicious corn pudding and wild cranberry relish to go with the goose.

Clara came bearing fruitcake and shortbread cookies made from butter she'd churned herself. "Merry Christmas," she beamed, handing her gifts of food to Paige, who'd greeted her and Theo at the door.

From the moment Theo carried her proudly into the house, the focus of everyone's attention was Ellie. Dressed in red velvet and long, ruffled white drawers, with a red ribbon holding her single curl on top of her golden head, she was the belle of the party and knew it. Fifteen months old now, she was just starting to walk, but she talked like a child twice her age.

"That girl's going to give Theo some bad moments when she's sixteen," Paige remarked, watching the dainty child openly flirt with one man after another even before Theo wrestled her out of her warm coat and hat. Small-boned and tiny for her age, Ellie was now the picture of health. The convulsions were nothing more than a distant memory.

The men, taking turns amusing Ellie, settled themselves in the parlor to discuss politics and farming and police matters.

Clara's face lit up when she walked into the kitchen and saw Tahny and her swollen stomach. She hurried over and embraced the other woman.

"You're in the family way. I sort of thought so when I last saw you in the fall, but I wasn't sure. When is it due?"

Tahnancoa glowed with health and pride. "Late in April."

"You must let me send you some of the loose dresses I made when I was expecting Ellie. They're my own design, and I found them very comfortable toward the end, when nothing else would fit. And of course, I'll make you a full layette."

"After you sew me a wedding dress, Clara," Paige said, trying for ultracasual, but aware that a blush was creeping up from the neck of her blue dress.

Clara and Tahnancoa stared at her for a moment, and then both erupted in delighted squeals. Paige showed off her ring, and they hugged her and demanded details and a date for the wedding.

Paige, her face bright pink, told them about Myles having to ask permission. "As soon as the commish gives his blessing, then we'll set a date," she promised. Of course, Tahnancoa already knew all about that quaint custom, and Clara wasn't at all surprised.

The news of the engagement was repeated when Abigail arrived, bearing pickled crab apples and an enormous tub of sugar doughnuts she'd made that morning.

"About time," Abigail exclaimed, her scrubbed little face alight with pleasure as she hugged Paige. "I told you long ago to set your sights on that handsome Dr. Baldwin."

Armand had brought his accordion, and while the women put the finishing touches to the dinner, making gravy and mashing potatoes, the strains of one lively Métis folk song after another filled the little house.

Christmas dinner was a huge success, in spite of the fact that the dressing in the goose was so peppery it made everyone sneeze.

Dennis and Tahnancoa left at dusk to ride home, but the Fletchers were staying until morning, so Paige went out to the barn with Myles when he was leaving to say a private good night as he saddled Major.

The night had turned cold, and frost gleamed on the windows. The sky was studded with faraway stars, and a half-moon was just rising over the town below them. Myles held her in his arms, and their breath puffed out above them and turned to steam.

He kissed her, deep and thorough and lingering.

"This leaving you at night is wearing me down," he grumbled. "I'm sending the commissioner a telegram in the morning saying that permission to marry is urgently requested."

"My God, Myles, he'll think I'm pregnant." She said the words without thinking, and a vivid image flashed into her mind of Myles holding Ellie on his lap tonight and making her giggle.

An old regret wormed its way into Paige's happiness. She whispered, "Do you mind terribly that we won't be able to have children of our own?"

"It's you I want, Paige." He bent his head and kissed her hard. "You're quite enough for me to handle, so don't start fretting about children. If we want some down the line, there's plenty of orphans that end up needing a home."

It was getting colder, and reluctantly he let her go and climbed on Major, leaning down to give her one last kiss.

She watched him ride off. He turned to wave at her when he reached the road that led to the fort, and she waved back and then scurried back into the warm house, shivering, silently chiding herself for being silly.

She was happy, wasn't she? Happier than she'd ever been. Her love for Myles was enough. It was foolish to have so very much and still long for what she knew couldn't ever be.

They'd made a makeshift crib for Ellie by shoving together two armchairs. Paige tiptoed in and looked at her. Ellie was on her stomach, round bottom stuck in the air, thumb plugged into her rosebud mouth.

Paige smoothed the blankets over the sleeping child, bending to press a kiss on her warm forehead, unable for one dangerous moment to stop herself from envisioning little girls with long-lashed gray eyes, and boys with black curls and their father's cleft chin.

Chapter Eighteen

Myles and Paige were married the twentieth of January, 1885, at two in the afternoon.

There'd been a blizzard the first week after Christmas, but when Paige awoke on her wedding morning and scratched away the frost on her bedroom window, the sky was periwinkle blue and sunshine sparkled like gems on the snowdrifts.

Her wedding dress hung on the wardrobe door, and she couldn't resist stroking it every time she passed. Clara had worked miracles in the short time she'd had for sewing. The dress was honey-colored taffeta, in the simple style that Paige had insisted upon. It had a simple V-neckline and close-fitting bodice that flowed gracefully into a paneled skirt. There was a long row of tiny pearl buttons up the back, and Clara had taken a few liberties with the sleeves, making them extravagantly full at the shoulder and then tapering them past the elbow into a long, narrow column that fastened on the forearm and wrist with more pearl buttons.

Somehow, Paige got through the hours until the wedding. She was far more nervous than she'd expected, and by the time Clara and Tahnancoa arrived at the house, Paige was wondering irritably why she hadn't insisted on the small civil ceremony she'd wanted in the beginning.

To her astonishment, Myles had insisted on a church wedding, with all the trimmings. "I only plan to do this once, Paige, and I don't want to rush through it. I want to have a celebration that everyone will remember. Leave the details of the party to me—we'll have it at the fort, and the mess hall will prepare the wedding supper."

It was his wedding too, Paige reminded herself. So she'd given in with good grace.

Myles had asked Dennis to be his best man, and she'd asked Clara and Tahnancoa to be her attendants, but Tahnancoa had gently refused.

"Thank you, my friend. It is a great honor to be asked, but my stomach is too big to stand with you in front of all those people," she'd demurred. "Maybe Clara will let me care for Ellie instead."

By one o'clock, Paige had bathed and donned her new underwear, slip, and the silk stockings she'd bought from the emporium.

Clara was helping Paige while Tahnancoa entertained Ellie in the kitchen.

Paige sat in front of the wavy mirror in her bedroom, trying desperately to bring some sort of order to her mass of black curling hair. She'd washed it that morning, and now it seemed impossible to tame.

"I should have had it cut long ago," she moaned. "Why hasn't someone thought yet of starting a beauty salon in Battleford?" She tugged a brush through the thick mass. "I knew it was getting too long, but I just kept tying it back out of the way, and now look at this mess. I'd give a lot for some mousse and a can of spray."

"Give me that brush." Clara, glasses perched on the end of her upturned nose, took charge, and within a few moments, Paige's hair was drawn and secured with hairpins into a high, loose knot at the crown of her head, with tendrils of curls escaping all around. Clara buttoned her into her dress, and then called Tahnancoa and Ellie in to admire the effect.

"Ooooohhh," Ellie crowed, clapping her tiny hands and rolling her eyes when she saw Paige.

The women laughed, and Paige relaxed a little.

But an hour later, entering the small church on Theo's arm, she could feel her knees shaking. She'd been collected and escorted to the church by what seemed to her an armed guard—four tall Mounties, resplendent in crimson dress uniform, had come for her in a carriage. The church was filled to overflowing. There were people standing at the back, and everywhere she looked were more crimson uniforms. There were familiar faces as well. She saw William Sweeney in a shiny black suit, and Abigail in a hat that looked as if a bird had nested on the brim.

Theo patted her hand and the organist began to play, and for a fleeting moment Paige's heart was torn apart with longing for her brother.

It should be Tony walking beside her down this aisle. . . .

But there at the alter stood Myles, ramrod straight, tall and incredibly handsome in a dress uniform embellished with gold braid, his tawny hair falling over his forehead, his gray eyes filled with light and love and admiration as he watched her come toward him.

Afterward, she remembered the moment when she said *I do,* and the moment when the minister pronounced them husband and wife. She remembered the adoring look in Myles's eyes when he bent his head and kissed her, but the rest of the ceremony seemed like a waking dream.

She floated back down the aisle on Myles's arm with the organ trumpeting the wedding march, and when the doors of the church opened, Paige could only stare in wonder.

A column of smartly uniformed mounted men, a guard of honor, sat at attention on either side of the path, horses facing one another, the steel tips of their ten-foot bamboo lances meeting in an archway under which she and Myles walked toward the decorated carriage that would take them to the fort for their wedding dinner.

Each lance bore a small pennant, red at the top and white at the bottom. Myles later explained to Paige the significance of the lances and the pennants.

"The archway of lances means that the North West Mounted have taken you under their protection because you're my wife. The pennant is a symbol from the time when lances were used in combat. Blood would run from the tip to the handle, making the lance difficult to hold, so bunting was wrapped around the tip to absorb the blood. Thus the red and white color of the pennant."

Myles didn't find anything gruesome about it, but Paige found herself wishing she'd never asked.

The elaborate dinner and the dancing that followed swallowed up the rest of the afternoon. Paige was whirled from one set of uniformed arms to the next as every member of the detachment claimed a dance with her, as well as Theo and Dennis and William Sweeney.

She was waltzing with a white-haired officer when Rob Cameron cut in and swirled her off, the top of his sandy head not quite reaching Paige's nose.

"Surgeon Baldwin's a lucky man," he said, his wide, freckled face somber, his steps just a trifle unsteady. Paige could smell whiskey on his breath.

"I trust ye'll be happy, Paige."

They'd never recaptured the easy friendship they'd shared, and Paige was sorry. "I know we will be, Rob," she said, adding impulsively, "I miss you, my friend. You must come over and visit soon."

He accepted politely, but Paige suspected he'd never really come. The waltz ended, and Rob bowed stiffly. "If ever the day comes ye need anything, ye've but to ask me, Paige," he blurted. With a clumsy half-salute, he turned away.

It was nearly dawn before Myles brought his weary bride home to the house on the hill.

He opened the front door and swept Paige into his arms, carrying her over the threshold. She clung to his neck, almost too tired to walk, her face buried in his tunic.

"It's warm in here, Myles." Her voice was filled with surprise. "Someone must have come over and restocked the fires."

"Dennis took care of all that for me." He carried her straight through to the bedroom, setting her down on the bed. A small lamp was already lit, the wick turned low.

She touched the cover and gasped. "Oh, Myles, look at this."

When she'd left that day, a worn patchwork quilt had adorned the freshly made bed. Now, the quilt was gone and in its place was a beautiful goose-down comforter, its white cotton cover hand-embroidered in bright and intricate Indian designs.

"Tahnancoa," Paige whispered, burying her face in the comforter. "She made this for us. Oh, Myles, everyone gave us such fabulous gifts today. You know, Clara sewed me a beautiful nightgown as well as this wedding dress."

"You're not about to wear it," he growled. He'd watched her every minute all afternoon, this breathtakingly beautiful

313

bride of his, and he'd seen the admiring faces of all his men as they whirled her, slender and radiant, around the dance floor.

It had been hard not to snatch her away hours ago. He'd fantasized about this moment, when at last the two of them were alone here in their own bedroom, when he could strip off her dress and claim her, once and for all, as his wife.

His fingers fumbled with the back of her dress, and impatience tinged his tone. "How the hell do these damnable buttons open, anyway? There must be fifty of the blasted things."

She shrugged. "I haven't a clue. Clara made the dress, and she fastened me into it."

He swore under his breath. "Between the nightgown and these buttons, I swear Clara's trying to preserve your virginity."

Paige giggled. "It's a bit late for that." But strangely enough, in spite of all the nights they'd lain in one another's arms, he sensed that she felt suddenly shy with him, and it touched his soul.

The back of the dress was open now, and he pressed a row of kisses along her spine. But when he tried to slip the dress off her arms, Paige presented each wrist, secured with another dozen buttons each, for him to undo.

He shook his head and muttered, "I always thought Clara Fletcher liked me." At last, the final tiny loop was undone, and he could slip the cool, smooth fabric down and off, allowing his hands to slide down her satiny skin, over her shoulders. He moved the straps of her petticoat down as well, and his eyebrows shot up when he caught sight of her new bra, flimsy and provocative, made of the same satin as the wedding dress.

He didn't comment until he'd stripped away both dress and petticoat, discovering in the process matching bikini panties and a flimsy garter belt, holding up her cream-colored silk stockings.

He looked into teasing green eyes, and noted the faint blush that rose up the slender column of her throat.

"Well," she said, just a little defensive, "I wasn't going to wear that tattered old underwear of mine to my wedding, and the emporium doesn't stock any like it, so I had Clara make me these."

Again, there was that delicious shyness in her look and her voice. "Do you—do you like them, Myles? I—" She paused and then said softly, "I sort of thought they could be my private wedding present for you." She gave a small, nervous giggle. "Clara was so scandalized when I showed her what I wanted, I thought she was going to have the vapors, but she made a good job of them after all."

"I can't imagine a finer gift." He decided he was going to buy Clara the largest box of chocolate bonbons the Hudson's Bay Company Store had in stock.

Paige's voluptuous beauty, revealed and yet concealed by the delicious underwear, took his breath away. He cupped her face in his hands and looked into her eyes, trying to convey a small part of the love and desire he felt for her.

"You are so beautiful," he whispered. "So very beautiful. I can't believe you're truly mine. My wife." He drew a shaky breath. "I love you, Paige. I'll be the best husband I know how to be. I'll love and cherish you all the days of my life."

The soft lantern light cast shadows across her skin, and he traced them with his lips, drawing her sweet fragrance into his nostrils, tasting the sweetness as his mouth traveled in leisurely paths across her lips, down over her chin, pausing at the pulse hammering in her throat.

He drew first one satin-covered nipple and then the other into his mouth, glorying in the sharp intake of her breath.

315

He searched for and found the hook that held the flimsy garment and undid it in one smooth motion.

He was getting better at this newfangled underwear, that was certain. All he'd needed was practice.

He traced the skin above the skimpy garter belt with his tongue, and with exquisite slowness tugged the tiny panties down and off. The effort of going slowly made him tremble.

When their bodies joined at last, he watched her eyes, open and heavy-lidded, search his countenance and seem to find whatever it was she was looking for. A smile tilted her lips, and he kissed it, making it his.

He called her name when he could wait no longer, and she answered with her body, finding the place he sought an instant ahead of him, drawing him with her into its glory.

The week after the wedding, Myles bought the little white house from Charlie Walker for a fair price and gave the deed to Paige as his wedding gift to her.

He moved all his belongings from the fort, and each night when he rode up to the house he marveled, This is home. I live here with my wife. And a grin would spread over his face, and unholy joy would fill his heart to bursting.

At the fort, however, there was little to smile about. Tension and unrest grew steadily as reports of Indian war drums and Métis anger intensified.

Myles had quietly begun stockpiling medicines, blankets, and quantities of dried food the previous fall, when Paige warned him about the coming rebellion.

After speaking with Dumont at Poundmaker's reserve in late September, Myles had written to the commissioner voicing his sympathy and concern for the Métis cause, warning of impending disaster should the government go on ignoring the demands of the native people and allowing their farms to be taken from them.

The only response he received was a reprimand, and a strongly worded suggestion that he mind his business and let the government mind theirs.

In December, Myles learned that Louis Riel had drawn up a bill of rights, asking in part for more liberal treatment for the Indians and free title for the land occupied by the Métis—reasonable and quite moderate requests, Myles believed.

He waited anxiously to hear of the results, and in early January, he learned that Sir John A. Macdonald had brushed these requests aside, just as he'd done all the others. Macdonald's exact words were incendiary, typical of the arrogance and disregard of the Canadian government for the native people.

"If you wait for an Indian or a half-breed to become contented," Macdonald had joked to his colleagues, "you may wait till the millennium."

But in February, as new reports of unrest filtered to the seat of government in Ottawa, Macdonald secretly ordered the Mounted Police to increase their forces at all the forts.

Of course, this secret spread like wildfire across the west. When the Métis heard that 500 more Mounties were on their way, Louis Riel assembled his men.

By late February, Myles knew beyond a doubt that the rebellion Paige had predicted was rapidly approaching, like a prairie fire sweeping across the land, threatening to destroy everything in its path. There was little to do but prepare and wait.

The second week in March, Paige was changing a burn dressing on a baby's arm one morning when a young Indian boy arrived with a message.

"Please come," it read in scrawled letters. "Tahnancoa needs you right away."

Instantly, visions of Tahnancoa in early labor, perhaps hemorrhaging, losing the child she carried and wanted so much, leaped into Paige's mind.

The baby was due in late April, Paige calculated. Surely it would survive if it were born now. Paige guessed it to be a big child; the last time she'd examined Tahnancoa was two weeks before, and the baby already seemed close to term.

Anxiety filled her as she told the boy, who said his name was Swift Runner, to sit in the kitchen and have milk and bread while she finished with the dressing. Fortunately, this was the last patient of the morning and her parlor was empty. Abigail was off on a maternity case and wasn't in this morning,

"Keep this dressing clean, change it every day, put this ointment on the burn," Paige instructed the young mother, handing her screaming baby to her and trying to curb her impatience as the woman fussed with the child.

The moment the door closed behind her, Paige turned to the boy. He looked about 15, and Paige thought he must be one of Tahnancoa's relatives from the reserve. "Do you know exactly what's wrong with Tahnancoa Quinlan?"

Naturally, he didn't know, but he was adamant that they leave right away. "Hurry," he insisted. "Big hurry. You want me saddle your horse?"

Paige accepted his offer, and he dashed out to the stables. In a frenzy, she gathered everything she could possibly think of for her medical bag, changed into her riding gear, packed an overnight bag, and scribbled a note for Myles, propping it on the table against the sugar bowl.

She forgot completely about the gun tucked in her underwear drawer.

Moments later, she was on Minnie, following the slender

figure of the Indian boy on his piebald pony out of town.

The boy was setting a rapid pace, and Paige urged Minnie into a trot. The trail still had patches of snow, but it was melting today—the sun had broken through the scattered clouds.

When the four rough-looking men on horseback appeared out of nowhere and surrounded her, Paige was mentally reviewing the problems she might encounter when at last she reached Tahnancoa, and at first she actually thought they were there to escort her the rest of the way to the Quinlan's farm.

"Bonjour, madame la docteur." The cheerful call came from a young man who rode up close beside her, then reached over and in one smooth motion snapped a lead rope to the bit on Minnie's bridle. Alarmed, Paige dug her heels into the pony's sides, trying to free herself, but the long rope held the pony fast.

"Let me go," she hollered at him. "Undo that rope this minute. Who are you, what the dickens do you think you're doing? I'm a doctor, I'm on my way to help a sick friend and I must get—" she stopped in midsentence.

Swift Runner, who was supposed to be taking her to Tahnancoa, had now joined the men, and they greeted him as one of them.

Horrified, Paige realized she'd been tricked. Horror gave way to terror.

Did they mean to murder her? Rape her? She looked at each of them. They were bearded, rough, dusty-looking men who looked as if they'd spent much time in the saddle. Besides Swift Runner, two were Indians, their long dark hair wild around their faces. The other two were half-breeds, wearing the distinctive red Métis sash.

One of the half-breed men urged his horse close to hers and lifted his hat in a gesture that might have seemed courtly under other circumstances. "Good day to you, Madame Paige." His English was good, lightly accented with his native French. "I am Urbain Langois, and this is my friend, Pierre Gervais. Please don't be afraid, we are Louis Riel's men, from Batoche. We will take you there to meet with him."

"Riel?" Paige's heart was hammering and her breath seemed stuck in her throat. "Louis Riel? But what—I don't understand. This is absolutely crazy. What does Riel want with me?"

He'd said they were taking her to Batoche. Wasn't Batoche at least a hundred miles away, somewhere to the east of Battleford?

Myles—oh, God, Myles, help me. . . .

The man shoved back his hat and studied her closely. "You are the one who traveled here from another time, no? From the years still ahead?"

"Yes, yes I did. But what—"

"You are *la docteur,* the friend of Armand LeClerc?"

"Yes, I know Armand. But what does this have to do—"

He held up a hand to quell the flow of her words. "Armand, he tells Louis all about you, from the time the police bring you to the fort. He says that you know the future, that you are a mighty shaman who cures fevers and even knows how to start a child when a woman is barren. Dumont, too, he knows you. He has heard of your powers from Poundmaker. So Louis sent us to bring you to him now. We need you, *madame docteur,* now and in the days to come."

Fear was rapidly giving way to outrage. "This is crazy, you can't just kidnap me like this. My husband will—"

"Ah, we know and respect your husband, madame, but he is one of the Mounted, he is now no longer our comrade.

He is one with the *Anglais*." He held out a hand and the other man tossed him the lead rope. He wound it around his saddle horn. "Come, now we must ride hard. Batoche, she is far from here."

Paige had no choice but to follow.

Myles lit a candle inside the back door, wondering where Paige might be. She hadn't said anything about going out when he left that morning. She'd been gone some time—he could tell because it was cold in the house. All the fires were out.

He took off his hat and undid his holster, laying it on the small table by the back door. He was tired, sick to his soul with the news that had reached the fort late that afternoon, via the telegraph wires. The news had electrified the entire detachment.

Louis Riel, with Dumont as his general, had assembled an army of Métis and Indians. He'd demanded that Major Crozier, in charge of the Mounted Police at Fort Carlton, 20 miles west of Batoche, surrender his government supplies and arms. Crozier had, of course, refused.

It was nothing less than a declaration of war, and Myles knew that at any moment there would be bloodshed. He wanted to talk it all over with Paige; he needed the comfort of her knowledge tonight—the assurance that there would come a time when the fighting ended, and peace would come again to the prairies.

It irritated him that she was gone, just when he most needed her. Where the hell was she?

He walked across to the table and took the glass chimney from the lamp and lit it, adjusting the wick, replacing the glass and blowing out the candle when the lamp's soft glow illuminated the room.

There was a note behind the sugar bowl, and he lifted it

and held it in the lamplight so he could read it.

"Dearest Myles, Tahnancoa may be miscarrying. Have gone to her, will be home soonest—love you, Paige."

Myles stared at the note, aghast. As its ramifications became clear, a fist seemed to reach into his chest and squeeze his heart.

Dennis had been at the fort late that very afternoon, making the weekly delivery of beef. Myles had asked after Tahnancoa.

"She's feeling just fine," Dennis had replied with a grin. "Big as a house, gonna get us a real bruiser of a boy, I reckon."

If Tahnancoa wasn't ill, then who had lured Paige away?

Myles ran to the examining room. Paige always marked down in a daily ledger what patients she treated. The book was lying open on the narrow shelf beside the table.

"Ten A.M., baby Fryer, burned arm."

It was the final entry. Myles racked his brain, trying to remember if he knew anyone by the name of Fryer. If the mother had still been here when the messenger came—

He buttoned his tunic, strapped his gun on, and just before he raced out the door, thought to check on the weapon he'd insisted Paige take along when she rode alone.

He opened the drawer where she kept it. It lay there, nestled in her lacy clothing.

It took precious moments to saddle Major again, and all the while Myles's brain worked frantically.

Charlie Walker, as factor at the Hudson's Bay Company store, would know where the Fryers lived. Charlie knew everyone.

It took more than an hour to track down the Fryers' homestead, a good ten miles out of town. Myles lost the trail twice in the darkness, and he had to summon every ounce of patience to keep from screaming when at last he talked to the pretty young mother. Wide-eyed and nervous, it took her precious long moments to stammer out the story of the Indian boy and the urgent message.

It was nearing midnight, black dark and cold, when Myles galloped back to the fort. He cursed at the sentry who challenged him and raced into the hospital.

He'd need a tracker, and Armand LeClerc was the best. Armand would help find the trail; he idolized Paige.

They'd have to wait for dawn, and then it might still be possible for Armand to discover how many there were, what direction they'd taken.

But Armand wasn't around. Myles burst into the small room at the back of the wards where the old Métis had always slept, but it was empty. Armand's clothes, bedroll, and rifle were missing, and with a sick feeling in his gut, Myles knew exactly where the old man was.

Armand had gone to join Riel's army.

Chapter Nineteen

By forenoon of the third day of constant riding, Paige was exhausted. The skin on her legs and buttocks was rubbed raw from the unaccustomed hours in the saddle, and it burned like fire with each new step Minnie took. There'd been no chance to bathe, and she felt filthy.

The men were pushing hard to get back to Batoche, and they rode from early morning until darkness forced a stop.

Physically, Paige was utterly miserable, but emotionally, she was numb. For the first two days, she'd agonized over Myles, wondering what he'd do when he found her gone, cursing herself for being such a gullible fool and racing off with the boy called Swift Runner. But as her physical exhaustion took over, the emotional turmoil became secondary.

Now, all she could think of was finishing this endless ride, reaching someplace where she could have a bath, where there was a bed to sleep in instead of a thin bedroll on hard-packed, cold earth, something to eat besides the revolting pemmican and rock-hard jerky which, along with bitter boiled tea and dried-out bannock, was all the men seemed to carry in the way of food.

Paige was no longer afraid of them—they'd treated her respectfully and done what little they could to make her more comfortable. They'd even brought along a thick buffalo hide on which to spread her bedroll at night, and they stopped every few hours to let her rest a few minutes and, on legs that would hardly carry her, head for whatever shelter there was to go to the bathroom.

In spite of her physical misery, she could hardly stay awake this morning. Her head nodded, and several times she came near falling off Minnie's back. The country had changed gradually during the long ride. Today they rode through wooded areas where the snow was still deep, and the horses had to work hard at breaking a path.

"Madame, we are nearly there." Pierre's announcement brought her jerking awake.

Ahead was a wide river, the South Saskatchewan, and on the other side Paige could see a few log cabins and two larger houses.

The men, delighted to be nearing home, urged their horses into a trot, and in a short while, they'd reached the spot among the poplar and aspen bluffs along the riverbank that the men called Gabriel's Crossing. Here, they informed Paige, Dumont operated a free ferry. Batoche was ten miles away.

The man who brought the ferry over to collect them wasn't Dumont, however. He called to Paige's captors long before the ferry drew close enough for them to board, his voice excited and his rapid French indecipherable to Paige. There were wild cheers from Urbain and Pierre, who swiftly translated whatever he'd said for the Indians.

Whatever the news was, it caused pandemonium among the men. They cheered and leaped about, all but upsetting

325

the flat-bottomed scow being used as a ferry.

"What is it? What's going on?" Paige tugged at Pierre's sleeve. "What did he say?"

"Riel and Dumont have attacked the trading posts and seized the ammunition we need for our cause. We are going to teach those damned *Anglais* a lesson now."

Paige gripped the side of the ferry, barely able to stand erect after the hours she'd spent on horseback. She shivered in the cold breeze coming from the river. Utter weariness and a feeling of unreality made her giddy. She began to giggle and couldn't stop, even though the men were staring at her and frowning.

Her history teacher would have been so impressed. Here she was in Batoche, in 1885, and it looked at though she was about to find herself in the exact middle of the Riel Rebellion. Professor Wood would be ecstatic if he knew.

Her laughter soon turned to tears she couldn't control. The men were unnerved by her collapse. They held a spirited discussion and when the scow reached the far side of the river, they hurried her over to a large, two-story log house.

A short, thin woman, her cheeks flushed scarlet, her graying dark hair braided and wound around her head in a coronet, came to the door. She was wearing a dark dress and a white apron, and what Paige noticed was how clean she looked. The men said something to her, obviously about Paige.

Paige, mortified by her tears but unable to stop, was still sobbing. The little woman clucked her tongue, put her arm around her, and led her gently inside the warm house. She turned to let loose a volley of angry French at the shamefaced men hovering on the porch. She shut the door on them and then conducted Paige into a large kitchen and sat her down on a chair, fishing inside the neckline of her dress and drawing out a large white handkerchief.

"Here, madame, wipe your eyes," she instructed in a gentle tone. "I am Madeleine Dumont, Gabriel's wife," she added. Her English was accented but good. She poured a cup of steaming coffee from an enamel pot on the back of the stove, added milk and a generous scoop of sugar, and handed it to Paige. From a pot, she ladeled out a bowl of thick soup.

"Drink, eat," she ordered. "It will warm you, and then we will fill the tub for a bath."

Famished, Paige spooned up the soup, swallowing between sobs that wouldn't quit. After a moment, the delicious warmth of the room and the comfort of the hot food allowed her to gain some control. She blew her nose and wiped her eyes on Madeleine's pristine handkerchief. The white cotton was smeared with dirt from her face and Paige realized her hands were filthy as well. Her hair felt as though it was caked with dirt, and the rest of her body felt itchy. She must look wrecked—she certainly felt it.

"Thank you so much, Madeleine," she choked out. "Lord, I need to wash. My name is—" she began, but Madeleine shook her head, motioning to the bowl.

"Hush now, and eat. I know who you are, *Madame Docteur*. We all know; Armand has spoken of you. Those stupid men have worn you out; you must eat and regain your strength. Then you can bathe and rest."

It sounded like heaven. For the first time in days, Paige was warm. There was good-tasting food, and the promise of hot water and soap, and even a bed with sheets and a pillow.

Those simple, everyday comforts now seemed like the most lavish of luxuries, and she couldn't think beyond them.

She relaxed slowly, surrendering herself to Madeleine's motherly care.

The news of Paige's disappearance traveled swiftly through the fort that first night, and just before dawn the next morning, Rob Cameron searched out Myles.

"Sir, I'm coming with ye. I want to help ye find her. I hunted with Armand last summer, and he taught me a fair bit about scouting and reading sign."

Myles looked at the young Scot and gratitude filled him. He was going to need help, and he knew that with the alarming reports now coming steadily over the telegraph wires concerning the uprising of the Métis and the Indians, few men could be spared to search for Paige.

He told Rob the few details he'd gathered. "I believe Paige and this Indian boy must have at least started towards the Quinlans' farm. We'll ride out that way as soon as dawn breaks."

Myles had paced through the hospital ward all night long, unable to sleep or even to sit. It was an enormous relief when at last the inky blackness outside the window slowly began to turn gray, and he and Rob could saddle their horses, load the saddlebags with the provisions Myles had gathered, and ride.

Because of the warm weather, the ground had thawed slightly, and Rob was able to easily pick out the marks of the unshod Indian pony once the town was behind them. He followed the tracks for a few miles, and then, near a small grove of willows, he drew his horse up and dismounted.

He walked around for some time, intent on the marks on the earth, and Myles tried to curb his impatience.

"Several other horses joined them right here." Rob's face was somber when at last he spoke. "They all veered off the trail and started riding due east. Two of the horses were shod, but I'd guess the others were Indian ponies."

Sick at heart, Myles turned Major toward the eastern horizon.

Their progress was sporadic, because Rob stopped often to make certain they were still on the trail. They'd been riding about two hours when the smell of smoke and the sound of guns drifted to them on the chill air.

"It's coming from just over that hill," Myles guessed. The flat prairie had given way to rolling hills and clumps of trees.

Myles and Rob urged their horses to a gallop and crested the hillside. The hill dropped away on the other side to a flat plain, and a settler had built a house and some outbuildings in a small grove of trees at the base of the hillside.

Myles stared down, hardly able to believe his eyes at the horrifying spectacle taking place on the homestead. It was immediately apparent that the settler and his family were in mortal danger.

Half a dozen Indians in war paint, whooping and firing their rifles from the back of ponies, were dodging in and out of the grove of small poplars that surrounded the log house. With fiery arrows, they'd set fire to the tar-paper roof. It was burning fiercely, and even as Myles and Rob gaped in horror, the door of the cabin burst open and a man with a rifle appeared, desperately trying to provide cover for the woman clutching two small children who cowered behind him. The roof was about to cave in, and they had to get out.

Quickly, Myles motioned to Rob to ride along the crest of the hillside and come down toward the Indians from a different angle, making it appear that there were more than just the two of them. As far as he could tell, the Indians weren't yet aware of their presence, although he and Rob were clearly outlined against the morning sky.

Myles drew his loaded rifle from the scabbard beside his saddle and aimed at one of the Indians. That bullet missed, but a second one sent an Indian careening from his horse, drawing the attention of the others and alerting them to his presence.

The marauders now turned their attention to Myles, and he urged Major into a gallop, riding low and dodging until he could throw himself from Major's back and take cover behind some low bushes.

The settler had shot one Indian, but his gun was now out of bullets, and he was desperately trying to reload. Myles did his best to provide cover and draw the Indians' aim toward himself, but even as he fired twice in rapid succession, Myles saw a whooping brave, hanging low on his horse's neck, head toward the burning building, raise his gun, draw aim, and fire.

The man in the doorway crumpled and fell. The Indian raised his gun again, aiming at the woman, now trying to run toward the shelter of a pole barn with one child clutched tight to her body, a second being half-dragged along by the hand.

Rob suddenly appeared from the opposite direction, riding at full gallop into the midst of the fighting, his revolver in his hand. Before the Indian could pull the trigger, Rob had shot him, but he was now in the very midst of the remaining three Indians, his scarlet tunic an obvious target.

"Rob, no, get back!" Myles wasn't aware he'd shouted.

Rifles roared, and almost instantaneously, Myles saw Rob topple from his saddle, his body sprawling facedown in the muddy farmyard.

Myles was on his feet now, oblivious to the target he provided. His rifle was out of bullets and he was firing his revolver, one shot after the other, desperately trying to hit the crazed Indian who, tomahawk in hand, was now racing his mount toward the woman and children, almost at the doorway of the barn.

The tomahawk sliced down through the woman's skull even as one of Myles's bullets found its mark. The woman fell to the ground and the child she was holding tumbled like a rag doll from her arms.

There were only two Indians left, and with bloodcurdling whoops they came riding straight up the incline toward Myles, rifles ready.

He took careful aim, aware that he was almost out of bullets. He squeezed the trigger, and the man he'd aimed at screamed and went flying from his horse. Myles tried to fire again at the remaining Indian galloping at full speed toward him, but his gun was empty. He dove behind Major as the screaming brave took aim and fired, and then disappeared over the crest of the hill.

The sudden silence was broken only by the sound of a child's hysterical crying. Myles got to his feet just as Major's forelegs gave under him, and the huge animal slowly toppled to the ground. The big horse was dead.

Quickly, Myles reloaded his revolver, aware every second that the Indian could return. He hurried over to where he'd dropped the rifle and reloaded it as well, and then ran down to the farmyard.

Bodies lay scattered everywhere. The Indians were all dead, and it was obvious the homesteader was as well, but Myles wasn't sure about Rob. Taking him by the sides of his tunic, just below the armpits, Myles dragged him quickly toward the barn, depositing him just inside the door. He then raced back outside for the children.

The boy was sitting in the dust, dazed and silent, but the little girl was clutching her mother's body and screaming at the top of her lungs.

Bobby Hutchinson

Myles scooped them up in his arms and hurried back into the shelter of the barn. The girl wailed and fought him like a small, fierce animal, struggling to go back to her mother. Myles was forced to pinion her small, squirming body against his shoulder while he scanned the hill. There was no sign of the Indian returning. Myles knelt beside Rob and was immediately aware that the young constable was dead.

His reckless bravery had saved the lives of the girl in Myles's arms and the little boy still crouched silently in the corner where Myles had set him. Looking at the freckled, young face of the constable, Myles could only feel an overwhelming rage at the circumstances that had brought Rob Cameron here to die.

It had been years since Indians were on the warpath, murdering settlers. There was no doubt in his mind that this tragedy was linked to the larger uprising of the Métis.

Myles stood in the doorway of the barn for a long time, watching and waiting, but there was no sign of the Indian returning, and at last the little girl quieted, her screams giving way to shuddering sobs against Myles's shoulder. The house was now engulfed in flames, the roaring of the fire the only sound in the sudden silence of the farmyard. All the dead Indians' horses and Rob's mount as well had bolted. A few chickens clucked from a fenced enclosure some distance away, but there was no sign of any other livestock.

Myles walked over to the boy and squatted down to the child's level. "What's your name, son?"

The boy's brown eyes were glassy with shock, and he was sitting with his arms wrapped tight around his legs. He stared at Myles, his throat convulsing as he tried to answer.

"Da-Danny."

"And what's your sister's name?"

"Mis-Missy."

"Well, Danny, you're a big, strong boy. How old are you anyway?"

"Si-six. Missy's only three." He gulped hard and then said in a quavery voice, "Are you a Mountie?"

Myles nodded. "I am, but I'm also a doctor."

Danny thought that over. "Should I call you Doc?"

"My name's Myles, but sure, you call me Doc. You know, son, you and I are gonna have to take care of Missy, us being men and all. You think you can help me out right now by sitting down here on this pile of hay and holding on to her for a few minutes? There's some things I've got to do outside."

Danny got to his feet and moved to the place Myles indicated, and Myles transferred the chubby little girl, hardly more than a baby, to her brother's arms. She turned her face into his dirty flannel shirt, taking a fistful of the cloth in her hand, and began to cry again, a soft and hopeless sound. She had a long, curling mop of brown hair, the same kind of wild, unmanageable curls Paige had.

Myles had to swallow hard, looking at the two children.

"She wants Ma." Danny's voice was desolate.

"I'm sorrier than I can say about what happened to your folks, Danny." Myles tousled the boy's sandy hair, wishing to God he could have somehow saved Dan's parents.

"Sometimes there doesn't seem much sense to these things, does there?" Myles thought of Paige, and had to swallow hard before he could summon up a reassuring wink for the wide-eyed boy cradling his sister. "Danny, I'm going to make certain those Indians are gone, so I've got to leave you alone with Missy for a few minutes in here. But I'll be right back, so you just stay put. All right, son?"

Danny nodded, and Myles slipped out the door of the

barn, moving from one bit of cover to the next. He made a full circuit of the barn and surrounding area. There was no sign of anyone.

He went from one body to the next and rapidly picked up guns and any ammunition he could see and put them inside the door of the barn. He'd find a safe hiding place for them later.

Back outside, he had neither the time nor the energy to dig graves, but mindful of the children, he carried the bodies of their parents over to a small shed that housed a buggy and some tools, and laid them on the floor. He went back into the barn and heaved Rob's body up and over his shoulder, putting him with the others in the shed. He shut his eyes and murmured a quick prayer, then went out and closed the door tight, bracing it with a rock.

He left the Indians lying where they'd fallen.

There was a ladder propped against the back of the barn, and he carried it around to the front and propped it against the wall. Climbing up it, he realized he could see quite a distance in three directions. There was no sign of any living thing, including Rob's horse.

He climbed down and went back inside. Missy had fallen asleep in her brother's arms, but both children were shivering in the chill air. They had no coats on, and only Danny wore boots. Missy was barefoot.

Myles slipped his bloodstained tunic off and wrapped it around the little girl, hollowing out a bed for her in the hay.

"We're gonna let Missy have a nap in here. You and I have work to do." He took Danny's hand and led him outside.

The boy looked immediately to where his parents had fallen.

"I put your ma and pa in the shed over there," Myles

explained gently. Danny's eyes filled with tears, but he nodded.

"I need your help, son. My horse got shot, and I have to go up the hill a ways and get my saddle and things. See, one of the first rules a policeman learns is never to leave any equipment for the enemy. Now I'll be right up there." Myles pointed to where Major lay. "I want you to climb up this ladder and keep a good eye out for anything moving. If you see anything at all, you holler to me, get down fast, and run in the barn."

Danny scrambled up the ladder, agile as a cat. Myles ran up the hillside. Major lay on his side, and it took a great deal of effort to release the saddle from underneath the horse's body. Myles had to use his knife and cut away the stirrup that was trapped under Major's side before he could heave it free.

He placed a hand on the horse's head in a final good-bye. Major had been a fine, faithful mount.

He carried saddle, saddlebags, medical bag, and bedroll down the hill again.

"You're a good sentry, son." Danny came down the ladder and helped carry some of the load into the barn.

Myles opened up his bedroll and wrapped it around Missy, putting his tunic back on. He took out the buckskin coat he carried in his saddlebags and held it for Danny.

"Best put this on so you don't freeze."

Danny shoved his arms into the sleeves. They hung down a good eight inches over his fingers. Myles wrapped the coat around the boy and used the tie from his bedroll as a belt. He turned the sleeves up as much as possible.

Myles felt as if he'd been here for endless hours already, but he knew it was only a couple of hours past noon. His brain flew from one thing to the next, trying to figure out a plan that might save his own life and those of the two children.

He had no doubt that sooner or later, the Indians would return to collect their dead. Somehow, he had to get these children out of here and back to the fort as fast as possible. If there'd been six rampaging Indians on the warpath, chances were good there were many more out there.

In daylight, Myles and the children would be easy targets on the open prairie. Their only chance for survival was to travel at night—but nights were still icy cold, and Myles was without a horse. On foot, the children might die of exposure before they ever reached the fort. Silently, Myles cursed Rob's mount—the horse was young and spooky, and there was little chance of it coming back the way Major would have done in similar circumstances.

Making his way back to the fort on foot with two small children in the black of night was next to impossible. He desperately needed a means of transportation.

"Danny, does your daddy have any horses?"

Danny nodded proudly. "We got Cody, he's our saddle horse, and we got Trooper and Buck, they're workhorses."

The horses had undoubtedly bolted because of the fire, along with Rob's mount and the Indian ponies. Chances were good that the Indian that escaped had rounded them up and taken them off with him.

"Were they all in the barn last night?"

"Cody was, but Pa keeps Trooper and Buck over in the back pasture." Tears flooded Danny's eyes again when he spoke of his father, and he swiped at them with the back of one grubby hand. "Pa used to keep 'em there," he corrected forlornly.

"Where would that be?" For the first time, Myles felt a faint stab of hope. Maybe the workhorses were still there.

"Not far. Just over beside the coulee."

Myles glanced at the sleeping baby. Her thumb was stuck in her mouth, and she was deeply asleep. He hated leaving her alone, but taking her with him would slow him down and make it almost impossible to catch the horses—if they were still there.

"We're gonna let Missy stay here and sleep and we'll hurry and see if we can find the horses." Myles filled an old tin pail with oats and grabbed a bridle, and he and Danny hurried off.

The path led through trees, and Myles was grateful for the cover, moving cautiously and as quickly as he dared with the boy stumbling along beside him, tripping on the too long coat, until they reached an open pasture beside a pool of stagnant water, still half frozen over.

"There's Trooper. Hey, Trooper, over here." Excited, Danny forgot Myles's admonition to be quiet, and the horse heard his voice and came trotting toward them. In a matter of seconds, Myles had the bridle over his ears. There was no sign of the other horse, and Myles assumed it had fled along with the others. Slinging Danny up on the horse, they started back.

Myles was relived to find that Missy hadn't stirred. He put Trooper in one of the stalls and forked hay to him, which started him thinking about food for himself and the children. He took dried biscuits and jerky from his bags and he and Danny chewed on them.

Again Myles cursed the loss of Rob's horse. Because of his medical bag, Rob had been carrying the largest portion of their rations on his mount. The cabin and whatever supplies had been in it were burned to the ground. Myles thought a moment and then an idea occurred to him.

"Did your ma have a root cellar, Danny?"

"Yup, I'll show you where."

The boy led Myles around the back of the cabin to a spot

by the hillside where bushes grew thick, partly masking double doors flush with the earth that marked the entrance to the cool, dark storehouse.

Myles opened the doors and stepped inside, and a wave of relief poured through him. At least the children wouldn't go hungry. Inside were slabs of dried beef, jars of preserved crab apples, strings of dried berries. Apples, shriveled and dried out, were in a bushel basket along with potatoes and turnips packed in sand.

"We're gonna make a big stew for dinner, Dan."

He remembered seeing an iron pot in the ashes of the cabin fire. A hot meal would help them all survive the cold, difficult night ahead—portions of the cabin were still burning. He could use the embers to cook over.

"You know how to cook, Doc?" Danny sounded doubtful, and Myles gave him a teasing look.

"Mounties have to learn how to do most everything, don't you know that?"

"Do you and your wife got kids at home like me and Missy? 'Cause if you don't, maybe we could come and be your kids."

Myles had to swallow the lump in his throat. "That's a fine offer, young man. We'll discuss it later, but right now I don't want you worrying about where you and Missy will end up, because I promise you I'll make certain you get a place where you're together and happy."

The baby slept, and when she awakened, she sat huddled inside the bedroll, watching with big dark eyes as Myles and Danny prepared a meal.

By the time they'd all eaten, it was dusk. Myles saddled Trooper and lifted Danny up on his broad back, handing him Missy, rolled tightly into the bedroll. He swung up himself, making certain his rifle was easily available, his revolver loaded and ready on his hip.

It had grown much colder as soon as evening came. It felt like snow. If they hit a bad snowstorm ... With an effort, Myles put the thought out of his mind.

He took Missy from Danny and cradled her for warmth between the boy's body and his own and clucked to the horse.

With luck, they'd reach the fort by dawn.

Somewhere out here were Paige's captors, Myles knew, heading further east if the tracks Rob had found were the right ones.

By now the trail was cold, and with every mile he traveled toward the fort, Myles was leaving her further and further behind.

Was she even still alive, or had they left her body somewhere out on the prairie, beaten, raped, tortured ... ?

Unbearable pain gnawed at his heart. He loved her more than life itself, and he'd lost her.

He'd failed her.

Paige, my darling, forgive me.

Chapter Twenty

With every mile they traveled, the temperature seemed to drop another degree.

It began to rain, and the rain became sleet and then snow.

Cold and wet even inside her blanket cocoon, Missy sobbed quietly for a time, but Danny didn't once complain.

The weather made the darkness almost impenetrable, and Myles could only hope that he was heading in the right direction.

At some point, the snow stopped and the sky cleared a little. Visibility improved. Myles, his arms clamped around the two groggy children, struggled to stay awake himself as the night progressed and the horse's steady, slow gait became dangerously hypnotic.

Once, far off to the west, he saw flames shooting skyward from some settler's cabin burning, and from then on he was wide-awake and cautious, looking out for any sign of an Indian encampment.

A wind sprang up before dawn, and Myles began to wonder if Danny and Missy would survive the bitter cold. Both children were shuddering, even though he held them against his body and tried to protect them from the worst of the icy wind.

Relief spilled through him when, shortly after dawn, he saw the first sign of light from houses in Battleford.

"Almost there, young ones," he murmured. "Just hold on, and we'll soon have you fed and in some dry, warm clothes."

Danny woke from his doze and sat up straighter, looking in the direction Myles indicated.

They'd ridden another quarter hour when the boy said, "It looks like somethin's on fire over there, Doc."

Myles had already pulled Trooper to a standstill. He stared, aghast, at the flames shooting high above the town, and his heart sank.

It could mean only one thing.

Just as Paige had predicted, Battleford was under siege.

Myles circled far around the town, approaching the stockade from the back. It added two hours to the trip, and it was forenoon and snowing again by the time the wide gates swung far enough open so that Trooper could slip through. The fort was filled to overflowing with settlers' horses and wagons.

"Find someone to take care of these children right away," Myles ordered as he handed Missy and Danny down from the horse and into the arms of a constable. He climbed stiffly down himself. "They need—"

"I'll take them, Myles." Carrying blankets, Clara Fletcher came running over and took Missy. She wrapped the child in one blanket and thrust the other at the constable who still held Danny.

"A policeman rode out early this morning and told us a

341

war party was murdering settlers. We came in to the fort right away, and I just heard about Paige being missing." She cradled the child against her. "You didn't find her?" Clara's voice was fearful.

Myles could only shake his head, and Clara, biting her lip hard to keep from crying, hurried the children away.

In Batoche, the small group of Métis women gathered in the kitchen tried not to flinch at the intermittent sound of guns and cannon fire, but Paige knew they were every bit as nervous and frightened as she was herself. Several of them were silently praying, their lips moving as they worked.

Paige's heart ached for them. They, as well as she, had so much at stake; their sons and husbands and brothers were in the middle of the fighting.

Myles was a surgeon, and if there was fighting she knew he'd be out on some battlefield just as these women's loved ones were right now. Today, their men were in danger of being blown to bits by the cannons the English had brought in to fight the Métis army.

Lord, but she missed Myles. Not an hour passed that she didn't think of him, long for him. She'd thought numerous times of trying to escape, but she knew she could never make her way alone across the hundred rugged miles that separated Batoche and Battleford.

Besides the terrain, she knew there were now Indian uprisings everywhere. The war drums throbbed, and everyone with white skin was at risk. There had been several horrifying accounts of white settlers attacked and murdered by the Indians.

"Drink this, Gigette, it will settle your stomach." Madeleine handed a potion she'd just mixed up to Marguerite, Riel's very pregnant young wife.

Marguerite—everyone affectionately called her Gigette—

342

had already bolted twice for the outhouse, nauseated from the tension created by the battle taking place less than 20 miles away.

Her baby was due in another month, and Madeleine was concerned about the nausea. Childless herself, Madeleine was fond godmother to dozens of the village's children.

"Gigette, it's not good to strain so at this stage, the *petit enfant* needs to spend these last few weeks safe inside you, is that not so, *madame la docteur?*" Madeleine smiled at Paige, her plain, dark features revealing the affection that had sprung up between the two women in the month since Paige's arrival at her door.

Madeleine had never once treated her as a prisoner. Rather, the older woman acted more like the loving mother Paige had never had.

Paige managed a reassuring smile in return, even though she was seriously concerned about Gigette's baby. She was fairly certain that Gigette, Madeleine, and several of the other Métis women had pulmonary tuberculosis, as well as some of the children playing quietly in another part of the house.

She'd done what little she could for them, educating them about the disease, stressing the need for healthy food, plenty of rest, fresh air, and most of all, the meticulous sterilizing of all dishes and utensils used by the affected person to prevent the bacteria from spreading.

Yet even as she listed the treatments, she realized how impossible it was for these poor people to abide by her suggestions; already, many of them had lost their homes to the invading army, and food was in dangerously short supply.

It made Paige furious to hear of houses burned and looted, food supplies stolen, possessions taken. In her opinion, the English army had a great deal to answer for in its treatment of the Métis homesteads.

The familiar feelings of frustration and helplessness haunted Paige, but there was absolutely nothing else she could do for the sick Métis women and children—antituberculous drugs were still a long way in the future.

"It's best if you can go full term, all right," she agreed now with a sorry attempt at a smile.

The smile was difficult for several reasons—her concern over the battle, Gigette's pregnancy, and also the fact that her own stomach was anything but stable this morning. But then, it hadn't been good for the past three weeks.

She wondered if perhaps there was a virus going around, causing the nausea from which she and Gigette seemed to be suffering.

The other women hadn't been affected, however. They moved efficiently around the table and the stove, stirring pots and kneading dough, their faces somber.

The kitchen was overly warm, filled with the smells of bread baking and beans cooking, smells which should have been pleasant, and instead made Paige's stomach heave.

For the past several weeks, Madeleine Dumont had gathered the women together every day like this in order to prepare whatever food they could devise, tear sheets into bandages, wash and mend warm clothing for the ragtag group of soldiers her husband had organized into an army.

For the women, the waiting was unbearable. Working together this way made it marginally easier.

The battle taking place today wasn't the first the women had waited through. Since Paige's arrival in Batoche, she'd treated more battle wounds than she could count, including a gaping four-inch gash in Gabriel Dumont's forehead which she'd had to stitch up without benefit of anesthetic—the meager supply of chloroform she'd brought with her was being hoarded for the worst of emergencies.

Gabriel had borne the pain in silence, with stoic bravery. Paige had never encountered men as physically tough as these Métis.

The wounds she'd treated were the results of skirmishes the Métis had with the English they considered their enemy. Paige had watched, sickened, as the men carried home their dead comrades from these encounters—already, six men and a boy had died, and the conflict seemed only to be accelerating.

The battle today was taking place barely 20 miles away, at a gully called Fish Creek, and Paige knew this was much more than a skirmish. The English army was advancing on the town of Batoche, and Dumont, with the Indian and Métis volunteers who had been pouring into town, was attempting to stop them.

She must check her meager medical supplies and get the women to cut and sterilize more dressings as soon as this debilitating nausea passed.

For a week now, scouts had arrived at the big white house in Batoche where the Dumonts and Paige were staying with Riel and his family.

"The English have gathered an army," the scouts reported fearfully. "It is said they have five thousand men, nine cannons, and a new weapon called a Gatling gun which shoots twelve hundred bullets a minute. They are even now marching across the prairie toward Batoche."

Gabriel and Louis listened without comment, and when the scouts were gone, they argued late into the night.

Paige had come to know Gabriel Dumont and Louis Riel. The two men made no effort to be secretive about their plans, and consequently Paige easily overheard the battle plans and strategies they argued about constantly.

The two strong leaders didn't agree at all with one another.

345

Dumont felt the only hope the Métis had was in guerrilla-type attacks, based on Indian methods. The Métis, masterful hunters of buffalo, knew the terrain intimately, and knew how to disappear into it. The approaching army, purportedly led by some aging retired British general, was unfamiliar with both Indian tactics and the rugged terrain. Despite their overwhelming numbers, Gabriel felt they could be defeated.

Riel, a mystic who put his faith in God and prayers and was squeamish about battles, refused to consider this type of warfare.

"We may be in danger of firing on our French-Canadian friends among the troops," he told Gabriel.

"But they have joined with the English to kill us, Louis," Gabriel roared in frustration.

"They are still our brothers," Riel insisted with a twisted sort of logic that eluded even Paige. "I have prayed to God. We must wait until the soldiers attack us. Then, with God's help, we will win."

Riel was a fascinating man, a brooding, serious dreamer who never seemed to sleep. Paige had heard him pacing at all hours of the night.

She had trouble sleeping herself. Her loneliness, her fear, and her longing for Myles were strongest at night. Missing him was a constant ache inside of her, and in the darkness she couldn't help but wonder if she'd ever see him again. Reason told her she'd be lucky to come through the rebellion alive.

Although she knew the Métis would never deliberately harm her, she also knew from her history lectures that there would be a fierce battle right here at Batoche, that the Métis would lose, and that there would be many fatalities.

Tired, but unable to sleep, she lit a candle and went to the kitchen one night to warm some milk. She found Louis sitting at the kitchen table composing a speech. His hair was rumpled, his handsome, somber face lined with fatigue. He smiled at her.

"Ahh, madame. Sit down, tell me what you think of this." He read her a rousing speech he'd written while she warmed two cups of milk, handing him one, praising his words honestly; he was a gifted orator.

"Please, Louis, can't you tell me what's happening at Battleford? You know my husband is there."

He sipped his milk, and for long moments she didn't think he was going to answer. Then he sighed and said, "Our brothers, the Cree, have joined the Assiniboin. The ways of the Indians are not our ways. Battleford is under siege by the Indians."

God help her, she'd known. She'd told Myles it would happen, but it didn't make it easier to bear. Tears filled her eyes, and Louis silently reached across and patted her hand.

She burst out, "Why can't you stop this now, Louis? You have the power to stop it. Believe me, it's only going to get worse. There are so few of you, you must know that in the end you can't win. Give up now, before it becomes a full-blown tragedy."

She tensed, expecting him to explode, to roar at her with all the passion she'd heard in his voice when he addressed his faithful followers.

Instead, he smiled a sad smile and shook his head. "I have prayed," he said simply. "And you and I both know there is no other way."

Since her arrival in Batoche, Riel had talked to her many times, asking her about the life she'd had in the future, about exactly how she'd come to travel through time. He asked repeatedly about her knowledge of the rebellion and its outcome. Paige had always been honest with him, repeating the scanty facts she remembered, always terrified that he'd want to know his own fate.

To her immense relief, he didn't ask. Paige had a feeling he knew.

Instead, he'd said with a quizzical smile, "So how did your people in that time view this rebellion of ours, this struggle of the native people of Canada against a government that wouldn't listen?"

She told him that he was regarded as a hero in her time, and that had pleased him a great deal. She told him about the claims of native people in the late 1900s, the slow but successful way in which they were reclaiming their heritage.

"Who would have believed," he said in a wondering tone, "that it would take so long?" He looked at her, and she felt as though his burning black gaze seared her with its passion. "And yet, in the eye of God, a day is the same as a century. You see, madame, why it is I can't stop this now. For their sake, all those relatives in some future time, it must go on. It is my destiny."

Paige had no answer.

Today, Gigette told the women proudly that Louis was praying for the men engaged in battle, that he'd begun long before daybreak. He stood in front of the church in the cold, sleeting rain, a short distance away from the house where the women worked, his arms spread wide in the shape of a cross, his face lifted to the gray and lowering sky. He stood unmoving hour after hour, and when his arms tired and threatened to drop, friends came forward to hold them up for him.

The guns boomed and the cannons roared hour after hour. Louis Riel prayed, and the women used what little stores they had left to prepare a kind of stew while they waited.

Late in the afternoon, two wounded men were brought

into the room Paige had set up as a surgery. The women gathered around to help, but also to hear the news of the battle. The wounds were not life-threatening—one man had a bullet in his shoulder, the other in his thigh.

"Gabriel set the grass on fire; you should have seen the *Anglais* run when the smoke and flames came at them," one of the men reported, trying to chuckle even as Paige cut away the tattered skin around his wound. "It was a great victory," he gasped, his face chalky. "Gabriel had only a hundred and fifty soldiers, and there were hundreds of the *Anglais,* and still we won."

One of the men who'd carried the injured took up the story. "Gabriel told us to go under cover of the smoke and pick up ammunition and arms they left in their flight. We shouted and sang, so they would think there were many more of us than there were."

"How many of our men died?" Madeleine was the only one brave enough to ask the question, and the room was silent with dread as the men looked at one another and then away.

"Five, at last count."

"Who?" The whispered question came from Amelie, recently married to the boy she loved. She pressed a trembling hand over her mouth, her eyes huge with terror. "Please, who?"

"I think Isadore Theilbault was the only one from Batoche."

Isadore was a bachelor, and Paige saw the guilty relief on the faces of the women. "One was Indian, and two were Métis from Montana. The other was the old man, Armand LeClerc."

"Armand?" The suture she was holding slipped from Paige's fingers. She knew it was partly Armand's fault that she'd been abducted and brought here, but she couldn't bring herself to blame the old man. She could only remember how kind he'd been to her when she first arrived at Battleford, and how he'd planted and tended her garden, her flowers, all summer long.

Tears blurred her eyes and she swiped them away with her sleeve so she could see to sew up the incision she'd made to remove the bullet.

"May God bless and keep them all," Madeleine murmured, crossing herself. The other women followed suit.

When the tired soldiers came back to the village later that night, they were exultant. The women distributed the meager food, and Paige treated minor injuries, but no more bullet wounds.

"I attribute our success to Riel's prayers," Dumont shouted to the excited crowd that gathered outside the house that night.

Paige was inside, kneeling on the rug and gratefully sorting through a leather bag that held an assortment of medical supplies. The Métis men had found it on the battlefield, abandoned by a fleeing medical officer, and brought it back to her.

She turned and looked up with a smile at Madeleine. The other woman had brought her a chunk of fresh bread and a plate of stew.

"Thanks, Madeleine, but I'm not hungry." The pesky nausea that had troubled her for so long now made her stomach ache. Paige knew she'd lost weight the last while.

"You must force yourself to eat," Madeleine scolded. "How can you hope to bear a healthy child unless you eat? You know as well as I that the sickness will pass soon now, but you must keep up your strength."

Paige gaped at her in amazement. "A child? Oh, Madeleine, but I'm not preg—" The denial died in her throat, and she stared at the Métis woman, the medical part of her mind going over the symptoms that had troubled her ever since she'd first arrived at Batoche.

Nausea, fatigue, sore breasts, dizziness, bloating, bouts of crying. She hadn't had a period since December, but she'd never been regular anyway, so she'd put it down to the excitement of her marriage, and then to the trauma of being abducted.

Pregnant. It couldn't be. Other possibilities, grim and dire, flitted through her mind, but she rejected them one by one. None of them fit except—

She stammered, "I can't—I mean, there's just no way I could be."

But the doctors had never said it was impossible, had they?

They'd used phrases like "highly unlikely," and "very little possibility." She'd never bothered with birth control, but she'd never had much reason to back in the nineties. Her sexual encounters had been few and very far between.

Until Myles.

Her heart began to thunder and her hands moved to her abdomen. In spite of her thinness, there was a definite swelling there.

She began to shake uncontrollably. She got to her feet, and instantly felt dizzy. The world began to turn dark, and she felt Madeleine grab her, guide her to a chair, force her head down between her knees.

Paige slumped, boneless, while the world turned topsy-turvy around her. Gradually the faintness passed and she looked up at Madeleine.

The other woman was standing over her, supporting her, stroking her hair, her smile warm and her expression tender.

"You really did not know, madame Paige? And you a *docteur?*"

Paige's tears began slowly, gathering and slipping one by one down her cheeks. Madeleine reached into her bosom and withdrew the snowy handkerchief that was always hiding there, reaching over to wipe Paige's face with gentle strokes.

"You do not wish it to be, this child?" There was sadness in Madeleine's voice, a frown on her dark face. She drew up a chair and sat down, then took both Paige's hands in hers and held them.

"Oh, yes, I do, that's not it at all. Oh, Madeleine, I do, I do want this, more than I can tell you. See, I lost a baby, long ago, before—long before I came here to this time, and I thought—the doctors all told me that I couldn't have another."

Madeleine smiled and gave her philosophical shrug. "So, the *docteurs,* even in your time, they do not always know everything."

Paige tried for a shaky smile. "That's certainly true."

"I, too, lost my babies." Madeleine's voice was soft. "Two babies, each of them lived no more than a day." She opened a tiny locket that she always wore, and showed Paige a few strands of fine hair. "This is all I have of them." She closed the locket again and tucked it inside the neckline of her dress.

Paige reached out and squeezed the work-worn, callused hand. "It's so painful, losing a child. I can't even imagine how hard it would be, losing two."

Madeleine nodded. "Gabriel and I, we both wanted children so much. But it is God's will."

"I wish I could be as philosophical as you are about death."

"Each of us comes to it in our own way, in our own

time." Madeleine smiled at her. "But this is no time for you to be thinking of death. This *enfant* will be fine, I feel it in my bones."

"I certainly hope your bones are right." Paige drew a deep, shaky breath, trying to curb the anxiety that was building in her.

She wasn't about to tell Madeleine how unlikely it was that the baby would survive. She was far too good an obstetrician to fool herself.

The stark truth was that there was a very real possibility that this pregnancy would mean her own death as well as the child's—because of the complications of her first delivery, the birth would have to be cesarean section, and, if she came through this rebellion alive, Myles would have to perform it.

She'd hemorrhaged the first time, needing blood transfusions. Even with the most modern of facilities, her baby had died.

What possible chance of survival did either of them have in this place and time, when cesarean section was practically unheard of, and blood transfusions not yet dreamed of, except by her?

Overwhelmed, terrified, she curled forward, her hands cradling the tiny life she and Myles had created, the life she would give anything in her power to save—even at the cost of her own.

A baby. She and Myles had started a new life with their love for one another. She longed as never before for her husband, to share this miracle with him, whatever the outcome. Her need for him became a kind of agony.

"Myles," she moaned aloud. "Oh, Myles, I need you now, I need you so terribly."

"Shhh." Madeleine stroked her hair, drawing Paige's head down to rest in her lap. "Soon now, this war will be over.

The Métis won today, a great victory. They will win again, and the *Anglais* will retreat. The government will recognize our people, and there will be peace."

Her voice took on the note of tenderness and pride it always held when she spoke of her husband. "Gabriel has told me this. He has also promised me no harm will come to you. You are a hostage; always the Métis take hostages in their wars, as a means of bargaining. But you will be returned safely to Battleford, to your husband, as soon as this final battle is won. Gabriel has given his word."

Madeleine was wrong. Paige thought of the final, bloody battle to be fought here at Batoche, the one she remembered from the history books, and a cold foreboding made her shudder. There was a good chance they'd all die in this battle of Batoche. The Métis would lose, Riel would hang for his dreams, Gabriel would flee to the United States— she racked her brains, trying to remember if she'd ever read what had become of Madeleine, but no memory surfaced.

She had to try to stop this, Paige thought frantically.

She'd once told Myles that history couldn't be changed, but maybe she'd been wrong. She had to make one last effort at convincing Louis Riel he must surrender now, before that final, bloody defeat that history decreed.

She raised her head from Madeleine's lap and got to her feet.

"I have to talk to Louis right now."

Madeleine looked at her, frowning. "He is out there with the people; he is still making speeches."

"I'll wait."

There had to be a way to make him see reason. She simply had to get back to Battleford alive.

She talked to Riel that night, quietly at first, relating again exactly what she remembered from the history books

354

about the Batoche battle, the bloodshed, the final surrender of the Métis.

Riel had remained unmoved. "We must go on," was all he would say.

She lost her temper finally and screamed at him that he would be hanged if he went on with the rebellion. He looked at her then and smiled, the sad, accepting smile of a martyr.

"Of course I will be hanged, madame," he said as though he were speaking to a child.

"Well, great, go ahead and commit suicide if that's your choice," she raged. "Just don't take the rest of us with you. You may want to die, but you have no right to make these women and children suffer because of your mad schemes. You have two children of your own, Gigette will have your third at any time, you must evacuate the town now, send the women and children away someplace safe."

He simply closed his eyes and began to pray, his response to almost everything. She felt like hitting him over the head with something heavy.

Louis Riel, she reminded herself too late, was mentally ill, probably schizophrenic. Reason simply didn't work with him.

Seventeen days later, frightened half to death and crouched on a cold dirt floor beside a suffering Gigette, Paige thought despairingly of the things she'd told Riel that night, wondering what else she might have said to make him see reason.

Probably nothing, she concluded in despair.

After her appeal to Riel, 12 days passed in ominous silence at Batoche.

The Métis celebrated, certain that they'd vanquished the enemy.

Then the scouts came running with the news that the English general was advancing on the village with 850 soldiers.

Gabriel mustered his army of 250, a pitiful collection of old men, boys, Indians, and his faithful buffalo hunters. Short of ammunition, but wise in the tricks of plains warfare, Dumont had miraculously repulsed the invading army for two days now. His men resorted to firing horseshoe nails and even stones from their muskets.

The women and children, Paige among them, were sent to hide in sand caves along the banks of the wide Saskatchewan River.

At night when the guns were silent, many of the women and all of the older children crept out to collect spent bullets on the battlefield, spending the midnight hours crouched over smoking fires, melting the metal into balls for their husband's muskets the next day.

Hungry, coughing endlessly, never complaining, they worked through the cold nights in spite of their pain and fatigue.

Paige could have wept at their bravery, except that her tears had dried up. Once again, she was numb, her emotions locked away in some safe place where tragedy couldn't touch them.

In the small, damp cave on the banks of the river, on the third morning of the siege, Gigette Riel went into labor.

Chapter Twenty-one

It was now past midnight. The pains had been coming at two-minute intervals for more than eight hours, and at last Paige felt Gigette was about to deliver.

She and Madeleine were alone with her—the other women had taken the children to sleep in a second, larger cave a short distance away after making what meager preparations they could for the birth. A small fire burned in one corner of the cave, and the smoke was nearly choking Paige. Shadows flickered like eerie ghosts on the walls, and from somewhere nearby, coyotes howled.

"Push, Gigette." Madeleine held the young woman's hands, and Paige crouched at the foot of the pallet, between her legs.

"I can't." The soft denial was followed by a moan as another pain began.

"I can see your baby's head, you should see all this lovely dark hair he has, one more good push and he'll be here,"

Paige pleaded. "Come on, Gigette." She raised her voice and ordered in a stern tone, "One good push, right now."

A sense of unreality filled Paige. Lord, what was she doing, delivering a baby in a cave? This girl belonged in a hospital, she couldn't draw a deep enough breath to push, she'd coughed up quantities of blood in between contractions, her heartbeat was so erratic Paige was terrified she was going to die during the delivery. Gigette's agonizing moan rose in volume and slowly became a scream.

"Push, that's good, great, again, Gigette, push."

The baby's head appeared, the small body slowly rotated into position, and with the next contraction, the tiny girl was propelled into Paige's waiting hands.

She didn't cry, and Paige worked over her with the familiar desperate intensity, blowing breath into the fragile body, elated when at last the infant gave a weak, wavering cry.

But all Paige's efforts were useless, after all, because within two hours of her birth, Riel's baby died.

For long hours after that, shivering in the damp chill of the early morning hours, Paige fought to keep Marguerite from accompanying her daughter.

Shortly after daybreak, she was reasonably sure that Gigette would live, but the sight of the baby's body, lying on a blanket on the ground in the dimly lit cave, tore her heart in pieces. She felt utterly defeated, drained of every bit of energy and hope.

Madeleine had washed the tiny girl and wrapped her in a clean, soft square of flannel.

"I wish I could have saved her," Paige whispered to Madeleine as they cleaned up as best they could. "There should have been something I could have done to save her."

Madeleine shook her head. "Hush," she ordered sternly.

"You are not God. You did the best you could, the best that anyone could have done; that is all any of us can ask of ourselves." She gave the baby to the mother, and Madeleine reached out a hand and gently stroked the tiny lifeless bundle Gigette cradled against her chest. Gigette's slow, exhausted tears dripped down on the small, still face.

As always, memories of her own baby girl, long ago and far away, came rushing into Paige's mind, and for a moment it felt as if the agony of her loss were fresh and new as she looked at Gigette's baby.

She knew that Madeleine too was grieving silently for her little lost children, but strangely, neither of them cried.

Perhaps, Paige thought in wonder, they'd each cried long and hard enough. Maybe now something in each of them realized the wounds had healed, that only scar tissue remained.

For the first time, Paige felt she wasn't alone in her grief. When her own child had died, and later each time she'd lost a baby, she'd always felt isolated, guilty, terribly alone.

Here, in this dismal cave, there was comfort. She felt the solace of unity, and it was healing.

Outside the cave, the sound of the river was steady and somehow soothing. The guns' intermittent bursts seemed unimportant and far away, part of a violent male universe of war and bloodshed.

For these few moments, here in a dismal cave, women were united in a ritual older even than war, of birth and death and sorrow and, finally, acceptance.

After a time, Madeleine took the baby's body and laid it on a blanket in a corner. She stirred up the small fire and boiled some water. She made tea, and the three women drank it.

There was absolutely nothing to do but wait for the battle to be finished. On her pallet, Gigette fell into a deep, exhausted slumber, and Paige and Madeleine talked softly, easily, women's talk about their families, their friends, their lives—words that brought smiles to their faces, and took them away from the harsh reality of the cave and the battle and the dead baby.

At dusk that day, Gabriel slipped through the narrow opening at the mouth of the cave, carrying a bag of provisions and some blankets. Madeleine spoke to him in French in a quiet voice and gestured at the baby's body, and he shook his head and crossed himself, holding out his arms. Madeleine moved close to him. He clasped her tight, patting her back with his hand in a clumsy gesture of solace and affection.

Over her shoulder, his fierce eyes met Paige's questioning gaze, and he shook his head.

"It is over," he said in his heavily accented English. "We are beaten. Riel, he has walked into da enemy camp and signed a note of surrender, but not I. Dumont will never surrender; dey must kill him first."

A tumult of emotions washed over Paige, among them relief that the fighting was over, mingled with compassion for the strong, brave Métis who'd fought so hard against such odds.

"Louis." From where she was lying, Gigette had heard what Gabriel was saying. She called her husband's name, over and over, and Gabriel went to kneel beside her.

"I am taking Madeleine now to my fadder's farm, where she will be safe," he told her. "Louis, he has asked dat you and your children come with us, Gigette. I know it is hard for you, and we must hurry." His eyes went to the tiny, blanketed baby. "I will see that da baby is taken to da priest for a proper burial, but we cannot wait. We must leave now."

He turned to Paige. "You, madame, are free to go. I tank

you for what you have done for my people. The *Anglais* general, he is even now in da village. I will make sure you reach him safely."

"Are there injured men, Gabriel? I'll do what I can for them first, if you like."

"*Merci,* madame, I would be very grateful. Tree of my faithful Métis are shot, twelve more are dead. They were taken to da church; the *Anglais* have burned da rest of da village."

Paige gathered together what few medical supplies she had left, and Madeleine helped Gigette to get up and dress. Both women, frail and poorly dressed, coughed violently in the cold, damp air, and Paige took two of the blankets Gabriel had brought and wrapped them around their shoulders.

The moment came when Paige had to say good-bye.

She pressed a small package of medications into Madeleine's hand, all she had to give her, and wrapped her arms around the frail older woman she'd come to love, unwilling to release her to what Paige knew could only be a tragic fate. Too emotional to speak, she hugged her close for long moments.

Madeleine's eyes were starry with tears. She drew away from Paige and impulsively took off the tiny locket she always wore and fastened it around Paige's neck.

"For good luck with your *enfant,*" she said in a tremulous voice. "Go with God, my friend."

By the middle of May spring had come to the prairies, and the residents of Battleford struggled to recover from the month they'd spent under siege inside the fort. While they'd been within its walls, many of their houses and businesses and most of the outlying homesteads had been burned by marauding Indians. The Hudson's Bay Company store had been looted and then burned to the ground.

Miraculously, Paige's house, up on the hill and away from the rest of the town, was one of the few buildings that survived the siege untouched, probably because of its proximity to the fort.

Myles visited it, but he couldn't bear to live there alone. He reclaimed his room at the fort and spent the sleepless night hours there, reading, pacing, trying alternately to think and not think of Paige.

The only way he could stay sane was by refusing to believe that she was dead. He convinced himself that she was being held hostage, and that when the rebellion ended, she'd come home.

Days ago, word had reached Battleford of Riel's surrender, so the rebellion was over.

Still she hadn't come. Day and night, Myles watched and waited for news of her. He questioned every injured soldier, every scout who reached the fort as to whether they'd seen or heard of her, but none had.

The time came when hope wore thin, and he felt totally disheartened. He'd spent the day writing urgent reports to the commissioner requesting medical supplies, blankets, cooking utensils, tools, and beds—the commanding officers at the fort had given the settlers as many supplies as they could.

The people were suffering. Their houses and farms and belongings were gone, and they were forced to start all over again, many of them with little more than the clothing they wore. They were disheartened, and the mounted policemen did whatever they could to help.

Myles forced himself to keep busy, treating the injured, composing reports, supervising cleanup details, taking inventory of what was left of his dispensary, but his mind wasn't on what he was doing.

He couldn't banish the terrible feeling that he was waiting in vain for Paige, that she'd died somewhere out on the prairies.

It was nearing evening. He was walking across the common, heading for the commander's residence to give him the reports for the morning's dispatch, when there was a commotion at the gates. He heard the sentry's challenge, and the gates swung open.

Two of the riders were male. Myles glanced at them, and then he looked at the third.

"Paige." His shout echoed through the stockade. "Paige." He dropped what he was carrying and ran toward her.

She slid off Minnie and into his arms.

He had to struggle to control the harsh sobs that left him speechless for long moments as he held her against him, his trembling hands relearning the shape of her skull, the delicate curve of her back.

He kissed her, once, fiercely, and then twice more, gently. Her lips were chapped, her face burned from the sun and wind. Her hair was long, curling in a wild frenzy across her shoulders, her face and arms alarmingly thin. She trembled like an aspen in his embrace, her arms locked around his neck as though she'd never let him go.

She tipped her head up to look at him, and through the tears raining down her face she laughed and wrinkled her sunburned and freckled nose at him, her green eyes immense. "You've grown a beard, Doctor. You'll have to shave it off; it tickles something awful when you kiss me."

His voice shook, but he was in control again. "Bossy wench. I guess I'll have to do it right away."

Hours later, they lay in their own bed, wrapped close in one another's arms. The gas lantern was turned low, casting long shadows over the familiar room. With their bodies, they'd bridged the time they'd spent apart and now, with words, they were filling in all the blank places.

Myles had tried to make her rest, insisting there was plenty of time to talk later. There were dark shadows underneath her eyes that troubled him, but when he insisted she sleep, she talked instead, and he understood that she needed to spill out the horror and fear of the past weeks.

In a mixture of tears and garbled phrases, she told him of Batoche, of Madeleine and the caves, of Gigette and the lost baby, of the tragic defeat of the courageous people she'd come to admire.

Myles could only hold her, aware that the words were cathartic.

"Now you must tell me what happened here while I was gone, please, Myles. I need to know everything."

He'd dreaded this moment, knowing the pain it would bring her, but it was obvious that she wouldn't rest until he did. Finally, his heart heavy, he began.

He told her of the day he'd come home to find her gone, and of how Rob Cameron had offered his help. Myles's voice faltered as he told her the rest, of the Indian attack and the children who survived, and, his voice thick with regret, of how Rob died in the attack.

She gasped and he felt her flinch, as if from a blow. He held her close when at last the tears came. "He was such a dear, good friend," she sobbed. "Rob was the first person I met that day on the prairie. He—he even asked me to marry him once."

He held her as the sobs shook her body.

"What—what became of the children, Myles?"

"Clara and Theo have Danny and Missy." It was a relief to have something good to tell her. "Clara insists Ellie needs brothers and sisters or she'll grow up spoiled, but from what

I saw, Clara and Theo'll just spoil all three of those tykes rotten. They're fine people, the Fletchers. Danny and Missy couldn't get better folks as parents. Their homestead was looted and burned, but at least the barn is still standing. They're all back out there now, getting started on spring planting."

"That's good." He felt her relax a little, but her next question sent his heart plummeting.

"Have you seen Tahny? How's the baby? Was it a boy like we thought? Did she and Dennis come in to the fort when the siege was on?"

Myles shut his eyes and tried to draw air past the lump in his throat. His voice was flat and empty. "They had a boy, but Dennis Quinlan's dead, Paige. He was murdered just over a week ago."

Again, her body jolted in his embrace, and he held her even closer, trying to cushion the shock, still hardly able himself to absorb the loss of his good friend.

"But why, Myles? How?" Her agonized whisper tore at him. "Why would the Indians murder Dennis? He was related to them by marriage. They wouldn't do that to Tahny, would they?"

He stroked her shoulders, resting a hand on her breast, aware of the erratic pounding of her heart. "Tahnancoa swears it wasn't Indians, my love." His voice was harsh. "She told me the men were white. She figures they were members of the Canadian army; they wore uniforms."

The burning rage he'd felt rose again inside of him, and he drew in a shaky breath, trying to control the desire to somehow find the men, avenge his friend's murder. But the ragtag army was dispersed now, the men long gone, their identities unknown.

"Why?" Paige's agonized question was the same one he'd asked.

"Tahny said they taunted and then killed Dennis because he was married to her. Called him an Indian lover. They burned the house and all the outbuildings and shot him when he fought back. Tahny was hiding with the baby. She got to her horse and managed to ride to the fort, but when I took her to the inspector to file charges against the army men, he didn't believe her story."

Myles had come close to assaulting a fellow officer that day.

"He figured Tahny was covering up for her people. There's bad feelings against the Indians because of the murder and looting that went on around here. When Tahny heard what he said, she got on her pony with the baby and rode off to Poundmaker's village. She's been there ever since."

"Have you seen her?"

Myles nodded. "I went to the reserve the very next day to see if I could help her." He sighed. "She refused to speak to me. She's angry and bitter, and now she's got even more reason to be."

The rest of the story sickened him. "Besides losing Dennis and being called a liar by the inspector, two of her cousins, young braves from the village, have been arrested by the Canadian army and charged with murder. They're in cells at the fort, awaiting execution. They're condemned to hang."

"Oh, my God. Oh, Myles, it's a nightmare. Are the charges legitimate? Did the men murder anyone?"

He shrugged and sighed. "Who can say? It was war. Indians, Métis, the army—everybody was shooting at everybody else. I still believe the Indians, and the Métis, were driven to it by the actions of the government. The Canadian army won, but it wasn't the easy victory they expected. I personally feel they're making scapegoats out

366

of Poundmaker and these two Indian braves. I said as much in a report to the commissioner, pleading for clemency, but I know my report will be ignored." His voice was bitter and sarcastic. "Naturally enough, the Mounted have to appear to support the army. And Tahny and her people are totally betrayed in the process."

Silence fell between them.

"I have to go and see her, Myles. Right away."

Myles traced the new hollows in Paige's cheeks with a finger, disturbed at the way the skin stretched tightly over her beautiful bones. "Not right away. You're going to get plenty of bedrest until I feel you're fit to travel," he stated in a harsh voice that brooked no argument. "And then you can only go out if I'm with you." He didn't think he could let her out of his sight, not for a long time to come. "You need to gain back the weight you've lost. It worries me that you're so thin."

He felt her draw her breath in sharply and then release it in a sigh. She was very still, and when she spoke her voice was trembling.

"I won't be thin for long, Myles." She took his hand and pressed it to her abdomen, turning her head so she could look directly into his eyes. "Feel here. I was sure you'd notice. Oh, Myles, I'm pregnant. We're going to have a baby."

For a moment, her words left him speechless and numb. He couldn't think, or breathe, or react. He felt as though a fist had punched him in the guts. At last, he stammered, "But I-I didn't think you could get pregnant."

"Well, neither did I." Her voice was strained, and she jerked away from him, her voice suddenly hurt and angry. "I'm sorry if you're disappointed, Myles. I guess I should have used those damned sponges I handed out so freely to my patients."

"Stop it." He reached out and yanked her back against him, his voice savage. "Damn you, Paige, don't be such a quick-tempered fool. Could you actually believe for an instant that I'm disappointed? I'm in shock. I never dreamed a child was possible for us. You told me it wasn't, more than once, and I believed you."

How could he not have noticed, when they'd made love a short time ago? He was half out of his mind with relief at having her back. He'd wondered at the fullness of her breasts when the rest of her looked starved, but when he removed the last of her clothing, she'd urged him on until his reason fled.

His voice lowered, and the passion he felt made his voice tremble. "My beautiful woman, having you as my wife is more than I ever dreamed life would hold for me. To have our child as well . . ." The thought sent shivers down his spine. He raised up on an elbow and placed the palm of his hand reverently on the slight swelling of her belly.

"But what about the delivery, Paige?" The doctor in him took over from the proud father, and he frowned at her. "You told me there were serious complications the first time you delivered. How will that affect you this time?"

She turned her head away, but not before he'd seen the stark fear in her eyes.

His own heart plummeted. "Paige? Talk to me. Don't shut me out." He took her chin and gently made her look at him again. "We're in this together. I'm a doctor, just as you are. It's our child. If there are problems, we can discuss them."

She nodded, her face troubled. "It'll be complicated. It'll definitely have to be cesarean." She saw the utter horror on his face and added quickly, "You can do it, Myles. It's a relatively easy operation." The words were confident, but she couldn't mask her own apprehension.

He was all too aware of what she wasn't saying. Cesarean might be an everyday procedure in her future time—here in his, it was performed only in the most extreme of emergencies, and only rarely did either the mother or the child survive.

He didn't have the equipment Paige had told him about, or the facilities she'd described. And having to perform it himself, on his own wife, his baby . . .

Memories of Beth, of the hemorrhage he couldn't stop, of the baby son born before its time, flashed before his eyes. How could he ever bring himself to open Paige, lift his child from her womb?

He shuddered, and icy sweat trickled down his spine.

Foreboding gripped him, even as he forced a reassuring smile and planted a gentle kiss on his wife's chapped lips. "We have plenty of time to prepare. When's our baby due?"

"Late September, early October."

A scant five months away. He reached over and turned down the wick on the lamp. Blessed darkness blanketed them, and he lay back down on the pillow and settled her head on his shoulder.

"We'll manage this together, my dearest." It took enormous effort to force confidence into his voice. "All you have to do is rest now, and eat, and regain your strength so our child will benefit. All that matters right now is that you're back with me, and safe." He stroked her hair, soothing her to sleep with his voice. "Having you here in my arms means everything to me. Sleep now, my love."

She sighed and burrowed down beside him, her hand on his chest, and before long he felt her body relax completely into slumber.

For a long time, he lay awake, staring up at the ceiling, his heart thundering.

He'd stopped believing in God when Beth died, but now he closed his eyes and tried to remember how to pray.

Myles was profoundly relieved when Paige took his advice for several weeks, doing little except sleeping and eating.

With the coming of June, summer exploded across the prairies and the days became hot.

Paige tended the patients who appeared at her office, but the energy she'd always had in excess was gone. The child growing within her made her languid and lazy.

In the first days after her return, Paige sent a message to Tahny, expressing her grief at Dennis's death and asking when she could come and see Tahnancoa and the baby, but there was no answer.

A second message brought a terse reply: "I have returned to my people," was all Tahny wrote.

It was obvious, as Myles had warned, that Tahnancoa wanted nothing more to do with anyone white. Saddened, Paige could only accept her friend's decision.

In early July, in the middle of a hot night, Abigail Donald sent a frantic young husband to ask Paige to come at once to an outlying farm where the man's wife had just delivered their first child.

"Lucy's bleeding somethin' fierce," the man babbled. "Mrs. Donald says to please hurry."

"I'm coming along," Myles said. He harnessed a team to the carriage he'd recently bought, and they set off across the prairie.

The trip brought back memories for Paige of the night Clara was in labor with Ellie, and she hoped this trip would have as happy an outcome.

But when she and Myles hurried into the tiny bedroom in the modest little cabin, her heart sank.

A baby girl lay squalling in a cradle, unwashed and hastily wrapped in a blanket. Abigail, normally cool and unflappable, was visibly upset.

The young mother was unconscious and despite all Abigail's efforts to stop the flow, blood still poured from her in great gushes, soaking the bed and mattress, dripping into pools on the rough wooden floor.

"The delivery was normal, the baby's healthy," Abigail explained as Paige and Myles hastily scrubbed at a basin in the corner. "The afterbirth came away, but the uterus wouldn't contract. I've given ergot, but it hasn't worked."

Paige examined the young woman. She'd lost a great deal of blood, and was already in shock. "We'll have to do an emergency hysterectomy," she decided.

For the remainder of the night, Paige and Myles fought for the young woman's life. With Myles assisting, Paige performed the operation as quickly and deftly as possible, and the bleeding was controlled, but it was evident almost from the beginning that Lucy had already lost far too much blood.

She died just after dawn.

Despondent, Paige and Myles helped Abigail clean up. They bathed the beautiful baby and gave her to the weeping young husband, and then Paige helped wash and prepare Lucy's body for burial.

Abigail promised to stay until the husband could find live-in help, and when there was nothing more to be done, Myles and Paige left.

They bounced over the rough prairie in silence for some time, and then Myles said in a quiet tone, "If this happened in your time, what more could have been done to save her?"

"A blood transfusion." Paige's voice was angry, and she smashed her fist down on the seat of the buggy. "All she needed was a lousy blood transfusion."

The harnesses jingled, and around them birds sang and gophers squawked.

"Did you require this blood transfusion when your first child was born?" His tone was conversational, but Paige knew how important her answer would be.

"Yes. I did." She looked out over the prairie and swiped at the perspiration on her forehead. "But that doesn't mean I'll need one again this time." Her tone was belligerent, covering her fear. "You know as well as I do that one birth is never the same as the next."

"Whoa." Myles brought the team to a halt, secured the reins, and pulled her into his arms.

There was a charged silence, and then he said, "I can't perform a cesarean on you, Paige. I just can't do it. I haven't had any experience at it, and you know yourself it's risky for a doctor to treat someone he loves. Will you agree to go and have the child at a hospital in Toronto?"

She struggled out of his arms and gaped at him, horrified. "Are you out of your mind? Myles, you know as well as I do that I wouldn't trust anyone but you to do this operation. Hospitals in this day and age are primitive; you've said yourself there's a high rate of infection and infant death. I absolutely wouldn't go to one to have my baby." All of a sudden her face crumpled and all her brave defenses were gone.

"I'm so afraid," she wailed. "I remember the last time, and God, I'm so scared. I want this baby more than anything. Oh, Myles, I just can't stand to have this baby die too. I can't stand it, and I can't figure out what to do to keep it from happening."

Her voice rose in a primitive wail, and she clung to him and cried, openmouthed and gasping, her terror starkly evident.

He'd known the answer for some time, although he hadn't allowed himself to put it into words until now.

He found his handkerchief and clumsily dabbed at her face. "You're going to have to try to go back, my love."

For a confused moment, she couldn't think what he meant, and she scowled at him through her tears.

His voice was quiet, maddeningly reasonable, but she could see the strain on his face. "I'm convinced that if you stay here, one or both of you will die." He touched her flushed cheek with a finger, smoothing away her tears. "I'd rather lose you to that other world than watch you die here in mine, darling. I'm going to try to find a way to send you back to your other life, so you and our child have a chance."

"But—but I don't want to go." A lump of dread congealed in her throat. "I won't go. I want to stay here with you. I won't go, and that's all there is to it."

He buried his face in her hair, his eyes squeezed shut. "My stubborn, impossible wife, don't you think I want you here with me? Don't you think I'd give my own life if it meant you and our baby would live?" His voice was agonized. "I've thought and thought about it, and when that poor girl died back there, I made up my mind. This is the only way to save you and our baby."

The plan must have been brewing in his subconscious, because it was fully formed. "I'm going to see Lame Owl. I'll beg her to try to send you back. If she can, maybe there's a chance you and the child could return. After all, it happened once already, didn't it?" He tried for a smile and failed.

"Then you must come with me, Myles." Her chin was set, her eyes determined. "The only way I'll go is if you come along."

He'd given it some thought. "I'll try. I'll talk to Lame

Owl, and I'll ask if it's possible. But either way, you have to go, Paige. With me or without me, you know it's our only chance."

"If you can't come, then make her promise to bring me back here." She couldn't control the note of hysteria in her voice.

This time he smiled at her, a sad smile that tore at her heart. "You have my word on that."

"It didn't sound to me as if Lame Owl had exactly perfected the technique." Ashamed of her earlier weakness, Paige tried for a shaky grin that didn't quite work. "You might just get stuck with delivering your kid after all, Doctor."

His eyes were haunted. "If that happens, then we'll have to make the best of it."

She fingered the locket at her throat, Madeleine's locket.

"God's will," she whispered. "Madeleine would say everything is just God's will. Do you believe that, Myles?"

Myles was silent.

Chapter Twenty-two

Lame Owl stared out over the valley, her obsidian eyes buried in a network of wrinkles, her hands folded in her lap.

Myles sat beside her on the grass, and sweat trickled uncomfortably down his back and under his arms as he fought against the sense of desperation that consumed him. He had to find a way to break through her silence. They'd been sitting here for more than an hour, and so far Lame Owl hadn't responded to one thing he'd said.

Difficult as it was for him to do, he'd bared his soul to the old woman, telling her about the war in the south, of coming back and finding his old way of life forever lost, all the people he loved dead or, like his mother, damaged beyond repair. He told her about Beth and the baby, and even though the words cut like glass, he'd described the way they'd died even as he'd fought to save them.

He told her about the love he'd found with Paige, the dreams he had for the child Paige was carrying, the problems surrounding its birth.

He might as well have confided in a rock. Lame Owl sat silent and unmoved by his monologue.

Without so much as flickering an eyelash, the old woman made it plain that he was intruding, and he knew he was—he'd come to her even though she wanted nothing to do with him.

He had to come up with something to bargain with, he told himself, something he could give back to Lame Owl in exchange for her help. Indians were great traders. There had to be something she needed, something he could exchange.

The answer came to him. It was dangerous, but it looked as though nothing else was going to work.

"Lame Owl, your grandsons are being held in the Battleford jail, charged with murder."

Finally the old woman turned her head and looked at him. She stared at him for a long time before she began to speak in a slow, measured voice, spraying spittle from her toothless mouth.

"My grandsons are being punished, and yet the English soldiers who murdered Tahnancoa's husband go free. My granddaughter's spirit is sick because her husband's own people deny the truth and blame Indians for what white men did."

Myles nodded, acknowledging the truth of what she said.

"Our race is disappearing. Already many tribes are no more." The old voice was filled with suffering. "The white man brought us diseases we knew nothing of, they killed our buffalo for sport instead of meat, they have made us captive in our own land. My people are sick, and hungry, and cold. Our hunting grounds are no more. No one listens when we speak. Your mounted men did not listen to Tahnancoa, just as no one listens when my grandsons say they are not murderers, that they protected their village when the English general crept up on us in the night and fired his cannons at our tipis."

"What you say is true, and it makes me ashamed for my people," he admitted. "As for Tahnancoa, I believe what she says. Dennis Quinlan was my friend, Lame Owl, and if I could find and punish the men who killed him, I would." Myles' voice was grim. "But those cowardly men are far away now, gone with the army that brought them here." He paused a moment and added in a deliberate tone, "I can't do anything about Dennis's murder, but I might be able to help your grandsons."

"They have been sentenced to hang."

Myles chose his words with care. "Perhaps they will have a chance to escape before that happens."

She gave him a questioning look, and he met her old eyes squarely.

"I can promise nothing, Lame Owl. I can only try. I will need your help."

She nodded once, and turned again to the view of the valley. After several moments, she said, "It is the same with me. I can promise nothing, but if you can free my grandsons, in turn I will try to open the gates and send your woman walking between the worlds."

He took a deep breath and let it out again. "Can you send me with her?"

She snorted and shook her head, and his hopes plummeted. "No. Only one may go, and you are a man. It is a woman's ceremony, and only women may walk between the worlds."

"Then can you bring her back again to me?"

She shrugged. "I can try. Who knows if the Great Spirit will allow it?"

It was less than he'd hoped for, but it was all there was.

Only one question remained. "When, Lame Owl?"

There wasn't much time. It was already August, and the baby was due in another six weeks. If it came early . . .

She shrugged again. "When the time is right." She shot him a challenging look. "When my grandsons are once again free. It must be before the frost, though. I will let you know."

"And—and when could you bring her back?"

She shrugged. "In spring, maybe. When the sun again warms the earth and the grasses grow."

A whole winter to get through before he'd even know if he'd ever see her, or his child. An eternity of waiting.

Myles thanked her and walked down the hill and into the village. He had one more thing to do, and he hoped for Paige's sake he'd be successful.

He searched for Tahnancoa, and finally found her down at the stream, kneeling beside it, washing clothes. A cradle holding a fat-cheeked, black-haired baby with astonishing crystal blue eyes was propped up against a willow close beside her.

Myles knew Tahnancoa had heard him approach, yet she didn't look up or acknowledge his presence. She went on sloshing baby clothes up and down in the clear water, rinsing soap from them.

He smiled and clucked to the baby, and was rewarded with a beaming smile.

"Dennis would be so proud of this fine son, Tahny," Myles said quietly. "I see he's inherited his father's blue eyes and your dark hair. He's part of each of you, isn't he? Half and half?"

She'd stopped scrubbing at the wet clothing, and although she didn't look up, Myles could see the way her lips quivered, the silver tears that began trickling down her cheeks when he mentioned Dennis. He hated hurting her, but he couldn't see any other way to break through the barrier she'd erected.

"Tahny, this beautiful baby is half Indian, half white." He put all the intensity of his feelings into his plea. "You can't change that. He's somehow going to have to learn to live in both worlds, and it'll be tough for him if you go on hating everyone with a white face, because he'll soon figure out that's half of what he is too. Do you want him to think there's part of him that isn't pleasing to you, Tahny?"

He waited. When she didn't respond he sighed and added, "Paige and I are your friends, Tahny. Let us help you, let us help your son learn that there's good as well as bad among his father's people."

The baby made soft, cooing sounds, turning his head to look as a butterfly floated past.

"What's his name, Tahnancoa?"

"Dennis," she responded in a whisper. "He will earn his Indian name as he grows. For now, he is named only for his father." She crumpled all of a sudden, covering her face with her hands. Her shoulders shook with sobs. "Myles Baldwin, sometimes I think I cannot go on without him."

Myles put an arm around her shoulders and dug a handkerchief from his pocket and handed it to her.

When the worst of the tears were over, he talked to her, telling her of Paige's pregnancy and of how much she missed Tahnancoa and longed to see her baby.

"Bring her here," Tahny said at last. "Tell her—" Her voice caught. "Tell her how happy I am about your child. Tell her she is my friend, and I miss her too."

Myles gave Paige Tahny's message, but he didn't mention the bargain he'd made with Lame Owl—he simply told her that Lame Owl had agreed to attempt the ceremony.

Immediately, he set about fulfilling his part of the agreement.

Myles understood all too well that the penalty for helping the Indian prisoners escape would be severe if he were caught. He'd be court-martialed, and probably sentenced to die by firing squad. The part that bothered him the most was that his failure would endanger Paige and his child.

He put the consequences firmly out of his mind as he studied the guard's routines and made his plans. As the fort's doctor, he was responsible for the prisoners' health, and it wasn't difficult to spirit away the spare key to the cell door where the Indians were imprisoned. Making a wax impression and painstakingly filing an exact match took much longer.

The execution was scheduled for Friday afternoon. On Wednesday, Lame Owl visited her grandsons and slipped them the key Myles had given her. She also relayed his instructions as to when it was to be used.

A dose of ipecac in the food the kitchen sent over for the guard and his prisoners' supper on Thursday night caused diarrhea and vomiting, and as he'd planned, Myles was called to treat the problem.

He knew the Indians hadn't eaten the drugged food, but they were doing a fine acting job, holding their stomachs and moaning.

He dispensed a tonic all around, making certain the guard's portion contained a strong sleeping powder. He'd told Lame Owl to have horses waiting at the back of the stockade at midnight. Scaling the wall would be child's play for the agile young men, and Myles had instructed them as to the timing of the sentry's rounds and the exact spot where it was safest to climb the wall.

Myles went home that evening a little later than usual.

He made love to Paige gently, holding her close until she

was deeply asleep. Then he got up and went outside, every nerve tense, his muscles aching from the strain of waiting for the alarm to be sounded from the fort.

Would there be time for the Indians to get clean away? As the huge summer moon inched its way across the sky, Myles counted the minutes, and then the hours. Silence reigned, and gradually, he relaxed.

It was nearly dawn before the commotion began, and he smiled grimly, knowing the escape had been successful. Lame Owl's grandsons had been gone for hours by now.

He went back to bed.

The next morning, the fort was buzzing with the news.

It had been four in the morning before the guard awoke enough to discover his prisoners gone and sound the alarm, and by then it was far too late to catch them, although patrols were dispatched and the best scouts employed to track the prisoners.

Myles went immediately to the inspector and explained that the guard and prisoners had been ill the previous night, and that because of the tonic he'd given out, it was probable that the young guard had slept more deeply than he should have done.

Myles apologized and insisted that if there was blame for the escape, he should share in it. He'd used a new sleeping powder, he explained, more potent than he'd realized.

"Asleep or not, it's a mystery how those savages ever got out of their cell," the inspector grumbled. "The chain was in place and the padlock still locked, but the cell was empty. It's enough to make a man believe in sorcery," he grumbled.

The guard was let off with a light reprimand, and the escape remained a mystery.

* * *

The days that followed were bittersweet. Myles knew the summons would come soon from Lame Owl, and he spent every moment he could with Paige.

Hand in hand, they walked their favorite paths beside the river, watching summer fade into fall. The baby in Paige's womb was growing larger day by day, and they laughed together at how big and active it was. Myles insisted it was a girl, but Paige said she knew it was a boy.

They talked endlessly about names, settling on Alexander for a boy, and Emily for a girl.

Late at night, wakeful beside his sleeping wife, Myles would place his palms on the mound of her stomach and feel his baby kick and turn inside her, and the tears he ruthlessly suppressed in the daylight trickled down his cheeks and soaked the pillowslip.

One morning he hitched up the buggy and they drove out to visit Clara and Theo, taking along a load of household goods they felt the Fletchers might need.

Myles knew their friends were living in what had been their barn, the only building on the farm that hadn't been burned by marauding Indians during the rebellion. Most of the Fletchers' possessions had been either burned or stolen, and with the two extra children to provide for, Myles and Paige were concerned about how they were managing.

They drove into the yard early in the morning, and Danny came hurtling out of a shed where he was helping Theo milk the cow.

"It's Doc." His brown eyes were huge and sparkling with excitement as he came racing over to the buggy, hollering, "Hey, Theo, come quick, Doc's here." He barely drew a breath. "Hey, Doc, guess what? Our cat had kittens last night, four of 'em. Theo says each of us kids can have one of our own, to keep. I'll show you mine. Theo says mine's the only boy cat; he says I need a boy cat 'cause him and me are outnumbered by girls in this fam'ly."

Myles laughed, helping Paige carefully down from the buggy and then ruffling the boy's sandy hair. He introduced Paige, and Danny smiled up at her shyly, his freckled countenance open and happy.

Myles looked at the boy, remembering bodies in another farmyard, a small girl screaming for her dead mother, a frightened little boy doing his best to pretend he was brave. It was wonderful to see Danny this way.

Theo walked over to them, his bearded, kind face split in a grin, and Myles noted how Danny imitated Theo's stance, standing with his legs apart and his hands stuck in the back pockets of his denims.

Clara, with Ellie on her hip and Missy by the hand, came rushing out to welcome them. Both little girls wore matching gingham dresses with white pinafores over them. As usual, Clara had been busy sewing.

"Come in." Her wide face was wreathed in smiles, her eyes behind the round lenses of her glasses filled with delight as she glanced discreetly at Paige's burgeoning stomach. "It's just so good to see you, the coffee's on, and I've just made a pan of fresh gingerbread."

The table was a plank set on two sawhorses, and the chairs were packing crates, but as the day sped past, it was obvious that Clara and Theo and their three children couldn't have been happier if they lived in a mansion.

Ellie and Missy tumbled about on the floor, giggling as only small girls can, playing with rag dolls Clara had made them. Danny stuck to Theo like a burr, very much the important big brother as he divided up the gumballs and suckers and molasses candy Myles and Paige had brought, rationing them out to the little girls.

Paige watched Myles take one sticky small girl after the

other up on his knee, gently teasing them and making them giggle. She saw his tender smile as he held them. She watched his eyes follow Danny, and she noted his wistful expression.

It was painfully obvious that he was a man who loved children.

The ache in her heart grew almost unbearable.

She'd give anything to be able to hand him their own child to hold. The closer the time came, the less she wanted to even try to leave.

But the bigger her unborn baby grew, the more certain she became that unless she had access to modern medical procedures, both she and the baby might die.

Sometimes, the irony of the situation twisted her mouth in a bitter smile. She remembered an expression that her partner, Sam Harris, used to use on occasion.

"Poor bastard," he'd say. "He's caught between a rock and a hard place."

Well, that was where she was right now.

Caught between a rock and a hard place.

Two weeks passed, and there was only a month left before the baby was due.

The search for the prisoners was called off.

Two days after that, Lame Owl sent Myles a message.

It was time for the ceremony. Myles would bring Paige as far as the Indian village, and then he must leave her.

The night before the trip, Paige talked for hours after they'd finally gone to bed, fighting sleep in the darkness of the room, trying to draw word pictures for Myles of where she'd be, what things would be like in the world she'd inhabit should Lame Owl's magic work.

Myles knew she was using words as a shield against the pain of emotion, the fear of the parting so close now.

" . . . and I never told you about disposable diapers, did I?"

"What about them, love?" Myles lay with her in his arms, her hand circling his waist, his arm underneath her head, their bodies pressed as close together as her swollen stomach would allow. The unborn child cradled between them kicked and somersaulted in his warm cocoon.

They'd been celibate for several weeks now, but there was a deep sensuality in lying together this way.

Myles rubbed her back, trailing his fingers along the curve of her spine, letting his hand cup her swollen breast, too large now with pregnancy to fit into his palm. He ran a finger along her temple, tracing the high cheekbone, the straight nose, the stubborn chin, the soft throat.

Memorizing her, for all the empty nights to come.

"They do away with so much washing, they're soft and easy on the baby's behind, but they're not biodegradable. The flannel, preformed ones are better. They close with Velcro; did I ever tell you about Velcro?"

He hadn't any idea what she was talking about. He hadn't listened to the words for some time now. Instead, he was absorbing the cadence of her voice, the timbre, the way she emphasized certain syllables. She was falling asleep; he could tell by the way her muscles slowly relaxed and her voice grew soft and fuzzy.

"It's this sticky stuff. . . ." She burrowed even closer to him. "You just press it together." She sighed and slipped into sleep as the deep weariness of advanced pregnancy overcame her.

Against him, the child inside her moved restlessly.

His child. He put his palm over the solid flesh of her abdomen.

Know that I love you, dear one. Know that you have a father who loves you, who loves your mother.

He held her, accommodating her restless slumber, moving when she moved so she always had enough room, enfolding her again as soon as her breathing deepened. He held her as the moon waned and the small hours of the morning grew. Dawn broke, and he leaned on an elbow and studied her sleeping face in the first gray light.

Ebony curls, wild as the prairie wind, strewn across the pillow. Golden skin, with tracings of freckles across the straight nose. Deep-set eyes, as green as the first spring grass. Long, curling lashes, gold-tipped from the hot sun, sooty at their base.

A stubborn chin. A wide, pink mouth, relaxed now in sleep, a mouth whose contours he knew as well as he knew his own, having traced every inch with his lips and his tongue.

His woman. His wife. His very life.

He hated waking her, but the sun was already up.

He bent his head and kissed her lips, and before her eyes opened her arms came up and clasped him to her.

"I love you, Myles." The sleepy murmur tore his heart nearly to shreds.

Later that morning, on the outskirts of the Indian village, they said good-bye. Tahnancoa had walked out to meet Paige, and she stood a polite distance away, waiting, her son securely strapped to her back.

They kissed, twice, three times, neither of them daring to speak, and when the final moment came, Paige lost her nerve. She clung to him, too devastated even to cry, her arms trembling, locked around his neck.

"I can't, Myles." Her whisper was frantic. "I can't leave you."

"Yes, you can. You must. Courage, my dearest love." He put a hand on her stomach. "Kiss my son for me, won't

386

you? I'll see you both when you get back, in the spring."
He drew a leather pouch with a drawstring out of his pocket
and looped it around her neck, over the locket she wore.
The weight of it made her gasp.

"You told me once that the money we use is different
than in your time, but that gold was still of value. These
are gold coins, for you and our child."

His thoughtfulness, his quiet strength, filtered through
to her, and by some strange kind of osmosis she became
calm.

He helped her down from the carriage, and in a poignant
gesture, took Paige's hand and placed it in Tahnancoa's.

He saluted formally, and he smiled with easy confidence,
as though he were leaving her to visit with Tahny for the
day and would come and get her when evening came.

He climbed in the buggy, shook the reins, and rode off
across the faint trail marked in the prairie grass. Paige
watched the outline of his head and shoulders grow
smaller and smaller, silhouetted against the intense blue
of the morning sky.

The ceremony would be at sunset. Paige spent the day
in preparation and in sleep.

She was taken to a tent where Tahnancoa helped her
bathe, and then her skin was rubbed with fragrant oil. She
was dressed in a loose white buckskin smock that came
down to her ankles, a comfortable, soft garment, made
incongruous by the worn Nikes on her feet. Myles had
knelt at her feet and laced them on that morning.

"They're good luck," he'd told her. "They brought you
to me, and they'll bring you safely back."

Paige was given a huge bowl of stew to eat. Then she
was shown to a pile of buffalo skins and told to rest. She
was far too nervous to even lie down, until Tahny gave her

bitter-tasting tea to drink. It must have had a narcotic in it, because Paige didn't awaken until late in the afternoon.

She felt logy and disoriented as Tahny led her and ten other women out of the village, a long, meandering, hot walk that seemed to Paige to lead straight across a barren strip of prairie. The women chatted softly to one another.

The sun was almost setting when they reached a large, circular depression in the ground. Lame Owl was sitting cross-legged on a blanket in the deepest section of the hollow, and she motioned to Paige to join her. An exact circle had been inscribed in the long prairie grass in an eight-foot circumference around the blanket. Inside the circle was a triangle, and a shiver of recognition skittered down Paige's spine.

It was a replica of the crop circle that had brought her here two long years before.

Awkward and heavy with her pregnancy, Paige sat beside Lame Owl, trying to find a comfortable position, the bag of gold coins heavy on her neck.

Lame Owl instructed her. "Look inside your soul and see the world you wish to enter. Make certain of the doorway, and when the time is right, go through it."

"But how will I know?" Paige felt both ridiculous and fearful, heavily pregnant, crouched like a frog inside the triangle and the circle.

Lame Owl gave her a disgusted look. "Trust your senses."

Paige reached out and gripped the old woman's sleeve. "I must know exactly what to do to come back again. You must bring me back, Lame Owl. Promise me, please."

Her face bland and impassive, the old woman gave her characteristic shrug, and Paige felt like punching her. "It is for the gods to decide who comes and goes."

"But at least tell me what to do."

Lame Owl was annoyed. "In the spring when the sun is warm again, find one of the gates and sit as you are now," she snapped. "See the time and place, make certain of the doorway."

Paige couldn't trust her. "But you'll work from this end to help me come back? Please?"

Lame Owl scowled at her. "I have given my word. I will do as I said. Be still now; go into your mind." Lame Owl rose, moving several feet outside the circle.

The women joined hands, and Lame Owl led them in a guttural, monotonous chant.

The sun had dipped to the horizon, and it sat poised, a fiery bubble, dropping slowly into the earth.

Paige tried to do as Lame Owl had instructed, but she was uncomfortable. She closed her eyes and in her mind, she visualized the calendar she'd always kept on her desk in her office, and with a red marking pen she circled the day, the year.

Nothing happened. She was aware of the women chanting, of the choking heat of the afternoon. A slight breeze arose that only occasionally cooled the sweat on her forehead.

Time passed, and the fear slowly faded to boredom. Her bottom ached from the hard ground. How insane it had been of her and Myles, to think that superstitious natives could pull off anything like time travel.

She yawned. She'd have to send a message, have Myles come and get her.

The women's humming was both hypnotic and haunting. Her head jerked as she dozed. The baby moved languidly inside her, and she folded her hands over him and smiled to herself.

Against her closed eyelids the light became scarlet and

then gold and orange. She imagined the calendar again and nodded, more than half asleep.

A hot wind blew over her, and she shivered with its searing heat and waited for it to subside. But it grew more intense, filling her ears with a whirling noise so loud it drowned out the voices of the women.

Startled, she opened her eyes and cried out. The wind swept around her, flattening the long prairie grass in its strange, circular pattern. She could see the women, but they shimmered in the wind, and she tried to call out to them, but the wind grew even stronger, snatching her voice away, whirling her into black nothingness.

A motor was running somewhere nearby.

Paige opened her eyes. She was on her back in the middle of a field. The familiar canopy of prairie sky stretched above her. She turned her head to the side and discovered tall stalks of grain surrounding the crop circle in which she lay.

The women were nowhere to be seen.

Her heart began to hammer. She struggled to sit up. The blanket was gone, but the leather bag was still around her neck. The grain immediately surrounding her was flattened in an exact, concentric pattern. She lumbered to her feet.

In a nearby field, a huge black tractor with an enclosed cab was pulling a machine that cut the tall grain in smooth, even swaths.

In the distance was a highway. Paige watched in wonder as a transport truck passed a blue car.

She could see power poles, stretching in long, unbroken lines into infinity.

"Myles." The tormented whisper died in her throat.

Myles was long ago and far away, and if she let herself think about him, she'd die from the pain.

She started walking slowly toward the tractor. She needed to find a telephone.

Chapter Twenty-three

"This is a big kid you're hatching, Paige." Sam Harris had his ample backside propped against his desk where the folder with all her test results lay open, and he tapped them with a finger.

"You can read these as well as I can. Your pelvis is definitely too narrow to deliver vaginally, so we go with a c-section. And because of the first stillbirth, I've got a neonatal specialist standing by, the best guy in the city. His name's Marvin Kent. And I don't have to tell you that things have changed a hell of a lot since you had your first baby. We're gonna make sure every last bit of technology is available, should you or this bruiser of a kid need it." He winked at her. "I've got a reputation to uphold, so don't think for a minute you'll get away with anything kinky."

"Thanks, Sam. You're the best, and that sets my mind at ease." Paige shifted uncomfortably on her chair. She really was huge. She'd told herself a dozen times these past few days that it would be a great relief to have this baby, even while some other part of her held back, insisting that only as long as her son was still inside her was he safe. The ultrasound results had confirmed what she'd thought all along—that the child she carried was a boy.

I told you so, Myles Baldwin.

"So go check into Grace tonight and first thing tomorrow morning we'll do it."

"Tomorrow?" Her heart gave a jolt and began pounding hard against her ribs. "I've got a million things to do tomorrow, Sam. Why not Wednesday, or—"

He shook his head and grinned at her. "Why is it doctors are always the worst when it comes to being patients? You're so close to delivering, tomorrow's even pushing it. I oughta drive you over there this minute, never mind tomorrow." There was both affection and concern in his brown eyes, and Paige was reminded again of how much Sam reminded her of Rob Cameron. They were physically alike, but it was this warm affection that made her remember Rob when she was around Sam.

"Okay, it's a date, see you tomorrow." She heaved herself to her feet, sounding far more nonchalant than she felt.

She turned to the door, dreading the moment when she'd have to pass the office that had been hers—and which now had someone else's name on the door.

"Paige, hold it." His hand on her arm stopped her. "How about some lunch? The deli down the street still makes those great subs, and I'm famished. No breakfast because one of my moms decided to deliver twins this morning, and then I had to race over here. And don't forget, this will be your last chance for solid food until after we get your kid out. 'Nothing by mouth after five,'" he quoted in a stern voice.

"Okay, Sam. Sure." Lunch would make one less hour to stare at the television in the small apartment she'd rented. "I can't remember, does the deli have decent chairs or only those little stools? Because if it's stools . . ." She patted her hips and shook her head.

Sam laughed and steered her quickly past the office that had been hers. "Chairs, guaranteed," he assured her.

The deli was crowded, but he found them a tiny table complete with the chairs he'd promised, and they ordered.

"So how're things going?" Sam took a gigantic bite from the foot-long sandwich and washed it down with a gulp of coffee.

"Not bad," she lied, nibbling at her own sub even though she wasn't at all hungry. She hadn't been really hungry since she'd come back, in spite of the convenience foods she'd longed for in Battleford. "I've got an apartment in Kerrisdale, all my things are now out of storage, and I rented a nice little red car. I call it Minnie."

She thought of her horse and smiled wistfully.

Sam chewed and swallowed. "Your sister-in-law still driving your Sunbird?"

"Yeah." Paige didn't meet his eyes. "I told her to go on using it for a while." She didn't tell Sam that Sharon also had most of her clothes and the few pieces of jewelry she'd owned. It had been a shock to find her sister-in-law using her things, and even more of a shock to find that her brother condoned it.

She told herself it didn't really matter—she'd be going back to Myles in the spring, wouldn't she? And she couldn't exactly take her car and a U-Haul along.

"Talk to your brother much? And by the way, give me his number; I'll get in touch with him the minute the baby's out."

"No, thanks." Paige shook her head and avoided Sam's questioning blue gaze. "I'll get in touch with him later. Maybe."

He lifted an eyebrow. "I thought you and Tony were real close. What's going on?"

"We were close." Paige frowned. "At least, I thought we were. But I was gone two years. He figured for sure I was dead. It changed things." More than she'd ever imagined.

"He managed all the legal stuff, cleaned out my apartment, put my things in storage, listed me as a missing person—I guess it was really tough for him, and I think he got used to the idea of me being dead," she said slowly, trying to understand it all herself.

"Then when I turned up again, and tried to tell him what had happened to me, he just couldn't accept it. He treats me as though I've had a major mental breakdown, and he told me straight out he doesn't want me filling my nephews' heads with what he considers my hallucinations." That had hurt worse than anything. "Lord, he was absolutely terrified some paper or television station would get wind of me and want an interview during those two days I spent there. He begged me not to say a word to anybody." She shoved her sandwich over toward him. "I can't eat this, Sam, you have it."

"Sure? Thanks." He wolfed down the last of his own and started on hers. "You've got to admit it's easier to believe you just went bonkers than it is to accept your story."

"Yeah, I know. There are times when I actually catch myself wondering if Tony's right, if the time I spent back then was only a dream." She put a palm on her belly. "But this isn't any dream, is it, Sam?" She fingered the wide wedding band on her left hand, the diamond-and-emerald engagement ring that rested beside it. "Or these." She touched Madeleine's locket at her throat. "Or this."

It was a routine she'd fallen into during the past days. They'd become her talismans, her visible links to the reality of that other life.

Sam wiped mayonnaise from his mouth and held up a hand, palm out. "Hey, you don't have to convince me. I believe you, remember?"

Paige nodded. Sam *did* believe her—and he was the only one who did. Her brother, her sister-in-law, the police—they'd listened to her story two or three times, and they'd all concluded that she was mentally deranged and pregnant to boot.

Not dangerous, or a threat to society, but definitely a fruitcake, found wandering around in the middle of a farmer's field dressed up as an Indian, wearing a worn pair of Nikes, clutching a fortune in gold coins and babbling her head off about time travel and the Riel Rebellion.

She'd realized quickly that she was an embarrassment to Tony. As soon as she could, she'd left her brother's house and flown home to Vancouver. She'd learned an important lesson those first couple of days. She stopped telling people the truth about what had happened to her. She learned to mumble something vague about a breakdown and amnesia, and she soon found that everyone accepted it.

Everyone except Sam.

Dear Sam. She'd had a panic attack when she arrived at the Vancouver airport—the stress of flying, the realization that she really had not one close friend she could get in touch with, that she no longer had an apartment to go to, or even an office—she knew even before Tony pointed it out that Sam would have had to activate the clause in their partnership that dealt with death or disappearance.

He couldn't operate the business alone, he couldn't possibly afford to wait around for her to turn up, of course he'd had to hire someone to take her place. But it hurt, all the same.

Sweating, shaking, nauseous from the flight and totally freaked by the crowds, the noise, the confusion, the *speed* of the modern day world compared to the one she'd left, Paige had called Sam from the airport, and he'd walked out on an office full of patients to come and collect her.

He'd loaded her into his turquoise Jeep and given her a smacking kiss on the cheek before he pulled out of the ambulance zone where he was parked.

"You look different." He'd reached over and patted her tummy. "Nice going, bringing home work for the firm just when things are slow. So where the hell you been, partner? I missed you."

She'd started to mumble the story about the breakdown and amnesia, and he'd put a hand over her mouth.

"C'mon, Paige, that's bullshit, right? Tell me the truth here. I'm a big boy, I can handle surprises. We worked together, remember?" He pointed at her pregnant belly and then to her wedding ring. "Who is he, Paige? He's got to be quite a guy to win you. And *where* is he? He's gotta be a louse to turn you loose alone in this condition. If you want me to hire a hit man and kill the bastard for you, I will, but I've gotta know the real story."

So she'd taken a deep breath and told him, and he'd asked questions, dozens of questions, in between taking her to a quiet hotel, booking her in, carrying her single suitcase up to the room, prying her new shoes from her swollen feet, ordering toast and tea for her and a giant-size pizza and a large coke for himself.

When she'd run out of both words and tears and he'd finished the pizza, she said without much hope, "Do you believe me, Sam?"

He'd raised one crooked eyebrow and given her a look. "Of course I believe you. It's just too damned farfetched not to believe. You were a great ob-gyn doc, but you never even read science fiction." He'd reached over and taken the toast she'd been unable to eat, smeared marmalade on it, and munched it down.

"Besides, I've got a cousin out at UBC who figures it won't be long before him and his partner have a working prototype for a time-travel device. You're just a little ahead of them, old girl. He's gonna be some excited when I drop the news about these crop circles on him."

She stumbled to her feet, upsetting the teapot, sending her cup flying to the carpet. Her whole body was trembling. "Then I could go back. I wouldn't have to wait; they could send me back right away, me and the baby—"

"Paige, hey, hold on there, this thing of theirs is a long way from being workable." Sam looked stricken. "I'm sorry, I wasn't thinking. Leo's a scientist, you know how those guys operate, ten years is nothing to them. Last I heard, that's about what he figures it's going to take to even build the contraption."

She sank back into the armchair, her disappointment so overwhelming it made her dizzy. She couldn't wait ten years.

She clung to Lame Owl's promise to try to bring her back in the spring—but right now, spring seemed forever away.

"Try taking things one day at a time," Sam had advised, and she'd been doing just that. One day at a time, day after day—and now her baby would be coming tomorrow.

Sam swallowed the last of her sub and glanced at his watch.

"Gotta run, kid." He got to his feet and gave her shoulder an affectionate squeeze. "Don't forget our early morning date, will ya?"

"Not a chance."

She waddled back to the parking garage and squeezed behind the wheel of her rented car, mentally listing the things she needed to do before she checked into the hospital.

She'd have to throw out the perishables from the fridge, and buy some shampoo. Pack an overnight bag, buy a paperback—what about baby clothes? She'd bought very little for the baby. Some superstitious part of her had refused to allow the purchase of all the things she knew the baby would need.

As if he were reprimanding her, he kicked, a solid wallop against her ribs that made her gasp.

Okay, so we'll go shopping for them together. After you're born, we'll go get you everything a baby could want or need.

Except your father. She rested her head on the steering wheel, swallowing hard against the anguish that threatened to overwhelm her, trying with her mind to send a message across endless space and time.

Myles, it's time, and I'm so scared. I'm going to have your baby within hours now, and I'm so alone. Myles, oh God, I miss you, I love you. I need you, my dearest love—make sure that crazy old woman keeps her part of the bargain, won't you?

Myles knelt inside the tipi beside the body of Lame Owl, frail now in death, and a feeling of utter hopelessness engulfed him, a desolation so deep he felt as if his very soul had died within him.

The old woman had been his only link to Paige, his only hope for the safe return of his wife and his child.

Now she was gone, dead in this terrible epidemic of scarlet fever that had raged through Poundmaker's camp for the past several weeks, taking many lives. The Indians had no natural defenses against diseases like scarlet fever.

You were right, old woman, when you said your race

398

was disappearing, and it was the fault of the white man.

With Lame Owl's passing, the village was without a shaman. Eventually, they would probably ask Tahnancoa to fill the role, but for the moment they were putting their trust in western medicine, and Myles felt unworthy of that trust.

He got heavily to his feet. There were others to tend to, and he must see to them. He'd have to tell Tahnancoa her grandmother was gone. So far, she and little Dennis and a few of the other natives had avoided infection, and he hoped that the strict sanitary rules he'd imposed and the quarantining of the sick in this one area of the village would keep the disease from infecting many more people. He was following Paige's example, putting into effect the things he'd learned from her about bacteria and infection.

Tahnancoa was working with him, implementing the treatments he suggested, adding to them her own herbal potions.

A bond of friendship had formed once again between him and Tahny, stronger than it had been. Now they were both alone, both mourning the loss of their beloved partners.

She'd been the one to send him word that day that the ceremony was successful, that Paige was gone. She'd also been the one to send for him when Lame Owl became ill—because of Paige, Tahnancoa had respect for western medicine.

Could Tahny have learned enough from Lame Owl to repeat the time-travel procedure? He was too tired and drained to even hope anymore.

He stood at the opening of the tipi, looking out at the rain that had been falling now for several days. It was the last day of September, and the prairie was sad and wet and lonely.

Had his child been born yet? Had both Paige and the

baby survived the birth? Would he even know if anything happened to her, far away in that other time? Surely he'd feel it, he'd sense that she was no longer alive on this green earth.

At this moment, he longed for whiskey the way a man parched by the desert longed for water. He wanted nothing more than the awful, mindless forgetfulness it afforded.

What good was he doing here, anyway? He had none of the magic drugs that Paige had spoken of so often. He could ride back to Battleford, to the saloon—

A small hand grasped his sleeve and tugged, and anxious obsidian eyes peered up at him from a small brown face. "My mother asks that you come to our tipi. My father is sick with the fever."

He couldn't turn his back on these people. He was all they had in the way of hope.

He took the boy's hand in his and attempted a smile. "Lead the way, son."

The anesthetic sent her spinning down into thick darkness, and Paige struggled through the corridors of time, searching for Myles. He was here somewhere, if she could only find him. . . .

"*Madame docteur,* this way, this way."

The urgent voice guided her, and then she was back in the caves on the river, and Madeleine was having a baby— but the baby was dead-dead-dead.

"Paige, wake up. You have a fine son, and he wants to meet you. Wake up now, Paige, your baby's here, he's a great big boy."

She forced her eyes to focus. Sam stood beside her, still in his green scrubs. His mask was down and his smile stretched from one ear to the other.

"Did he—" Her throat was parched. "Did my baby breathe?"

"Breathe? You bet. He was bawling before we even had him properly out. Told you this kid of yours was a heavyweight. He's nine pounds fifteen, healthy as can be, went right off the scale on the Apgar, obviously inherited his mommy's brains. Both of you did really well. You awake enough to meet him?"

Paige nodded, and Annette Evans, who'd insisted on being present when Paige's baby was born, held up a bundle swathed in flannel.

Paige stared at her son. His hair was as dark as her own, but she could already see Myles in his features, the elegant bone structure, the way his eyes were set, the shape of his ears.

Was she still dreaming? She reached out a hand toward him, aware that there was an IV in her arm.

It was real. Her baby was here, and he was alive.

Myles, you have a son—my love, we have a son.

Annette wound up the head of the bed and placed him in Paige's arms.

"You look just like your daddy," Paige whispered to him, tracing the tiny face with one trembling finger. She touched his cheek with her lips, marveling at the feel and smell of him. He was warm and squirming, opening his eyes and closing them again, batting his fists.

Her son. Myles's son. He made a tiny sound and turned his mouth eagerly toward her flesh, already wanting to eat, and the nurse laughed.

"Famished already."

The enormity of the feelings that rolled over Paige made her close her eyes for an instant.

The overwhelming love she felt for him was frightening in its intensity.

Nothing must ever harm him.

She had to keep him safe, and the responsibility of it was entirely hers.

She longed for Myles, ached as never before to have him see and hold this beautiful child they'd made between them, but she shuddered when she thought of her recent dream, of the caves, of how near her son had come to being born into that primitive world. The dangers to babies back then were endless.

Like a waking nightmare, she saw children with tuberculosis, diphtheria, felt again the helplessness, the galling frustration of not having drugs or facilities to treat them.

She counted the months in her mind, and apprehension filled her. He'd only be seven months by spring. Would he be old enough, strong enough, to withstand the dangers?

"What's his name?" Annette's voice finally penetrated.

"Alexander," Paige said. "Alexander Myles Baldwin. After his father."

"Well, c'mon, young Alex." Annette scooped him up. "Your mommy needs to rest a while, and then she can try feeding you."

Paige reached out and squeezed Sam's hand. "Thanks, partner. You did a great job."

He reddened and bent to plant a kiss on her cheek. "Nothing to it. I'll be in to see you a little later, as soon as they get you back in your room. Rest now."

With the miracle of her son's tiny face in her mind, she slid into sleep.

There were carnations and roses when she awoke, from Sam and the nursing staff. They brought rattles and stuffed toys and baby pajamas and popped in at all hours to ooh and aah over Alex.

Paige knew they were trying to make up for the fact

that she had no other visitors during the days she spent in hospital, and she was both touched and grateful to them for their thoughtfulness.

There were no doting grandparents hovering over Alex's crib, no husband to hold on to and sympathize when she took the first, painful steps after surgery, no friends sneaking burgers and fries into her room.

The strange thing was that she noticed, but she didn't really care, because her world revolved around one tiny boy. All the years she'd been an obstetrician, all the babies she'd delivered, hadn't prepared her for the way she felt about Alex. Time after time, she unwrapped him, examined every inch of him, reassuring herself again and again that he was perfect.

He was more than perfect—he was the picture of health. From the beginning, he drank prodigious amounts of her milk, slept regular hours, and gained weight at an incredible rate.

She took him home when she was strong enough, and the apartment that had been so quiet and lonely was filled with the music of a baby's hungry cries. She bought a rocking chair and sat in front of the window, nursing him. She talked to him, telling him about his father, about that other world where he'd been conceived, and outside the window she watched the bustle of a modern city and compared it to Battleford.

October became November, and on the sixteenth, Alex was six weeks old. She knew it was crazy, but she made a cake and celebrated by buying him a stroller so they could go for walks.

On November 16, 1885, Louis Riel was hanged as a traitor, despite petitions for his pardon from France, England, Ireland, and the United States. Even Queen Victoria asked for clemency for him, but the prime minister would not be moved.

"Riel shall hang," Sir John A. Macdonald declared, "though every dog in Quebec bark in his favor."

The news flew over the telegraph wires from Ottawa to Battleford, and Myles spent that long night alone with a bottle of whiskey, trying to obliterate the savage loneliness in his soul and his disillusionment in his fellow men.

"You grow fine babies, Paige," Sam pronounced, grinning down at a wriggling Alex and trying to refasten his diaper. "This fellow's in perfect health, and you're not far behind yourself. You've made a great recovery in three months. All that walking you're doing is paying off. You're thin as a rail again. Darn, now this thing's too tight; the poor kid's belly is all squashed. Here, you do it." He gave up on the diaper's tabs and stepped aside so Paige could take over. "So when are you going to get bored and come back to work?"

Paige stuffed Alex's plump legs into his red terry playsuit and shot Sam a surprised look. "I'm pretty busy with Alex. Besides, I thought you didn't need a third doctor here, Sam."

He looked embarrassed. "Actually, we don't just yet. But a friend's starting a woman's drop-in clinic downtown, right after Christmas, and there's a good nursery right next door. He's a colleague of ours; you remember Nathan Fielding? I mentioned you to him, so if he calls you'll know what it's all about. It's regular hours, no night calls, you could pretty much decide how much or little you wanted to work. It'd ease you back in, and then later on, if you wanted to come back and work here—or are you still going to try to disappear again, come spring?"

Paige didn't meet his eyes. "I-I think so. I don't know. I

haven't really made up my mind yet." Her love for Myles was counterbalanced now by her urgent need to protect her son from the dangers of that earlier time.

She picked Alex up and cuddled him, burying her nose in his soft curly hair. Each time she thought of taking him back she became anxious and uneasy, and yet the thought of never seeing Myles again was unbearable, a physical pain in her chest.

"I miss Myles, but Alex is still so little. And my chances of getting back are slim at best."

It was the truth, but what she didn't tell Sam was how she'd begun to question whether or not she wanted even to try. Instead of abating, that first powerful reaction she'd had when Alex was born was now growing stronger, the overwhelming desire to give her son all the advantages of modern medicine and modern times.

Sam didn't comment. "The only reason I asked, besides the job, of course, is because of my cousin Leo. You remember I told you about Leo, the scientist out at the university? Well, I've mentioned you to him, and he keeps bugging me to introduce him. Because of the machine he's working on, he's really keen to hear firsthand about your experience."

She frowned at him and shook her head. "Oh, Sam, I don't know. You're the only one I feel comfortable with talking about it."

"It's entirely up to you, but Leo's easy to be around. He's not hooked into the popular concepts of possible and impossible, that's for sure."

She shook her head.

"Look, Paige, you know it's our big Christmas bash at the hospital this Friday, you can't miss that, so why not let me pick you up, we'll stay an hour or so, and then we'll meet Leo afterward for dinner or something?"

Paige shook her head again. "I don't have a sitter for Alex."

"So bring him along. It's a family thing anyhow, you remember how these Christmas parties go, they're a zoo. All the nurses keep asking about you, especially Annette. And there'll be lots of other kids there. There'll be Santa Claus; you don't want to deprive Alex of meeting Santa, do you?"

Paige was tempted. She'd tried to ignore the shop windows, the decorated streets, the music on the radio. She was finding this Christmas season torturously lonely.

Memories of the previous year kept surfacing, the party she'd had for all her friends, the memory of Myles proposing. Dennis had been at her house that day, and Armand too, and no one had thought that joy-filled night that the two men would be dead within a few short months.

That was the trouble with Battleford. Life was so unpredictable back then, so many unforeseen things happened, tragic things, that no one had any control over.

But good things happened as well, she reminded herself.

There was Myles and the love they'd shared. He was always just at the edge of her consciousness, combined with the nostalgic ache that accompanied her memories.

What the heck. She needed to get out; she spent too much time alone with Alex, too much time thinking and worrying.

"All right, Sam. We'll be ready about three."

Her sudden acceptance left him looking both amazed and delighted. "Paige, my love, I do believe this is the first time we've ever had a formal date."

She winked at him. "You've forgotten Alex's birth. And this is a group date, don't forget. There's three of us. Four, counting your cousin."

He nodded and assumed a doleful expression. "Beggars can't be choosers, as my sainted mother used to say. I'll take whatever I can get."

Paige smiled at his nonsense, but she also noted the wistful expression in his eyes when he looked at Alex. She knew Sam was more than half in love with her, and it made her sad.

Why did life have to be so damned complicated? Everything would have been so easy if she could have only fallen in love with Sam instead of Myles.

But she hadn't, had she?

And Myles was waiting, somewhere out there.

Sometime.

Chapter Twenty-four

The party was fun.

Just as Sam had predicted, the hospital staff all made a huge fuss over Alex, and Paige found herself relaxing, laughing at the inevitable hospital jokes, even enjoying the glass of wine Sam brought her.

By the time they left for the restaurant, Paige had even stopped being nervous about meeting Sam's cousin.

"Paige Randolph—sorry, Paige Baldwin, my cousin, Leo Clauson." Sam introduced them, and Leo reached out and took her hand, holding it in his own large grasp for a long moment.

Leo was younger than Paige had imagined, and also better-looking, in an Abe Lincolnesque sort of way. For some obscure reason, she'd thought he'd resemble a much older version of Sam, short and bald and comfortably plump, but Leo was very tall and angular, with thick, long brown hair that drooped attractively on his neck. He wore an expensive-looking gray suit and a conservative blue-striped tie—with bright blue joggers on decidedly large bare feet, as if he'd become absentminded and forgotten about shoes and socks.

He had nice eyes, soft and brown and expressive, and just as Sam had promised, he was easy to talk to.

He studied Alex, who was in his baby carrier and getting squirmy and desperate because he was going to need to be fed very soon. Alex took his mealtimes seriously.

"I've never been around babies very much," Leo remarked. "How do you ever know what they need?"

Paige laughed, because it was a problem she'd never really considered until she had a baby of her own. "Mostly you guess," she said. "Before I had Alex, I thought I knew everything there was to know about babies. Now I realize how little I knew."

They ordered, and while they waited for the food Paige took Alex into the ladies' room and nursed him. When she returned to the table, Leo asked if he could hold him, and she placed the groggy baby in his arms.

From the beginning, Alex had put so much violent energy into eating, he was exhausted and panting by the time each feeding was done. Happy now that he was full, he gave Leo a goofy, cross-eyed grin and instantly fell asleep.

"Hard to believe we all start this way," Leo commented in a wondering tone, cradling the baby, endearingly awkward and careful with him. "His hands and feet have never been used, have they?"

Paige and Sam laughed, but it was obvious that Leo was quite serious.

When the food came, Paige settled the limp baby back in the carrier. Leo smiled at her. "Thanks for letting me hold him. It must have taken a great deal of courage for you to come back here and have him. I'd love to hear what it felt like, traveling through time."

Leo's total acceptance of her experience wiped away

any lingering hesitations Paige might have had, and for the rest of the meal, she talked freely about Battleford and her experiences there.

"It's astonishing, talking to someone who actually met Louis Riel," Leo marveled. "That's the very reason time travel fascinates and obsesses me, because it would give us firsthand knowledge of historical people and events."

"Do you know of any books about Riel and the rebellion?" Paige had planned to search some out in a library, but she hadn't done so yet.

"I'll bring you some of the best from the university library," Leo promised.

For the rest of the meal, Leo entertained her with absurd stories of mad scientists and their exploits at the university.

Sam was unusually quiet, and his mood lasted as he drove her home. He brought Alex's baby carrier into her apartment and set him on the couch.

"Would you like coffee, Sam?"

He shook his head. "I can't stay; I've got to drop by the hospital. One of my patients was admitted this afternoon and I want to check on her before I head home."

Paige kissed him on the cheek. "Thanks so much for everything; I had a wonderful time. It was a great evening, and I enjoyed meeting Leo."

"It was great, until I realized that damned cousin of mine was falling in love with you over the pasta. Then I wanted to stab him in the aorta with a fork."

Paige laughed. "You're nuts, you know that?"

He grinned his old familiar grin. "You're right, I am. First I talk you into meeting old Leo, and then I turn green when you like him. Go figure." He turned to the door. "I'll call you soon."

The following day was Christmas Eve, and Paige decided

there was no point ignoring the season. She went out and bought a small tree and hung a stocking for Alex.

Tony phoned in the afternoon, and Paige tried and failed to break through the barrier that had somehow come between them. She'd sent gifts for Jason and Matthew, Nintendo games that she knew her nephews coveted, and Sharon had dutifully airmailed a box containing a giant-size fuzzy rabbit for Alex.

Tony thanked her for the gifts, asked dutifully about Alex, whom he'd never seen, and turned the phone over to the boys as if he couldn't wait to end the conversation.

Paige had barely hung up, feeling as though she was about to bawl for the rest of the day, when the phone rang again.

She snatched it up, certain that Tony had had second thoughts.

"Hi, Tone, I'm so glad you called back." Her voice was still choked with tears, and her relief was evident in her voice.

There was a small silence, and then a man's voice said, "Paige, it's Leo Clauson here. I hope this isn't a bad time to call?"

It took her several seconds to regain some composure and answer him. They exchanged polite greetings and then he said, "I wondered, I mean, tell me if this is an imposition, but I—well, I wondered if you and Alex might like to have dinner with me tonight. I have those books I promised you, and I don't know if I mentioned that I live alone"—His voice went on and on, betraying his nervousness—"I'm divorced, years ago. The only time it bothers me is holidays, and I know it's Christmas Eve, you've probably got a house full of friends and relatives, it's stupid of me to even ask, it was just an impulse—"

"I don't." She interrupted his monologue, thinking that

411

if she didn't he could possibly go on all afternoon. "I don't have anybody here, I mean." She took a moment to think about his invitation and remembered what Sam had said about his cousin falling for her. She'd have to make her situation very clear, she decided.

"Leo, I'd like to spend the evening with you, but I don't want you to misunderstand me. I'm very much in love with my husband, and I plan to return to him as soon as I can."

Did she plan that? God help her, she wasn't sure, but she didn't want to mislead Leo.

"Of course." She could hear the embarrassment in his voice. "I knew that by the way you spoke of him the other night. I thought we could simply be friends. Would that be all right, Paige?"

"Sure. I'd like that." God knew she could use friends; she hadn't realized until she was back how few friends she really had here—or how many she'd left behind in Battleford. There were times when she ached to talk to Clara or Tahny.

"I can bring dinner over, or take you and Alex out, whatever is best for you."

He brought dinner, and she was astonished. He'd ordered a ready-cooked, full-course, gourmet meal for them from one of the most expensive restaurants in Vancouver. He also brought white wine, chocolates, mandarin oranges, a huge bouquet of hothouse spring flowers, a new tape by a Western singer named Clint Black, and a set of beginner's cloth books for Alex, as well as a bag full of library books for her that dealt with Riel and the 1880s.

"Leo, this is far too much," she protested, her arms full of packages.

"I was afraid maybe it was, but I didn't know for sure," he admitted with an innocent candor that touched her. "Figure

412

out what you don't want and I'll take it back."

"It's not that I don't want it, Leo, it's just—look, at least let me pay for half the dinner, okay?"

He looked horrified. "Absolutely not. I invited you."

She gave in.

They ate and talked and laughed, and after dinner he put Clint Black on her tape player and sang in an off-key baritone, which totally delighted Alex, so Leo took him in his arms and sang, and the baby stared into Leo's face for a moment and then laughed out loud.

"The child has excellent taste in music," Leo pronounced.

When Alex fell asleep she asked Leo about his work, about the machine he and his fellow scientist were working on.

"We used our own money at first, but of course it's a very expensive venture, and considered risky. Last year, we attracted the attention of a wealthy entrepreneur, and he's financed the project, which speeded up our research. We hope to have a working model by the turn of the century. Einstein, of course, laid down the basic equations for the concept of time travel; we simply progressed from his foundations." Brown eyes glowing, he lapsed into technical details that Paige couldn't begin to decipher. He seemed to love talking about it, so she listened and nodded and allowed her thoughts to wander back to Battleford.

Later, Leo asked again to hold Alex, and he sat cradling the baby for a good half-hour, frowning down at him as though he were another complicated equation that needed deciphering.

"You never had children?" Paige was curious. It was obvious Leo was fascinated by babies.

"Alice couldn't have any. We applied for adoption, but then our marriage fell apart. It was pretty much my fault.

413

I have a tendency to forget about time and work around the clock when I find something that interests me. And our interests were different. Alice enjoyed parties and the symphony. I'm more inclined toward long walks and books and Clint Black."

"How long have you been divorced?"

"Ten years now." He caught the look of surprise on her face and smiled at her. "I'm forty-six. After Alice left, I decided I wasn't very good marriage material, so I never really tried again." He looked down at Alex, cooing and smiling up at him. "I rather regret that at times."

"Heavens, Leo, you're still young, there's plenty of time to meet someone and have kids. I felt much the same as you before I met Myles."

He smiled at her again, a quizzical smile. "But you have to admit that was an unusual occurrence."

"Yes, it was." The ache that was never really gone from her heart came back with wrenching intensity, and she wondered what she was doing, sitting here watching one man hold her son when her heart and soul longed for another.

Alex began to fuss anxiously and devour his fist, and Leo handed him over. "Why don't I go and clean up in the kitchen while he has his supper," he suggested tactfully.

Paige took the baby into the bedroom, opened her blouse, and put him to her breast. In his usual frenzy, Alex snorted and batted at her with his tiny fists, gulping in great mouthfuls of milk, choking and crying and coughing before he could relax enough to nurse comfortably. He attacked each feeding as if he were starving to death, and then halfway through he'd stop for an instant and give Paige a wide, grateful grin, like an abashed apology, before he began gobbling again.

"Piglet." Paige laughed at her funny, frantic child, and then her eyes filled with tears.

She wanted so badly to share all the funny, intimate details about Alex with Myles. At first, when Alex was new, she'd talked to Myles as if he were nearby and somehow could hear and laugh with her at their son's idiosyncrasies.

But as time passed, her husband and his world seemed to draw further and further away, and with increasing regularity she couldn't find him to talk to anymore.

In February when Alex was five months old, he'd grown two teeth. He knew how to roll from his back to his stomach, and he had a plastic set of keys he adored. He was good-natured about everything except his meals, and he resembled Myles more than ever.

The only obvious part of Paige he'd inherited was her hair—Alex's sooty curls were as wild and unmanageable as her own, but the shape of his skull, the color and shape of his eyes, the curve of his chin, the way his ears lay flat against his head—all of these were miniature replicas of his father.

Nathan Fielding called one day and asked Paige to come work with him at the drop-in clinic he'd established in the heart of downtown Vancouver.

She was beginning to worry a little about money, and after some deliberating about hours, and a great deal of agonizing about leaving Alex at the nursery next door to the clinic, she agreed to take the job.

She'd had money in her account when she disappeared, but when she got back much of it had gone to pay the storage expenses on her furniture and to set herself up again in another apartment. There'd been the expenses of the baby, and she'd also bought a car—Sharon hadn't offered to return her Sunbird, and Paige had decided against asking. It seemed too shoddy, somehow, nagging her sister-in-law for her car.

The gold coins Myles had given her were still untouched, sitting in a safety-deposit box at her bank. She couldn't bring herself to use them. She thought of them as Alex's only legacy from his father.

Leo Clauson had become a good friend. He'd fallen into the habit of dropping by once or twice a week. He always brought dinner, and he was endlessly fascinated by Alex.

After her first week at the clinic, Leo came by on Friday night with cardboard containers of Chinese food.

"So how did it go?" He'd learned where she kept everything in the kitchen, and he set out plates and forks and wineglasses while she settled Alex in his jumper.

"The clinic's in a low-income area; a lot of the patients are immigrants. I've treated severe burns, six cases of intestinal flu, three women with venereal infection, done countless prenatal workups. There was also a woman who's HIV positive and pregnant, and two other pregnant women who are drug addicts."

"Sounds like an ambitious first week." Leo looked over at Alex, squealing and leaping up and down like a jackrabbit in his jumper. "Were you satisfied with the nursery?"

"Absolutely. It's right next door. Whenever there's a break I can pop over and visit him. And feed him, of course."

"To his immense relief."

They laughed together. By now, Leo had often witnessed Alex's frenzy at mealtimes.

"It was the strangest feeling, treating those women and children," Paige mused. "I have moments when I feel as though I'm back in my clinic in Battleford."

Leo raised a quizzical eyebrow.

"Oh, the physical problems then were different," she explained. "No AIDS, no drug addicts, but the emotions were exactly the same. And back then I used to curse at the lack of available treatments."

Leo indicated he was listening.

"Well, damned if it isn't exactly the same now. Y'know, Leo, there's a whole new crop of diseases we still don't have any magic drugs for. Some I can help, some I can't, just like it was back then. It's the damnedest thing."

She wished so much she could tell Myles. How often had she raged because his time didn't have the miracles hers did? Had she ever told him about AIDS, about drug addiction? She couldn't remember.

"The more things change, the more they stay the same," Leo said, spooning stir-fried vegetables on her plate.

Alex was six months old in March. He could move himself around the floor now, pulling himself from one fascinating object to the next. He had six teeth, and a whole vocabulary of sounds. He was impossible to diaper; he couldn't stand to be still for an instant. He could sit up on his own, and he'd learned how to play pat-a-cake.

He had Myles's bone structure, and would probably be a tall man. His huge gray-green eyes were fringed with indecently long, curling lashes. Strangers smiled at him on the street, unable to resist his wide grin.

His passion for food had never changed; the only time he howled in misery was when there was a slight delay with his meal.

Then one morning in early April, he woke with a fever and refused to eat the pabulum Paige tried to spoon into him. She was still nursing him, but after two or three gulps of milk, he turned his head away from her breast.

It was the first time he'd ever been ill, and definitely

417

the first time he'd refused to eat. Alarmed, Paige took his temperature. It was high, alarmingly so. She gave him aspirin, sponged him in tepid water, and called the clinic to say she wouldn't be in.

By late afternoon, Alex's fever had risen alarmingly in spite of medication, sponging, and even ice-water packs to the groin. He was flushed and listless, his breath coming in short pants. He wouldn't swallow even water, and Paige was beginning to be concerned about dehydration. She'd checked his throat and ears, and neither seemed inflamed.

Feeling foolish at herself for being a nervous mother, she called the pediatrician Sam had recommended, who confirmed that she was doing exactly what he'd have done himself, adding, "If he doesn't improve, bring him in to the office first thing in the morning and I'll have a look at him. If you're concerned during the night, call me."

Trying to stay calm and rational, but needing reassurance and support, Paige dialed Sam's office number.

"I've got two more patients to see, and then I'll be there," he promised, and she was too grateful to protest.

She'd seen Sam only a few times since Christmas. When she opened the door for him, he gave her a hug before he even said hello.

"Kid's probably just teething, and the two best doctors in Vancouver are unable to diagnose the problem," he teased her, bending over Alex's crib.

Sam performed the exact examination Paige had done herself a number of times that day and reached the same conclusion.

"He's spiking a pretty good fever all right, but damned if I know why. I brought along a different medication; we'll maybe give it a try."

The drug was administered rectally, and Sam stayed to see if it would be effective. Paige tried to visit with him, but her every nerve was attuned to the baby dozing in his crib.

"I saw Leo the other day. He said you guys see quite a lot of each other." Sam's voice was nonchalant.

"We do, but it's a friendship and nothing more, Sam." It made her irritable to have to be defensive.

He got up and walked over to the window, staring down at the tiny park and the daffodils that were in bloom. "You decided yet about going back, Paige? Didn't you say it had to be in the spring?"

His question struck a bull's-eye, right at the center of everything that had plagued her all winter. "Why are you asking me all these questions?" Her voice was shrill, and she knew she was being unreasonable, but the strain of worrying about Alex combined with the guilty knowledge that she was avoiding making a decision about trying to return to Battleford made her snap at him. "I don't go around prying into your personal affairs."

He turned from the window, but instead of getting angry, he came over and rubbed her shoulders. "Easy, Doc. I'm not very diplomatic, am I? See, I'm trying to tell you something here, and I ought to just blurt it out. The thing is, I've met a woman I kinda like. Besides you, that is. Which is why I haven't been around much this last while. I didn't want you to think I had my nose out of joint over Leo or anything."

Paige was already ashamed of her outburst. "Oh, Sam, that's just great. I'm really happy for you, and I'd love to meet her, as soon as Alex is better. Is she a doctor? A nurse?"

He shook his head. "She's a policeperson. A Mountie, actually."

Paige's mouth dropped. "A Mountie?"

He grinned, enjoying her surprise. "She was visiting her

sister, who's one of my patients. She wanted to be in the delivery room when her nephew was born, and we sort of hit it off. Her name's Christine."

"Christine." Paige saw the color deepen in Sam's cheeks, the expression in his eyes change. He was in love, and it made her long for Myles.

"I wanted to say something to you about Leo." He sat down on the couch beside her and took her hand. "Don't take this the wrong way, but the guy's in love with you, and you really ought to think carefully about this whole idea you've got about trying to get back to Battleford."

She started to protest, but he interrupted. "It's dangerous, Paige. I don't have the foggiest notion how the hell it works, but Leo says it could be really dangerous, and I believe him. You've got Alex to think of; it's not just you anymore. And Leo's a good guy—he's an eccentric, but his heart's in the right place. That first wife of his was an absolute bitch, but the guy never once says anything bad about her. He's even rich, not that money matters that much to you. He inherited money from his mother's family, a lot of money. He's bonkers about Alex, and if you gave him the slightest encouragement, I know he'd be there for you."

Paige felt miserable. "I know. I know all that, Sam. The trouble is, I don't love Leo. I'm in love with my husband. I'm in love with Surgeon Myles Baldwin." Repeating his name and title made him seem closer to her for a second.

"And you're going to try to go back?"

Alex began to cry, and she shot to her feet and hurried in to pick him up.

Sam came too, and they both felt the baby's head. It was clear that Alex was cooler, that the medication Sam brought had worked. The thermometer confirmed it. Alex's temperature was down.

Paige felt weak with relief. She sat in the rocking chair

and lifted her sweatshirt and nursed him, and this time Alex drank, not with his usual gusto, but at least not refusing the way he'd done before.

Sam was exuberant. "There now, he's back on the rails again. Like I said, he's probably cutting a molar, and we're too dumb to know." Sam grinned at her, as relieved as she was that the baby was better. He glanced at his watch. "Oops, I've got to go; Christine's waiting for me. Call if you need me."

"Thanks, Sam."

He hesitated. "Think about what I've said, okay? Because I'm so darned happy myself, I'd like to see you settled and content. In this century."

She heard the outside door close behind him, leaving her alone with her baby. She stroked Alex's forehead, nearly sick with relief and gratitude, smoothing the damp, dark curls. He was cooler, and he was eating again.

Her underarms were damp with perspiration, her stomach, empty and knotted all day, rumbled with hunger now that her fear had subsided.

The question that haunted her days and nights was there in her mind, demanding an answer.

What would have happened if Alex had spiked that kind of temperature in Battleford?

He lay heavily against her stomach, warm and damp and fragrant, one small hand resting on her breast, his eyes meeting hers in silent communion as he swallowed her milk. As he did so often, he stopped nursing for a moment and smiled up at her, his wonderful, trusting baby smile.

He was more precious to her than her own life, and she knew in that instant that she couldn't take him back. She couldn't deliberately expose him to danger, to a place where she had no tools to protect him, no resources to fall back on.

She felt her heart tearing in two, knowing she was forsaking Myles for their child.

Forgive me, my dearest love. Understand, and forgive.

Slow tears dripped down on the baby's soft skin, and with a fingertip, she wiped them away, along with hopes and dreams and the searing memory of a love that she instinctively knew she'd find only once in this lifetime— a love she'd have to sacrifice for the sake of the child in her arms.

Chapter Twenty-five

Part of her knew it was only the dream, but the sand caves smelled real, damp, filled with the pungent odor of woodsmoke and hot, coppery blood, and in her ears echoed the sound of Marguerite groaning, the muffled screams that were bringing her child, the frightened hammering of her own heart in her chest—

Paige came out of the dream, but the sound continued.

"Alex. My God, Alex."

She wrestled out from the sheet, somehow wrapped in a tight shroud around her body. She leaped up from the bed, fumbling on the bedside light. His crib was only a few feet away, yet it seemed to take an eternity to reach it.

The sound he was making. God, the sound he was making.

His face was scarlet, his eyes rolled back in his skull. Milky foam bubbled from his mouth. His body was rigid, and even as she stared in horror, his limbs jerked and shook.

He was convulsing. Her baby was convulsing.

Paige fought back the primitive, immobilizing terror that gripped her. She forced her finger into Alex's mouth, making certain his tongue wasn't choking him. His temperature had shot up again; his skin was like fire against her hand. With her free hand she loosened the snaps on his blanket sleeper, waiting through the eternity the seizure took to subside and allow his small form to relax.

At last he opened his eyes and recognized her, and his mouth quivered. He pouted and then gave a helpless, wavering cry, and she scooped him up, held him tight against her as she dialed the number for Children's Hospital.

"It's okay, my darling, Mommy's here," she crooned, and when the switchboard answered she asked that they alert Alex's pediatrician and have him meet her at the hospital immediately.

She stuffed a bag with the things Alex needed, pulled on a pair of sweats and a jacket, and within half an hour, her son was being admitted.

For the next five days, Alex's temperature fluctuated. The increasing number of specialists called in to consult on his case couldn't agree on a diagnosis, and Paige existed in a narrow world that consisted of a small room painted a cheerful yellow, a high-sided crib with a mobile that played a lullaby, and an unnamed atrocity that threatened to consume her child.

She stayed with Alex every possible moment, snatching brief moments of sleep on a cot in his room and eating whatever the kitchen supplied, caring for him herself, supervising each and every useless treatment the specialists prescribed.

She felt nauseated all the time, but she forced herself to eat because she refused to stop nursing Alex. He was drinking enough to avoid dehydration, and she knew the value of breast milk, but she also knew that the moments spent with her listless baby at her breast were the closest she came to sanity during those days. Her milk seemed to be the only thing she could give her child that had any value.

She understood the hospital system, she knew exactly what the barrage of specialists who converged on his crib were searching for—positive signs that her son had some nameable, treatable disease.

She also knew that after five days they had no more idea than she what was wrong with her baby, and she knew too that they'd come to resent her involvement—she was a doctor and she understood their limitations.

They ordered more tests, a barrage of tests.

Paige refused to allow any of them unless the experts explained to her exactly what they thought to gain by each and every one, exactly what effects these tests would have on Alex.

This was her child; each needle in his tiny veins had to have a valid explanation, each exposure to some new machine had to be worth the risk it posed to his system. They were forced to cancel several procedures because Paige knew they were both painful and unproductive.

The tests she agreed to showed that Alex's liver and spleen were enlarged. There was no sign of malignancy, but something was very wrong. The fevers continued in no predictable pattern, and Alex grew weaker and more listless.

Sam came far more often than she suspected he had time for, and from the first day, Leo spent hours with her in Alex's small room. He talked or was quiet, depending on what she needed. He insisted that Paige go outside, walk in the rain for ten minutes, have soup in the cafeteria down the street, shower, do any one of the many things she needed or wanted to do, while he sat beside the crib and held Alex's tiny hand or walked up and down with Alex on his shoulder, singing the baby some Western song about love gone wrong.

Instead of the things he suggested, Paige spent the time away from Alex at the computer, studying every obscure childhood illness she could locate that had similar symptoms.

Not trusting even the computer, she went to the medical library and hauled back armloads of textbooks, reading them while Alex slept. There were countless conditions that had similar symptoms, but none that were identical. Alex tested negative to those few that were even possible.

On the fifth afternoon, after eight hours of near normality that aroused cautious hope inside of her, Alex's temperature shot up higher than ever before, and the familiar routine of drugs, tepid baths, ice-water packs, hypothermia blankets began all over again. This time, a drip was inserted in his tiny foot to allow massive doses of broad-base antibiotics, on the chance that they'd subdue whatever was causing the infection.

When Leo arrived that evening, she slipped out of the room and walked into a storage closet down the hall. She locked the door behind her, buried her face in a stack of fresh towels, and screamed until her throat was sore and her body shook so hard she could barely stand.

The following morning, the doctors admitted that they still had no idea what was wrong, but whatever it was seemed to be progressing at a rapid rate; Alex's blood cells now showed definite signs of some general massive infection.

Paige no longer felt like one of the doctors; she was a mother, she couldn't discuss any part of this dispassionately. She listened as they summed up their conclusions.

"Whatever is wrong with your son has become life-threatening. We feel the time has come for more aggressive measures, Dr. Baldwin." The chief pediatrician was an older man, probably a grandfather, Paige mused. In his gentle voice he listed all the possibilities, the drug therapy that he thought might perhaps help.

His voiced faded in and out. In Paige's head, like a videotape automatically turned on, she saw herself, frantic because of her helpless, hopeless feeling about little Ellie. She heard herself ask Myles a question.

"If she was your child, Myles, what would you do?"

"I'd take her to a shaman," he'd replied.

The pediatrician was still talking, speculating about an obscure form of leukemia, about chemotherapy, about bone-marrow transplants, about environmental diseases so new they had no name.

"This would seem to be a nineties phenomenon," he concluded. "We must begin treatment as soon as possible."

"No." Paige looked at him, looked at the other doctors, and said again, in a stronger voice, "No. I'll be discharging Alex within the hour. Thank you for all your efforts on our behalf."

A babble of protest rose like static, but she didn't bother explaining.

A clarity had come to her mind through the weariness, and terror, and pain. It was as if Myles stood at her elbow, shaking his head and telling her where she'd gone wrong.

She'd made such a grave mistake, thinking she could protect Alex. Keeping him in the twentieth century hadn't kept him safe. Instead, it had deprived both him and Myles of knowing and loving one another. She'd been incredibly selfish, incredibly weak and stupid and self-serving.

She'd forgotten that Alex was a special child, a child conceived of love in another time. Perhaps keeping him here was like attempting to transplant a delicate seed that needed different air in order to grow.

The tape flicked on again, and Paige saw Clara, desperate about her child, and then she saw Tahnancoa, performing a mystical ritual over the fragile baby that somehow healed her.

Could it work for Alex the way it had for Ellie?

She was unaware of walking down the hallway, of opening the door to Alex's room.

Leo, his kind face marked with weariness and strain just as her own was, sat beside the crib, his hand through the bars, one finger stretched out to stroke Alex's cheek. He got up, alarmed when he saw the expression on her face.

"What is it, Paige? Is there anything I can do?"

"Yes. Please call all the airlines for me and make a reservation for Alex and me on the first flight available to Saskatchewan. And somehow, I have to find out where there's a crop circle."

"You're going back." There was resignation in his voice, and acceptance. He hesitated and then blurted, "Do you mind if I fly to Saskatchewan with you and Alex? I don't want to intrude, but if I could help in any way . . ."

She'd been trying not to worry about the mechanics of it all, the physical problems involved with taking a sick baby on a trip, of finding a crop circle and getting herself and Alex there at the right time.

Having Leo with her would be a huge relief. She put her arms around him and gave him an impulsive hug. "There's nothing I'd appreciate more. Thanks, friend."

Without another word, he hurried off to the phones down the hall. She stuffed Alex's belongings into a bag and then made a detailed list of the medical supplies she'd need for him.

She bent over the crib. He was lying on his back, his

small foot attached to the drip at his bedside, his eyes flickering behind his closed eyelids in some baby dream. Paige touched the silky hair that curled around his ears.

"Hold on, my darling," she whispered. "Be strong, and I'll take you home."

She glanced toward the window. The trees were in bloom, the spring season well advanced. Had she waited too long? Had Lame Owl performed the ceremony many times already and finally given up? She'd been very explicit about performing the ceremony only in the spring and the fall.

Spring was almost over, and fall would be too late—too late for Alex.

Apprehension grew, and Paige fought it down.

She had to have faith; she had to trust. There was nothing else.

Leo stuck his head in the door. "I have two seats on a Canadian Airlines flight at three this afternoon. I told the agent to hold the line until I checked with you."

Paige took a deep breath and then unhooked the IV from Alex's foot. It was terrifying, this turning away from the medical services she'd always depended upon, but there was also a knowledge inside of her, fragile still but insistent, that this was the right thing to do. "Confirm the reservations, Leo."

She dressed Alex and then scooped him into her arms.

"C'mon, little boy." She forced confidence and strength into her voice, even though she felt neither. "You and I are going to see your daddy."

Her child in her arms, she walked out of the hospital into the warmth of the April day.

Everyone in Poundmaker's village welcomed the changing season. Spring had come to the prairies early this year, and the people rejoiced because the winter had been filled with sickness and hardship.

Now crocuses bloomed and the patches of snow that lay scattered on the brown earth like dirty laundry were shrinking, melting away in the welcome warmth of the sun. Women brought sleeping robes out of tipis to air, and small brown children shed their heavy winter clothing and ran half-naked, wild in the warmth of the sun.

As she'd done at dawn and dusk for many days now, Tahnancoa summoned the women once again this afternoon to join her in the ceremony that she hoped would bring Paige back through the corridors of time.

Far from the village, in the sacred area, she traced the charmed circle on the earth and scattered the magic potions in the particular way Lame Owl had taught her. She chanted the rhythms and tried to clear her mind of all but the ceremony, but deep in her heart Tahnancoa was afraid.

The more times she tried this and failed, the less confidence she had in herself and her ability. She was afraid she didn't have the power Lame Owl had possessed. She did everything her grandmother had said to do, but still she couldn't seem to locate the dream pathway between the worlds that would open the gateway and capture the spirits and bodies of Paige and her child and transport them from then to now.

She imagined she could hear her grandmother's petulant old voice, instructing her. "Open your mind and allow the four winds to blow through you. Call on the earth mother to open the door, and then trust in her power."

Tahnancoa had tried all those things, but there was still a part of her that doubted her own ability, and that part grew more powerful each time she tried and failed.

Myles had been in the Indian village for many days, waiting.

Each night when she walked back into the village the awful disappointment and pain in his eyes when he saw she was alone called out to her, made her ashamed of her inadequacy.

Her heart ached for the tall doctor in the policeman's scarlet tunic, but knowing he was there put pressure on her, and that pressure made it even more difficult to concentrate.

Myles watched from a hilltop as Tahnancoa and the small group of women straggled back toward the village in the early dusk. He knew Paige wasn't with them, but in spite of himself he studied each figure over and over again, just in case he'd somehow missed her.

Of course she wasn't there, and it felt as if more shreds of his soul dried up and blew away in the cool evening air. He'd told himself all winter that his wife and child were lost to him forever, that he was a fool to think otherwise, but hope died hard.

He walked down to the women. When he saw the dejection on Tahny's face, the compassion in her eyes, he knew there was no point in hoping any longer.

"Tahny, I'm riding back to the fort tonight." He reached out and took her hand in his own. "Thank you for all your efforts, my dear. It wasn't meant to be, so don't fret over it."

Her dark eyes were agonized and ashamed. "I'm sorry, Myles Baldwin."

He squeezed her hand. One of the young boys brought his horse and his medical bag, and he thanked the boy and then swung into the saddle. He lifted his wide-brimmed hat to Tahnancoa and turned away from the village.

Raw anguish filled him, and he urged his horse to a gallop

even though he knew it was dangerous to race across the rough ground in the fading light.

He'd welcome death. It was living with this aching loneliness he couldn't bear.

There was no longer any hope, he knew that now. He'd write to the superintendent in the morning, requesting a transfer that would take him far away from Battleford.

The field Paige had Leo drive to was wet and soggy, the first green sprigs of grass just beginning to tinge the prairie soil. The crop circle was like an old, half-healed scar on the surface of the dark earth.

In distant fields, a tractor plowed the earth for spring planting, but here it was still too wet, and the earth was undisturbed, the stubble of last fall's crop still lying on the ground. Paige was wearing her worn old Nikes, and the mud rose almost to their tops.

For the past three days, Leo had brought Paige and Alex here well before dawn and again in the hour before sunset. In the center of the circle, Paige stood and waited, Alex, wrapped in thick blankets, clutched close in her arms. At her feet was a bulging carryall of medical supplies and over her shoulder was Alex's diaper bag. Around her neck was the pouch with the gold coins and her locket. In her heart was a desperate hope.

Twice each day, Leo would patiently carry her bags to the spot Paige indicated and then go back and stand by the rented car, his shoulders bent against the chill prairie wind, as immobile as Paige for the hour it took the sun to rise or set. One of the days had been overcast, and they'd had to guess at the right moment.

Time after time Paige ignored the icy wind and waited. She prayed and tried to visualize Battleford. She searched for Myles's face in her memory, she tried with her mind to reach Lame Owl and let her know they were waiting here, but fear and the knowledge that the listless child in her arms was growing weaker each day made her impotent.

When dawn was over, when sunset was only a streak of crimson in the western sky, Leo would come and silently take Alex from her aching arms.

"We'll try again in the morning," he'd say reassuringly.

Alex had been blessedly free of fever during those first days, but on the fourth night, the fever came back with raging intensity.

All night, in her sparse room in the little motel in the middle of nowhere, Paige worked over the baby, sponging, giving antibiotics, making bargains with God, sickeningly aware that her son's small body couldn't withstand such ravages much longer.

Leo had seen the light on in her room and tapped at the door just after midnight.

"Can I help?" He wrung out cool towels, made coffee, held Alex so Paige could gulp down a cupful. He talked about everyday things: a man he'd met in the coffee shop, the evening weather report, a movie he'd once seen on television, and once in a while, Paige was able to respond.

When dawn came, Alex was still far too feverish to risk the trip to the distant field. Leo was holding him, and Paige stood at the window, her arms wrapped around her body, watching the inky darkness change to gray, and then to palest blue. Urgency was an illness inside of her.

"Leo, what if this was our chance, and I've missed it?" Her voice quavered, and she fought the tears that threatened. If she once started to cry, she was afraid she'd never have the strength to stop again.

Leo was silent, walking back and forth and back again across the stained green carpet, humming to Alex. At last,

433

in a voice as gentle as the dawn, he said, "My dear, don't you think that perhaps soon we should give up and go home? This can't be the best thing for the baby, or for you."

He was right. Her brain knew he was right, but her heart resisted. "I want to try again," she insisted. "Just once more."

He looked at her, and she saw the love and desire in his eyes, despite the fact that she was still in the mud-stained jeans she'd worn the day before, and she hadn't washed her face or brushed her hair in far too long.

"You're a good man, Leo. You deserve better than this."

He smiled at her. "Let me be the judge of what I deserve."

Alex had fallen asleep, and Leo tenderly laid him in the small crib the motel had provided. "Go have a shower now. I'll sit here and watch him. Then I'll bring us some breakfast from the coffee shop, and after that, you lie down and sleep. I'll stay here in the armchair and if there's any problem I'll wake you immediately."

She agreed, knowing it was selfish; Leo hadn't slept any more than she. She was simply too exhausted to protest.

The baby moved restlessly, kicking off his blanket, and Leo leaned into the crib and carefully tucked it back around the little boy. He tiptoed back to the armchair and picked up the paperback mystery he'd been staring at for several hours.

It was late afternoon, and he'd have to wake Paige soon if they were going to have time to drive out to that godforsaken field in time for sunset.

Once more, he told himself. If she tried once more and failed, maybe there'd be a chance. He glanced over at Paige, her too slender body wrapped in a peach-colored blanket, her breath making tiny sighing sounds as she breathed.

He'd fallen in love with her the first day they'd met. It had been as though he'd spent his life in some dispassionate gray dream, and then all of a sudden he'd awakened to color and life and feeling. He hadn't realized what was missing in his life until he'd seen the play of expression across her face, or watched the way she ran her fingers distractedly through her mass of black hair. He hadn't realized he'd longed for the warm, fragrant weight of a baby in his arms until he'd held Alex.

Alex. He rose again and laid his palm across the baby's forehead. He was still too warm, but not burning up the way he'd been before.

Was Alex going to die?

Leo could hardly stand to pose the question even to himself. He loved Alex, in a different way than he loved Paige, but just as much.

The child was gravely ill, he knew that. He'd called Sam and asked him about Alex, asked him to be honest about Alex's chances of recovery.

"The prognosis isn't good," Sam had told him in that maddening jargon that doctors used on laypeople. "But Paige is an excellent doctor; she can do as much for him as any hospital could."

"Is there anywhere else in the world where the doctors could do something more?" Leo was prepared to hire a Concord, take the baby anywhere, if it meant help for him.

But Sam said no. The specialists at Children's Hospital had consulted by telephone and computer with experts all over the world, and no one had any answers to Alex's illness.

Sam had paused and then added, "Take her where she wants to go, Leo. You know as well as I do that the chances of this crazy time-travel thing working again are well below zero. But if she doesn't try, she's always going to blame herself. Take her, let her put this thing to rest once and for all, and then you can make a new start with her."

"And the baby? What'll happen if she loses him, Sam? He's her whole life."

"She'll need you then. She'll need you badly."

Whatever happened, Leo vowed he'd be there for her.

He reached over and touched Paige's shoulder, alarmed at how thin she'd grown. It was time to drive out to the field. At least this was the last time, he reminded himself.

Lame Owl came to Tahnancoa in a dream, her thin mouth set in lines of displeasure, her voice angry. "What's the matter with you, daughter of my daughter? Did I not tell you that the path between the worlds is one of no resistance? You try, and with such trying, naturally you fail. Why are you being so stupid? Be one with the earth spirits and forget the rest. It will come of its own will." The old woman went over every detail of the ceremony, making Tahnancoa repeat the ritual after her.

As the last of Lame Owl's words faded, Tahnancoa woke up, her heart hammering. Little Dennis slept cuddled against her, and she was careful to leave him asleep as she slid out of the warm robes and drew on her clothing.

It was already dawn. She'd missed the gateway of the morning. She'd go in the afternoon instead, make her way to the sacred hollow and perform the ceremony once again, using Lame Owl's instructions. Filled with new resolve, Tahnancoa set about her daily chores, waiting for the hour of sunset. She didn't eat all day, and in the afternoon, she went to the sweat lodge to purify herself as Lame Owl had instructed.

When the time came, she left Dennis with her cousin, took the shaman's pouch Lame Owl had left her, and set off alone toward the hollow.

Paige knew it was hopeless. For the first time, she left her medical bag and Alex's diaper bag in the car. She wandered alone out to the center of the field, carrying Alex. The worst of the fever had passed, and he was drowsy and irritable, rubbing his eyes and struggling against the blanket.

Tonight the sky was clear, the sun dropping steadily toward the horizon. With the orange light glimmering behind her closed eyelids, Paige stood facing the west.

She could see Myles clearly this time, his beloved face smiling at her. She could feel the ring he'd put on her finger biting into her flesh.

She thought of Madeleine, of Gabriel and Riel and Tahnancoa and Lame Owl. She thought of Clara and Ellie and all the friends she'd made in Battleford.

She'd never see them again, she knew that now. She was saying good-bye.

A pervasive peace seeped through her as she thought of them, and for an instant she remembered exactly how it felt to be held tight in Myles's arms.

A plane soared high overhead.

Lost in her daydream, Paige wasn't aware of it.

Alex fussed a little and quieted again.

Leo heard the baby and started toward Paige, but she was so intensely still he paused, turned, and went back to the car. His heart was torn by her hopeless, lonely vigil, but it was something she had to do alone.

He glanced up for a moment and watched the jet make its way across the wide sky and into the hot colors the sun created as it dipped toward the horizon.

And when he looked toward Paige again, a hoarse cry rose in his throat, and he raced across the field to where she had been an instant before, but she and Alex were gone.

Chapter Twenty-six

For the first time, Tahnancoa knew beyond doubt she was one with the earth spirits.

In this last moment between day and evening, she sensed from the depths of her trance that she was no longer alone.

Paige's image shimmered before her closed eyelids, trying to find form and shape and substance, struggling to escape from the space between the worlds and enter the door that Tahnancoa's passive will held open for her.

Tahnancoa resisted the urge to reach out and try to help her friend, mindful of Lame Owl's lecture. Instead, she allowed the gateway in her mind to open even wider, and as Paige's image gradually became stronger, Tahnancoa realized that Paige wasn't alone.

She had a baby clutched to her breast, a small boy child.

Tahnancoa knew he was terribly sick, and even in the midst of her joy, she was afraid for her friend.

The little boy's spirit was already beginning to slip away.

When she was certain it was safe, she opened her eyes, and her arms reached out to encircle Paige and the child.

Paige, her face ravaged with tears of gratitude, placed her baby in Tahnancoa's arms.

"His name is Alex. Please, Tahny, can you help him?"

Tahnancoa touched the beautiful boy's face with her fingers.

"It is for the gods to decide, but I will try," she said.

In Poundmaker's village, Paige waited as the dusk faded and night fell. A messenger had been sent to the fort, and she heard Myles's horse approaching before she saw her husband.

"Paige? Oh, my beloved . . ." He threw himself down before the animal had fully stopped, and then his arms were around her, holding her against him in an embrace so tight she was certain her ribs were cracking.

"My darling, my darling."

He kissed her, and she felt the warmth of his tears mingle with her own, and neither of them could speak for long moments.

"Our baby?" His voice was a fearful whisper, and she gestured toward the sweat lodge where Tahnancoa had taken Alex hours before.

"He's sick. Oh, Myles, our son is so sick." In broken sentences, she told him all about their child's illness, and for the first time there was comfort, because the awful pain and responsibility were shared between them.

Alex was theirs, flesh of their flesh. Whatever happened to him affected them equally. As the bright stars filled the prairie sky and a full moon waxed and waned again, she told Myles about their son, healing words that filled the spaces time had stretched between them.

It was almost dawn when Tahnancoa brought Alex to them.

"The fever is gone for now," she said. "As for tomorrow, I can promise nothing. The illness he has is powerful. We will have to wait and see." She handed the baby to Myles.

Paige saw the wonder on her husband's face as he held his son for the first time. Seeing them together, the likeness between their two faces was uncanny.

Alex was wide-awake, more cheerful than she'd seen him for a long time. He studied Myles's face, his huge gray eyes searching the strange features, assessing them. He reached a tentative hand up and tried to put his fingers into his father's mouth. Myles pretended to nibble them.

At that, Alex smiled his goofy, crooked grin and reached up, tugging at his father's hair as though he'd known him always.

There was a brightness, an alertness in the baby that had been missing since he became ill, and the fear that had been all-consuming in Paige began to ease.

Alex looked from Myles to Paige, and seemed to remember all of a sudden that it had been hours since he'd eaten, and that she was his major food source. He squirmed and held his arms out to his mother, and his mouth pouted and then formed the outraged square shape it always assumed when he was hungry.

His whimper became a cry, and then a full-fledged tantrum. His hungry screams ringing in her ears, she and Myles ducked into Tahny's tipi and Paige sat down to open her shirt and nurse him.

Frantic, he gobbled and choked and sputtered and fought with all the wonderful spirit she'd missed so much the past few weeks.

Myles watched his fierce, small son in disbelief. When the usual choking fits and flailing of arms and thrashing of feet finally settled down and Alex stopped swallowing long enough to look up and give Paige his apologetic grin, Myles laughed with delight. "He's just like you, my darling. Stubborn and determined and single-minded, until he gets what he wants."

She opened her mouth to object, and then realized that Myles was right about Alex. He had Myles's looks and her nature. He was part of each of them—and so much more.

Born only with the sophisticated help of the most advanced medical technology, still Alex would be a young man before the horse and buggy even gave way to the automobile.

A chromium child, growing up in a candlelight age.

"He's going to be just fine, this boy of ours," Myles declared, and Paige knew it was the truth. A great peace came over her.

Myles sat down beside her, his strong arm supporting them both.

"Welcome home," he whispered.

Time's Healing Heart

Marti Jones

No man has ever swept Madeline St. Thomas off her feet, and after she buries herself in her career, she loses hope of finding one. But when a freak accident propels her to the Old South, Maddie is rescued by a stranger with the face of an angel and the body of an Adonis—a stranger whose burning touch and smoldering kisses awaken forgotten longings in her heart.

Devon Crowe has had enough of women. His dead wife betrayed him, his fiancee despises him, and Maddie drives him to distraction with her claims of coming from another era. But the more Devon tries to convince himself that Maddie is aptly named, the more he believes her preposterous story. And when she makes him a proposal no lady would make, he doesn't know whether he should wrap her in a straitjacket—or lose himself in desires that promise to last forever.

_51954-2 $4.99 US/$5.99 CAN

Timeswept passion...timeless love

FLORA SPEER

When he is accidentally thrust back to the eighth century by a computer genius's time-travel program, Mike Bailey falls from the sky and lands near Charlemagne's camp. Knocked senseless by the crash, he can't remember his name, address, or occupation, but no shock can make his body forget how to respond when he awakens to the sight of an enchanting angel on earth.

Headstrong and innocent, Danise is already eighteen and almost considered an old maid by the Frankish nobles who court her. Yet the stubborn beauty would prefer to spend the rest of her life cloistered in a nunnery rather than marry for any reason besides love. Unexpectedly mesmerized by the stranger she discovers unconscious in the forest, Danise is quickly arroused by an all-consuming passion—and a desire that will conquer time itself.

_51948-8 $4.99 US/$5.99 CAN

**TIMESWEPT
PASSION...
TIMELESS
LOVE**

THE RELUCTANT VIKING

SANDRA HILL

*"Picture yourself floating out of your body—
floating...floating...floating..."* The hypnotic voice on the
self-motivation tape is supposed to help Ruby Jordan solve
her problems, not create new ones. Instead, she is lulled from
a life full of a demanding business, a neglected home, and
a failing marriage—to an era of hard-bodied warriors and
fair maidens, fierce fighting and fiercer wooing. But the
world ten centuries in the past doesn't prove to be all mead
and mirth. Even as Ruby tries to update medieval times, she
has to deal with a Norseman whose view of women is stuck
in the Dark Ages. And what is worse, brawny Thork has
her husband's face, habits, and desire to avoid Ruby.
Determined not to lose the same man twice, Ruby plans a
bold seduction that will conquer the reluctant Viking—and
make him an eager captive of her love.

_51983-6 $4.99 US/$5.99 CAN

A TIMESWEPT ROMANCE

Timeswept passion...timeless love.

Time-Spun Treasure

Thomasina Ring

When she takes part in a reenactment of Patrick Henry's "Give me liberty or give me death" speech, thoroughly modern Meredith Davis never expects to be thrown back in time to the real thing. Caught up in a bewildering tangle of events from which there seems no escape, Meredith finds herself marrying the most exasperating Colonial she could ever imagine. She longs to return to her own time—until a night in her new husband's bed shows her that men have lost a lot over the centuries.

_3334-8 $4.50 US/$5.50 CAN

A TIMESWEPT ROMANCE

Timeswept passion...timeless love.

A Tryst in Time

EUGENIA RILEY

Devastated by her brother's death in Vietnam, Sarah Jennings retreats to a crumbling Civil War plantation house, where a dark-eyed lover calls to her from across the years. Damien too has lost a brother to war—the War Between the States—yet in Sarah's embrace he finds a sweet ecstasy that makes life worth living. But if Sarah and Damien cannot unravel the secret of her mysterious arrival at Belle Fontaine, their brief tryst in time will end forever.

_3198-1 $4.50 US/$5.50 CAN

ENCHANTED CROSSINGS

Three captivating stories of love in another time, another place.

MADELINE BAKER
"Heart of the Hunter"

A Lakota warrior must defy the boundaries of life itself to claim the spirited beauty he has sought through time.

ANNE AVERY
"Dream Seeker"

On faraway planets, a pilot and a dreamer learn that passion can bridge the heavens, no matter how vast the distance from one heart to another.

KATHLEEN MORGAN
"The Last Gatekeeper"

To save her world, a dazzling temptress must use her powers of enchantment to open a stellar portal—and the heart of a virile but reluctant warrior.

__51974-7 *Enchanted Crossings* (three unforgettable love stories in one volume) $4.99 US/
$5.99 CAN